WILLA CATHER is best known for her superb American
novels, but she also wrote over sixty short stories. The
first of these was written in 1892, when she was nineteen; the last was published in 1948, the year after her
death. Yet, until now, there has been no substantial
collection of these stories. Cather's tales range from short,
vivid sketches to novellas. They tell of the bitter lives of
Nebraskan immigrants, of the pull between provincial
America and the cosmopolitan world of art. Her marvellous late stories eloquently describe the tensions and
complications of family life. And she lets herself go in the
stories in ways she did not in the longer fiction, with
harsh satires on New York life, chilling glimpses of the
supernatural, and strong expressions of sexual feeling.
This rich selection, the first to be published in Britain,
mixes the little-known with the much anthologised. It
adds immeasurably to our perception of Cather's range
and complexity.

Hermione Lee grew up in London and was educated at St
Hilda's College, Oxford. Her publications include *The
Novels of Virginia Woolf* (1977); *Elizabeth Bowen: An Esti-
mation* (1981) and *Philip Roth* (1982). She is also the
editor of *Stevie Smith: A Selection* (1983) and of works by
Trollope and Kipling, and she has edited anthologies of
short stories by women, *The Secret Self 1* and *2*. Her
selection of Elizabeth Bowen's writings, *The Mulberry Tree*
(1986) and *Willa Cather: A Life Saved Up* (1989) are
published by Virago. She is currently a Senior Lecturer in
English at the University of York, and reviews for the
Observer. She lives in Yorkshire.

THE
SHORT STORIES OF
WILLA CATHER

SELECTED AND INTRODUCED BY

HERMIONE LEE

VIRAGO

Published by VIRAGO PRESS Limited 1989
20–23 Mandela Street, Camden Town, London NW1 0HQ

Selection, Introduction and Notes copyright Hermione Lee 1989

A CIP catalogue record for this book
is available from the British Library

Typeset by Goodfellow & Egan Ltd, Cambridge
Printed in Great Britain by Billings & Sons Ltd.

CONTENTS

ACKNOWLEDGEMENTS

ANYONE working on Cather's short fiction is indebted to the pioneering work of Bernice Slote, Virginia Faulkner, and James Woodress, as the 'Note on Editions' makes clear. Permission to reproduce the following stories is gratefully acknowledged: 'Lou, the Prophet', 'On the Divide', 'Tommy, the Unsentimental', 'The Sentimentality of William Tavener', '"A Death in the Desert"', 'A Wagner Matinée', 'The Sculptor's Funeral', and 'Paul's Case' from *Willa Cather's Collected Short Fiction, 1892–1912*, edited by Virginia Faulkner, introduced by Mildred R. Bennett, by permission of University of Nebraska Press, copyright © 1965, 1970 by University of Nebraska Press; 'The Enchanted Bluff', 'The Bohemian Girl', 'Consequences', 'Ardessa' and 'Uncle Valentine' copyright © by The Estate of Willa Cather; 'Coming, Aphrodite!' from *Youth and the Bright Medusa* by Willa Cather, copyright © 1920 by Willa Cather and renewed 1948 by the Executors of the Estate of Willa Cather, reprinted by permission of Alfred A. Knopf, Inc.; 'Neighbour Rosicky', 'Two Friends', and 'Old Mrs Harris' from *Obscure Destinies* by Willa Cather, copyright © 1930, 1932 by Willa Cather and renewed 1958, 1960 by the Executors of the Estate of Willa Cather, reprinted by permission of Alfred A. Knopf, Inc.; 'The Old Beauty', 'Before Breakfast', and 'The Best Years' from *The Old Beauty and Others* by Willa Cather, copyright © 1948 by Alfred A. Knopf, Inc., reprinted by kind permission of Alfred A. Knopf, Inc.

INTRODUCTION

'*E*VERY great story', Willa Cather wrote in the preface to her selection of stories by her mentor and friend, Sarah Orne Jewett, 'must leave in the mind . . . an intangible residuum of pleasure; a cadence, a quality of voice that is exclusively the writer's own, individual, unique. A quality that one can remember without the volume at hand, can experience over and over again in the mind but can never absolutely define . . .'[1] That emphasis on the intangible and the indefinable is the key to Cather's thoughts about writing. It is there in her famous essay of 1922, 'The Novel Démeublé', on the need for simplification and suggestion in fiction, as opposed to over-documented realism, to create 'the inexplicable presence of the thing not named'.[2] It is there again in her eloquent appreciation of Katherine Mansfield, which singles out her New Zealand stories for their 'powerful slightness', for something indefinable, a 'magic', an 'overtone',[3] which communicates more than is actually written.

This aesthetic of suggestiveness is an ideal one for the writer of short stories. And Cather's models for the genre were exemplary. Sarah Orne Jewett and Katherine Mansfield gave her a female tradition; but, characteristically crossing between the sexes, she also absorbed the examples of Stephen Crane and Kipling, Hawthorne, Maupassant, Henry James and Flaubert. Technically, she took all she could from them: James's 'perfect frameworks' and 'polish without flaw', Crane's 'vividness' and 'constructive perfection', Kipling's brilliant mastery of detail and his 'amazingly original use of it'.[4] She learnt from her reading that 'in constructing a story as in building an airship the first problem is to get something that will lift its own weight'.[5] The pragmatic masculinity of this is a typical early pose; but it shows how much thought she gave, from the start, to the thermodynamics of story-writing.

Some of these influences went in phases. Cather was not the only young writer to be overcome, at one stage, by Jamesian mannerisms, or to be Maupassant-mad at another. (When, as a young journalist, she met Stephen Crane, he commented sardonically on her literary enthusiasm: 'Oh, you're Moping, are you?')[6] But some, like her passion for the integrity and coldness of Flaubert, her sympathy for Hawthorne's shadowy allegories, or her attraction to Jewett's rootedness in 'a native language',[7] lasted all her life, and fed into her treatment of the 'obscure destinies' of her American characters.

Like these mentors, Cather interspersed the writing of novels and stories throughout her career. She started to write stories in the 1890s, and she wrote the last (of over sixty stories, ranging from short sketches to extensive novellas) just before her death in 1947. Among these are some of the finest American stories of the century. And yet Willa Cather is known much more – and thought of herself much more – as a novelist. Though three collections were published in her lifetime, and one posthumously in 1948, it is only in the last twenty years that the stories she did not choose to reprint have been made available. And her reputation still rests on *My Ántonia* or *A Lost Lady*, *The Professor's House* or *Death Comes for the Archbishop*, rather than on the outstanding stories, 'Paul's Case' or 'The Enchanted Bluff', 'Neighbour Rosicky' or 'Old Mrs Harris'. The reasons for this intriguing imbalance in her reputation have partly to do with Cather's life and temperament, partly with the status of the short story in American publishing history.

Cather began her writing career as a very young, ambitious, passionately literary student journalist in Nebraska, fresh from the prairies and avid for all the culture she could lay hands on. She was also in need of an income: the early 1890s were depression years in the mid-West, and her father (as in 'Old Mrs Harris') had had to borrow to send her to college. Within two years of arriving at Lincoln she was a regular columnist and theatre reviewer (notorious for her hatchet jobs) for the *Nebraskan State Journal*. In 1896, at only twenty-three, she moved east for a job as managing editor of a genteel Pittsburgh magazine, the *Home Monthly* (which she filled largely with her own contributions) and then on the *Pittsburgh Daily Leader*. Her output in these early years of journalism, much of it pseudonymous, was prodigious, and covered all the theatre and opera productions she could see locally, and all the new literature of her time. From the start, and increasingly towards the end of her Pittsburgh years, when she was teaching and free-lancing, it included short stories. It was these which attracted the attention of S. S. McClure, a dynamic force in the magazine-publishing world, who, with characteristic impetuousness and determination, whisked Cather off in 1906 to New York and a high-powered editorial job on *McClure's*, with, as a bribe, the publication of her first volume of stories, *The Troll Garden*. But, working all out for McClure between 1906 and 1912, her own writing suffered, and there were fewer stories. Her first novel wasn't published until 1912, when she was thirty-nine, and only then did she take the plunge into full-time writing. It had been a long apprenticeship, which had seemed at times like imprisonment, but from which she had certainly learned her craft. In the next decade she would occasionally supplement her income from the novels with stories; that these were primarily commercial ventures (like the magazine serial-isation of some of her novels) is shown up by her suggestion to one editor, in 1917, that she should do a series of stories called 'Office Wives'.[8] (Nothing came of it.) Only the later stories of the 1930s and 1940s were written entirely for her own pleasure, not from financial need.

As Cather became more famous and secure as a novelist, she also came to feel more at odds with post-war America.

Her 1936 volume of essays even had, as its first title, *Not Under Forty*, with a grumpily reactionary introduction which said that, as the world had broken in two in 1922 'or thereabouts', no one under forty would be interested in what she had to say; this book was for 'the backward'. The idea of a split (an idea which took different but persistent forms in her writing) came to be applied to her own life too. Increasingly wary of self-exposure and betrayals of privacy (Cather's will, notoriously, forbids all quotations from those letters she did not succeed in having destroyed), she turned her back on her earlier, more outgoing and commercially opportunistic writings.

This dissociation from the early work had a great deal to do with her complex and changing feelings for the place she came from. The brutal picture of immigrant Nebraskan life in the young stories such as 'On the Divide' or 'Lou, the Prophet', and the painful clash between claustrophobic provincial desolation and artistic aspirations in *The Troll Garden* volume (much toned down in later alterations), contrast dramatically with the late stories' more benign and nostalgic retrospect on the Nebraskan childhood pastoral as 'the best years'. But compounding these personal reasons was a professional distaste for her journeyman work.

Cather was not the only American writer to have mixed feelings about the work she did for the magazines. Her career coincided with, and was partly shaped by, an expansive period in American publishing, when the fiction writer could at once profit hugely from, and be intensely frustrated by, the boom in popular periodicals. Following on from the early nineteenth-century fashions for annuals and gift books, mostly directed at women readers (like *Godey's Lady's Book*), there had been a big rise in demand, after the Civil War, for rapid and easy entertainment in the form of popular periodicals filled with short stories: and the shorter the better. By the 1880s, when 'the short story' (as opposed to the 'tale' or the 'sketch') was becoming a common term, and handbooks on how to write them were starting to appear, magazines like

Harper's Monthly proudly advertised 'No continued stories'.[9] But, while the popular market was being fed with brisk sensation stories, local colour stories, humorous stories, and so on, high standards were being preserved by magazines such as the *Atlantic Monthly, Century, Scribner's,* or *The Yellow Book,* where Henry James could find a haven for 'the beautiful and blest *nouvelle*'.

So the short story, which had come to be seen as a distinctively American genre, was at the centre of the battle between the traditionalists – accused of gentility and Europeanism by their opponents – and the raw 'native' writers such as Jack London, whose advice to his fellow-practitioners was:

> Make it concrete, to the point, with snap and go and life, crisp and crackling and interesting . . . Put a snapper at the end, so if they are crowded for space they can cut off your contents anywhere, reattach the snapper, and the story will still retain form.[10]

The gap between highbrow and lowbrow was being dramatically filled, just at the time when Cather started publishing, by McClure himself. When (making use of the new cheap photo-engraving methods) he cut the price of his 'muck-raking' magazine from 15 cents to 10 cents, in 1895, with a circulation of 300,000, he was in the vanguard of the new, popular mass-circulation periodicals like the *Ladies' Home Journal* or the *Saturday Evening Post,* challenging the staid old 35 cent subscription monthlies. Frank Norris, one of the all-American democratic school of novelists (much admired by the young Cather), approved of the trend: 'A literature that cannot be vulgarised is no literature at all,' he wrote.[11] O. Henry, the most popular story-writer of the day, said he was writing 'for Mr Everybody'.[12]

Cather's earliest stories show a consciousness of popular demands. They contain abductions and elopements, hauntings, scandals and suicides. But at the same time – more like Henry James than O. Henry – she is working out her own way of treating her own subject, and frequently ignoring the recommendation for 'No continued stories'. This pull between the needs of the American public and of the American writer is part of Cather's doubleness, but also part of the times.

Popular magazines meant syndicated short stories, big prize contests, and lavish opportunities for writers. McClure, for instance (who, with his investigative articles, published fiction by O. Henry alongside Kipling, Stevenson, Bret Harte, Conan Doyle – and Cather) advertising 'one hundred short stories by one hundred authors in one hundred days'.[13] Prices were high – the *New York World* paid O. Henry $100 a week, whatever he wrote. Cather, who naively turned down $750 for 'The Bohemian Girl' in 1912, saying that *McClure's* never paid that much for fiction (she took $500), would usually be paid $450 for shorter stories.

But the form had its disadvantages. Publishers wanted novels rather than collections of stories (since if the stories had already appeared in cheap magazines, collections were hard to sell). Reviewers tended to disparage them as an inferior art form: Carl Van Doren, for instance, hoped that Miss Cather would consider *Youth and the Bright Medusa*, 'striking though it is, but an interlude in her brilliant progress' as a novelist.[14] But most damage was done by censorship. Popular magazines for the home were strait-jacketed by what Frank Norris bitterly called the 'family center table' standard:

> The great merit of the stories of these 'magazinists' – the one quality which endears them to the editors, is that they are what in editorial slang is called 'safe' . . . They adorn the center table. They do not 'call a blush to the cheek of the young'. They can be placed – Oh crowning virtue, Oh supreme encomium – they can be 'safely' placed in the hands of any young girl in the country over.[15]

Such complaints were heard from writers as different as Norris, James, and Hardy (*Jude the Obscure* was savagely blue-pencilled by *Harper's*), and from Cather too. She had had early practice in censorship when she was editing the 'namby-pamby' Pittsburgh *Home Monthly*. And she herself fell foul of what H. L. Mencken, editor of the *Smart Set*, called 'Comstockery'. Anthony Comstock and his Society for the Suppression of Vice, the Mary Whitehouses of their day, had succeeded in having Dreiser censored (Cather had signed a petition of protest supporting Dreiser in 1916). In 1921 Mencken remarked that the *Century* had had to turn down something by Cather because 'the Comstocks are in violent eruption, and the *Century* has been taking too many chances.'[16] Mencken took 'Coming, Aphrodite!', but it appeared as 'Coming, Eden Bower!', greatly bowdlerised. The 'wholly unclad' Eden appears in the magazine 'clad in a pink chiffon cloud', with thighs and breasts missing, and 'perspiration' replacing 'sweat'. In the erotic Mexican story her lover tells, 'maimed' is substituted for 'gelded'.

That Cather let her stories be 'gelded' in ways she would not have allowed her novels to be, suggests that she attached less importance to them: and the reasons for that were, as I've suggested, partly personal and partly circumstantial. Yet the two kinds of writing were closely interrelated. Cather began to write novels out of her stories. Her first successful novel, *O Pioneers!*, took shape as two separate stories which she joined together to make 'a two-part pastoral', and some of her best mature works, *A Lost Lady* and *My Mortal Enemy*, have the length and shape of novellas. Her longer novels, like classical epics, graft self-contained stories onto the main plot: Tom Outland's story set inside *The Professor's House*, the legends that accumulate as the narrative of *Death Comes for the Archbishop* the gentle sequence of episodes in *Shadows on the Rock*. Several of Cather's stories provide versions – try-outs or recapitulations – of what is in the novels. A harsh, early Nebraskan story like 'Lou, the Prophet', will be softened for old Ivar in *O Pioneers!* The boys' legend of the Indian cliff-city, told in 'The Enchanted Bluff' before Cather had been to the South west and seen the cliff-dwellings for herself, was saved up for *The Song of the Lark* and *The Professor's House*. Sometimes, material from the novels spilled over into later stories.

'Coming, Aphrodite!' shows some left-over feelings for opera singers after *The Song of the Lark*; 'Neighbour Rosicky' returns, years later, to the Nebraskan Bohemian family of *My Ántonia*.

But the stories are not just of interest as adjuncts to the novels. One of their attractions is that they open windows onto scenes of Cather's life, and are sometimes more self-revealing than the novels. The change over the years from a harsh, grotesque Nebraskan pastoral to a serene, nostalgic one shows up one kind of conflict in Cather. So does the recurrent and unresolved preoccupation with the choices for the American artist, who needs to 'tear loose', go abroad, acquire a metropolitan and European culture, but who knows, however ruefully (as in 'The Sculptor's Funeral') that 'it rather seems as though we ought to go back to the place we came from in the end'. Cather used other models than herself – the redoubtable opera singer Olive Fremstad, the Pittsburgh composer Ethelbert Nevin, who died young – for her argument. But when she says of 'Uncle Valentine', with Nevin in mind, 'Some artists profit by exile. He was one of those who do not,' she is evidently thinking of herself.

The stories chart her own journeys, not only through Nebraska, but to dark, solid, materialist Pittsburgh, cultured decorous Boston, the picturesque New York of her first years there, living in Washington Square, (as well as the city's more frightening, claustrophobic side). Later, they move to Provence, Cather's favourite place in Europe (in 'The Old Beauty'), and, at the end, to Grand Manan, the remote Maine island where she and her friend Edith Lewis had a house built, and which is the setting for a strange late story, 'Before Breakfast', wrily resigning herself to man's small but energetic part in 'the immense design of things'. Only the South west is relatively under-represented in the stories, though it's brought in by the legends told in 'The Enchanted Bluff' and 'Coming, Aphrodite!'

Her professional journey is illustrated, too: teaching (in 'Paul's Case' and 'The Best Years'), journalism ('Ardessa' is a sharp satire on *McClure's*), and minding about money. Paul, who steals from the bank to fulfil his fantasy of an escapist aesthetic paradise, learns in the end that 'money was everything'; and Cather's stories are always tough and realistic about who's got it, how it's come by, and how it changes people's lives. In spite of 'the disappointed strugglers in a bitter, dead little Western town' of 'A Sculptor's Funeral', she has a good deal of sympathy – as in 'Two Friends' – for bankers, businessmen and people with financial acumen, like 'Tommy', who knows how to stop a run on a country bank. The wonderful long late story of family life, 'Old Mrs Harris', takes a contemplative, almost visionary, tone, from its title character, but is firmly rooted in the economic facts of the family's situation.

'Old Mrs Harris' takes her back, late in life, to the beginning of her journey as an American writer. It gives a remarkable picture of Cather's childhood home in Red Cloud, Nebraska, at once intimately revealing and impersonally distanced. It evokes everyone's feelings, not just Vickie as the young Cather, but the discontented mother, the stoical grandmother, the 'bound girl', the little boys, even the cat. And it marvellously gives the sense, which Cather describes in her essay on Katherine Mansfield, of the tension in families between the 'group life' and the hidden life of the individuals – 'secret and passionate and intense' – always pulling against the 'social unit'.

More tormented, extreme versions of the young girl's passionate desire to get away are found in *The Troll Garden* stories, 'Paul's Case', 'A Wagner Matinée', 'A Death in the Desert'. But the title of that collection (which Cather took from Charles Kingsley's fable of the primitive children of the forest tempted by, and at last destroying, the kingdom of the trolls, full of precious valuable things) suggests the dangers of art, and of the 'world-shine' which seduces Paul. (So does *Youth and the Bright Medusa*, the title of the 1920 collection.) Cather's passion for artists, musicians, theatre, is always tempered by her fear of mere 'bohemianism'. Like Don Hedger in 'Coming, Aphrodite!', she knows that 'true' art means hard grind and sacrifice.

The tension, in her treatment of the artist's profession, between romance and realism, is characteristic of Cather's doubleness. That sense of strain partly has to do with her sexuality. Cather, who was deeply in love with one woman, Isabelle McClung, for many years, and spent most of her life living companionably with another, Edith Lewis, would never have used the word 'lesbian' of herself, and certainly cannot be described as a feminist. Attempts to co-opt her can only be made with difficulty. Readings which explicate Cather's fiction entirely as an encoding of covert, repressed lesbian sexuality seem to me simplistic, even patronising. Cather works *best* through indirection and suppression, and through her idiosyncratic refusal to be enlisted, in her life and in her work, to any group or cause. Nevertheless, the stories reveal a great deal – sometimes more than the novels – of these strategies and indirections, from the jaunty 'cross-dressing', like the young 'William Cather Jr's', of 'Tommy, the Unsentimental', to the practised, self-disguising adoption of, or identification with, a male *persona* in 'Neighbour Rosicky', 'Two Friends', or 'Before Breakfast'. Sexual roles are constantly shifted away from the expected: the stories are full of powerful matriarchs or female guardians, weak fathers, and feminine men. (There are a significant number, too, of cheery, matter-of-fact 'principal boy' types among Cather's performers, like the splendid balloonist in 'Coming, Aphrodite!', and Cherry Beamish in 'The Old Beauty'.) Nowhere in the novels is there an erotic moment of such voyeuristic intensity – carefully translated into aesthetic pleasure – as Don Hedger's spying on the naked Eden in 'Coming, Aphrodite!', a love story which fleetingly brings a chaste, untouchable 'Diana' figure down to a dark, troll-like passion. No wonder Mencken took fright.

Cather's sense of sexual doubleness extends to the insistence on doubles in many of the stories. The ghost story 'Consequences' plays on the Wildean idea of twin brothers, one a healthy outdoor Western type who died young, taking with him all the goodness from the New York playboy brother, who is haunted by a mocking image of his own old age. The like-unlikeness of brothers or twins – as in 'A Death in the Desert', or 'Uncle Valentine', where the successful musician has a pathetic, degenerate family of uncles and brothers, brilliantly done – makes plain the theme of the double self. But that can be expressed in other ways too, sometimes by the tension between two kinds of life, as in a neurotically split character such as Paul, sometimes in the way the narrative divides itself between past and present, experience and memory. Many of Cather's stories, like her novels, end with a coda which moves us on in time and returns us to the scene of the story as to something long vanished. The effect is to give a serene, appeased, elegiac quality to a story which may be a painful one of loss, death or suffering.

Much of the brilliance of Cather's writing lies in her detailing, with almost imperceptible skill, scenes from ordinary, 'obscure' lives: the Norwegian and Bohemian pastorals in 'The Bohemian Girl', the rhythms of Rosicky's life, the local rituals of the 'two friends', the constricted life of the family in 'Old Mrs Harris'. These scenes are patterned with scrupulous minuteness. The ridges of ripple marks on the island in the river of 'The Enchanted Bluff', 'strewn with the tiny skeletons of turtles and fish, all as white and dry as if they had been expertly cured'; the painful irruption into Paul's fantasy life of 'his father, at the top of the stairs, his hairy legs sticking out from his night-shirt, his feet thrust into carpet slippers'; the Herculean brown, dark-veined hands of the old ladies at Olaf Ericson's barn-raising in 'The Bohemian Girl'; the soft dust in the road on the summer nights where the 'two friends' sit talking; Mrs Harris's swollen legs, thin cotton mattress, ragged 'comforter', and night-time memories of her lemon tree, back in Tennessee, 'in a tub on the front porch, which bore little lemons almost every summer, and folks would come for miles to see it': these selected, ordered details make for a language of authenticity that can't be quarrelled with.

Yet the stories are, also, always pulling out and away, so that we look back on their inhabitants as if in another dimension of time and space. The boys in 'The Enchanted Bluff', discussing astrological orderings and pre-historic legends; Mr Trueman and Mr Dillon, in 'Two Friends', watching the transit of Venus and contemplating the distance of the moon from the earth; Rosicky viewing with satisfaction the 'nice' graveyard in which he is to be buried, 'so near home' and yet on the edge of 'so much open country', and the businessman in 'Before Breakfast', coming to terms with himself as an infinitesimal speck in geological time, seem to be turned into mythological figures, at once near and far, at once mundane and heroic. So in the very greatest of Cather's stories – 'The Enchanted Bluff', 'Old Mrs Harris', 'Neighbour Rosicky' – it is hard to tell whether we are reading a story of loss and defeat, or of taking possession.

Hermione Lee, York, 1989

Notes

1. Preface to *The Best Stories of Sarah Orne Jewett*, Selected and Arranged by Willa Cather, Houghton Mifflin (Boston & New York, 1925), p. xi. Revised as 'Miss Jewett' in *Not Under Forty*, Knopf (New York, 1936), pp. 85–108.
2. *Not Under Forty*, p. 54.
3. *ibid.*, p. 164.
4. From *The World and the Parish: Willa Cather's Articles and Reviews, 1893–1902*, ed. William M. Curtin, University of Nebraska Press, 2 vols. (Lincoln, 1970), pp. 275, 560, 777.
5. *ibid.*, p. 728.
6. *ibid.*, p. 773.
7. *Not Under Forty*, p. 93.
8. James Woodress, *Willa Cather: a Literary Life*, University of Nebraska Press (Lincoln & London, 1987), p. 286. For Cather's mixed feelings about her magazine work, see Curtis Bradford, 'Willa Cather's uncollected short stories', *American Literature*, vol. 26, 1954–55, pp. 537–551.
9. Fred Lewis Pattee, *The Development of the American Short Story*, Biblo & Tannen (New York, 1966), p. 193.
10. *ibid.*, p. 340.
11. *The Literary Criticism of Frank Norris*, ed. Donald Pizer, Russell & Russell (New York, 1964), 'September 1902', p. 221.
12. Pattee, *op. cit.*, p. 361.
13. *ibid.*, p. 311.
14. *ibid.*, p. 376.
15. Frank Norris, *op. cit.*, 'January 30 1897', p. 28. For censorship and gentility in American magazines, see Larzer Ziff, *The American 1890s*, Chatto & Windus (London, 1967), Ch. 6, pp. 120–145.
16. Woodress, *op. cit.*, p. 315; Bernice Slote, ed., *Uncle Valentine and Other Stories: Willa Cather's Uncollected Short Fiction, 1915–1929*, University of Nebraska Press (Lincoln & London, 1973), 'Introduction', p. xviii. Slote's 'Appendix', pp. 177–8, gives the magazine variants for 'Coming, Aphrodite!'

LOU, THE PROPHET

IT HAD been a very trying summer to every one, and most of all to Lou. He had been in the West for seven years, but he had never quite gotten over his homesickness for Denmark. Among the northern people who emigrate to the great west, only the children and the old people ever long much for the lands they have left over the water. The men only know that in this new land their plow runs across the field tearing up the fresh, warm earth, with never a stone to stay its course. That if they dig and delve the land long enough, and if they are not compelled to mortgage it to keep body and soul together, some day it will be theirs, their very own. They are not like the southern people; they lose their love for their fatherland quicker and have less of sentiment about them. They have to think too much about how they shall get bread to care much what soil gives it to them. But among even the most blunted, mechanical people, the youths and the aged always have a touch of romance in them.

Lou was only twenty-two; he had been but a boy when his family left Denmark, and had never ceased to remember it. He was a rather simple fellow, and was always considered less promising than his brothers; but last year he had taken up a claim of his own and made a rough dugout upon it and he lived there all alone. His life was that of many another young man in our country. He rose early in the morning, in the summer just before daybreak; in the winter, long before. First he fed his stock, then himself, which was a much less important matter. He ate the same food at dinner that he ate at breakfast, and the same at supper that he ate at dinner. His bill of fare never changed the year round; bread, coffee, beans and sorghum molasses, sometimes a little salt pork. After breakfast he worked until dinner time, ate, and then worked again. He always went to bed soon after the sunset, for he was always tired, and it saved oil. Sometimes, on Sundays, he would go over home after he had done his washing and house cleaning, and sometimes he hunted. His life was as sane and as uneventful as the life of his plow horses, and it was as hard and thankless. He was thrifty for a simple, thickheaded fellow, and in the spring he was to have married Nelse Sorenson's daughter, but he had lost all his cattle during the winter, and was not so prosperous as he had hoped to be; so, instead she married her cousin, who had an 'eighty' of his own. That hurt Lou more than anyone ever dreamed.

A few weeks later his mother died. He had always loved his mother. She had been kind to him and used to come over to see him sometimes, and shake up his hard bed for him, and sweep, and make his bread. She had a strong affection for the boy, he was her youngest, and she always felt sorry for him; she had danced a great deal before his birth, and an old woman in Denmark had told her that was the cause of the boy's weak head.

Perhaps the greatest calamity of all was the threatened loss of his corn crop. He had bought a new corn planter on time that spring, and had intended that his corn should pay for it. Now, it looked as though he would not have corn enough to feed his horses. Unless rain fell within the next two weeks, his entire crop would be ruined; it was half gone now. All these things together were too much for poor Lou, and one morning he felt a strange loathing for the bread and sorghum which he usually ate as mechanically as he slept. He kept thinking about the strawberries he used to gather on the mountains after the snows were gone, and the cold water in the mountain streams. He felt hot someway, and wanted cold water. He had no well, and he hauled his water from a neighbor's well every Sunday, and it got warm in the barrels those hot summer days. He worked at his haying all day; at night, when he was through feeding, he stood a long time by the pig stye with a basket on his arm. When the moon came up, he sighed restlessly and tore the buffalo pea flowers with his bare toes. After a while, he put his basket away, and went into his hot, close, little dugout. He did not sleep well, and he dreamed a horrible dream. He thought he saw the Devil and all his angels in the air holding back the rain clouds, and they loosed all the damned in Hell, and they came, poor tortured things, and drank up whole clouds of rain. Then he thought a strange light shone from the south, just over the river bluffs, and the clouds parted, and Christ and all his angels were descending. They were coming, coming, myriads and myriads of them, in a great blaze of glory. Then he felt something give way in his poor, weak head, and with a cry of pain he awoke. He lay shuddering a long time in the dark, then got up and lit his lantern and took from the shelf his mother's Bible. It opened of itself at Revelation, and Lou began to read, slowly indeed, for it was hard work for him. Page by page, he read those burning, blinding, blasting words, and they seemed to shrivel up his poor brain altogether. At last the book slipped from his hands and he sank down upon his knees in prayer, and stayed so until the dull gray dawn stole over the land and he heard the pigs clamoring for their feed.

He worked about the place until noon, and then prayed and read again. So he went on several days, praying and reading and fasting, until he grew thin and haggard. Nature did not comfort him any, he knew nothing about nature, he had never seen her; he had only stared into a black plow furrow all his life. Before, he had only seen in the wide, green lands and the open blue the possibilities of earning his bread; now, he only saw in them a great world ready for the judgment, a funeral pyre ready for the torch.

One morning, he went over to the big prairie dog town, where several little Danish boys herded their fathers' cattle. The boys were very fond of Lou; he never teased them as the other men did, but used to help them with their cattle, and let them come over to his dugout to make sorghum taffy. When they saw him coming, they ran to meet him and asked him where he had been all these days. He did not answer their questions, but said: 'Come into the cave, I want to see you.'

Some six or eight boys herded near the dog town every summer, and by their combined efforts they had dug a cave in the side of a high bank. It was large enough to hold them all comfortably, and high enough to stand in. There the boys used to go when it rained or when it was cold in the fall. They followed Lou silently and sat down on the floor. Lou stood up and looked tenderly down into the little faces before him. They were old-faced little fellows, though they were not over twelve or thirteen years old, hard work matures boys quickly.

'Boys,' he said earnestly, 'I have found out why it don't rain, it's because of the sins of the world. You don't know how wicked the world is, it's all bad, all, even Denmark. People have been sinning a long time, but they won't much longer. God has been watching and watching for thousands of years, and filling up the phials of wrath, and now he is going to pour out his vengeance and let Hell loose upon the world. He is burning up our corn now, and worse things will happen; for the sun shall be as sackcloth, and the moon shall be like blood, and the stars of heaven shall fall, and the heavens shall part like a scroll, and the mountains shall be moved out of their places, and the great day of his wrath shall come, against which none may stand. Oh, boys! the floods and the flames shall come down upon us together and the whole world shall perish.' Lou paused for breath, and the little boys gazed at him in wonder. The sweat was running down his haggard face, and his eyes were staring wildly. Presently, he resumed in a softer tone, 'Boys, if you want rain, there is only one way to get it, by prayer. The people of the world won't pray, perhaps if they did God would not hear them, for they are so wicked; but he will hear you, for you are little children and are likened unto the kingdom of heaven, and he loved ye.'

Lou's haggard, unshaven face bent toward them and his blue eyes gazed at them with terrible earnestness.

'Show us how, Lou,' said one little fellow in an awed whisper. Lou knelt down in the cave, his long, shaggy hair hung down over his face, and his voice trembled as he spoke:

'Oh God, they call thee many long names in thy book, thy prophets; but we are only simple folk, the boys are all little and I am weak headed ever since I was born, therefore, let us call thee Father, for thy other names are hard to remember. O Father, we are so thirsty, all the world is thirsty; the creeks are all dried up, and the river is so low that the fishes die and rot in it; the corn is almost gone; the hay is light; and even the little flowers are no more beautiful. O God! our corn may yet be saved. O, give us rain! Our corn means so much to us, if it fails, all our pigs and cattle will die, and we ourselves come very near it; but if you do not send rain, O Father, and if the end is indeed come, be merciful to thy great, wicked world. They do many wrong things, but I think they forget thy word, for it is a long book to remember, and some are little and some are born weak headed, like me, and some are born very strong headed, which is near as bad. Oh, forgive them their abominations in all the world, both in Denmark and here, for the fire hurts so, O God! Amen.'

The little boys knelt and each said a few blundering words. Outside, the sun shone brightly and the cattle nibbled at the short, dry grass, and the hot wind blew through the shriveled corn; within the cave, they knelt as many another had knelt before them, some in temples, some in prison cells, some in the caves of earth, and One, indeed, in the garden, praying for the sin of the world.

The next day, Lou went to town, and prayed in the streets. When the people saw his emaciated frame and wild eyes, and heard his wild words, they told the sheriff to do his duty, the man must be mad. Then Lou ran away; he ran for miles, then walked and limped and stumbled on, until he reached the cave; there the boys found him in the morning. The officials hunted him for days, but he hid in the cave, and the little Danes kept his secret well. They shared their dinners with him, but now they would have gone straight through fire for him, any one of them, they almost worshipped him.

He had about him that mysticism which always appeals so quickly to children. I have always thought that bear story which the Hebrews used to tell their children very improbable. If it was true, then I have my doubts about the prophet; no one in the world will hoot at insincere and affected piety sooner than a child, but no one feels the true prophetic flame quicker, no one is more readily touched by simple goodness. A very young child can tell a sincere man better than any phrenologist.

One morning, he told the boys that he had had another 'true dream.' He was not going to die like other men, but God was going to take him to himself as he was. The end of the world was close at hand, too very close. He prayed more than usual that day, and when they sat eating their dinner in the sunshine, he suddenly sprang to his feet and stared wildly south, crying, 'See, see, it is the great light! the end comes!! and they do not know it; they will keep on sinning, I must tell them, I must!'

'No, no, Lou, they will catch you; they are looking for you, you must not go!'

'I must go, my boys; but first let me speak once more to you. Men would not heed me, or believe me, because my head is weak, but you have always believed in me, that God has revealed his word to me, and I will pray God to take you to himself quickly, for ye are worthy. Watch and pray always, boys, watch the light over the bluffs, it is breaking, breaking, and shall grow brighter. Goodbye, my boys, I must leave ye in the world yet awhile.' He kissed them all tenderly and blessed them, and started south. He walked at first, then he ran, faster and faster he went, all the while shouting at the top of his voice, 'The sword of the Lord and of Gideon!'

The police officers heard of it, and set out to find him. They hunted the country over and even dragged the river, but they never found him again, living or dead. It is thought that he was drowned and the quicksands of the river sucked his body under. But the little Dane boys in our country firmly believed that he was translated like Enoch of old. On stormy nights, when the great winds sweep down from the north they huddle together in their beds and fancy that in the wind they still hear that wild cry, 'The sword of the Lord and of Gideon.'

First published in *The Hesperian*, 15 October 1892

ON THE DIVIDE

NEAR Rattlesnake Creek, on the side of a little draw, stood Canute's shanty. North, east, south, stretched the level Nebraska plain of long rust-red grass that undulated constantly in the wind. To the west the ground was broken and rough, and a narrow strip of timber wound along the turbid, muddy little stream that had scarcely ambition enough to crawl over its black bottom. If it had not been for the few stunted cottonwoods and elms that grew along its banks, Canute would have shot himself years ago. The Norwegians are a timber-loving people, and if there is even a turtle pond with a few plum bushes around it they seem irresistibly drawn toward it.

As to the shanty itself, Canute had built it without aid of any kind, for when he first squatted along the banks of Rattlesnake Creek there was not a human being within twenty miles. It was built of logs split in halves, the chinks stopped with mud and plaster. The roof was covered with earth and was supported by one gigantic beam curved in the shape of a round arch. It was almost impossible that any tree had ever grown in that shape. The Norwegians used to say that Canute had taken the log across his knee and bent it into the shape he wished. There were two rooms, or rather there was one room with a partition made of ash saplings interwoven and bound together like big straw basket work. In one corner there was a cook stove, rusted and broken. In the other a bed made of unplaned planks and poles. It was fully eight feet long, and upon it was a heap of dark bed clothing. There was a chair and a bench of colossal proportions. There was an ordinary kitchen cupboard with a few cracked dirty dishes in it, and beside it on a tall box a tin washbasin. Under the bed was a pile of pint flasks, some broken, some whole, all empty. On the wood box lay a pair of shoes of almost incredible dimensions. On the wall hung a saddle, a gun, and some ragged clothing, conspicuous among which was a suit of dark cloth, apparently new, with a paper collar carefully wrapped in a red silk handkerchief and pinned to the sleeve. Over the door hung a wolf and a badger skin, and on the door itself a brace of thirty or forty snake skins whose noisy tails rattled ominously every time it opened. The strangest things in the shanty were the wide window sills. At first glance they looked as though they had been ruthlessly hacked and mutilated with a hatchet, but on closer inspection all the notches and holes in the wood took form and shape. There seemed to be a series of pictures. They were, in a rough way, artistic, but the figures were heavy and labored, as though they had been cut very slowly and with very awkward instruments. There were men plowing with little horned imps sitting on their shoulders and on their horses' heads. There were men praying with a skull hanging over their heads and little demons behind them mocking their attitudes. There were men fighting with big serpents, and skeletons dancing together. All about these pictures were blooming vines and foliage such as never grew in this world, and coiled among the branches of the vines there was always the scaly body of a serpent, and behind every flower there was a serpent's head. It was a veritable Dance of Death by one who had felt its sting. In the wood box lay some boards, and every inch of them was cut up in the same manner. Sometimes the work was very rude and careless, and looked as though the hand of the workman had trembled. It would sometimes have been hard to distinguish the men from their evil geniuses but for one fact, the men were always grave and were either toiling or praying, while the devils were always smiling and dancing. Several of these boards had been split for kindling and it was evident that the artist did not value his work highly.

It was the first day of winter on the Divide. Canute stumbled into his shanty carrying a basket of cobs, and after filling the stove, sat down on a stool and crouched his seven foot frame over the fire, staring drearily out of the window at the wide gray sky. He knew by heart every individual clump of bunch grass in the miles of red shaggy prairie that stretched before his cabin. He knew it in all the deceitful loveliness of its early summer, in all the bitter barrenness of its autumn. He had seen it smitten by all the plagues of Egypt. He had seen it parched by drought, and sogged by rain, beaten by hail, and swept by fire, and in the grasshopper years he had seen it eaten as bare and clean as bones that the vultures have left. After the great fires he had seen it stretch for miles and miles, black and smoking as the floor of hell.

He rose slowly and crossed the room, dragging his big feet heavily as though they were burdens to him. He looked out of the window into the hog corral and saw the pigs burying themselves in the straw before the shed. The leaden gray clouds were beginning to spill themselves, and the snow-flakes were settling down over the white leprous patches of frozen earth where the hogs had gnawed even the sod away. He shuddered and began to walk, trampling heavily with his ungainly feet. He was the wreck of ten winters on the Divide and he knew what they meant. Men fear the winters of the Divide as a child fears night or as men in the North Seas fear the still dark cold of the polar twilight.

His eyes fell upon his gun, and he took it down from the wall and looked it over. He sat down on the edge of his bed and held the barrel towards his face, letting his forehead rest upon it, and laid his finger on the trigger. He was perfectly calm, there was neither passion nor despair in his face, but the thoughtful look of a man who is considering. Presently he laid down the gun, and reaching into the cupboard, drew out a pint bottle of raw white alcohol. Lifting it to his lips, he drank greedily. He washed his face in the tin basin and combed his rough hair and shaggy blond beard. Then he stood in uncertainty before the suit of dark clothes that hung on the wall. For the fiftieth time he took them in his hands and tried to summon courage to put them on. He took the paper collar that was pinned to the sleeve of the coat and cautiously slipped it under his rough beard, looking with timid expectancy into the cracked, splashed glass that hung over the bench. With a short laugh he threw it down on the bed, and pulling on his old black hat, he went out, striking off across the level.

It was a physical necessity for him to get away from his cabin once in a while. He had been there for ten years, digging and plowing and sowing, and reaping what little the hail and the hot winds and the frosts left him to reap. Insanity and suicide are very common things on the Divide. They come on like an epidemic in the hot wind season. Those scorching dusty winds that blow up over the bluffs from Kansas seem to dry up the blood in men's veins as they do the sap in the corn leaves. Whenever the yellow scorch creeps down over the tender inside leaves about the ear, then the coroners prepare for active duty; for the oil of the country is burned out and it does not take long for the flame to eat up the wick. It causes no great sensation there when a Dane is found swinging to his own windmill tower, and most of the Poles after they have become too careless and discouraged to shave themselves keep their razors to cut their throats with.

It may be that the next generation on the Divide will be very happy, but the present one came too late in life. It is useless for men that have cut hemlocks among the mountains of Sweden for forty years to try to be happy in a country as flat and gray and as naked as the sea. It is not easy for men that have spent their youths fishing in the Northern seas to be content with following a plow, and men that have served in the Austrian army hate hard work and coarse clothing and the loneliness of the plains, and long for marches and excitement and tavern company and pretty barmaids. After a man has passed his fortieth birthday it is not easy for him to change the habits and conditions of his life. Most men bring with them to the Divide only the dregs of the lives that they have squandered in other lands and among other peoples.

Canute Canuteson was as mad as any of them, but his madness did not take the form of suicide or religion but of alcohol. He had always taken liquor when he wanted it, as all Norwegians do, but after his first year of solitary life he settled down to it steadily. He exhausted whisky after a while, and went to alcohol, because its effects were speedier and surer. He was a big man with a terrible amount of resistant force, and it took a great deal of alcohol even to move him. After nine years of drinking, the quantities he could take would seem fabulous to an ordinary drinking man. He never let it interfere with his work, he generally drank at night and on Sundays. Every night, as soon as his chores were done, he began to drink. While he was able to sit up he would play on his mouth harp or hack away at his window sills with his jackknife. When the liquor went to his head he would lie down on his bed and stare out of the window until he went to sleep. He drank alone and in solitude not for pleasure or good cheer, but to forget the awful loneliness and level of the Divide. Milton made a sad blunder when he put mountains in hell. Mountains postulate faith and aspiration. All mountain peoples are religious. It was the cities of the plains that, because of their utter lack of spirituality and the mad caprice of their vice, were cursed of God.

Alcohol is perfectly consistent in its effects upon man. Drunkenness is merely an exaggeration. A foolish man drunk becomes maudlin; a bloody man, vicious; a coarse man, vulgar. Canute was none of these, but he was morose and gloomy, and liquor took him through all the hells of Dante. As he lay on his giant's bed all the horrors of this world and every other were laid bare to his chilled senses. He was a man who knew no joy, a man who toiled in silence and bitterness. The skull and the serpent were always before him, the symbols of eternal futileness and of eternal hate.

When the first Norwegians near enough to be called neighbors came, Canute rejoiced, and planned to escape from his bosom vice. But he was not a social man by nature and had not the power of drawing out the social side of other people. His new neighbors rather feared him because of his great strength and size, his silence and his lowering brows. Perhaps, too, they knew that he was mad, mad from the eternal treachery of the plains, which every spring stretch green and rustle with the promises of Eden, showing long grassy lagoons full of clear water and cattle whose hoofs are stained with wild roses. Before autumn the lagoons are dried up, and the ground is burnt dry and hard until it blisters and cracks open.

So instead of becoming a friend and neighbor to the men that settled about him, Canute became a mystery and a terror. They told awful stories of his size and strength and of the alcohol he drank. They said that one night, when he went out to see to his horses just before he went to bed, his steps were unsteady and the rotten planks of the floor gave way and threw him behind the feet of a fiery young stallion. His foot was caught fast in the floor, and the nervous horse began kicking frantically. When Canute felt the blood trickling down into his eyes from a scalp wound in his head, he roused himself from his kingly indifference, and with the quiet stoical courage of a drunken man leaned forward and wound his arms about the horse's hind legs and held them against his breast with crushing embrace. All through the darkness and cold of the night he lay there, matching strength against strength. When little Jim Peterson went over the next morning at four o'clock to go with him to the Blue to cut wood, he found him so, and the horse was on its foreknees, trembling and whinnying with fear. This is the story the Norwegians tell of him, and if it is true it is no wonder that they feared and hated this Holder of the Heels of Horses.

One spring there moved to the next 'eighty' a family that made a great change in Canute's life. Ole Yensen was too drunk most of the time to be afraid of anyone, and his wife Mary was too garrulous to be afraid of any one who listened to her talk, and Lena, their pretty daughter, was not afraid of man nor devil. So it came about that Canute went over to take his alcohol with Ole oftener than he took it alone. After a while the report spread that he was going to marry Yensen's daughter, and the Norwegian girls began to tease Lena about the great bear she was going to keep house for. No one could quite see how the affair had come about, for Canute's tactics of courtship were somewhat peculiar. He apparently never spoke to her at all: he would sit for hours with Mary chattering on one side of him and Ole drinking on the other and watch Lena at her work. She teased him, and threw flour in his face and put vinegar in his coffee, but he took her rough jokes with silent wonder, never even smiling. He took her to church occasionally, but the most watchful and curious people never saw him speak to her. He would sit staring at her while she giggled and flirted with the other men.

Next spring Mary Lee went to town to work in a steam laundry. She came home every Sunday, and always ran across to Yensens to startle Lena with stories of ten cent theatres, firemen's dances, and all the other esthetic delights of metropolitan life. In a few weeks Lena's head was completely turned, and she gave her father no rest until he let her go to town to seek her fortune at the ironing board. From the time she came home on her first visit she began to treat Canute with contempt. She had bought a plush cloak and kid gloves, had her clothes made by the dressmaker, and assumed airs and graces that made the other women of the neighborhood cordially detest her. She generally brought with her a young man from town who waxed his mustache and wore a red necktie, and she did not even introduce him to Canute.

The neighbors teased Canute a good deal until he knocked one of them down. He gave no sign of suffering from her neglect except that he drank more and avoided the other Norwegians more carefully than ever. He lay around in his den and no one knew what he felt or thought, but little Jim Paterson, who had seen him glowering at Lena in church one Sunday when she was there with the town man, said that he would not give an acre of his wheat for Lena's life or the town chap's either; and Jim's wheat was so wondrously worthless that the statement was an exceedingly strong one.

Canute had bought a new suit of clothes that looked as

nearly like the town man's as possible. They had cost him half a millet crop; for tailors are not accustomed to fitting giants and they charge for it. He had hung those clothes in his shanty two months ago and had never put them on, partly from fear of ridicule, partly from discouragement, and partly because there was something in his own soul that revolted at the littleness of the device.

Lena was at home just at this time. Work was slack in the laundry and Mary had not been well, so Lena stayed at home, glad enough to get an opportunity to torment Canute once more.

She was washing in the side kitchen, singing loudly as she worked. Mary was on her knees, blacking the stove and scolding violently about the young man who was coming out from town that night. The young man had committed the fatal error of laughing at Mary's ceaseless babble and had never been forgiven.

'He is no good, and you will come to a bad end by running with him! I do not see why a daughter of mine should act so. I do not see why the Lord should visit such a punishment upon me as to give me such a daughter. There are plenty of good men you can marry.'

Lena tossed her head and answered curtly, 'I don't happen to want to marry any man right away, and so long as Dick dresses nice and has plenty of money to spend, there is no harm in my going with him.'

'Money to spend? Yes, and that is all he does with it I'll be bound. You think it very fine now, but you will change your tune when you have been married for five years and see your children running naked and your cupboard empty. Did Anne Hermanson come to any good end by marrying a town man?'

'I don't know anything about Anne Hermanson, but I know any of the laundry girls would have Dick quick enough if they could get him.'

'Yes, and a nice lot of store clothes huzzies you are too. Now there is Canuteson who has an 'eighty' proved up and fifty head of cattle and — '

'And hair that ain't been cut since he was a baby, and a big dirty beard, and he wears overalls on Sundays, and drinks like a pig. Besides he will keep. I can have all the fun I want, and when I am old and ugly like you he can have me and take care of me. The Lord knows there ain't nobody else going to marry him.'

Canute drew his hand back from the latch as though it were red hot. He was not the kind of man to make a good eavesdropper, and he wished he had knocked sooner. He pulled himself together and struck the door like a battering ram. Mary jumped and opened it with a screech.

'God! Canute, how you scared us! I thought it was crazy Lou – he has been tearing around the neighborhood trying to convert folks. I am afraid as death of him. He ought to be sent off, I think. He is just as liable as not to kill us all, or burn the barn, or poison the dogs. He has been worrying even the poor minister to death, and he laid up with the rheumatism, too! Did you notice that he was too sick to preach last Sunday? But don't stand there in the cold – come in. Yensen isn't here, but he just went over to Sorenson's for the mail; he won't be gone long. Walk right in the other room and sit down.'

Canute followed her, looking steadily in front of him and not noticing Lena as he passed her. But Lena's vanity would not allow him to pass unmolested. She took the wet sheet she was wringing out and cracked him across the face with it, and ran giggling to the other side of the room. The blow stung his cheeks and the soapy water flew in his eyes, and he involuntarily began rubbing them with his hands. Lena giggled with delight at his discomfiture, and the wrath in Canute's face grew blacker than ever. A big man humiliated is vastly more undignified than a little one. He forgot the sting of his face in the bitter consciousness that he had made a fool of himself. He stumbled blindly into the living room, knocking his head against the door jamb because he forgot to stoop. He dropped into a chair behind the stove, thrusting his big feet back helplessly on either side of him.

Ole was a long time in coming, and Canute sat there, still

and silent, with his hands clenched on his knees, and the skin of his face seemed to have shriveled up into little wrinkles that trembled when he lowered his brows. His life had been one long lethargy of solitude and alcohol, but now he was awakening, and it was as when the dumb stagnant heat of summer breaks out into thunder.

When Ole came staggering in, heavy with liquor, Canute rose at once.

'Yensen,' he said quietly, 'I have come to see if you will let me marry your daughter today.'

'Today!' gasped Ole.

'Yes, I will not wait until tomorrow. I am tired of living alone.'

Ole braced his staggering knees against the bedstead, and stammered eloquently: 'Do you think I will marry my daughter to a drunkard? a man who drinks raw alcohol? a man who sleeps with rattlesnakes? Get out of my house or I will kick you out for your impudence.' And Ole began looking anxiously for his feet.

Canute answered not a word, but he put on his hat and went out into the kitchen. He went up to Lena and said without looking at her, 'Get your things on and come with me!'

The tone of his voice startled her, and she said angrily, dropping the soap, 'Are you drunk?'

'If you do not come with me, I will take you – you had better come,' said Canute quietly.

She lifted a sheet to strike him, but he caught her arm roughly and wrenched the sheet from her. He turned to the wall and took down a hood and shawl that hung there, and began wrapping her up. Lena scratched and fought like a wild thing. Ole stood in the door, cursing, and Mary howled and screeched at the top of her voice. As for Canute, he lifted the girl in his arms and went out of the house. She kicked and struggled, but the helpless wailing of Mary and Ole soon died away in the distance, and her face was held down tightly on Canute's shoulder so that she could not see whither he was taking her. She was conscious only of the north wind whistling in her ears, and of rapid steady motion and of a great breast that heaved beneath her in quick, irregular breaths. The harder she struggled the tighter those iron arms that had held the heels of horses crushed about her, until she felt as if they would crush the breath from her, and lay still with fear. Canute was striding across the level fields at a pace at which man never went before, drawing the stinging north wind into his lungs in great gulps. He walked with his eyes half closed and looking straight in front of him, only lowering them when he bent his head to blow away the snow-flakes that settled on her hair. So it was that Canute took her to his home, even as his bearded barbarian ancestors took the fair frivolous women of the South in their hairy arms and bore them down to their war ships. For ever and anon the soul becomes weary of the conventions that are not of it, and with a single stroke shatters the civilized lies with which it is unable to cope, and the strong arm reaches out and takes by force what it cannot win by cunning.

When Canute reached his shanty he placed the girl upon a chair, where she sat sobbing. He stayed only a few minutes. He filled the stove with wood and lit the lamp, drank a huge swallow of alcohol and put the bottle in his pocket. He paused a moment, staring heavily at the weeping girl, then he went off and locked the door and disappeared in the gathering gloom of the night.

Wrapped in flannels and soaked with turpentine, the little Norwegian preacher sat reading his Bible, when he heard a thundering knock at his door, and Canute entered, covered with snow and with his beard frozen fast to his coat.

'Come in, Canute, you must be frozen,' said the little man, shoving a chair towards his visitor.

Canute remained standing with his hat on and said quietly, 'I want you to come over to my house tonight to marry me to Lena Yensen.'

'Have you got a license, Canute?'

'No, I don't want a license. I want to be married.'

'But I can't marry you without a license, man. It would not be legal.'

A dangerous light came in the big Norwegian's eye. 'I want you to come over to my house to marry me to Lena Yensen.'

'No, I can't, it would kill an ox to go out in a storm like this, and my rheumatism is bad tonight.'

'Then if you will not go I must take you,' said Canute with a sigh.

He took down the preacher's bearskin coat and bade him put it on while he hitched up his buggy. He went out and closed the door softly after him. Presently he returned and found the frightened minister crouching before the fire with his coat lying beside him. Canute helped him put it on and gently wrapped his head in his big muffler. Then he picked him up and carried him out and placed him in his buggy. As he tucked the buffalo robes around him he said: 'Your horse is old, he might flounder or lose his way in this storm. I will lead him.'

The minister took the reins feebly in his hands and sat shivering with the cold. Sometimes when there was a lull in the wind, he could see the horse struggling through the snow with the man plodding steadily beside him. Again the blowing snow would hide them from him altogether. He had no idea where they were or what direction they were going. He felt as though he were being whirled away in the heart of the storm, and he said all the prayers he knew. But at last the long four miles were over, and Canute set him down in the snow while he unlocked the door. He saw the bride sitting by the fire with her eyes red and swollen as though she had been weeping. Canute placed a huge chair for him, and said roughly,

'Warm yourself.'

Lena began to cry and moan afresh, begging the minister to take her home. He looked helplessly at Canute. Canute said simply,

'If you are warm now, you can marry us.'

'My daughter, do you take this step of your own free will?' asked the minister in a trembling voice.

'No sir, I don't, and it is disgraceful he should force me into it! I won't marry him.'

'Then, Canute, I cannot marry you,' said the minister, standing as straight as his rheumatic limbs would let him.

'Are you ready to marry us now, sir?' said Canute, laying one iron hand on his stooped shoulder. The little preacher was a good man, but like most men of weak body he was a coward and had a horror of physical suffering, although he had known so much of it. So with many qualms of conscience he began to repeat the marriage service. Lena sat sullenly in her chair, staring at the fire. Canute stood beside her, listening with his head bent reverently and his hands folded on his breast. When the little man had prayed and said amen, Canute began bundling him up again.

'I will take you home, now,' he said as he carried him out and placed him in his buggy, and started off with him through the fury of the storm, floundering among the snow drifts that brought even the giant himself to his knees.

After she was left alone, Lena soon ceased weeping. She was not of a particularly sensitive temperament, and had little pride beyond that of vanity. After the first bitter anger wore itself out, she felt nothing more than a healthy sense of humiliation and defeat. She had no inclination to run away, for she was married now, and in her eyes that was final and all rebellion was useless. She knew nothing about a license, but she knew that a preacher married folks. She consoled herself by thinking that she had always intended to marry Canute someday, anyway.

She grew tired of crying and looking into the fire, so she got up and began to look about her. She had heard queer tales about the inside of Canute's shanty, and her curiosity soon got the better of her rage. One of the first things she noticed was the new black suit of clothes hanging on the wall. She was dull, but it did not take a vain woman long to interpret anything so decidedly flattering, and she was pleased in spite of herself. As she looked through the cupboard, the general air of neglect and discomfort made her pity the man who lived there.

'Poor fellow, no wonder he wants to get married to get somebody to wash up his dishes. Batchin's pretty hard on a man.'

It is easy to pity when once one's vanity has been tickled. She looked at the window sill and gave a little shudder and wondered if the man were crazy. Then she sat down again and sat a long time wondering what her Dick and Ole would do.

'It is queer Dick didn't come right over after me. He surely came, for he would have left town before the storm began and he might just as well come right on as go back. If he'd hurried he would have gotten here before the preacher came. I suppose he was afraid to come, for he knew Canuteson could pound him to jelly, the coward!' Her eyes flashed angrily.

The weary hours wore on and Lena began to grow horribly lonesome. It was an uncanny night and this was an uncanny place to be in. She could hear the coyotes howling a little way from the cabin, and more terrible still were all the unknown noises of the storm. She remembered the tales they told of the big log overhead and she was afraid of those snaky things on the window sills. She remembered the man who had been killed in the draw, and she wondered what she would do if she saw crazy Lou's white face glaring into the window. The rattling of the door became unbearable, she thought the latch must be loose and took the lamp to look at it. Then for the first time she saw the ugly brown snake skins whose death rattle sounded every time the wind jarred the door.

'Canute, Canute!' she screamed in terror.

Outside the door she heard a heavy sound as of a big dog getting up and shaking himself. The door opened and Canute stood before her, white as a snow drift.

'What is it?' he asked kindly.

'I am cold,' she faltered.

He went out and got an armful of wood and a basket of cobs and filled the stove. Then he went out and lay in the snow before the door. Presently he heard her calling again.

'What is it?' he said, sitting up.

'I'm so lonesome, I'm afraid to stay in here all alone.'

'I will go over and get your mother.' And he got up.

'She won't come.'

'I'll bring her,' said Canute grimly.

'No, no. I don't want her, she will scold all the time.'

'Well, I will bring your father.'

She spoke again and it seemed as though her mouth was close up to the key hole. She spoke lower than he had ever heard her speak before, so low that he had to put his ear up to the lock to hear her.

'I don't want him either, Canute – I'd rather have you.'

For a moment she heard no noise at all, then something like a groan. With a cry of fear she opened the door, and saw Canute stretched in the snow at her feet, his face in his hands, sobbing on the door step.

First published in *Overland Monthly*, January 1896.

TOMMY, THE UNSENTIMENTAL

'YOUR father says he has no business tact at all, and of course that's dreadfully unfortunate.'

'Business,' replied Tommy, 'he's a baby in business; he's good for nothing on earth but to keep his hair parted straight and wear that white carnation in his buttonhole. He has 'em sent down from Hastings twice a week as regularly as the mail comes, but the drafts he cashes lie in his safe until they are lost, or somebody finds them. I go up occasionally and send a package away for him myself. He'll answer your notes promptly enough, but his business letters – I believe he destroys them unopened to shake the responsibility of answering them.'

'I am at a loss to see how you can have such patience with him, Tommy, in so many ways he is thoroughly reprehensible.'

'Well, a man's likeableness don't depend at all on his virtues or acquirements, nor a woman's either, unfortunately. You like them or you don't like them, and that's all there is to it. For the why of it you must appeal to a higher oracle than I. Jay is a likeable fellow, and that's his only and sole acquirement, but after all it's a rather happy one.'

'Yes, he certainly is that,' replied Miss Jessica, as she deliberately turned off the gas jet and proceeded to arrange her toilet articles. Tommy watched her closely and then turned away with a baffled expression.

Needless to say, Tommy was not a boy, although her

keen gray eyes and wide forehead were scarcely girlish, and she had the lank figure of an active half grown lad. Her real name was Theodosia, but during Thomas Shirley's frequent absences from the bank she had attended to his business and correspondence signing herself 'T. Shirley,' until everyone in Southdown called her 'Tommy.' That blunt sort of familiarity is not unfrequent in the West, and is meant well enough. People rather expect some business ability in a girl there, and they respect it immensely. That, Tommy undoubtedly had, and if she had not, things would have gone at sixes and sevens in the Southdown National. For Thomas Shirley had big land interests in Wyoming that called him constantly away from home, and his cashier, little Jay Ellington Harper, was, in the local phrase, a weak brother in the bank. He was the son of a friend of old Shirley's, whose papa had sent him West, because he had made a sad mess of his college career, and had spent too much money and gone at too giddy a pace down East. Conditions changed the young gentleman's life, for it was simply impossible to live either prodigally or rapidly in Southdown, but they could not materially affect his mental habits or inclinations. He was made cashier of Shirley's bank because his father bought in half the stock, but Tommy did his work for him.

The relation between these two young people was peculiar; Harper was, in his way, very grateful to her for keeping him out of disgrace with her father, and showed it by a hundred little attentions which were new to her and much more agreeable than the work she did for him was irksome. Tommy knew that she was immensely fond of him, and she knew at the same time that she was thoroughly foolish for being so. As she expressed it, she was not of his sort, and never would be. She did not often take pains to think, but when she did she saw matters pretty clearly, and she was of a peculiarly unfeminine mind that could not escape meeting and acknowledging a logical conclusion. But she went on liking Jay Ellington Harper, just the same. Now Harper was the only foolish man of Tommy's acquaintance.

She knew plenty of active young business men and sturdy ranchers, such as one meets about live western towns, and took no particular interest in them, probably just because they were practical and sensible and thoroughly of her own kind. She knew almost no women, because in those days there were few women in Southdown who were in any sense interesting, or interested in anything but babies and salads. Her best friends were her father's old business friends, elderly men who had seen a good deal of the world, and who were very proud and fond of Tommy. They recognized a sort of squareness and honesty of spirit in the girl that Jay Ellington Harper never discovered, or, if he did, knew too little of its rareness to value highly. Those old speculators and men of business had always felt a sort of responsibility for Tom Shirley's little girl, and had rather taken her mother's place, and been her advisers on many points upon which men seldom feel at liberty to address a girl.

She was just one of them; she played whist and billiards with them, and made their cocktails for them, not scorning to take one herself occasionally. Indeed, Tommy's cocktails were things of fame in Southdown, and the professional compounders of drinks always bowed respectfully to her as though acknowledging a powerful rival.

Now all these things displeased and puzzled Jay Ellington Harper, and Tommy knew it full well, but clung to her old manner of living with a stubborn pertinacity, feeling somehow that to change would be both foolish and disloyal to the Old Boys. And as things went on, the seven Old Boys made greater demands upon her time than ever, for they were shrewd men, most of them, and had not lived fifty years in this world without learning a few things and unlearning many more. And while Tommy lived on in the blissful delusion that her role of indifference was perfectly played and without a flaw, they suspected how things were going and were perplexed as to the outcome. Still, their confidence was by no means shaken, and as Joe Elsworth said to Joe Sawyer one evening at billiards, 'I think we can pretty nearly depend on Tommy's good sense.'

They were too wise to say anything to Tommy, but they said just a word or two to Thomas Shirley, Sr., and combined to make things very unpleasant for Mr Jay Ellington Harper.

At length their relations with Harper became so strained that the young man felt it would be better for him to leave town, so his father started him in a little bank of his own up in Red Willow. Red Willow, however, was scarcely a safe distance, being only some twenty-five miles north, upon the Divide, and Tommy occasionally found excuse to run up on her wheel to straighten out the young man's business for him. So when she suddenly decided to go East to school for a year, Thomas Sr., drew a sigh of great relief. But the seven Old Boys shook their heads; they did not like to see her gravitating toward the East; it was a sign of weakening, they said, and showed an inclination to experiment with another kind of life, Jay Ellington Harper's kind.

But to school Tommy went, and from all reports conducted herself in a most seemly manner; made no more cocktails, played no more billiards. She took rather her own way with the curriculum, but she distinguished herself in athletics, which in Southdown counted for vastly more than erudition.

Her evident joy on getting back to Southdown was appreciated by everyone. She went about shaking hands with everybody, her shrewd face, that was so like a clever wholesome boy's, held high with happiness. As she said to old Joe Elsworth one morning, when they were driving behind his stud through a little thicket of cottonwood scattered along the sun-parched bluffs, 'It's all very fine down East there, and the hills are great, but one gets mighty homesick for this sky, the old intense blue of it, you know. Down there the skies are all pale and smoky. And this wind, this hateful, dear, old everlasting wind that comes down like the sweep of cavalry and is never tamed or broken, O Joe, I used to get hungry for this wind! I couldn't sleep in that lifeless stillness down there.'

'How about the people, Tom?'

'O, they are fine enough folk, but we're not their sort, Joe, and never can be.'

'You realize that, do you, fully?'

'Quite fully enough, thank you, Joe.' She laughed rather dismally, and Joe cut his horse with the whip.

The only unsatisfactory thing about Tommy's return was that she brought with her a girl she had grown fond of at school, a dainty, white, languid bit of a thing, who used violet perfumes and carried a sunshade. The Old Boys said it was a bad sign when a rebellious girl like Tommy took to being sweet and gentle to one of her own sex, the worst sign in the world.

The new girl was no sooner in town than a new complication came about. There was no doubt of the impression she made on Jay Ellington Harper. She indisputably had all those little evidences of good breeding that were about the only things which could touch the timid, harassed young man who was so much out of his element. It was a very plain case on his part, and the souls of the seven were troubled within them. Said Joe Elsworth to the other Joe, 'The heart of the cad is gone out to the little muff, as is right and proper and in accordance with the eternal fitness of things. But there's the other girl who has the blindness that may not be cured, and she gets all the rub of it. It's no use, I can't help her, and I am going to run down to Kansas City for awhile. I can't stay here and see the abominable suffering of it.' He didn't go, however.

There was just one other person who understood the hopelessness of the situation quite as well as Joe, and that was Tommy. That is, she understood Harper's attitude. As to Miss Jessica's she was not quite so certain, for Miss Jessica, though pale and languid and addicted to sunshades, was a maiden most discreet. Conversations on the subject usually ended without any further information as to Miss Jessica's feelings, and Tommy sometimes wondered if she were capable of having any at all.

At last the calamity which Tommy had long foretold descended upon Jay Ellington Harper. One morning she received a telegram from him begging her to intercede with her father; there was a run on his bank and he must have help before noon. It was then ten thirty, and the one sleepy little train that ran up to Red Willow daily had crawled out of the station an hour before. Thomas Shirley, Sr., was not at home.

'And it's a good thing for Jay Ellington he's not, he might be more stony hearted than I,' remarked Tommy, as she closed the ledger and turned to the terrified Miss Jessica. 'Of course we're his only chance, no one else would turn their hand over to help him. The train went an hour ago and he says it must be there by noon. It's the only bank in the town, so nothing can be done by telegraph. There is nothing left but to wheel for it. I may make it, and I may not. Jess, you scamper up to the house and get my wheel out, the tire may need a little attention. I will be along in a minute.'

'O, Theodosia, can't I go with you? I must go!'

'You go! O, yes, of course, if you want to. You know what you are getting into, though. It's twenty-five miles uppish grade and hilly, and only an hour and a quarter to do it in.'

'O, Theodosia, I can do anything now!' cried Miss Jessica, as she put up her sunshade and fled precipitately. Tommy smiled as she began cramming bank notes into a canvas bag. 'May be you can, my dear, and may be you can't.'

The road from Southdown to Red Willow is not by any means a favorite bicycle road; it is rough, hilly and climbs from the river bottoms up to the big Divide by a steady up grade, running white and hot through the scorched corn fields and grazing lands where the long-horned Texan cattle browse about in the old buffalo wallows. Miss Jessica soon found that with the pedaling that had to be done there was little time left for emotion of any sort, or little sensibility for anything but the throbbing, dazzling heat that had to be endured. Down there in the valley the distant bluffs were vibrating and dancing with the heat, the cattle, completely overcome by it, had hidden under the shelving banks of the 'draws' and the prairie dogs had fled to the bottom of their holes that are said to reach to water. The whirr of the seventeen-year locust was the only thing that spoke of animation, and that ground on as if only animated and enlivened by the sickening, destroying heat. The sun was like hot brass, and the wind that blew up from the south was hotter still. But Tommy knew that wind was their only chance. Miss Jessica began to feel that unless she could stop and get some water she was not much longer for this vale of tears. She suggested this possibility to Tommy, but Tommy only shook her head, 'Take too much time,' and bent over her handle bars, never lifting her eyes from the road in front of her. It flashed upon Miss Jessica that Tommy was not only very unkind, but that she sat very badly on her wheel and looked aggressively masculine and professional when she bent her shoulders and pumped like that. But just then Miss Jessica found it harder than ever to breathe, and the bluffs across the river began doing serpentines and skirt dances, and more important and personal considerations occupied the young lady.

When they were fairly over the first half of the road, Tommy took out her watch. 'Have to hurry up, Jess, I can't wait for you.'

'O, Tommy, I can't,' panted Miss Jessica, dismounting and sitting down in a little heap by the roadside. 'You go on, Tommy, and tell him – tell him I hope it won't fail, and I'd do anything to save him.'

By this time the discreet Miss Jessica was reduced to tears, and Tommy nodded as she disappeared over the hill laughing to herself. 'Poor Jess, anything but the one thing he needs. Well, your kind have the best of it generally, but in little affairs of this sort my kind come out rather strongly. We're rather better at them than at dancing. It's only fair, one side shouldn't have all.'

Just at twelve o'clock, when Jay Ellington Harper, his collar crushed and wet about his throat, his eyeglass dimmed with perspiration, his hair hanging damp over his forehead, and even the ends of his moustache dripping with moisture, was attempting to reason with a score of angry

Bohemians, Tommy came quietly through the door, grip in hand. She went straight behind the grating, and standing screened by the book-keeper's desk, handed the bag to Harper and turned to the spokesman of the Bohemians.

'What's all this business mean, Anton? Do you all come to bank at once nowadays?'

'We want 'a money, want 'a our money, he no got it, no give it,' bawled the big beery Bohemian.

'O, don't chaff 'em any longer, give 'em their money and get rid of 'em, I want to see you,' said Tommy carelessly, as she went into the consulting room.

When Harper entered half an hour later, after the rush was over, all that was left of his usual immaculate appearance was his eyeglass and the white flower in his buttonhole.

'This has been terrible!' he gasped. 'Miss Theodosia, I can never thank you.'

'No,' interrupted Tommy. 'You never can, and I don't want any thanks. It was rather a tight place, though, wasn't it? You looked like a ghost when I came in. What started them?'

'How should I know? They just came down like the wolf on the fold. It sounded like the approach of a ghost dance.'*

'And of course you had no reserve? O, I always told you this would come, it was inevitable with your charming methods. By the way, Jess sends her regrets and says she would do anything to save you. She started out with me, but she has fallen by the wayside. O, don't be alarmed, she is not hurt, just winded. I left her all bunched up by the road like a little white rabbit. I think the lack of romance in the escapade did her up about as much as anything; she is essentially romantic. If we had been on fiery steeds bespattered with foam I think she would have made it, but a wheel hurt her dignity. I'll tend bank; you'd better get your

*The ghost dance, a ritualistic worship of Wovoka, a self-appointed Indian Messiah, was associated with the so-called Sioux Uprising of 1890, which culminated in the battle of Wounded Knee, in South Dakota near the Nebraska border, on December 29, 1890.

wheel and go and look her up and comfort her. And as soon as it is convenient, Jay, I wish you'd marry her and be done with it, I want to get this thing off my mind.'

Jay Ellington Harper dropped into a chair and turned a shade whiter.

'Theodosia, what do you mean? Don't you remember what I said to you last fall, the night before you went to school? Don't you remember what I wrote you – '

Tommy sat down on the table beside him and looked seriously and frankly into his eyes.

'Now, see here, Jay Ellington, we have been playing a nice little game, and now it's time to quit. One must grow up sometime. You are horribly wrought up over Jess, and why deny it? She's your kind, and clean daft about you, so there is only one thing to do. That's all.'

Jay Ellington wiped his brow, and felt unequal to the situation. Perhaps he really came nearer to being moved down to his stolid little depths than he ever had before. His voice shook a good deal and was very low as he answered her.

'You have been very good to me, I didn't believe any woman could be at once so kind and clever. You almost made a man of even me.'

'Well, I certainly didn't succeed. As to being good to you, that's rather a break, you know; I am amiable, but I am only flesh and blood after all. Since I have known you I have not been at all good, in any sense of the word, and I suspect I have been anything but clever. Now, take mercy upon Jess – and me – and go. Go on, that ride is beginning to tell on me. Such things strain one's nerve ... Thank Heaven he's gone at last and had sense enough not to say anything more. It was growing rather critical. As I told him I am not at all superhuman.'

After Jay Ellington Harper had bowed himself out, when Tommy sat alone in the darkened office, watching the flapping blinds, with the bank books before her, she noticed a white flower on the floor. It was the one Jay Ellington Harper had worn in his coat and had dropped in his nervous agitation. She picked it up and stood holding it a moment, biting her lip. Then she dropped it into the grate and turned away, shrugging her thin shoulders.

'They are awful idiots, half of them, and never think of anything beyond their dinner. But O, how we do like 'em!'

First published in *Home Monthly*, August 1896.

THE SENTIMENTALITY OF
WILLIAM TAVENER

IT TAKES a strong woman to make any sort of success of living in the West, and Hester undoubtedly was that. When people spoke of William Tavener as the most prosperous farmer in McPherson County, they usually added that his wife was a 'good manager.' She was an executive woman, quick of tongue and something of an imperatrix. The only reason her husband did not consult her about his business was that she did not wait to be consulted.

It would have been quite impossible for one man, within the limited sphere of human action, to follow all Hester's advice, but in the end William usually acted upon some of her suggestions. When she incessantly denounced the 'shift-lessness' of letting a new threshing machine stand unprotected in the open, he eventually built a shed for it. When she sniffed contemptuously at his notion of fencing a hog corral with sod walls, he made a spiritless beginning on the structure – merely to 'show his temper,' as she put it – but in the end he went off quietly to town and bought enough barbed wire to complete the fence. When the first heavy rains came on, and the pigs rooted down the sod wall and made little paths all over it to facilitate their ascent, he heard his wife relate with relish the story of the little pig that built a mud house, to the minister at the dinner table, and William's gravity never relaxed for an instant. Silence, indeed, was William's refuge and his strength.

William set his boys a wholesome example to respect their

mother. People who knew him very well suspected that he even admired her. He was a hard man towards his neighbors, and even towards his sons: grasping, determined and ambitious.

There was an occasional blue day about the house when William went over the store bills, but he never objected to items relating to his wife's gowns or bonnets. So it came about that many of the foolish, unnecessary little things that Hester bought for boys, she had charged to her personal account.

One spring night Hester sat in a rocking chair by the sitting room window, darning socks. She rocked violently and sent her long needle vigorously back and forth over her gourd, and it took only a very casual glance to see that she was wrought up over something. William sat on the other side of the table reading his farm paper. If he had noticed his wife's agitation, his calm, clean-shaven face betrayed no sign of concern. He must have noticed the sarcastic turn of her remarks at the supper table, and he must have noticed the moody silence of the older boys as they ate. When supper was but half over little Billy, the youngest, had suddenly pushed back his plate and slipped away from the table, manfully trying to swallow a sob. But William Tavener never heeded ominous forecasts in the domestic horizon, and he never looked for a storm until it broke.

After supper the boys had gone to the pond under the willows in the big cattle corral, to get rid of the dust of plowing. Hester could hear an occasional splash and a laugh ringing clear through the stillness of the night, as she sat by the open window. She sat silent for almost an hour reviewing in her mind many plans of attack. But she was too vigorous a woman to be much of a strategist, and she usually came to her point with directness. At last she cut her thread and suddenly put her darning down, saying emphatically:

'William, I don't think it would hurt you to let the boys go to that circus in town tomorrow.'

William continued to read his farm paper, but it was not Hester's custom to wait for an answer. She usually divined his arguments and assailed them one by one before he uttered them.

'You've been short of hands all summer, and you've worked the boys hard, and a man ought to use his own flesh and blood as well as he does his hired hands. We're plenty able to afford it, and it's little enough our boys ever spend. I don't see how you can expect 'em to be steady and hard workin', unless you encourage 'em a little. I never could see much harm in circuses, and our boys have never been to one. Oh, I know Jim Howley's boys get drunk an' carry on when they go, but our boys ain't that sort, an' you know it, William. The animals are real instructive, an' our boys don't get to see much out here on the prairie. It was different where we were raised, but the boys have got no advantages here, an' if you don't take care, they'll grow up to be greenhorns.'

Hester paused a moment, and William folded up his paper, but vouchsafed no remark. His sisters in Virginia had often said that only a quiet man like William could ever have lived with Hester Perkins. Secretly, William was rather proud of his wife's 'gift of speech,' and of the fact that she could talk in prayer meetings as fluently as a man. He confined his own efforts in that line to a brief prayer at Covenant meetings.

Hester shook out another sock and went on.

'Nobody was ever hurt by goin' to a circus. Why, law me! I remember I went to one myself once, when I was little. I had most forgot about it. It was over at Pewtown, an' I remember how I had set my heart on going. I don't think I'd ever forgiven my father if he hadn't taken me, though that red clay road was in a frightful way after the rain. I mind they had an elephant and six poll parrots, an' a Rocky Mountain lion, an' a cage of monkeys, an' two camels. My! but they were a sight to me then!'

Hester dropped the black sock and shook her head and smiled at the recollection. She was not expecting anything from William yet, and she was fairly startled when he said gravely, in much the same tone in which he announced the hymns in prayer meeting:

'No, there was only one camel. The other was a dromedary.'

She peered around the lamp and looked at him keenly.

'Why, William, how come you to know?'

William folded his paper and answered with some hesitation, 'I was there, too.'

Hester's interest flashed up. 'Well, I never, William! To think of my finding it out after all these years! Why, you couldn't have been much bigger'n our Billy then. It seems queer I never saw you when you was little, to remember about you. But then you Back Creek folks never have anything to do with us Gap people. But how come you to go? Your father was stricter with you than you are with your boys.'

'I reckon I shouldn't 'a gone,' he said slowly, 'but boys will do foolish things. I had done a good deal of fox hunting the winter before, and father let me keep the bounty money. I hired Tom Smith's Tap to weed the corn for me, an' I slipped off unbeknownst to father an' went to the show.'

Hester spoke up warmly: 'Nonsense, William! It didn't do you no harm, I guess. You was always worked hard enough. It must have been a big sight for a little fellow. That clown must have just tickled you to death.'

William crossed his knees and leaned back in his chair.

'I reckon I could tell all that fool's jokes now. Sometimes I can't help thinkin' about 'em in meetin' when the sermon's long. I mind I had on a pair of new boots that hurt me like the mischief, but I forgot all about 'em when that fellow rode the donkey. I recall I had to take them boots off as soon as I got out of sight o' town, and walked home in the mud barefoot.'

'O poor little fellow!' Hester ejaculated, drawing her chair nearer and leaning her elbows on the table. 'What cruel shoes they did use to make for children. I remember I went up to Back Creek to see the circus wagons go by. They came down from Romney, you know. The circus men stopped at the creek to water the animals, an' the elephant got stubborn an' broke a big limb off the yellow willow tree that grew

there by the toll house porch, an' the Scribners were 'fraid as
death he'd pull the house down. But this much I saw him do;
he waded in the creek an' filled his trunk with water and
squirted it in at the window and nearly ruined Ellen Scribner's
pink lawn dress that she had just ironed an' laid out on the bed
ready to wear to the circus.'

'I reckon that must have been a trial to Ellen,' chuckled
William, 'for she was mighty prim in them days.'

Hester drew her chair still nearer William's. Since the
children had begun growing up, her conversation with her
husband had been almost wholly confined to questions of
economy and expense. Their relationship had become purely
a business one, like that between landlord and tenant. In her
desire to indulge her boys she had unconsciously assumed a
defensive and almost hostile attitude towards her husband.
No debtor ever haggled with his usurer more doggedly than
did Hester with her husband in behalf of her sons. The
strategic contest had gone on so long that it had almost
crowded out the memory of a closer relationship. This
exchange of confidences tonight, when common recollections
took them unawares and opened their hearts, had all the
miracle of romance. They talked on and on; of old neighbors,
of old familiar faces in the valley where they had grown up, of
long forgotten incidents of their youth – weddings, picnics,
sleighing parties and baptizings. For years they had talked of
nothing else but butter and eggs and the prices of things, and
now they had as much to say to each other as people who
meet after a long separation.

When the clock struck ten, William rose and went over to
his walnut secretary and unlocked it. From his red leather
wallet he took out a ten dollar bill and laid it on the table
beside Hester.

'Tell the boys not to stay late, an' not to drive the horses
hard,' he said quietly, and went off to bed.

Hester blew out the lamp and sat still in the dark a long time.
She left the bill lying on the table where William had placed it.
She had a painful sense of having missed something, or lost
something; she felt that somehow the years had cheated her.

The little locust trees that grew by the fence were white with blossoms. Their heavy odor floated in to her on the night wind and recalled a night long ago, when the first whippoorwill of the Spring was heard, and the rough, buxom girls of Hawkins Gap had held her laughing and struggling under the locust trees, and searched in her bosom for a lock of her sweetheart's hair, which is supposed to be on every girl's breast when the first whippoorwill sings. Two of those same girls had been her bridesmaids. Hester had been a very happy bride. She rose and went softly into the room where William lay. He was sleeping heavily, but occasionally moved his hand before his face to ward off the flies. Hester went into the parlor and took the piece of mosquito net from the basket of wax apples and pears that her sister had made before she died. One of the boys had brought it all the way from Virginia, packed in a tin pail, since Hester would not risk shipping so precious an ornament by freight. She went back to the bedroom and spread the net over William's head. Then she sat down by the bed and listened to his deep, regular breathing until she heard the boys returning. She went out to meet them and warn them not to waken their father.

'I'll be up early to get your breakfast, boys. Your father says you can go to the show.' As she handed the money to the eldest, she felt a sudden throb of allegiance to her husband and said sharply, 'And you be careful of that, an' don't waste it. Your father works hard for his money.'

The boys looked at each other in astonishment and felt that they had lost a powerful ally.

First published in *The Library*, 12 May 1900.

'A DEATH IN THE DESERT'

*E*VERETT Hilgarde was conscious that the man in the seat across the aisle was looking at him intently. He was a large, florid man, wore a conspicuous diamond solitaire upon his third finger, and Everett judged him to be a travelling salesman of some sort. He had the air of an adaptable fellow who had been about the world and who could keep cool and clean under almost any circumstances.

The 'High Line Flyer,' as this train was derisively called among railroad men, was jerking along through the hot afternoon over the monotonous country between Holdrege and Cheyenne. Besides the blond man and himself the only occupants of the car were two dusty, bedraggled-looking girls who had been to the Exposition at Chicago, and who were earnestly discussing the cost of their first trip out of Colorado. The four uncomfortable passengers were covered with a sediment of fine, yellow dust which clung to their hair and eyebrows like gold powder. It blew up in clouds from the bleak, lifeless country through which they passed, until they were one colour with the sage-brush and sand-hills. The grey and yellow desert was varied only by occasional ruins of deserted towns, and by the little red boxes of station-houses, where the spindling trees and sickly vines in the blue-grass yards made little green reserves fenced off in that confusing wilderness of sand.

As the slanting rays of the sun beat in stronger and stronger through the car-windows, the blond gentleman asked the ladies' permission to remove his coat, and sat in his lavender striped shirt-sleeves, with a black silk handkerchief tucked carefully about his collar. He had seemed interested in Everett since they had boarded the train at Holdrege, and kept glancing at him curiously and then looking reflectively out of the window, as though he were trying to recall something. But wherever Everett went some one was almost sure to look at him with that curious interest, and it had ceased to embarrass or annoy him. Presently the stranger, seeming satisfied with his observation, leaned back in his seat, half closed his eyes, and began softly to whistle the Spring Song from *Proserpine*, the cantata that a dozen years before had made its young composer famous in a night. Everett had heard that air on guitars in Old Mexico, on mandolins at college glees, on cottage organs in New England hamlets, and only two weeks ago he had heard it played on sleighbells at a variety theatre in Denver. There was literally no way of escaping his brother's precocity. Adriance could live on the other side of the Atlantic, where his youthful indiscretions were forgotten in his mature achievements, but his brother had never been able to outrun *Proserpine*, and here he found it again in the Colorado sand-hills. Not that Everett was exactly ashamed of *Proserpine*; only a man of genius could have written it, but it was the sort of thing that a man of genius outgrows as soon as he can.

Everett unbent a trifle, and smiled at his neighbour across the aisle. Immediately the large man rose and coming over dropped into the seat facing Hilgarde, extending his card.

'Dusty ride, isn't it? I don't mind it myself; I'm used to it. Born and bred in de briar patch, like Br'er Rabbit. I've been trying to place you for a long time; I think I must have met you before.'

'Thank you,' said Everett, taking the card; 'my name is Hilgarde. You've probably met my brother, Adriance; people often mistake me for him.'

The travelling-man brought his hand down upon his knee with such vehemence that the solitaire blazed.

'So I was right after all, and if you're not Adriance Hilgarde you're his double. I thought I couldn't be mistaken. Seen him? Well, I guess! I never missed one of his recitals at the Auditorium, and he played the piano score of *Proserpine* through to us once at the Chicago Press Club. I used to be on the *Commercial* there before I began to travel for the publishing department of the concern. So you're Hilgarde's brother, and here I've run into you at the jumping-off place. Sounds like a newspaper yarn, doesn't it?'

The travelling-man laughed and offered Everett a cigar and plied him with questions on the only subject that people ever seemed to care to talk to Everett about. At length the salesman and the two girls alighted at a Colorado station, and Everett went on to Cheyenne alone.

The train pulled into Cheyenne at nine o'clock, late by a matter of four hours or so; but no one seemed particularly concerned at its tardiness except the station agent, who grumbled at being kept in the office over time on a summer night. When Everett alighted from the train he walked down the platform and stopped at the track crossing, uncertain as to what direction he should take to reach a hotel. A phaeton stood near the crossing and a woman held the reins. She was dressed in white, and her figure was clearly silhouetted against the cushions, though it was too dark to see her face. Everett had scarcely noticed her, when the switch-engine came puffing up from the opposite direction, and the headlight threw a strong glare of light on his face. Suddenly the woman in the phaeton uttered a low cry and dropped the reins. Everett started forward and caught the horse's head, but the animal only lifted its ears and whisked its tail in impatient surprise. The woman sat perfectly still, her head sunk between her shoulders and her handkerchief pressed to her face. Another woman came out of the depot and hurried toward the phaeton, crying 'Katharine, dear, what is the matter?'

Everett hesitated a moment in painful embarrassment, then lifted his hat and passed on. He was accustomed to sudden recognitions in the most impossible places, especially by women, but this cry out of the night had shaken him.

While Everett was breakfasting the next morning, the head waiter leaned over his chair to murmur that there was a gentleman waiting to see him in the parlour. Everett finished his coffee, and went in the direction indicated, where he found his visitor restlessly pacing the floor. His whole manner betrayed a high degree of agitation, though his physique was not that of a man whose nerves lie near the surface. He was something below medium height, square-shouldered and solidly built. His thick, closely cut hair was beginning to show grey about the ears, and his bronzed face was heavily lined. His square brown hands were locked behind him, and he held his shoulders like a man conscious of responsibilities, yet, as he turned to greet Everett, there was an incongruous diffidence in his address.

'Good-morning, Mr Hilgarde,' he said, extending his hand; 'I found your name on the hotel register. My name is Gaylord. I'm afraid my sister startled you at the station last night, Mr Hilgarde, and I've come around to apologize.'

'Ah! the young lady in the phaeton? I'm sure I didn't know whether I had anything to do with her alarm or not. If I did, it is I who owe the apology.'

The man coloured a little under the dark brown of his face.

'Oh, it's nothing you could help, sir, I fully understand that. You see, my sister used to be a pupil of your brother's, and it seems you favour him; and when the switch-engine threw a light on your face it startled her.'

Everett wheeled about in his chair. 'Oh! *Katharine* Gaylord! Is it possible! Now it's you who have given me a turn. Why I used to know her when I was a boy. What on earth – '

'Is she doing here?' said Gaylord, grimly filling out the pause. 'You've got at the heart of the matter. You knew my sister had been in bad health for a long time?'

'No, I had never heard a word of that. The last I knew of her she was singing in London. My brother and I correspond infrequently, and seldom get beyond family matters. I am deeply sorry to hear this. There are many more reasons why I am concerned than I can tell you.'

The lines in Charley Gaylord's brow relaxed a little.

'What I'm trying to say, Mr Hilgarde, is that she wants to see you. I hate to ask you, but she's so set on it. We live several miles out of town, but my rig's below, and I can take you out any time you can go.'

'I can go now, and it will give me real pleasure to do so,' said Everett, quickly. 'I'll get my hat and be with you in a moment.'

When he came downstairs Everett found a cart at the door, and Charley Gaylord drew a long sight of relief as he gathered up the reins and settled back into his own element.

'You see, I think I'd better tell you something about my sister before you see her, and I don't know just where to begin. She travelled in Europe with your brother and his wife, and sang at a lot of his concerts; but I don't know just how much you know about her.'

'Very little, except that my brother always thought her the most gifted of his pupils, and that when I knew her she was very young and very beautiful and turned my head sadly for a while.'

Everett saw that Gaylord's mind was quite engrossed by his grief. He was wrought up to the point where his reserve and sense of proportion had quite left him, and his trouble was the one vital thing in the world. 'That's the whole thing,' he went on, flicking his horses with the whip.

'She was a great woman, as you say, and she didn't come of a great family. She had to fight her own way from the first. She got to Chicago, and then to New York, and then to Europe, where she went up like lightning, and got a taste for it all; and now she's dying here like a rat in a hole, out of her own world, and she can't fall back into ours. We've grown apart, some way – miles and miles apart – and I'm afraid she's fearfully unhappy.'

'It's a very tragic story that you are telling me, Gaylord,' said Everett. They were well out into the country now, spinning along over the dusty plains of red grass, with the ragged blue outline of the mountains before them.

'Tragic!' cried Gaylord, starting up in his scat, 'my God, man, nobody will ever know how tragic. It's a tragedy I live with and eat with and sleep with, until I've lost my grip on everything. You see she had made a good bit of money, but she spent it all going to health resorts. It's her lungs, you know. I've got money enough to send her anywhere, but the doctors all say it's no use. She hasn't the ghost of a chance. It's just getting through the days now. I had no notion she was half so bad before she came to me. She just wrote that she was all run down. Now that she's here, I think she'd be happier anywhere under the sun, but she won't leave. She says it's easier to let go of life here, and that to go East would be dying twice. There was a time when I was a brakeman with a run out of Bird City, Iowa, and she was a little thing I could carry on my shoulder, when I could get her everything on earth she wanted, and she hadn't a wish my $80 a month didn't cover; and now, when I've got a little property together, I can't buy her a night's sleep!'

Everett saw that, whatever Charlie Gaylord's present status in the world might be, he had brought the brakeman's heart up the ladder with him, and the brakeman's frank avowal of sentiment. Presently Gaylord went on:

'You can understand how she has outgrown her family. We're all a pretty common sort, railroaders from away back. My father was a conductor. He died when we were kids. Maggie, my other sister, who lives with me, was a telegraph operator here while I was getting my grip on things. We had no education to speak of. I have to hire a stenographer because I can't spell straight – the Almighty couldn't teach me to spell. The things that make up life to Kate are all Greek to me, and there's scarcely a point where we touch any more, except in our recollections of the old times when we were all young and happy together, and Kate sang in a church choir in Bird City. But I believe, Mr Hilgarde, that if she can see just one person like you, who knows about the things and people she's interested in, it will give her about the only comfort she can have now.'

The reins slackened in Charley Gaylord's hands as they drew up before a showily painted house with many gables and a round tower. 'Here we are,' he said, turning to Everett, 'and I guess we understand each other.'

They were met at the door by a thin, colourless woman, whom Gaylord introduced as 'My sister, Maggie.' She asked her brother to show Mr Hilgarde into the music-room, where Katharine wished to see him alone.

When Everett entered the music-room he gave a start of surprise, feeling that he had stepped from the glaring Wyoming sunlight into some New York studio that he had always known. He wondered which it was of those countless studios, high up under the roofs, over banks and shops and wholesale houses, that this room resembled, and he looked incredulously out of the window at the grey plain which ended in the great upheaval of the Rockies.

The haunting air of familiarity about the room perplexed him. Was it a copy of some particular studio he knew, or was it merely the studio atmosphere that seemed so individual and poignantly reminiscent here in Wyoming? He sat down in a reading-chair and looked keenly about him. Suddenly his eye fell upon a large photograph of his brother above the piano. Then it all became clear to him: this was veritably his brother's room. If it were not an exact copy of one of the many studios that Adriance had fitted up in various parts of the world, wearying of them and leaving almost before the renovator's varnish had dried, it was at least in the same tone. In every detail Adriance's taste was so manifest that the room seemed to exhale his personality.

Among the photographs on the wall there was one of Katharine Gaylord, taken in the days when Everett had known her, and when the flash of her eye or the flutter of her skirt was enough to set his boyish heart in tumult. Even now, he stood before the portrait with a certain degree of embarrassment. It was the face of a woman already old in her first youth, thoroughly sophisticated and a trifle hard, and it told of what her brother had called her fight. The *camaraderie* of her frank, confident eyes was qualified by the deep lines about her mouth and the curve of the lips, which was both sad and cynical. Certainly she had more good-will than confidence toward the world, and the bravado of her smile could not conceal the shadow of an unrest that was almost discontent. The chief charm of the woman, as Everett had known her, lay in her superb figure and in her eyes, which possessed a warm, life-giving quality like the sunlight; eyes which glowed with a sort of perpetual *salutat* to the world. Her head, Everett remembered as peculiarly well shaped and proudly poised. There had been always a little of the imperatrix about her, and her pose in the photograph revived all his old impressions of her unattachedness, of how absolutely and valiantly she stood alone.

Everett was still standing before the picture, his hands behind him and his head inclined, when he heard the door open. A very tall woman advanced toward him, holding out her hand. As she started to speak she coughed slightly, then, laughing, said in a low, rich voice, a trifle husky: 'You see I make the traditional Camille entrance – with the cough. How good of you to come, Mr Hilgarde.'

Everett was acutely conscious that while addressing him she was not looking at him at all, and, as he assured her of his pleasure in coming, he was glad to have an opportunity to collect himself. He had not reckoned upon the ravages of a long illness. The long, loose folds of her white gown had been especially designed to conceal the sharp outlines of her emaciated body, but the stamp of her disease was there; simple and ugly and obtrusive, a pitiless fact that could not be disguised or evaded. The splendid shoulders were stooped, there was a swaying unevenness in her gait, her arms seemed disproportionately long, and her hands were transparently white, and cold to the touch. The changes in her face were less obvious; the proud carriage of the head, the warm, clear eyes, even the delicate flush of colour in her cheeks, all defiantly remained, though they were all in a lower key – older, sadder, softer.

She sat down upon the divan and began nervously to arrange the pillows. 'I know I'm not an inspiring object to look upon, but you must be quite frank and sensible about that and get used to it at once, for we've no time to lose. And if I'm a trifle irritable you won't mind? – for I'm more than usually nervous.'

'Don't bother with me this morning, if you are tired,' urged Everett. 'I can come quite as well to-morrow.'

'Gracious, no!' she protected, with a flash of that quick, keen humour that he remembered as a part of her. 'It's solitude that I'm tired to death of – solitude and the wrong kind of people. You see, the minister, not content with reading the prayers for the sick, called on me this morning. He happened to be riding by on his bicycle and felt it his duty to stop. Of course, he disapproves of my profession, and I think he takes it for granted that I have a dark past. The funniest feature of his conversation is that he is always excusing my own vocation to me – condoning it, you know – and trying to patch up my peace with my conscience by suggesting possible noble uses for what he kindly calls my talent.'

Everett laughed. 'Oh! I'm afraid I'm not the person to call after such a serious gentleman – I can't sustain the situation. At my best I don't reach higher than low comedy. Have you decided to which one of the noble uses you will devote yourself?'

Katharine lifted her hands in a gesture of renunciation and exclaimed: 'I'm not equal to any of them, not even the least noble. I didn't study that method.'

She laughed and went on nervously: 'The parson's not so bad. He has read Gibbon's "Decline and Fall," all five volumes, and that's something. Then, he has been to New York, and that's a great deal. But how we are losing time! Do tell me about New York; Charley says you're just on from there. How does it look and taste and smell just now? I think a whiff of the Jersey ferry would be as flagons of cod-liver oil to me. Who conspicuously walks the Rialto now, and what does he or she wear? Are the trees still green in Madison Square, or have they grown brown and dusty? Does the chaste Diana on the Garden Theatre still keep her vestal vows through all the exasperating changes of weather? Who has your brother's old studio now, and what misguided aspirants practise their scales in the rookeries about Carnegie Hall? What do people go to see at the theatres, and what do they eat and drink there in the world nowadays? You see, I'm homesick for it all, from the Battery to Riverside. Oh, let me die in Harlem!' she was interrupted by a violent attack of coughing, and Everett, embarrassed by her discomfort, plunged into gossip about the professional people he had met in town during the summer, and the musical outlook for the winter. He was diagramming with his pencil, on the back of an old envelope he found in his pocket, some new mechanical device to be used at the Metropolitan in the production of the *Rheingold*, when he became conscious that she was looking at him intently, and that he was talking to the four walls.

Katharine was lying back among the pillows, watching him through half-closed eyes, as a painter looks at a picture. He finished his explanation vaguely enough and put the envelope back in his pocket. As he did so, she said, quietly: 'How wonderfully like Adriance you are!' and he felt as though a crisis of some sort had been met and tided over.

He laughed, looking up at her with a touch of pride in his eyes that made them seem quite boyish. 'Yes, isn't it absurd? It's almost as awkward as looking like Napoleon – But, after all, there are some advantages. It has made some of his friends like me, and I hope it will make you.'

Katharine smiled and gave him a quick, meaning glance from under her lashes. 'Oh, it did that long ago. What a haughty, reserved youth you were then, and how you used to stare at people, and then blush and look cross if they paid you back in your own coin. Do you remember that night when you took me home from a rehearsal, and scarcely spoke a word to me?'

'It was the silence of admiration,' protested Everett, 'very crude and boyish, but very sincere and not a little painful. Perhaps you suspected something of the sort? I remember you saw fit to be very grown up and worldly.'

'I believe I suspected a pose; the one that college boys usually affect with singers – "an earthen vessel in love with a star," you know. But it rather surprised me in you, for you must have seen a good deal of your brother's pupils. Or had you an omnivorous capacity, and elasticity that always met the occasion?'

'Don't ask a man to confess the follies of his youth,' said Everett, smiling a little sadly; 'I am sensitive about some of them even now. But I was not so sophisticated as you imagined. I saw my brother's pupils come and go, but that was about all. Sometimes I was called on to play accompaniments, or to fill out a vacancy at a rehearsal, or to order a carriage for an infuriated soprano who had thrown up her part. But they never spent any time on me, unless it was to notice the resemblance you speak of.'

'Yes,' observed Katharine, thoughtfully. 'I noticed it then, too; but it has grown as you have grown older. That is rather strange, when you have lived such different lives. It's not merely an ordinary family likeness of feature, you know, but a sort of interchangeable individuality; the suggestion of the other man's personality in your face – like an air transposed to another key. But I'm not attempting to define it; it's beyond me; something altogether unusual and a trifle – well, uncanny,' she finished, laughing.

'I remember,' Everett said, seriously, twirling the pencil between his fingers and looking, as he sat with his head thrown back, out under the red window-blind which was raised just a little, and as it swung back and forth in the wind revealed the glaring panorama of the desert – a blinding stretch of yellow, flat as the sea in dead calm, splotched here and there with deep purple shadows; and, beyond, the ragged white clouds – 'I remember, when I was a little fellow I used to be very sensitive about it. I don't think it exactly displeased me, or that I would have had it otherwise if I could, but it seemed to me like a birthmark, or something not to be lightly spoken of. People were naturally always fonder of Ad than of me, and I used to feel the chill of reflected light pretty often. It came into even my relations with my mother. Ad went abroad to study when he was absurdly young, you know, and mother was all broken up over it. She did her whole duty by each of us, but it was sort of generally understood among us that she'd have made burnt offerings of us all for Ad any day. I was a little fellow then, and when she sat alone on the porch in the summer dusk, she used sometimes to call me to her and turn my face up in the light that streamed out through the shutters and kiss me, and then I always knew she was thinking of Adriance.'

'Poor little chap,' said Katharine, and her tone was a trifle huskier than usual. 'How fond people have always been of Adriance! Now tell me the latest news of him. I haven't heard, except through the press, for a year or more. He was in Algiers then, in the valley of the Chelif, riding horseback night and day in an Arabian costume, and in his usual enthusiastic fashion he had quite made up his mind to adopt the Mahometan faith and become as nearly an Arab as possible. How many countries and faiths has he adopted, I wonder? Probably he was playing Arab to himself all the time. I remember he was a sixteenth-century duke in Florence once for weeks together.'

'Oh, that's Adriance,' chuckled Everett. 'He is himself barely long enough to write checks and be measured for his clothes. I didn't hear from him while he was an Arab; I missed that.'

'He was writing an Algerian *suite* for the piano then; it must be in the publisher's hands by this time. I have been too ill to answer his letter, and have lost touch with him.'

Everett drew a letter from his pocket. 'This came about a month ago. It's chiefly about his new opera which is to be brought out in London next winter. Read it at your leisure.'

'I think I shall keep it as a hostage, so that I may be sure you will come again. Now I want you to play for me. Whatever you like; but if there is anything new in the world, in mercy let me hear it. For nine months I have heard nothing but "The Baggage Coach Ahead" and "She is My Baby's Mother."'

He sat down at the piano, and Katharine sat near him, absorbed in his remarkable physical likeness to his brother, and trying to discover in just what it consisted. She told

herself that it was very much as though a sculptor's finished
work had been rudely copied in wood. He was of a larger
build than Adriance, and his shoulders were broad and
heavy, while those of his brother were slender and rather
girlish. His face was of the same oval mould, but it was grey,
and darkened about the mouth by continual shaving. His
eyes were of the same inconstant April colour, but they were
reflective and rather dull; while Adriance's were always
points of high light, and always meaning another thing than
the thing they meant yesterday. But it was hard to see why
this earnest man should so continually suggest that lyric,
youthful face that was as gay as his was grave. For Adriance,
though he was ten years the elder, and though his hair was
streaked with silver, had the face of a boy of twenty, so
mobile that it told his thoughts before he could put them into
words. A contralto, famous for the extravagance of her vocal
methods and of her affections had once said of him that the
shepherd-boys who sang in the Vale of Tempe must certainly
have looked like young Hilgarde; and the comparison had
been appropriated by a hundred shyer women who preferred to quote.

As Everett sat smoking on the veranda of the Inter-Ocean
House that night, he was a victim to random collections. His
infatuation for Katharine Gaylord, visionary as it was, had
been the most serious of his boyish love-affairs, and had long
disturbed his bachelor dreams. He was painfully timid in
everything relating to the emotions, and his hurt had with-
drawn him from the society of women. The fact that it was
all so done and dead and far behind him, and that the
woman had lived her life out since then, gave him an
oppressive sense of age and loss. He bethought himself of
something he had read about 'sitting by the hearth and
remembering the faces of women without desire,' and felt
himself an octogenarian.

He remembered how bitter and morose he had grown
during his stay at his brother's studio when Katharine
Gaylord was working there, and how he had wounded

Adriance on the night of his last concert in New York. He had sat there in the box while his brother and Katharine were called back again and again after the last number, watching the roses go up over the footlights until they were stacked half as high as the piano, brooding, in his sullen boy's heart, upon the pride those two felt in each other's work – spurring each other to their best and beautifully contending in song. The footlights had seemed a hard, glittering line drawn sharply between their life and his; a circle of flame set about those splendid children of genius. He walked back to his hotel alone, and sat in his window staring out on Madison Square until long after midnight, resolving to beat no more at doors that he could never enter, and realizing more keenly than ever before how far this glorious world of beautiful creations lay from the paths of men like himself. He told himself that he had in common with this woman only the baser uses of life.

Everett's week in Cheyenne stretched to three, and he saw no prospect of release except through the thing he dreaded. The bright, windy days of the Wyoming autumn passed swiftly. Letters and telegrams came urging him to hasten his trip to the coast, but he resolutely postponed his business engagements. The mornings he spent on one of Charley Gaylord's ponies, or fishing in the mountains, and in the evenings he sat in his room writing letters or reading. In the afternoon he was usually at his post of duty. Destiny, he reflected, seems to have very positive notions about the sort of parts we are fitted to play. The scene changes and the compensation varies, but in the end we usually find that we have played the same class of business from first to last. Everett had been a stop-gap all his life. He remembered going through a looking-glass labyrinth when he was a boy, and trying gallery after gallery, only at every turn to bump his nose against his own face – which, indeed, was not his own, but his brother's. No matter what his mission, east or west, by land or sea, he was sure to find himself employed in his brother's business, one of the tributary lives which helped to swell the shining current of Adriance Hilgarde's. It was not the first time that his duty had been to comfort, as best he could, one of the broken things his brother's imperious speed had cast aside and forgotten. He made no attempt to analyse the situation or to state it in exact terms; but he felt Katharine Gaylord's need for him, and he accepted it as a commission from his brother to help this woman to die. Day by day he felt her demands on him grow more imperious, her need for him grow more acute and positive; and day by day he felt that in his peculiar relation to her, his own individuality played a smaller and smaller part. His power to minister to her comfort, he saw, lay solely in his link with his brother's life. He understood all that his physical resemblance meant to her. He knew that she sat by him always watching for some common trick of gesture, some familiar play of expression, some illusion of light and shadow, in which he should seem wholly Adriance. He knew that she lived upon this and that her disease fed upon it; that it sent shudders of remembrance through her and that in the exhaustion which followed this turmoil of her dying senses, she slept deep and sweet, and dreamed of youth and art and days in a certain old Florentine garden, and not of bitterness and death.

The question which most perplexed him was, 'How much shall I know? How much does she wish me to know?' A few days after his first meeting with Katharine Gaylord, he had cabled his brother to write her. He had merely said that she was mortally ill; he could depend on Adriance to say the right thing – that was a part of his gift. Adriance always said not only the right thing, but the opportune, graceful, exquisite thing. His phrases took the colour of the moment and the then present condition, so that they never savoured of perfunctory compliment or frequent usage. He always caught the lyric essence of the moment, the poetic suggestion of every situation. Moreover, he usually did the right thing, the opportune, graceful, exquisite thing – except, when he did very cruel things – bent upon making people happy when their existence touched his, just as he insisted that his material environment should be beautiful; lavishing upon those near him all the warmth and radiance of his rich nature, all the homage of the poet and troubadour, and, when they were no longer near, forgetting – for that also was a part of Adriance's gift.

Three weeks after Everett had sent his cable, when he made his daily call at the gayly painted ranch-house, he found Katharine laughing like a school-girl. 'Have you ever thought,' she said, as he entered the music-room, 'how much these séances of ours are like Heine's "Florentine Nights," except that I don't give you the opportunity to monopolize the conversation as Heine did?' She held his hand longer than usual as she greeted him, and looked searchingly up into his face. 'You are the kindest man living, the kindest,' she added, softly.

Everett's grey face coloured faintly as he drew his hand away, for he felt that this time she was looking at him, and not at a whimsical caricature of his brother. 'Why, what have I done now?' he asked, lamely. 'I can't remember having sent you any stale candy or champagne since yesterday.'

She drew a letter with a foreign postmark from between the leaves of a book and held it out, smiling. 'You got him to write it. Don't say you didn't, for it came direct, you see, and the last address I gave him was a place in Florida. This deed shall be remembered of you when I am with the just in Paradise. But one thing you did not ask him to do, for you didn't know about it. He has sent me his latest work, the new sonata, the most ambitious thing he has ever done, and you are to play it for me directly, though it looks horribly intricate. But first for the letter; I think you would better read it aloud to me.'

Everett sat down in a low chair facing the window-seat in which she reclined with a barricade of pillows behind her. He opened the letter, his lashes half-veiling his kind eyes, and saw to his satisfaction that it was a long one; wonderfully tactful and tender, even for Adriance, who was tender with his valet and his stable-boy, with his old gondolier and the beggar-women who prayed to the saints for him.

The letter was from Granada, written in the Alhambra, as he sat by the fountain of the Patio di Lindaraxa. The air was heavy with the warm fragrance of the South and full of the sound of splashing, running water, as it had been in a certain old garden in Florence, long ago. The sky was one great turquoise, heated until it glowed. The wonderful Moorish arches threw graceful blue shadows all about him. He had sketched an outline of them on the margin of his note-paper. The subtleties of Arabic decoration had cast an unholy spell over him, and the brutal exaggerations of Gothic art were a bad dream, easily forgotten. The Alhambra itself had, from the first, seemed perfectly familiar to him, and he knew that he must have trod that court, sleek and brown and obsequious, centuries before Ferdinand rode into Andalusia. The letter was full of confidences about his work, and delicate allusions to their old happy days of study and comradeship, and of her own work, still so warmly remembered and appreciatively discussed everywhere he went.

As Everett folded the letter he felt that Adriance had divined the thing needed and had risen to it in his own wonderful way. The letter was consistently egotistical, and seemed to him even a trifle patronizing, yet it was just what she had wanted. A strong realization of his brother's charm and intensity and power came over him; he felt the breath of that whirlwind of flame in which Adriance passed, consuming all in his path, and himself even more resolutely than he consumed others. Then he looked down at this white, burnt-out brand that lay before him. 'Like him, isn't it?' she said, quietly.

'I think I can scarcely answer his letter, but when you see him next you can do that for me. I want you to tell him many things for me, yet they can all be summed up in this: I want him to grow wholly into his best and greatest self, even at the cost of the dear boyishness that is half his charm to you and me. Do you understand me?'

'I know perfectly well what you mean,' answered Everett, thoughtfully. 'I have often felt so about him myself. And yet it's difficult to prescribe for those fellows; so little makes, so little mars.'

Katharine raised herself upon her elbow, and her face flushed with feverish earnestness. 'Ah, but it is the waste of himself that I mean; his lashing himself out on stupid and uncomprehending people until they take him at their own estimate. He can kindle marble, strike fire from putty, but is it worth what it costs him?'

'Come, come,' expostulated Everett, alarmed at her excitement. 'Where is the new sonata? Let him speak for himself.'

He sat down at the piano and began playing the first movement which was indeed the voice of Adriance, his proper speech. The sonata was the most ambitious work he had done up to that time, and marked the transition from his purely lyric vein to a deeper and nobler style. Everett played intelligently and with that sympathetic comprehension which seems peculiar to a certain lovable class of men who never accomplish anything in particular. When he had finished he turned to Katharine.

'How he has grown!' she cried. 'What the three last years have done for him! He used to write only the tragedies of passion; but this is the tragedy of the soul, the shadow coexistent with the soul. This is the tragedy of effort and failure, the thing Keats called hell. This is my tragedy, as I lie here spent by the race-course, listening to the feet of the runners as they pass me – ah, God! the swift feet of the runners!'

She turned her face away and covered it with her straining hands. Everett crossed over to her quickly and knelt beside her. In all the days he had known her she had never before, beyond an occasional ironical jest, given voice to the bitterness of her own defeat. Her courage had become a point of pride with him, and to see it going sickened him.

'Don't do it,' he gasped. 'I can't stand it, I really can't, I feel it too much. We mustn't speak of that; it's too tragic and too vast.'

When she turned her face back to him there was a ghost of the old, brave, cynical smile on it, more bitter than the tears she could not shed. 'No, I won't be so ungenerous; I will save that for the watches of the night when I have no better

company. Now you may mix me another drink of some sort.
Formerly, when it was not *if* I should ever sing Brunhilda,
but quite simply when I *should* sing Brunhilda, I was always
starving myself, and thinking what I might drink and what I
might not. But broken music-boxes may drink whatsoever
they list, and no one cares whether they lose their figure.
Run over that theme at the beginning again. That, at least, is
not new. It was running in his head when we were in Venice
years ago, and he used to drum it on his glass at the
dinner-table. He had just begun to work it out when the late
autumn came on, and the paleness of the Adriatic oppressed
him, and he decided to go to Florence for the winter, and lost
touch with the theme during his illness. Do you remember
those frightful days? All the people who have loved him are
not strong enough to save him from himself! When I got
word from Florence that he had been ill, I was in Nice filling
a concert engagement. His wife was hurrying to him from
Paris, but I reached him first. I arrived at dusk, in a terrific
storm. They had taken an old palace there for the winter, and
I found him in the library – a long, dark room full of old Latin
books and heavy furniture and bronzes. He was sitting by a
wood fire at one end of the room, looking, oh so worn and
pale! – as he always does when he is ill, you know. Ah, it is so
good that you *do* know! Even his red smoking-jacket lent no
colour to his face. His first words were not to tell me how ill
he had been, but that that morning he had been well enough
to put the last strokes to the score of his *"Souvenirs d'Au-
tomne,"* and he was, as I most like to remember him; so calm
and happy and tired; not gay, as he usually is, but just
contented and tired with that heavenly tiredness that comes
after a good work done at last. Outside, the rain poured
down in torrents, and the wind moaned for the pain of all
the world and sobbed in the branches of the shivering olives
and about the walls of that desolate old palace. How that
night comes back to me! There were no lights in the room,
only the wood fire which glowed upon the hard features of
the bronze Dante like the reflection of purgatorial flames,
and threw long black shadows about us; beyond us it

scarcely penetrated the gloom at all. Adriance sat staring at the fire with the weariness of all his life in his eyes, and of all the other lives that must aspire and suffer to make up one such life as his. Somehow the wind with all its world-pain had got into the room, and the cold rain was in our eyes, and the wave came up in both of us at once – that awful vague, universal pain, that cold fear of life and death and God and hope – and we were like two clinging together on a spar in mid-ocean after the shipwreck of everything. Then we heard the front door open with a great gust of wind that shook even the walls, and the servants came running with lights, announcing that Madame had returned, *"and in the book we read no more that night."'*

She gave the old line with a certain bitter humour, and with the hard, bright smile in which of old she had wrapped her weakness as in a glittering garment. That ironical smile, worn like a mask through so many years, had gradually changed even the lines of her face completely, and when she looked in the mirror she saw not herself, but the scathing critic, the amused observer and satirist of herself. Everett dropped his head upon his hand and sat looking at the rug. 'How much you have cared!' he said.

'Ah, yes, I cared,' she replied, closing her eyes with a long-drawn sight of relief; and lying perfectly still, she went on: 'You can't imagine what a comfort it is to have you know how I cared, what a relief it is to be able to tell it to some one. I used to want to shriek it out to the world in the long nights when I could not sleep. It seemed to me that I could not die with it. It demanded some sort of expression. And now that you know, you would scarcely believe how much less sharp the anguish of it is.'

Everett continued to look helplessly at the floor. 'I was not sure how much you wanted me to know,' he said.

'Oh, I intended you should know from the first time I looked into your face, when you came that day with Charley. I flatter myself that I have been able to conceal it when I chose, though I suppose women always think that. The more observing ones may have seen, but discerning people are usually discreet and often kind, for we usually bleed a little before we begin to discern. But I wanted you to know; you are so like him that it is almost like telling him himself. At least, I feel now that he will know some day, and then I shall be quite sacred from his compassion, for we none of us dare pity the dead. Since it was what my life has chiefly meant, I should like him to know. On the whole, I am not ashamed of it. I have fought a good fight.'

'And has he never known at all?' asked Everett, in a thick voice.

'Oh! never at all in the way you mean. Of course, he is accustomed to looking into the eyes of women and finding love there; when he doesn't find it there he thinks he must have been guilty of some discourtesy and is miserable about it. He has a genuine fondness for every one who is not stupid or gloomy, or old or preternaturally ugly. Granted youth and cheerfulness, and a moderate amount of wit and some tact, and Adriance will always be glad to see you coming round the corner. I shared with the rest; shared the smiles and the gallantries and the droll little sermons. It was quite like a Sunday-school picnic; we wore our best clothes and a smile and took our turns. It was his kindness that was hardest. I have pretty well used my life up at standing punishment.'

'Don't; you'll make me hate him,' groaned Everett.

Katharine laughed and began to play nervously with her fan. 'It wasn't in the slightest degree his fault; that is the most grotesque part of it. Why, it had really begun before I ever met him. I fought my way to him, and I drank my doom greedily enough.'

Everett rose and stood hesitating. 'I think I must go. You ought to be quiet, and I don't think I can hear any more just now.'

She put out her hand and took his playfully. 'You've put in three weeks at this sort of thing, haven't you? Well, it may never be to your glory in this world, perhaps, but it's been the mercy of heaven to me, and it ought to square accounts for a much worse life than yours will ever be.'

Everett knelt beside her, saying, brokenly: 'I stayed

because I wanted to be with you, that's all. I have never cared about other women since I met you in New York when I was a lad. You are a part of my destiny, and I could not leave you if I would.'

She put her hands on his shoulders and shook her head. 'No, no; don't tell me that. I have seen enough of tragedy, God knows: don't show me any more just as the curtain is going down. No, no, it was only a boy's fancy, and your divine pity and my utter pitiableness have recalled it for a moment. One does not love the dying, dear friend. If some fancy of that sort had been left over from boyhood, this would rid you of it, and that were well. Now go, and you will come again tomorrow, as long as there are to-morrows, will you not?' She took his hand with a smile that lifted the mask from her soul, that was both courage and despair, and full of infinite loyalty and tenderness, as she said softly:

'For ever and for ever, farewell, Cassius;
If we do meet again, why, we shall smile;
If not, why then, this parting was well made.'

The courage in her eyes was like the clear light of a star to him as he went out.

On the night of Adriance Hilgarde's opening concert in Paris, Everett sat by the bed in the ranch-house in Wyoming, watching over the last battle that we have with the flesh before we are done with it and free of it forever. At times it seemed that the serene soul of her must have left already and found some refuge from the storm, and only the tenacious animal life were left to do battle with death. She laboured under a delusion at once pitiful and merciful, thinking that she was in the Pullman on her way to New York, going back to her life and her work. When she aroused from her stupor, it was only to ask the porter to waken her half an hour out of Jersey City, or to remonstrate with him about the delays and the roughness of the road. At midnight Everett and the nurse were left alone with her. Poor Charley Gaylord had lain down on a couch outside the door. Everett sat looking at the sputtering night-lamp until it made his eyes ache. His head dropped forward on the foot of the bed, and he sank into a heavy, distressful slumber. He was dreaming of Adriance's concert in Paris, and of Adriance, the troubadour, smiling and debonair, with his boyish face and the touch of silver grey in his hair. He heard the applause and he saw the roses going up over the footlights until they were stacked half as high as the piano, and the petals fell and scattered, making crimson splotches on the floor. Down this crimson pathway came Adriance with his youthful step, leading his prima donna by the hand; a dark woman this time, with Spanish eyes.

The nurse touched him on the shoulder, he started and awoke. She screened the lamp with her hand. Everett saw that Katharine was awake and conscious, and struggling a little. He lifted her gently upon his arm and began to fan her. She laid her hands lightly on his hair and looked into his face with eyes that seemed never to have wept or doubted. 'Ah, dear Adriance, dear, dear,' she whispered.

Everett went to call her brother, but when they came back the madness of art was over for Katharine.

Two days later Everett was pacing the station siding, waiting for the west-bound train. Charley Gaylord walked beside him, but the two men had nothing to say to each other. Everett's bags were piled on the truck, and his step was hurried and his eyes were full of impatience, as he gazed again and again up the track, watching for the train. Gaylord's impatience was not less than his own; these two, who had grown so close, had now become painful and impossible to each other, and longed for the wrench of farewell.

As the train pulled in, Everett wrung Gaylord's hand among the crowd of alighting passengers. The people of a German opera company, *en route* for the coast, rushed by them in frantic haste to snatch their breakfast during the stop. Everett heard an exclamation in a broad German dialect, and a massive woman whose figure persistently escaped from her stays in the most improbable places rushed up to him, her blond hair disordered by the wind, and glowing with joyful surprise she caught his coat-sleeve with her tightly gloved hands.

'*Herr Gott*, Adriance, *lieber Freund*,' she cried, emotionally.

Everett quickly withdrew his arm, and lifted his hat, blushing. 'Pardon me, madame, but I see that you have mistaken me for Adriance Hilgarde. I am his brother,' he said, quietly, and turning from the crestfallen singer he hurried into the car.

First published in *Scribner's*, January 1903.

A WAGNER MATINÉE

I RECEIVED one morning a letter, written in pale ink on glassy, blue-lined note-paper, and bearing the postmark of a little Nebraska village. This communication, worn and rubbed, looking as though it had been carried for some days in a coat pocket that was none too clean, was from my uncle Howard and informed me that his wife had been left a small legacy by a bachelor relative who had recently died, and that it would be necessary for her to go to Boston to attend to the settling of the estate. He requested me to meet her at the station and render her whatever services might be necessary. On examining the date indicated as that of her arrival, I found it no later than to-morrow. He had characteristically delayed writing until, had I been away from home for a day, I must have missed the good woman altogether.

The name of my Aunt Georgiana called up not alone her own figure, at once pathetic and grotesque, but opened before my feet a gulf of recollection so wide and deep that, as the letter dropped from my hand, I felt suddenly a stranger to all the present conditions of my existence, wholly ill at ease and out of place amid the familiar surroundings of my study. I became, in short, the gangling farmer-boy my aunt had known, scourged with chilblains and bashfulness, my hands cracked and sore from the corn husking. I felt the knuckles of my thumb tentatively, as though they were raw again. I sat again before her parlour organ, fumbling the scales with my stiff, red hands, while she, beside me, made canvas mittens for the huskers.

The next morning, after preparing my landlady somewhat, I set out for the station. When the train arrived I had some difficulty in finding my aunt. She was the last of the passengers to alight, and it was not until I got her into the carriage that she seemed really to recognize me. She had come all the way in a day coach; her linen duster had become black with soot and her black bonnet grey with dust during the journey. When we arrived at my boarding-house the landlady put her to bed at once and I did not see her again until the next morning.

Whatever shock Mrs Springer experienced at my aunt's appearance, she considerately concealed. As for myself, I saw my aunt's misshapen figure with that feeling of awe and respect with which we behold explorers who have left their ears and fingers north of Franz Josef Land, or their health somewhere along the Upper Congo. My Aunt Georgiana had been a music teacher at the Boston Conservatory, somewhere back in the latter sixties. One summer, while visiting in the little village among the Green Mountains where her ancestors had dwelt for generations, she had kindled the callow fancy of the most idle and shiftless of all the village lads, and had conceived for this Howard Carpenter one of those extravagant passions which a handsome country boy of twenty-one sometimes inspires in an angular, spectacled woman of thirty. When she returned to her duties in Boston, Howard followed her, and the upshot of this inexplicable infatuation was that she eloped with him, eluding the reproaches of her family and the criticisms of her friends by going with him to the Nebraska frontier. Carpenter, who, of course, had no money, had taken a homestead in Red Willow County, fifty miles from the railroad. There they had measured off their quarter section themselves by driving across the prairie in a wagon, to the wheel of which they had tied a red cotton handkerchief, and counting off its revolutions. They built a dugout in the red hillside, one of those cave dwellings whose inmates so often reverted to primitive conditions. Their water they got from the lagoons where the buffalo drank, and their slender stock of provisions was always at the mercy of bands of roving Indians. For thirty years my aunt had not been farther than fifty miles from the homestead.

But Mrs Springer knew nothing of all this, and must have been considerably shocked at what was left of my kinswoman. Beneath the soiled linen duster which, on her arrival, was the most conspicuous feature of her costume, she wore a black stuff dress, whose ornamentation showed that she had surrendered herself unquestioningly into the hands of a country dressmaker. My poor aunt's figure, however, would have presented astonishing difficulties to any dressmaker. Originally stooped, her shoulders were now almost bent together over her sunken chest. She wore no stays, and her gown, which trailed unevenly behind, rose in a sort of peak over her abdomen. She wore ill-fitting false teeth, and her skin was as yellow as a Mongolian's from constant exposure to a pitiless wind and to the alkaline water which hardens the most transparent cuticle into a sort of flexible leather.

I owed to this woman most of the good that ever came my way in my boyhood, and had a reverential affection for her. During the years when I was riding herd for my uncle, my aunt, after cooking the three meals — the first of which was ready at six o'clock in the morning — and putting the six children to bed, would often stand until midnight at her ironing-board, with me at the kitchen table beside her, hearing me recite Latin declensions and conjugations, gently shaking me when my drowsy head sank down over a page of irregular verbs. It was to her, at her ironing or mending, that I read my first Shakespere, and her old text-book on mythology was the first that ever came into my empty hands. She taught me my scales and exercises, too — on the little parlour organ which her husband had bought her after fifteen years, during which she had not so much as seen any instrument, but an accordion that belonged to one of the Norwegian farm-hands. She would sit beside me by the hour, darning and counting, while I struggled with the 'Joyous Farmer,' but she seldom talked to me about music, and I understood why. She was a pious woman; she had the consolations of religion and, to her at least, her martyrdom was not wholly sordid. Once when I had been doggedly beating out some easy passages from an old score of *Euryanthe* I had found among her music books, she came up to me and, putting her hands over my eyes, gently drew my head back upon her shoulder, saying tremulously, 'Don't love it so well, Clark, or it may be taken from you. Oh! dear boy, pray that whatever your sacrifice may be, it be not that.'

When my aunt appeared on the morning after her arrival, she was still in a semi-somnambulant state. She seemed not to realize that she was in the city where she had spent her youth, the place longed for hungrily half a lifetime. She had been so wretchedly train-sick throughout the journey that she had no recollection of anything but her discomfort, and, to all intents and purposes, there were but a few hours of nightmare between the farm in Red Willow County and my study on Newbury Street. I had planned a little pleasure for her that afternoon, to repay her for some of the glorious moments she had given me when we used to milk together in the strawthatched cowshed and she, because I was more than usually tired, or because her husband had spoken sharply to me, would tell me of the splendid performance of the *Huguenots* she had seen in Paris, in her youth. At two o'clock the Symphony Orchestra was to give a Wagner programme, and I intended to take my aunt; though, as I conversed with her, I grew doubtful about her enjoyment of it. Indeed, for her own sake, I could only wish her taste for such things quite dead, and the long struggle mercifully ended at last. I suggested our visiting the Conservatory and the Common before lunch, but she seemed altogether too timid to wish to venture out. She questioned me absently about various changes in the city, but she was chiefly concerned that she had forgotten to leave instructions about feeding half-skimmed milk to a certain weakling calf, 'old

Maggie's calf, you know, Clark,' she explained, evidently having forgotten how long I had been away. She was further troubled because she had neglected to tell her daughter about the freshly-opened kit of mackerel in the cellar, which would spoil if it were not used directly.

I asked her whether she had ever heard any of the Wagnerian operas, and found that she had not, though she was perfectly familiar with their respective situations, and had once possessed the piano score of *The Flying Dutchman*. I began to think it would have been best to get her back to Red Willow County without waking her, and regretted having suggested the concert.

From the time we entered the concert hall, however, she was a trifle less passive and inert, and for the first time seemed to perceive her surroundings. I had felt some trepidation lest she might become aware of the absurdities of her attire, or might experience some painful embarrassment at stepping suddenly into the world to which she had been dead for more than a quarter of a century. But, again, I found how superficially I had judged her. She sat looking about her with eyes as impersonal, almost as stony, as those with which the granite Rameses in a museum watches the froth and fret that ebbs and flows about his pedestal – separated from it by the lonely stretch of centuries. I have seen this same aloofness in old miners who drift into the Brown Hotel at Denver, their pockets full of bullion, their linen soiled, their haggard faces unshaven; standing in the thronged corridors as solitary as though they were still in a frozen camp on the Yukon, conscious that certain experiences have isolated them from their fellows by a gulf no haberdasher could bridge.

We sat at the extreme left of the first balcony, facing the arc of our own and the balcony above us, veritable hanging gardens, brilliant as tulip beds. The matinée audience was made up chiefly of women. One lost the contour of faces and figures, indeed any effect of line whatever, and there was only the colour of bodices past counting, the shimmer of fabrics soft and firm, silky and sheer; red, mauve, pink, blue, lilac, purple, ecru, rose, yellow, cream, and white, all the colours that an impressionist finds in a sunlit landscape, with here and there the dead shadow of a frock coat. My Aunt Georgiana regarded them as though they had been so many daubs of tube-paint on a palette.

When the musicians came out and took their places, she gave a little stir of anticipation, and looked with quickening interest down over the rail at that invariable grouping, perhaps the first wholly familiar thing that had greeted her eye since she had left old Maggie and her weakling calf. I could feel how all those details sank into her soul, for I had not forgotten how they had sunk into mine when I came fresh from ploughing forever and forever between green aisles of corn, where, as in a treadmill, one might walk from daybreak to dusk without perceiving a shadow of change. The clean profiles of the musicians, the gloss of their linen, the dull black of their coats, the beloved shapes of the instruments, the patches of yellow light thrown by the green shaded lamps on the smooth, varnished bellies of the 'cellos and the bass viols in the rear, the restless, wind-tossed forest of fiddle necks and bows – I recalled how, in the first orchestra I had ever heard, those long bow strokes seemed to draw the heart out of me, as a conjurer's stick reels out yards of paper ribbon from a hat.

The first number was the *Tannhäuser* overture. When the horns drew out the first strain of the Pilgrim's chorus, my Aunt Georgiana clutched my coat sleeve. Then it was I first realized that for her this broke a silence of thirty years; the inconceivable silence of the plains. With the battle between the two motives, with the frenzy of the Venusberg theme and its ripping of strings, there came to me an overwhelming sense of the waste and wear we are so powerless to combat; and I saw again the tall, naked house on the prairie, black and grim as a wooden fortress; the black pond where I had learned to swim, its margin pitted with sun-dried cattle tracks; the rain gullied clay banks about the naked house, the four dwarf ash seedlings where the dish-cloths were always hung to dry before the kitchen door.

The world there was the flat world of the ancients; to the east, a cornfield that stretched to daybreak; to the west, a corral that reached to sunset; between, the conquests of peace, dearer bought than those of war.

The overture closed, my aunt released my coat sleeve, but she said nothing. She sat staring at the orchestra through a dullness of thirty years, through the films made little by little by each of the three hundred and sixty-five days in every one of them. What, I wondered, did she get from it? She had been a good pianist in her day I knew, and her musical education had been broader than that of most music teachers of a quarter of a century ago. She had often told me of Mozart's operas and Meyerbeer's, and I could remember hearing her sing, years ago, certain melodies of Verdi's. When I had fallen ill with a fever in her house she used to sit by my cot in the evening – when the cool, night wind blew in through the faded mosquito netting tacked over the window and I lay watching a certain bright star that burned red above the cornfield – and sing 'Home to our mountains, O, let us return!' in a way fit to break the heart of a Vermont boy near dead of homesickness already.

I watched her closely through the prelude to *Tristan and Isolde*, trying vainly to conjecture what that seething turmoil of strings and winds might mean to her, but she sat mutely staring at the violin bows that drove obliquely downward, like the pelting streaks of rain in a summer shower. Had this music any message for her? Had she enough left to at all comprehend this power which had kindled the world since she had left it? I was in a fever of curiosity, but Aunt Georgiana sat silent upon her peak in Darien. She preserved this utter immobility throughout the number from *The Flying Dutchman*, though her fingers worked mechanically upon her black dress, as though, of themselves, they were recalling the piano score they had once played. Poor old hands! They had been stretched and twisted into mere tentacles to hold and lift and knead with; the palm, unduly swollen, the fingers bent and knotted – on one of them a thin, worn band that had once been a wedding ring. As I pressed and gently quieted one of those groping hands, I remembered with quivering eyelids their services for me in other days.

Soon after the tenor began the 'Prize Song', I heard a quick drawn breath and turned to my aunt. Her eyes were closed, but the tears were glistening on her cheeks, and I think, in a moment more, they were in my eyes as well. It never really died, then – the soul that can suffer so excruciatingly and so interminably; it withers to the outward eye only; like that strange moss which can lie on a dusty shelf half a century and yet, if placed in water, grows green again. She wept so throughout the development and elaboration of the melody.

During the intermission before the second half of the concert, I questioned my aunt and found that the 'Prize Song' was not new to her. Some years before there had drifted to the farm in Red Willow County a young German, a tramp cow-puncher, who had sung in the chorus at Bayreuth, when he was a boy, along with the other peasant boys and girls. Of a Sunday morning he used to sit on his gingham-sheeted bed in the hands' bedroom which opened off the kitchen, cleaning the leather of his boots and saddle, singing the 'Prize Song,' while my aunt went about her work in the kitchen. She had hovered about him until she had prevailed upon him to join the country church, though his sole fitness for this step, in so far as I could gather, lay in his boyish face and his possession of this divine melody. Shortly afterward he had gone to town on the Fourth of July, been drunk for several days, lost his money at a faro table, ridden a saddled Texas steer on a bet, and disappeared with a fractured collar-bone. All this my aunt told me huskily, wanderingly, as though she were talking in the weak lapses of illness.

'Well, we have come to better things than the old *Trovatore* at any rate, Aunt Georgie?' I queried, with a well meant effort at jocularity.

Her lip quivered and she hastily put her handkerchief up

to her mouth. From behind it she murmured, 'And you have been hearing this ever since you left me, Clark?' Her question was the gentlest and saddest of reproaches.

The second half of the programme consisted of four numbers from the *Ring*, and closed with Siegfried's funeral march. My aunt wept quietly, but almost continuously, as a shallow vessel overflows in a rain-storm. From time to time her dim eyes looked up at the lights which studded the ceiling, burning softly under their dull glass globes; doubtless they were stars in truth to her. I was still perplexed as to what measure of musical comprehension was left to her, she who had heard nothing but the singing of Gospel Hymns at Methodist services in the square frame schoolhouse on Section Thirteen for so many years. I was wholly unable to gauge how much of it had been dissolved in soapsuds, or worked into bread, or milked into the bottom of a pail.

The deluge of sound poured on and on; I never knew what she found in the shining current of it; I never knew how far it bore her, or past what happy islands. From the trembling of her face I could well believe that before the last numbers she had been carried out where the myriad graves are, into the grey, nameless burying grounds of the sea; or into some world of death vaster yet, where, from the beginning of the world, hope has lain down with hope and dream with dream and, renouncing, slept.

The concert was over; the people filed out of the hall chattering and laughing, glad to relax and find the living level again, but my kinswoman made no effort to rise. The harpist slipped its green felt cover over his instrument; the flute-players shook the water from their mouthpieces; the men of the orchestra went out one by one, leaving the stage to the chairs and music stands, empty as a winter cornfield.

I spoke to my aunt. She burst into tears and sobbed pleadingly. 'I don't want to go, Clark, I don't want to go!'

I understood. For her, just outside the door of the concert

hall, lay the black pond with the cattle-tracked bluffs; the tall, unpainted house, with weather-curled boards; naked as a tower, the crook-backed ash seedlings where the dish-cloths hung to dry; the gaunt, moulting turkeys picking up refuse about the kitchen door. ·

First published in *Everybody's Magazine*, February 1904.

THE SCULPTOR'S FUNERAL

A GROUP of the townspeople stood on the station siding of a little Kansas town, awaiting the coming of the night train, which was already twenty minutes overdue. The snow had fallen thick over everything; in the pale starlight the line of bluffs across the wide, white meadows south of the town made soft, smoke-coloured curves against the clear sky. The men on the siding stood first on one foot and then on the other, their shoulders screwed up with the cold; and they glanced from time to time toward the southeast, where the railroad track wound along the river shore. They conversed in low tones and moved about restlessly, seeming uncertain as to what was expected of them. There was but one of the company who looked as though he knew exactly why he was there; and he kept conspicuously apart; walking to the far end of the platform, returning to the station door, then pacing up the track again, his chin sunk in the high collar of his overcoat, his burly shoulders drooping forward, his gait heavy and dogged. Presently he was approached by a tall, spare, grizzled man clad in a faded Grand Army suit, who shuffled out from the group and advanced with a certain deference, craning his neck forward until his back made the angle of a jack-knife three-quarters open.

'I reckon she's a-goin' to be pretty late agin to-night, Jim,' he remarked in a squeaky falsetto. 'S'pose it's the snow?'

'I don't know,' responded the other man with a shade of

annoyance, speaking from out an astonishing cataract of red beard that grew fiercely and thickly in all directions.

The spare man shifted the quill toothpick he was chewing to the other side of his mouth. 'It ain't likely that anybody from the East will come with the corpse, I s'pose,' he went on reflectively.

'I don't know,' responded the other, more curtly than before.

'It's too bad he didn't belong to some lodge or other. I like an order funeral myself. They seem more appropriate for people of some repytation,' the spare man continued, with an ingratiating concession in his shrill voice, as he carefully placed his toothpick in his vest pocket. He always carried the flag at the G.A.R. funerals in the town.

The heavy man turned on his heel, without replying, and walked up the siding. The spare man shuffled back to the uneasy group. 'Jim's ez full ez a tick, ez ushel,' he commented commiseratingly.

Just then a distant whistle sounded, and there was a shuffling of feet on the platform. A number of lanky boys of all ages appeared as suddenly and slimily as eels wakened by the crack of thunder; some came from the waiting-room, where they had been warming themselves by the red stove, or half asleep on the slat benches; others uncoiled themselves from baggage trucks or slid out of express wagons. Two clambered down from the driver's seat of a hearse that stood backed up against the siding. They straightened their stooping shoulders and lifted their heads, and a flash of momentary animation kindled their dull eyes at that cold, vibrant scream, the world-wide call for men. It stirred them like the note of a trumpet; just as it had often stirred the man who was coming home to-night, in his boyhood.

The night express shot, red as a rocket, from out the eastward marsh lands and wound along the river shore under the long lines of shivering poplars that sentinelled the meadows, the escaping steam hanging in grey masses against the pale sky and blotting out the Milky Way. In a moment the red glare from the headlight streamed up the snow-covered track before the siding and glittered on the wet, black rails. The burly man with the dishevelled red beard walked swiftly up the platform toward the approaching train, uncovering his head as he went. The group of men behind him hesitated, glanced questioningly at one another, and awkwardly followed his example. The train stopped, and the crowd shuffled up to the express car just as the door was thrown open, the spare man in the G.A.R. suit thrusting his head forward with curiosity. The express manager appeared in the doorway, accompanied by a young man in a long ulster and travelling cap.

'Are Mr Merrick's friends here?' inquired the young man.

The group on the platform swayed and shuffled uneasily. Philip Phelps, the banker, responded with dignity: 'We have come to take charge of the body. Mr Merrick's father is very feeble and can't be about.'

'Send the agent out here,' growled the express manager, 'and tell the operator to lend a hand.'

The coffin was got out of its rough box and down on the snowy platform. The townspeople drew back enough to make room for it and then formed a close semicircle about it, looking curiously at the palm leaf which lay across the black cover. No one said anything. The baggage man stood by his truck, waiting to get at the trunks. The engine panted heavily, and the fireman dodged in and out among the wheels with his yellow torch and long oil-can, snapping the spindle boxes. The young Bostonian, one of the dead sculptor's pupils who had come with the body, looked about him helplessly. He turned to the banker, the only one of that black, uneasy, stoop-shouldered group who seemed enough of an individual to be addressed.

'None of Mr Merrick's brothers are here?' he asked uncertainly.

The man with the red beard for the first time stepped up and joined the group. 'No, they have not come yet; the family is scattered. The body will be taken directly to the house.' He stooped and took hold of one of the handles of the coffin.

'Take the long hill road up, Thompson, it will be easier on the horses,' called the liveryman as the undertaker snapped the door of the hearse and prepared to mount to the driver's seat.

Laird, the red-bearded lawyer, turned again to the stranger: 'We didn't know whether there would be any one with him or not,' he explained. 'It's a long walk, so you'd better go up in the hack.' He pointed to a single battered conveyance, but the young man replied stiffly: 'Thank you, but I think I will go up with the hearse. If you don't object,' turning to the undertaker, 'I'll ride with you.'

They clambered up over the wheels and drove off in the starlight up the long, white hill toward the town. The lamps in the still village were shining from under the low, snow-burdened roofs; and beyond, on every side, the plains reached out into emptiness, peaceful and wide as the soft sky itself, and wrapped in a tangible, white silence.

When the hearse backed up to a wooden sidewalk before a naked, weather-beaten frame house, the same composite, ill-defined group that had stood upon the station siding was huddled about the gate. The front yard was an icy swamp, and a couple of warped planks, extending from the sidewalk to the door, made a sort of rickety footbridge. The gate hung on one hinge, and was opened wide with difficulty. Steavens, the young stranger, noticed that something black was tied to the knob of the front door.

The grating sound made by the casket, as it was drawn from the hearse, was answered by a scream from the house; the front door was wrenched open, and a tall, corpulent woman rushed out bareheaded into the snow and flung herself upon the coffin, shrieking: 'My boy, my boy! And this is how you've come home to me!'

As Steavens turned away and closed his eyes with a shudder of unutterable repulsion, another woman, also tall, but flat and angular, dressed entirely in black, darted out of the house and caught Mrs Merrick by the shoulders, crying sharply: 'Come, come, mother; you mustn't go on like this!' Her tone changed to one of obsequious solemnity as she turned to the banker: 'The parlour is ready, Mr Phelps.'

The bearers carried the coffin along the narrow boards, while the undertaker ran ahead with the coffin-rests. They bore it into a large, unheated room that smelled of dampness and disuse and furniture polish, and set it down under a hanging lamp ornamented with jingling glass prisms and before a 'Rogers group' of John Alden and Priscilla, wreathed with smilax. Henry Steavens stared about him with the sickening conviction that there had been some horrible mistake, and that he had somehow arrived at the wrong destination. He looked painfully about over the clover-green Brussels, the fat plush upholstery; among the hand-painted china placques and panels and vases, for some mark of identification, for something that might once conceivably have belonged to Harvey Merrick. It was not until he recognized his friend in the crayon portrait of a little boy in kilts and curls, hanging above the piano, that he felt willing to let any of these people approach the coffin.

'Take the lid off, Mr Thompson; let me see my boy's face,' wailed the elder woman between her sobs. This time Steavens looked fearfully, almost beseechingly into her face, red and swollen under its masses of strong, black, shiny hair. He flushed, dropped his eyes, and then, almost incredulously, looked again. There was a kind of power about her face – a kind of brutal handsomeness, even; but it was scarred and furrowed by violence, and so coloured and coarsened by fiercer passions that grief seemed never to have laid a gentle finger there. The long nose was distended and knobbed at the end, and there were deep lines on either side of it; her heavy, black brows almost met across her forehead, her teeth were large and square, and set far apart – teeth that could tear. She filled the room; the men were obliterated, seemed tossed about like twigs in an angry water, and even Steavens felt himself being drawn into the whirlpool.

The daughter – the tall, raw-boned woman in crêpe, with a mourning comb in her hair which curiously lengthened her face – sat stiffly upon the sofa, her hands, conspicuous for their large knuckles, folded in her lap, her mouth and eyes drawn down, solemnly awaiting the opening of the coffin. Near the door stood a mulatto woman, evidently a servant in the house, with a timid bearing and an emaciated face pitifully sad and gentle. She was weeping silently, the corner of her calico apron lifted to her eyes, occasionally suppressing a long, quivering sob. Steavens walked over and stood beside her.

Feeble steps were heard on the stairs, and an old man, tall and frail, odorous of pipe smoke, with shaggy, unkept grey hair and a dingy beard, tobacco stained about the mouth, entered uncertainly. He went slowly up to the coffin and stood rolling a blue cotton handkerchief between his hands, seeming so pained and embarrassed by his wife's orgy of grief that he had no consciousness of anything else.

'There, there, Annie, dear, don't take on so,' he quavered timidly, putting out a shaking hand and awkwardly patting her elbow. She turned with a cry, and sank upon his shoulder with such violence that he tottered a little. He did not even glance toward the coffin, but continued to look at her with a dull, frightened, appealing expression, as a spaniel looks at the whip. His sunken cheeks slowly reddened and burned with miserable shame. When his wife rushed from the room, her daughter strode after her with set lips. The servant stole up to the coffin, bent over it for a moment, and then slipped away to the kitchen, leaving Steavens, the lawyer, and the father to themselves. The old man stood trembling and looking down at his dead son's face. The sculptor's splendid head seemed even more noble in its rigid stillness than in life. The dark hair had crept down upon the wide forehead; the face seemed strangely long, but in it there was not that beautiful and chaste repose which we expect to find in the faces of the dead. The brows were so drawn that there were two deep lines above the beaked nose, and the chin was thrust forward defiantly. It was as though the strain of life had been so sharp and bitter that death could not at once wholly relax the tension and smooth the countenance into perfect peace – as though he were still guarding something precious and holy, which might even yet be wrested from him.

The old man's lips were working under his stained beard. He turned to the lawyer with timid deference: 'Phelps and the rest are comin' back to set up with Harve, ain't they?' he asked. 'Thank 'ee, Jim, thank 'ee.' He brushed the hair back gently from his son's forehead. 'He was a good boy, Jim; always a good boy. He was ez gentle ez a child and the kindest of 'em all – only we didn't none of us ever onderstand him.' The tears trickled slowly down his beard and dropped upon the sculptor's coat.

'Martin, Martin. Oh, Martin! come here,' his wife wailed from the top of the stairs. The old man started timorously: 'Yes, Annie, I'm coming.' He turned away, hesitated, stood for a moment in miserable indecision; then reached back and patted the dead man's hair softly, and stumbled from the room.

'Poor old man, I didn't think he had any tears left. Seems as if his eyes would have gone dry long ago. At his age nothing cuts very deep,' remarked the lawyer.

Something in his tone made Steavens glance up. While the mother had been in the room, the young man had scarcely seen any one else; but now, from the moment he first glanced into Jim Laird's florid face and blood-shot eyes, he knew that he had found what he had been heartsick at not finding before – the feeling, the understanding, that must exist in some one, even here.

The man was red as his beard, with features swollen and blurred by dissipation, and a hot, blazing blue eye. His face was strained – that of a man who is controlling himself with difficulty – and he kept plucking at his beard with a sort of fierce resentment. Steavens, sitting by the window, watched him turn down the glaring lamp, still its jangling pendants with an angry gesture, and then stand with his hands locked behind him, staring down into the master's face. He could not help wondering what link there could have been between the porcelain vessel and so sooty a lump of potter's clay.

From the kitchen an uproar was sounding; when the dining-room door opened, the import of it was clear. The mother was abusing the maid for having forgotten to make the dressing for the chicken salad which had been prepared for the watchers. Steavens had never heard anything in the least like it; it was injured, emotional, dramatic abuse, unique and masterly in its excruciating cruelty, as violent and unrestrained as had been her grief of twenty minutes before. With a shudder of disgust the lawyer went into the dining-room and closed the door into the kitchen.

'Poor Roxy's getting it now,' he remarked when he came back. 'The Merricks took her out of the poor-house years ago; and if her loyalty would let her, I guess the poor old thing could tell tales that would curdle your blood. She's the mulatto woman who was standing in here a while ago, with her apron to her eyes. The old woman is a fury; there never was anybody like her for demonstrative piety and ingenious cruelty. She made Harvey's life a hell for him when he lived at home; he was so sick ashamed of it. I never could see how he kept himself so sweet.'

'He was wonderful,' said Steavens slowly, 'wonderful; but until to-night I have never known how wonderful.'

'That is the true and eternal wonder of it, anyway; that it can come even from such a dung heap as this,' the lawyer cried, with a sweeping gesture which seemed to indicate much more than the four walls within which they stood.

'I think I'll see whether I can get a little air. The room is so close I am beginning to feel rather faint,' murmured Steavens, struggling with one of the windows. The sash was stuck, however, and would not yield, so he sat down dejectedly and began pulling at his collar. The lawyer came over, loosened the sash with one blow of his red fist and sent the window up a few inches. Steavens thanked him, but the nausea which had been gradually climbing into his throat for the last half hour left him with but one desire – a desperate feeling that he must get away from this place with what was left of Harvey Merrick. Oh, he comprehended well enough now the quiet bitterness of the smile that he had seen so often on his master's lips!

He remembered that once, when Merrick returned from a

visit home, he brought with him a singularly feeling and suggestive bas-relief of a thin, faded old woman, sitting and sewing something pinned to her knee; while a full-lipped, full-blooded little urchin, his trousers held up by a single gallows, stood beside her, impatiently twitching her gown to call her attention to a butterfly he had caught. Steavens, impressed by the tender and delicate modelling of the thin, tired face, had asked him if it were his mother. He remembered the dull flush that had burned up in the sculptor's face.

The lawyer was sitting in a rocking-chair beside the coffin, his head thrown back and his eyes closed. Steavens looked at him earnestly, puzzled at the line of the chin, and wondering why a man should conceal a feature of such distinction under that disfiguring shock of beard. Suddenly, as though he felt the young sculptor's keen glance, he opened his eyes.

'Was he always a good deal of an oyster?' he asked abruptly. 'He was terribly shy as a boy.'

'Yes, he was an oyster, since you put it so,' rejoined Steavens. 'Although he could be very fond of people, he always gave one the impression of being detached. He disliked violent emotion; he was reflective, and rather distrustful of himself – except, of course, as regarded his work. He was sure-footed enough there. He distrusted men pretty thoroughly and women even more, yet somehow without believing ill of them. He was determined, indeed, to believe the best, but he seemed afraid to investigate.'

'A burnt dog dreads the fire,' said the lawyer grimly, and closed his eyes.

Steavens went on and on, reconstructing that whole miserable boyhood. All this raw, biting ugliness had been the portion of the man whose tastes were refined beyond the limits of the reasonable – whose mind was an exhaustless gallery of beautiful impressions, and so sensitive that the mere shadow of a poplar leaf flickering against a sunny wall would be etched and held there forever. Surely, if ever a man had the magic word in his finger tips, it was Merrick. Whatever he touched, he revealed its holiest secret; liberated it from enchantment and restored it to its pristine loveliness, like the Arabian prince who fought the enchantress spell for spell. Upon whatever he had come in contact with, he had left a beautiful record of the experience – a sort of ethereal signature; a scent, a sound, a colour that was his own.

Steavens understood now the real tragedy of his master's life; neither love nor wine, as many had conjectured; but a blow which had fallen earlier and cut deeper than these could have done – a shame not his, and yet so unescapably his, to hide in his heart from his very boyhood. And without – the frontier warfare; the yearning of a boy, cast ashore upon a desert of newness and ugliness and sordidness, for all that is chastened and old, and noble with traditions.

At eleven o'clock the tall, flat woman in black crêpe entered and announced that the watchers were arriving, and asked them 'to step into the dining-room.' As Steavens rose, the lawyer said dryly: 'You go on – it'll be a good experience for you, doubtless; as for me, I'm not equal to that crowd to-night; I've had twenty years of them.'

As Steavens closed the door after him he glanced back at the lawyer, sitting by the coffin in the dim light, with his chin resting on his hand.

The same misty group that had stood before the door of the express car shuffled into the dining-room. In the light of the kerosene lamp they separated and became individuals. The minister, a pale, feeble-looking man with white hair and blond chin-whiskers, took his seat beside a small side table and placed his Bible upon it. The Grand Army man sat down behind the stove and tilted his chair back comfortably against the wall, fishing his quill toothpick from his waistcoat pocket. The two bankers, Phelps and Elder, sat off in a corner behind the dinner-table, where they could finish their discussion of the new usury law and its effect on chattel security loans. The real estate agent, an old man with a smiling, hypocritical face, soon joined them. The coal and lumber dealer and the cattle shipper sat on opposite sides of the hard coal-burner, their feet on the nickel-work. Steavens took a book from his pocket and began to read. The talk around him ranged through various topics of local interest while the house was quieting down. When it was clear that the members of the family were in bed, the Grand Army man hitched his shoulders and, untangling his long legs, caught his heels on the rounds of his chair.

'S'pose there'll be a will, Phelps?' he queried in his weak falsetto.

The banker laughed disagreeably, and began trimming his nails with a pearl-handled pocket-knife.

'There'll scarcely be any need for one, will there?' he queried in his turn.

The restless Grand Army man shifted his position again, getting his knees still nearer his chin. 'Why, the ole man says Harve's done right well lately,' he chirped.

The other banker spoke up. 'I reckon he means by that Harve ain't asked him to mortgage any more farms lately, so as he could go on with his education.'

'Seems like my mind don't reach back to a time when Harve wasn't bein' edycated,' tittered the Grand Army man.

There was a general chuckle. The minister took out his handkerchief and blew his nose sonorously. Banker Phelps closed his knife with a snap. 'It's too bad the old man's sons didn't turn out better,' he remarked with reflective authority. 'They never hung together. He spent money enough on Harve to stock a dozen cattle-farms, and he might as well have poured it into Sand Creek. If Harve had stayed at home and helped nurse what little they had, and gone into stock on the old man's bottom farm, they might all have been well fixed. But the old man had to trust everything to tenants and was cheated right and left.'

'Harve never could have handled stock none,' interposed the cattleman. 'He hadn't it in him to be sharp. Do you remember when he bought Sander's mules for eight-year olds, when everybody in town knew that Sander's father-in-law gave 'em to his wife for a wedding present eighteen years before, an' they was full-grown mules then?'

Every one chuckled, and the Grand Army man rubbed his knees with a spasm of childish delight.

'Harve never was much account for anything practical,

and he shore was never fond of work,' began the coal and lumber dealer. 'I mind the last time he was home; the day he left, when the old man was out to the barn helpin' his hand hitch up to take Harve to the train, and Cal Moots was patchin' up the fence, Harve, he come out on the step and sings out, in his ladylike voice: "Cal Moots, Cal Moots! please come cord my trunk."'

'That's Harve for you,' approved the Grand Army man gleefully. 'I kin hear him howlin' yet, when he was a big feller in long pants and his mother used to whale him with a rawhide in the barn for lettin' the cows git foundered in the cornfield when he was drivin' 'em home from pasture. He killed a cow of mine that-a-way onct – a pure Jersey and the best milker I had, an' the ole man had to put up for her. Harve, he was watchin' the sun set acrost the marshes when the anamile got away; he argued that sunset was oncommon fine.'

'Where the old man made his mistake was in sending the boy East to school,' said Phelps, stroking his goatee and speaking in a deliberate, judicial tone. 'There was where he got his head full of trapseing to Paris and all such folly. What Harve needed, of all people, was a course in some first-class Kansas City business college.'

The letters were swimming before Steavens's eyes. Was it possible that these men did not understand, that the palm on the coffin meant nothing to them? The very name of their town would have remained forever buried in the postal guide had it not been now and again mentioned in the world in connection with Harvey Merrick's. He remembered what his master had said to him on the day of his death, after the congestion of both lungs had shut off any probability of recovery, and the sculptor had asked his pupil to send his body home. 'It's not a pleasant place to be lying while the world is moving and doing and bettering,' he had said with a feeble smile, 'but it rather seems as though we ought to go back to the place we came from in the end. The townspeople will come in for a look at me; and after they have had their say, I shan't have much to fear from the judgment of God.

The wings of the Victory, in there' – with a weak gesture toward his studio – 'will not shelter me.'

The cattleman took up the comment. 'Forty's young for a Merrick to cash in; they usually hang on pretty well. Probably he helped it along with whisky.'

'His mother's people were not long lived, and Harvey never had a robust constitution,' said the minister mildly. He would have liked to say more. He had been the boy's Sunday-school teacher, and had been fond of him; but he felt that he was not in a position to speak. His own sons had turned out badly, and it was not a year since one of them had made his last trip home in the express car, shot in a gambling-house in the Black Hills.

'Nevertheless, there is no disputin' that Harve frequently looked upon the wine when it was red, also variegated, and it shore made an oncommon fool of him,' moralized the cattleman.

Just then the door leading into the parlour rattled loudly and every one started involuntarily, looking relieved when only Jim Laird came out. His red face was convulsed with anger, and the Grand Army man ducked his head when he saw the spark in his blue, blood-shot eye. They were all afraid of Jim; he was a drunkard, but he could twist the law to suit his client's needs as no other man in all western Kansas could do; and there were many who tried. The lawyer closed the door gently behind him, leaned back against it and folded his arms, cocking his head a little to one side. When he assumed this attitude in the court-room, ears were always pricked up, as it usually foretold a flood of withering sarcasm.

'I've been with you gentlemen before,' he began in a dry, even tone, 'when you've sat by the coffins of boys born and raised in this town; and, if I remember rightly, you were never any too well satisfied when you checked them up. What's the matter, anyhow? Why is it that reputable young men are as scarce as millionaires in Sand City? It might almost seem to a stranger that there was some way something the matter with your progressive town. Why did

Ruben Sayer, the brightest young lawyer you ever turned out, after he had come home from the university as straight as a die, take to drinking and forge a check and shoot himself? Why did Bill Merrit's son die of the shakes in a saloon in Omaha? Why was Mr Thomas's son, here, shot in a gambling-house? Why did young Adams burn his mill to beat the insurance companies and go to the pen?'

The lawyer paused and unfolded his arms, laying one clenched fist quietly on the table. 'I'll tell you why. Because you drummed nothing but money and knavery into their ears from the time they wore knickerbockers; because you carped away at them as you've been carping here to-night, holding our friends Phelps and Elder up to them for their models, as our grandfathers held up George Washington and John Adams. But the boys, worse luck, were young, and raw at the business you put them to; and how could they match coppers with such artists as Phelps and Elder? You wanted them to be successful rascals; they were only unsuccessful ones – that's all the difference. There was only one boy ever raised in this borderland between ruffianism and civilization who didn't come to grief, and you hated Harvey Merrick more for winning out than you hated all the other boys who got under the wheels. Lord, Lord, how you did hate him! Phelps, here, is fond of saying that he could buy and sell us all out any time he's a mind to; but he knew Harve wouldn't have given a tinker's damn for his bank and all his cattle-farms put together; and a lack of appreciation, that way, goes hard with Phelps.

'Old Nimrod, here, thinks Harve drank too much; and this from such as Nimrod and me!

'Brother Elder says Harve was too free with the old man's money – fell short in filial consideration, maybe. Well, we can all remember the very tone in which brother Elder swore his own father was a liar, in the county court; and we all know that the old man came out of that partnership with his son as bare as a sheared lamb. But maybe I'm getting personal, and I'd better be driving ahead at what I want to say.'

The lawyer paused a moment, squared his heavy shoulders, and went on: 'Harvey Merrick and I went to school together, back East. We were dead in earnest, and we wanted you all to be proud of us some day. We meant to be great men. Even I, and I haven't lost my sense of humour, gentlemen, I meant to be a great man. I came back here to practise, and I found you didn't in the least want me to be a great man. You wanted me to be a shrewd lawyer – oh, yes! Our veteran here wanted me to get him an increase of pension, because he had dyspepsia; Phelps wanted a new county survey that would put the widow Wilson's little bottom farm inside his south line; Elder wanted to lend money at 5 per cent a month, and get it collected; old Stark here wanted to wheedle old women up in Vermont into investing their annuities in real-estate mortgages that are not worth the paper they are written on. Oh, you needed me hard enough, and you'll go on needing me; and that's why I'm not afraid to plug the truth home to you this once.

'Well, I came back here and became the damned shyster you wanted me to be. You pretend to have some sort of respect for me; and yet you'll stand up and throw mud at Harvey Merrick, whose soul you couldn't dirty and whose hands you couldn't tie. Oh, you're a discriminating lot of Christians! There have been times when the sight of Harvey's name in some Eastern paper has made me hang my head like a whipped dog; and, again, times when I liked to think of him off there in the world, away from all this hog-wallow, doing his great work and climbing the big, clean up-grade he'd set for himself.

'And we? Now that we've fought and lied and sweated and stolen, and hated as only the disappointed strugglers in a bitter, dead little Western town know how to do, what have we got to show for it? Harvey Merrick wouldn't have given one sunset over your marshes for all you've got put together, and you know it. It's not for me to say why, in the inscrutable wisdom of God, a genius should ever have been called from this placc of hatred and bitter waters; but I want this Boston man to know that the drivel he's been hearing here to-night is the only tribute any truly great man could ever have from such a lot of sick, side-tracked, burnt-dog, land-poor sharks as the here-present financiers of Sand City – upon which town may God have mercy!'

The lawyer thrust out his hand to Steavens as he passed him, caught up his overcoat in the hall, and had left the house before the Grand Army man had had time to lift his ducked head and crane his long neck about at his fellows.

Next day Jim Laird was drunk and unable to attend the funeral services. Steavens called twice at his office, but was compelled to start East without seeing him. He had a presentiment that he would hear from him again, and left his address on the lawyer's table; but if Laird found it, he never acknowledged it. The thing in him that Harvey Merrick had loved must have gone under ground with Harvey Merrick's coffin; for it never spoke again, and Jim got the cold he died of driving across the Colorado mountains to defend one of Phelps's sons who had got into trouble out there by cutting government timber.

First published in *McClure's*, January 1905.

PAUL'S CASE
A STUDY IN TEMPERAMENT

IT WAS Paul's afternoon to appear before the faculty of the Pittsburgh High School to account for his various misdemeanours. He had been suspended a week ago, and his father had called at the Principal's office and confessed his perplexity about his son. Paul entered the faculty room suave and smiling. His clothes were a trifle out-grown and the tan velvet on the collar of his open overcoat was frayed and worn; but for all that there was something of the dandy about him, and he wore an opal pin in his neatly knotted black four-in-hand, and a red carnation in his button-hole. This latter adornment the faculty somehow felt was not properly significant of the contrite spirit befitting a boy under the ban of suspension.

Paul was tall for his age and very thin, with high, cramped shoulders and a narrow chest. His eyes were remarkable for a certain hysterical brilliancy, and he continually used them in a conscious, theatrical sort of way, peculiarly offensive in a boy. The pupils were abnormally large, as though he were addicted to belladonna, but there was a glassy glitter about them which that drug does not produce.

When questioned by the Principal as to why he was there, Paul stated, politely enough, that he wanted to come back to school. This was a lie, but Paul was quite accustomed to lying; found it, indeed, indispensable for overcoming friction. His teachers were asked to state their respective charges against him, which they did with such a rancour and aggrievedness as evinced that this was not a usual case. Disorder and impertinence were among the offences named, yet each of his instructors felt that it was scarcely possible to put into words the real cause of the trouble, which lay in a sort of hysterically defiant manner of the boy's; in the contempt which they all knew he felt for them, and which he seemingly made not the least effort to conceal. Once, when he had been making a synopsis of a paragraph at the blackboard, his English teacher had stepped to his side and attempted to guide his hand. Paul had started back with a shudder and thrust his hands violently behind him. The astonished woman could scarcely have been more hurt and embarrassed had he struck at her. The insult was so involuntary and definitely personal as to be unforgettable. In one way and another, he had made all his teachers, men and women alike, conscious of the same feeling of physical aversion. In one class he habitually sat with his hand shading his eyes; in another he always looked out of the window during the recitation; in another he made a running commentary on the lecture, with humorous intention.

His teachers felt this afternoon that his whole attitude was symbolized by his shrug and his flippantly red carnation flower, and they fell upon him without mercy, his English teacher leading the pack. He stood through it smiling, his pale lips parted over his white teeth. (His lips were continually twitching, and he had a habit of raising his eyebrows that was contemptuous and irritating to the last degree.) Older boys than Paul had broken down and shed tears under that baptism of fire, but his set smile did not once desert him, and his only sign of discomfort was the nervous trembling of the fingers that toyed with the buttons of his overcoat, and an occasional jerking of the other hand that held his hat. Paul was always smiling, always glancing about him, seeming to feel that people might be watching him and trying to detect something. This conscious expression, since it was as far as possible from boyish mirthfulness, was usually attributed to insolence or 'smartness.'

As the inquisition proceeded, one of his instructors

repeated an impertinent remark of the boy's, and the Principal asked him whether he thought that a courteous speech to have made a woman. Paul shrugged his shoulders slightly and his eyebrows twitched.

'I don't know,' he replied. 'I didn't mean to be polite or impolite, either. I guess it's a sort of way I have of saying things regardless.'

The Principal, who was a sympathetic man, asked him whether he didn't think that a way it would be well to get rid of. Paul grinned and said he guessed so. When he was told that he could go, he bowed gracefully and went out. His bow was but a repetition of the scandalous red carnation.

His teachers were in despair, and his drawing master voiced the feeling of them all when he declared there was something about the boy which none of them understood. He added: 'I don't really believe that smile of his comes altogether from insolence; there's something sort of haunted about it. The boy is not strong, for one thing. I happen to know that he was born in Colorado, only a few months before his mother died out there of a long illness. There is something wrong about the fellow.'

The drawing master had come to realize that, in looking at Paul, one saw only his white teeth and the forced animation of his eyes. One warm afternoon the boy had gone to sleep at his drawing-board, and his master had noted with amazement what a white, blue-veined face it was; drawn and wrinkled like an old man's about the eyes, the lips twitching even in his sleep, and stiff with a nervous tension that drew them back from his teeth.

His teachers left the building dissatisfied and unhappy; humiliated to have felt so vindictive toward a mere boy, to have uttered this feeling in cutting terms, and to have set each other on, as it were, in the grewsome game of intemperate reproach. Some of them remembered having seen a miserable street cat set at bay by a ring of tormentors.

As for Paul, he ran down the hill whistling the Soldiers' Chorus from *Faust* looking wildly behind him now and then to see whether some of his teachers were not there to writhe under his light-heartedness. As it was now late in the afternoon and Paul was on duty that evening as usher at Carnegie Hall, he decided that he would not go home to supper. When he reached the concert hall the doors were not yet open and, as it was chilly outside, he decided to go up into the picture gallery — always deserted at this hour — where there were some of Raffaelli's gay studies of Paris streets and an airy blue Venetian scene or two that always exhilarated him. He was delighted to find no one in the gallery but the old guard, who sat in one corner, a newspaper on his knee, a black patch over one eye and the other closed. Paul possessed himself of the place and walked confidently up and down, whistling under his breath. After a while he sat down before a blue Rico and lost himself. When he bethought him to look at his watch, it was after seven o'clock, and he rose with a start and ran downstairs, making a face at Augustus, peering out from the cast-room, and an evil gesture at the Venus of Milo as he passed her on the stairway.

When Paul reached the ushers' dressing-room half-a-dozen boys were there already, and he began excitedly to tumble into his uniform. It was one of the few that at all approached fitting, and Paul thought it very becoming — though he knew that the tight, straight coat accentuated his narrow chest, about which he was exceedingly sensitive. He was always considerably excited while he dressed, twanging all over to the tuning of the strings and the preliminary flourishes of the horns in the music-room; but to-night he seemed quite beside himself, and he teased and plagued the boys until, telling him that he was crazy, they put him down on the floor and sat on him.

Somewhat calmed by his suppression, Paul dashed out to the front of the house to seat the early comers. He was a model usher; gracious and smiling he ran up and down the aisles; nothing was too much trouble for him; he carried messages and brought programmes as though it were his greatest pleasure in life, and all the people in his section thought him a charming boy, feeling that he remembered and admired them. As the house filled, he grew more and more vivacious and animated, and the colour came to his cheeks and lips. It was very much as though this were a great reception and Paul were the host. Just as the musicians came out to take their places, his English teacher arrived with checks for the seats which a prominent manufacturer had taken for the season. She betrayed some embarrassment when she handed Paul the tickets, and a *hauteur* which subsequently made her feel very foolish. Paul was startled for a moment, and had the feeling of wanting to put her out; what business had she here among all these fine people and gay colours? He looked her over and decided that she was not appropriately dressed and must be a fool to sit downstairs in such togs. The tickets had probably been sent her out of kindness, he reflected as he put down a seat for her, and she had about as much right to sit there as he had.

When the symphony began Paul sank into one of the rear seats with a long sigh of relief, and lost himself as he had done before the Rico. It was not that symphonies, as such, meant anything in particular to Paul, but the first sigh of the instruments seemed to free some hilarious and potent spirit within him; something that struggled there like the Genius in the bottle found by the Arab fisherman. He felt a sudden zest of life; the lights danced before his eyes and the concert hall blazed into unimaginable splendour. When the soprano soloist came on, Paul forgot even the nastiness of his teacher's being there and gave himself up to the peculiar stimulus such personages always had for him. The soloist chanced to be a German woman, by no means in her first youth, and the mother of many children; but she wore an elaborate gown and a tiara, and above all she had that indefinable air of achievement, that world-shine upon her, which, in Paul's eyes, made her a veritable queen of Romance.

After a concert was over Paul was always irritable and wretched until he got to sleep, and to-night he was even more than usually restless. He had the feeling of not being able to let down, of its being impossible to give up this delicious excitement which was the only thing that could be called living at all. During the last number he withdrew and, after hastily changing his clothes in the dressing-room, slipped out to the side door where the soprano's carriage stood. Here he began pacing rapidly up and down the walk, waiting to see her come out.

Over yonder the Schenley, in its vacant stretch, loomed big and square through the fine rain, the windows of its twelve stories glowing like those of a lighted card-board house under a Christmas tree. All the actors and singers of the better class stayed there when they were in the city, and a number of the big manufacturers of the place lived there in the winter. Paul had often hung about the hotel, watching the people go in and out, longing to enter and leave school-masters and dull care behind him forever.

At last the singer came out, accompanied by the conductor, who helped her into her carriage and closed the door with a cordial *auf wiedersehen*, which set Paul to wondering whether she were not an old sweetheart of his. Paul followed the carriage over to the hotel, walking so rapidly as not to be far from the entrance when the singer alighted and disappeared behind the swinging glass doors that were opened by a negro in a tall hat and a long coat. In the moment that the door was ajar, it seemed to Paul that he, too, entered. He seemed to feel himself go after her up the steps, into the warm, lighted building, into an exotic, a tropical world of shiny, glistening surfaces and basking ease. He reflected upon the mysterious dishes that were brought into the dining-room, the green bottles in buckets of ice, as he had seen them in the supper party pictures of the *Sunday World* supplement. A quick gust of wind brought the rain down with sudden vehemence, and Paul was startled to find that he was still outside in the slush of the gravel driveway; that his boots were letting in the water and his scanty overcoat was clinging wet about him; that the lights in front of the concert hall were out, and that the rain was driving in sheets between him and the orange glow of the windows above him. There it was, what he wanted – tangibly before him,

like the fairy world of a Christmas pantomime, but mocking
spirits stood guard at the doors, and, as the rain beat in his
face, Paul wondered whether he were destined always to
shiver in the black night outside, looking up at it.

He turned and walked reluctantly toward the car tracks.
The end had to come sometime; his father in his night-
clothes at the top of the stairs, explanations that did not
explain, hastily improvised fictions that were forever tripping
him up, his upstairs room and its horrible yellow wall-paper,
the creaking bureau with the greasy plush collar-box, and
over his painted wooden bed the pictures of George Washington and John Calvin, and the framed motto, 'Feed my
Lambs,' which had been worked in red worsted by his
mother.

Half an hour later, Paul alighted from his car and went
slowly down one of the side streets off the main thor-
oughfare. It was a highly respectable street, where all the
houses were exactly alike, and where business men of
moderate means begot and reared large families of children,
all of whom went to Sabbath-school and learned the shorter
catechism, and were interested in arithmetic; all of whom
were as exactly alike as their homes, and of a piece with the
monotony in which they lived. Paul never went up Cordelia
Street without a shudder of loathing. His home was next to
the house of the Cumberland minister. He approached it
to-night with the nerveless sense of defeat, the hopeless
feeling of sinking back forever into ugliness and commonness that he had always had when he came home. The
moment he turned into Cordelia Street he felt the waters
close above his head. After each of these orgies of living, he
experienced all the physical depression which follows a
debauch; the loathing of respectable beds, of common food,
of a house permeated by kitchen odours; a shuddering
repulsion for the flavourless, colourless mass of every-day
existence; a morbid desire for cool things and soft lights and
fresh flowers.

The nearer he approached the house, the more absolutely
unequal Paul felt to the sight of it all; his ugly sleeping

chamber; the cold bathroom with the grimy zinc tub, the cracked mirror, the dripping spiggots; his father, at the top of the stairs, his hairy legs sticking out from his night-shirt, his feet thrust into carpet slippers. He was so much later than usual that there would certainly be inquiries and reproaches. Paul stopped short before the door. He felt that he could not be accosted by his father to-night; that he could not toss again on that miserable bed. He would not go in. He would tell his father that he had no car fare, and it was raining so hard he had gone home with one of the boys and stayed all night.

Meanwhile, he was wet and cold. He went around to the back of the house and tried one of the basement windows, found it open, raised it cautiously, and scrambled down the cellar wall to the floor. There he stood, holding his breath, terrified by the noise he had made, but the floor above him was silent, and there was no creak on the stairs. He found a soap-box, and carried it over to the soft ring of light that streamed from the furnace door, and sat down. He was horribly afraid of rats, so he did not try to sleep, but sat looking distrustfully at the dark, still terrified lest he might have awakened his father. In such reactions, after one of the experiences which made days and nights out of the dreary blanks of the calendar, when his senses were deadened, Paul's head was always singularly clear. Suppose his father had heard him getting in at the window and had come down and shot him for a burglar? Then, again, suppose his father had come down, pistol in hand, and he had cried out in time to save himself, and his father had been horrified to think how nearly he had killed him? Then, again, suppose a day should come when his father would remember that night, and wish there had been no warning cry to stay his hand? With this last supposition Paul entertained himself until daybreak.

The following Sunday was fine; the sodden November chill was broken by the last flash of autumnal summer. In the morning Paul had to go to church and Sabbath-school, as always. On seasonable Sunday afternoons the burghers of

Cordelia Street always sat out on their front 'stoops,' and talked to their neighbours on the next stoop, or called to those across the street in neighbourly fashion. The men usually sat on gay cushions placed upon the steps that led down to the sidewalk, while the women, in their Sunday 'waists,' sat in rockers on the cramped porches, pretending to be greatly at their ease. The children played in the streets; there were so many of them that the place resembled the recreation grounds of a kindergarten. The men on the steps – all in their shirt sleeves, their vests unbuttoned – sat with their legs well apart, their stomachs comfortably protruding, and talked of the prices of things, or told anecdotes of the sagacity of their various chiefs and overlords. They occasionally looked over the multitude of squabbling children, listened affectionately to their high-pitched, nasal voices, smiling to see their own proclivities reproduced in their offspring, and interspersed their legends of the iron kings with remarks about their sons' progress at school, their grades in arithmetic, and the amounts they had saved in their toy banks.

On this last Sunday of November, Paul sat all the afternoon on the lowest step of his 'stoop,' staring into the street, while his sisters, in their rockers, were talking to the minister's daughters next door about how many shirt-waists they had made in the last week, and how many waffles some one had eaten at the last church supper. When the weather was warm, and his father was in a particularly jovial frame of mind, the girls made lemonade, which was always brought out in a red-glass pitcher, ornamented with forget-me-nots in blue enamel. This the girls thought very fine, and the neighbours always joked about the suspicious colour of the pitcher.

To-day Paul's father sat on the top step, talking to a young man who shifted a restless baby from knee to knee. He happened to be the young man who was daily held up to Paul as a model, and after whom it was his father's dearest hope that he would pattern. This young man was of a ruddy complexion, with a compressed, red mouth, and faded, near-sighted eyes, over which he wore thick spectacles, with gold bows that curved about his ears. He was clerk to one of the magnates of a great steel corporation, and was looked upon in Cordelia Street as a young man with a future. There was a story that, some five years ago – he was now barely twenty-six – he had been a trifle dissipated, but in order to curb his appetites and save the loss of time and strength that a sowing of wild oats might have entailed, he had taken his chief's advice, oft reiterated to his employees, and at twenty-one had married the first woman whom he could persuade to share his fortunes. She happened to be an angular school-mistress, much older than he, who also wore thick glasses, and who had now borne him four children, all near-sighted, like herself.

The young man was relating how his chief, now cruising in the Mediterranean, kept in touch with all the details of the business, arranging his office hours on his yacht just as though he were at home, and 'knocking off work enough to keep two stenographers busy.' His father told, in turn, the plan his corporation was considering, of putting in an electric railway plant at Cairo. Paul snapped his teeth; he had an awful apprehension that they might spoil it all before he got there. Yet he rather liked to hear these legends of the iron kings, that were told and retold on Sundays and holidays; these stories of palaces in Venice, yachts on the Mediterranean, and high play at Monte Carlo appealed to his fancy, and he was interested in the triumphs of these cash boys who had become famous, though he had no mind for the cash-boy stage.

After supper was over, and he had helped to dry the dishes, Paul nervously asked his father whether he could go to George's to get some help in his geometry, and still more nervously asked for car fare. This latter request he had to repeat, as his father, on principle, did not like to hear requests for money, whether much or little. He asked Paul whether he could not go to some boy who lived nearer, and told him that he ought not to leave his school work until Sunday; but he gave him the dime. He was not a poor man, but he had a worthy ambition to come up in the world. His only reason for allowing Paul to usher was, that he thought a boy ought to be earning a little.

Paul bounded upstairs, scrubbed the greasy odour of the dish-water from his hands with the ill-smelling soap he hated, and then shook over his fingers a few drops of violet water from the bottle he kept hidden in his drawer. He left the house with his geometry conspicuously under his arm, and the moment he got out of Cordelia Street and boarded a downtown car, he shook off the lethargy of two deadening days, and began to live again.

The leading juvenile of the permanent stock company which played at one of the downtown theatres was an acquaintance of Paul's, and the boy had been invited to drop in at the Sunday-night rehearsals whenever he could. For more than a year Paul had spent every available moment loitering about Charley Edwards's dressing-room. He had won a place among Edwards's following not only because the young actor, who could not afford to employ a dresser, often found him useful, but because he recognized in Paul something akin to what churchmen term 'vocation.'

It was at the theatre and at Carnegie Hall that Paul really lived; the rest was but a sleep and a forgetting. This was Paul's fairy tale, and it had for him all the allurement of a secret love. The moment he inhaled the gassy, painty, dusty odour behind the scenes, he breathed like a prisoner set free, and felt within him the possibility of doing or saying splendid, brilliant, poetic things. The moment the cracked orchestra beat out the overture from *Martha*, or jerked at the serenade from *Rigoletto*, all stupid and ugly things slid from him, and his senses were deliciously, yet delicately fired.

Perhaps it was because, in Paul's world, the natural nearly always wore the guise of ugliness, that a certain element of artificiality seemed to him necessary in beauty. Perhaps it was because his experience of life elsewhere was so full of Sabbath-school picnics, petty economies, wholesome advice as to how to succeed in life, and the unescapable odours of cooking, that he found this existence so alluring, these smartly-clad men and women so attractive, that he was so moved by these starry apple orchards that bloomed perennially under the lime-light.

It would be difficult to put it strongly enough how convincingly the stage entrance of that theatre was for Paul the actual portal of Romance. Certainly none of the company ever suspected it, least of all Charley Edwards. It was very like the old stories that used to float about London of fabulously rich Jews, who had subterranean halls there, with palms, and fountains, and soft lamps and richly apparelled women who never saw the disenchanting light of London day. So, in the midst of that smoke-palled city, enamoured of figures and grimy toil, Paul had his secret temple, his wishing carpet, his bit of blue-and-white Mediterranean shore bathed in perpetual sunshine.

Several of Paul's teachers had a theory that his imagination had been perverted by garish fiction, but the truth was that he scarcely ever read at all. The books at home were not such as would either tempt or corrupt a youthful mind, and as for reading the novels that some of his friends urged upon him – well, he got what he wanted much more quickly from music; any sort of music, from an orchestra to a barrel organ. He needed only the spark, the indescribable thrill that made his imagination master of his senses, and he could make plots and pictures enough of his own. It was equally true that he was not stage-struck – not, at any rate, in the usual acceptation of that expression. He had no desire to become an actor, any more than he had to become a musician. He felt no necessity to do any of these things; what he wanted was to see, to be in the atmosphere, float on the wave of it, to be carried out, blue league after blue league, away from everything.

After a night behind the scenes, Paul found the schoolroom more than ever repulsive; the bare floors and naked walls; the prosy men who never wore frock coats, or violets in their button-holes; the women with their dull gowns, shrill voices, and pitiful seriousness about prepositions that govern the dative. He could not bear to have the other pupils think, for a moment, that he took these people seriously; he must convey to them that he considered it all trivial, and was there only by way of a jest, anyway. He had autograph pictures of all the members of the stock company which he showed his classmates, telling them the most incredible stories of his familiarity with these people, of his acquaintance with the soloists who came to Carnegie Hall, his suppers with them and the flowers he sent them. When these stories lost their effect, and his audience grew listless, he became desperate and would bid all the boys good-bye, announcing that he was going to travel for awhile; going to Naples, to Venice, to Egypt. Then, next Monday, he would slip back, conscious and nervously smiling; his sister was ill, and he should have to defer his voyage until spring.

Matters went steadily worse with Paul at school. In the itch to let his instructors know how heartily he despised them and their homilies, and how thoroughly he was appreciated elsewhere, he mentioned once or twice that he had no time to fool with theorems; adding – with a twitch of the eyebrows and a touch of that nervous bravado which so perplexed them – that he was helping the people down at the stock company; they were old friends of his.

The upshot of the matter was, that the Principal went to Paul's father, and Paul was taken out of school and put to work. The manager at Carnegie Hall was told to get another usher in his stead; the doorkeeper at the theatre was warned not to admit him to the house; and Charley Edwards remorsefully promised the boy's father not to see him again.

The members of the stock company were vastly amused when some of Paul's stories reached them – especially the women. They were hard-working women, most of them supporting indigent husbands or brothers, and they laughed rather bitterly at having stirred the boy to such fervid and florid inventions. They agreed with the faculty and with his father that Paul's was a bad case.

The east-bound train was ploughing through a January snow-storm; the dull dawn was beginning to show grey when the engine whistled a mile out of Newark. Paul started up from the seat where he had lain curled in uneasy slumber, rubbed the breath-misted window glass with his hand, and peered out. The snow was whirling in curling eddies above the white bottomlands, and the drifts lay already deep in the fields and along the fences, while here and there the long dead grass and dried weed stalks protruded black above it. Lights shone from the scattered houses, and a gang of labourers who stood beside the track waved their lanterns.

Paul had slept very little, and he felt grimy and uncomfortable. He had made the all-night journey in a day coach, partly because he was ashamed, dressed as he was, to go into a Pullman, and partly because he was afraid of being seen there by some Pittsburgh business man, who might have noticed him in Denny & Carson's office. When the whistle awoke him, he clutched quickly at his breast pocket, glancing about him with an uncertain smile. But the little, clay-bespattered Italians were still sleeping, the slatternly women across the aisle were in open-mouthed oblivion, and even the crumby, crying babies were for the nonce stilled. Paul settled back to struggle with his impatience as best he could.

When he arrived at the Jersey City station, he hurried through his breakfast, manifestly ill at ease and keeping a sharp eye about him. After he reached the Twenty-third Street station, he consulted a cabman, and had himself driven to a men's furnishing establishment that was just opening for the day. He spent upward of two hours there, buying with endless reconsidering and great care. His new street suit he put on in the fitting-room; the frock coat and dress clothes he had bundled into the cab with his linen. Then he drove to a hatter's and a shoe house. His next errand was at Tiffany's, where he selected his silver and a new scarf-pin. He would not wait to have his silver marked, he said. Lastly, he stopped at a trunk shop on Broadway, and had his purchases packed into various traveling bags.

It was a little after one o'clock when he drove up to the Waldorf, and after settling with the cabman, went into the office. He registered from Washington; said his mother and father had been abroad, and that he had come down to await the arrival of their steamer. He told his story plausibly and had no trouble, since he volunteered to pay for them in advance, in engaging his rooms, a sleeping-room, sitting-room and bath.

Not once, but a hundred times Paul had planned this entry into New York. He had gone over every detail of it with Charley Edwards, and in his scrap book at home there were pages of description about New York hotels, cut from the Sunday papers. When he was shown to his sitting-room on the eighth floor, he saw at a glance that everything was as it should be; there was but one detail in his mental picture that the place did not realize, so he rang for the bell boy and sent him down for flowers. He moved about nervously until the boy returned, putting away his new linen and fingering it delightedly as he did so. When the flowers came, he put them hastily into water, and then tumbled into a hot bath. Presently he came out of his white bath-room, resplendent in his new silk underwear, and playing with the tassels of his red robe. The snow was whirling so fiercely outside his windows that he could scarcely see across the street, but within the air was deliciously soft and fragrant. He put the violets and jonquils on the taboret beside the couch, and threw himself down, with a long sigh, covering himself with a Roman blanket. He was thoroughly tired; he had been in such haste, he had stood up to such a strain, covered so much ground in the last twenty-four hours, that he wanted to think how it had all come about. Lulled by the sound of the wind, the warm air, and the cool fragrance of the flowers, he sank into deep, drowsy retrospection.

It had been wonderfully simple; when they had shut him out of the theatre and concert hall, when they had taken away his bone, the whole thing was virtually determined. The rest was a mere matter of opportunity. The only thing that at all surprised him was his own courage – for he realized well enough that he had always been tormented by fear, a sort of apprehensive dread that, of late years, as the meshes of the lies he had told closed about him, had been pulling the muscles of his body tighter and tighter. Until now, he could not remember the time when he had not been dreading something. Even when he was a little boy, it was always there – behind him, or before, or on either side. There had always been the shadowed corner, the dark place into which he dared not look, but from which something seemed always to be watching him – and Paul had done things that were not pretty to watch, he knew.

But now he had a curious sense of relief, as though he had at last thrown down the gauntlet to the thing in the corner.

Yet it was but a day since he had been sulking in the traces; but yesterday afternoon that he had been sent to the bank with Denny & Carson's deposit, as usual – but this time he was instructed to leave the book to be balanced. There was above two thousand dollars in checks, and nearly a thousand in the bank notes which he had taken from the book and quietly transferred to his pocket. At the bank he had made out a new deposit slip. His nerves had been steady enough to permit of his returning to the office, where he had finished his work and asked for a full day's holiday to-morrow, Saturday, giving a perfectly reasonable pretext. The bank book, he knew, would not be returned before Monday or Tuesday, and his father would be out of town for the next week. From the time he slipped the bank notes into his pocket until he boarded the night train for New York, he had not known a moment's hesitation. It was not the first time Paul had steered through treacherous waters.

How astonishingly easy it had all been; here he was, the thing done; and this time there would be no awakening, no figure at the top of the stairs. He watched the snow flakes whirling by his window until he fell asleep.

When he awoke, it was three o'clock in the afternoon. He bounded up with a start; half of one of his precious days gone already! He spent more than an hour in dressing, watching every stage of his toilet carefully in the mirror. Everything was quite perfect; he was exactly the kind of boy he had always wanted to be.

When he went downstairs, Paul took a carriage and drove up Fifth Avenue toward the Park. The snow had somewhat abated; carriages and tradesmen's wagons were hurrying soundlessly to and fro in the winter twilight; boys in woolen mufflers were shovelling off the door-steps; the avenue stages made fine spots of colour against the white street. Here and there on the corners were stands, with whole flower gardens blooming under glass cases, against the sides of which the snow flakes stuck and melted; violets, roses, carnations, lilies of the valley – somehow vastly more lovely and alluring that they blossomed thus unnaturally in the snow. The Park itself was a wonderful stage winter-piece.

When he returned, the pause of the twilight had ceased, and the tune of the streets had changed. The snow was falling faster, lights streamed from the hotels that reared their dozen stories fearlessly up into the storm, defying the raging Atlantic winds. A long, black stream of carriages poured down the avenue, intersected here and there by other streams, tending horizontally. There were a score of cabs about the entrance of his hotel, and his driver had to wait. Boys in livery were running in and out of the awning stretched across the sidewalk, up and down the red velvet carpet laid from the door to the street. Above, about, within it all was the rumble and roar, the hurry and toss of thousands of human beings as hot for pleasure as himself, and on every side of him towered the glaring affirmation of the omnipotence of wealth.

The boy set his teeth and drew his shoulders together in a spasm of realization; the plot of all dramas, the text of all romances, the nerve-stuff of all sensations was whirling about him like the snow flakes. He burnt like a faggot in a tempest.

When Paul went down to dinner, the music of the orchestra came floating up the elevator shaft to greet him. His head whirled as he stepped into the thronged corridor, and he sank back into one of the chairs against the wall to get his breath. The lights, the chatter, the perfumes, the bewildering medley of colour – he had, for a moment, the feeling of not being able to stand it. But only for a moment; these were his own people, he told himself. He went slowly about the corridors, through the writing-rooms, smoking-rooms, reception-rooms, as though he were exploring the chambers of an enchanted palace, built and peopled for him alone.

When he reached the dining-room he sat down at a table near a window. The flowers, the white linen, the many-coloured wine glasses, the gay toilettes of the women, the low popping of corks, the undulating repetitions of the *Blue Danube* from the orchestra, all flooded Paul's dream with bewildering radiance. When the roseate tinge of his champagne was added – that cold, precious bubbling stuff that creamed and foamed in his glass – Paul wondered that there were honest men in the world at all. This was what all the world was fighting for, he reflected; this was what all the struggle was about. He doubted the reality of his past. Had he ever known a place called Cordelia Street, a place where fagged-looking business men got on the early car; mere rivets in a machine they seemed to Paul, – sickening men, with combings of children's hair always hanging to their coats, and the smell of cooking in their clothes. Cordelia Street – Ah! that belonged to another time and country; had he not always been thus, had he not sat here night after night, from as far back as he could remember, looking pensively over just such shimmering textures, and slowly twirling the stem of a glass like this one between his thumb and middle finger? He rather thought he had.

He was not in the least abashed or lonely. He had no especial desire to meet or to know any of these people; all he demanded was the right to look on and conjecture, to watch the pageant. The mere stage properties were all he contended for. Nor was he lonely later in the evening, in his loge at the Metropolitan. He was now entirely rid of his nervous misgivings, of his forced aggressiveness, of the imperative desire to show himself different from his surroundings. He felt now that his surroundings explained him. Nobody questioned the purple; he had only to wear it passively. He had only to glance down at his attire to reassure himself that here it would be impossible for any one to humiliate him.

He found it hard to leave his beautiful sitting-room to go to bed that night, and sat long watching the raging storm from his turret window. When he went to sleep, it was with the lights turned on in his bedroom; partly because of his old timidity, and partly so that, if he should wake in the night, there would be no wretched moment of doubt, no horrible suspicion of yellow wall-paper, or of Washington and Calvin above his bed.

Sunday morning the city was practically snow-bound. Paul breakfasted late, and in the afternoon he fell in with a wild San Francisco boy, a freshman at Yale, who said he had run down for a 'little flyer' over Sunday. The young man offered to show Paul the night side of the town, and the two boys went out together after dinner, not returning to the hotel until seven o'clock the next morning. They had started out in the confiding warmth of a champagne friendship, but their parting in the elevator was singularly cool. The freshman pulled himself together to make his train, and Paul went to bed. He awoke at two o'clock in the afternoon, very thirsty and dizzy, and rang for ice-water, coffee, and the Pittsburgh papers.

On the part of the hotel management, Paul excited no suspicion. There was this to be said for him, that he wore his spoils with dignity and in no way made himself conspicuous. Even under the glow of his wine he was never boisterous, though he found the stuff like a magician's wand for wonder-building. His chief greediness lay in his ears and eyes, and his excesses were not offensive ones. His dearest pleasures were the grey winter twilights in his sitting-room; his quiet enjoyment of his flowers, his clothes, his wide divan, his cigarette and his sense of power. He could not remember a time when he had felt so at peace with himself. The mere release from the necessity of petty lying, lying every day and every day, restored his self-respect. He had never lied for pleasure, even at school; but to be noticed and admired, to assert his difference from other Cordelia Street boys; and he felt a good deal more manly, more honest, even, now that he had no need for boastful pretensions, now that he could, as his actor friends used to say, 'dress the part.' It was characteristic that remorse did nor occur to him. His golden days went by without a shadow, and he made each as perfect as he could.

On the eighth day after his arrival in New York, he found the whole affair exploited in the Pittsburgh papers, exploited with a wealth of detail which indicated that local news of a sensational nature was at a low ebb. The firm of Denny & Carson announced that the boy's father had refunded the full amount of the theft, and that they had no intention of prosecuting. The Cumberland minister had been interviewed, and expressed his hope of yet reclaiming the motherless lad, and his Sabbath-school teacher declared that she would spare no effort to that end. The rumour had reached Pittsburgh that the boy had been seen in a New York hotel, and his father had gone East to find him and bring him home.

Paul had just come in to dress for dinner; he sank into a chair, weak to the knees, and clasped his head in his hands. It was to be worse than jail, even; the tepid waters of Cordelia Street were to close over him finally and forever. The grey monotony stretched before him in hopeless, unrelieved years; Sabbath-school, Young People's Meeting, the yellow-papered room, the damp dish-towels; it all rushed back upon him with a sickening vividness. He had the old feeling that the orchestra had suddenly stopped, the sinking sensation that the play was over. The sweat broke out on his face, and he sprang to his feet, looked about him with his white, conscious smile, and winked at himself in the mirror. With something of the old childish belief in miracles with which he had so often gone to class, all his lessons unlearned, Paul dressed and dashed whistling down the corridor to the elevator.

He had no sooner entered the dining-room and caught the measure of the music than his remembrance was lightened by his old elastic power of claiming the moment, mounting with it, and finding it all sufficient. The glare and glitter about him, the mere scenic accessories had again, and for the last time, their old potency. He would show himself that he was game, he would finish the thing splendidly. He doubted, more than ever, the existence of Cordelia Street, and for the first time he drank his wine recklessly. Was he not, after all, one of those fortunate beings born to the purple, was he not still himself and in his own place? He drummed a nervous accompaniment to the Pagliacci music and looked about him, telling himself over and over that it had paid.

He reflected drowsily, to the swell of the music and the chill sweetness of his wine, that he might have done it more wisely. He might have caught an outbound steamer and been well out of their clutches before now. But the other side of the world had seemed too far away and too uncertain then; he could not have waited for it; his need had been too sharp. If he had to choose over again, he would do the same thing to-morrow. He looked affectionately about the dining-room, now gilded with a soft mist. Ah, it had paid indeed!

Paul was awakened next morning by a painful throbbing in his head and feet. He had thrown himself across the bed without undressing, and had slept with his shoes on. His limbs and hands were lead heavy, and his tongue and throat were parched and burnt. There came upon him one of those fateful attacks of clear-headedness that never occurred except when he was physically exhausted and his nerves hung loose. He lay still and closed his eyes and let the tide of things wash over him.

His father was in New York; 'stopping at some joint or other,' he told himself. The memory of successive summers on the front stoop fell upon him like a weight of black water. He had not a hundred dollars left; and he knew now, more than ever, that money was everything, the wall that stood between all he loathed and all he wanted. The thing was winding itself up; he had thought of that on his first glorious day in New York, and had even provided a way to snap the thread. It lay on his dressing-table now; he had got it out last night when he came blindly up from dinner, but the shiny metal hurt his eyes, and he disliked the looks of it.

He rose and moved about with a painful effort, succumbing now and again to attacks of nausea. It was the old depression exaggerated; all the world had become Cordelia Street. Yet somehow he was not afraid of anything, was absolutely calm; perhaps because he had looked into the dark corner at last and knew. It was bad enough, what he saw there, but somehow not so bad as his long fear of it had been. He saw everything clearly now. He had a feeling that he had made the best of it, that he had lived the sort of life he was meant to live, and for half an hour he sat staring at the revolver. But he told himself that was not the way, so he went downstairs and took a cab to the ferry.

When Paul arrived at Newark, he got off the train and took another cab, directing the driver to follow the Pennsylvania tracks out of the town. The snow lay heavy on the roadways and had drifted deep in the open fields. Only here and there the dead grass or dried weed stalks projected, singularly black, above it. Once well into the country, Paul dismissed the carriage and walked, floundering along the tracks, his mind a medley of irrelevant things. He seemed to hold in his brain an actual picture of everything he had seen that morning. He remembered every feature of both his drivers, of the toothless old woman from whom he had bought the red flowers in his coat, the agent from whom he had got his ticket, and all of his fellow-passengers on the ferry. His mind, unable to cope with vital matters near at hand, worked feverishly and deftly at sorting and grouping these images. They made for him a part of the ugliness of the world, of the ache in his head, and the bitter burning on his tongue. He stooped and put a handful of snow into his mouth as he walked, but that, too, seemed hot. When he reached a little hillside, where the tracks ran through a cut some twenty feet below him, he stopped and sat down.

The carnations in his coat were drooping with the cold, he noticed; their red glory all over. It occurred to him that all the flowers he had seen in the glass cases that first night must have gone the same way, long before this. It was only one splendid breath they had, in spite of their brave mockery at the winter outside the glass; and it was a losing game in the end, it seemed, this revolt against the homilies by which the world is run. Paul took one of the blossoms carefully from his coat and scooped a little hole in the snow, whre he covered it up. Then he dozed a while, from his weak condition, seeming insensible to the cold.

The sound of an approaching train awoke him, and he started to his feet, remembering only his resolution, and afraid lest he should be too late. He stood watching the approaching locomotive, his teeth chattering, his lips drawn away from them in a frightened smile; once or twice he glanced nervously sidewise, as though he were being watched. When the right moment came, he jumped. As he fell, the folly of his haste occurred to him with merciless clearness, the vastness of what he had left undone. There flashed through his brain, clearer than ever before, the blue of Adriatic water, the yellow of Algerian sands.

He felt something strike his chest, and that his body was being thrown swiftly through the air, on and on, immeasurably far and fast, while his limbs were gently relaxed. Then, because the picture making mechanism was crushed, the disturbing visions flashed into black, and Paul dropped back into the immense design of things.

First published in *McClure's*, May 1905.

THE ENCHANTED BLUFF

WE HAD our swim before sundown, and while we were cooking our supper the oblique rays of light made a dazzling glare on the white sand about us. The translucent red ball itself sank behind the brown stretches of corn field as we sat down to eat, and the warm layer of air that had rested over the water and our clean sand bar grew fresher and smelled of the rank ironweed and sunflowers growing on the flatter shore. The river was brown and sluggish, like any other of the half-dozen streams that water the Nebraska corn lands. On one shore was an irregular line of bald clay bluffs where a few scrub oaks with thick trunks and flat, twisted tops threw light shadows on the long grass. The western shore was low and level, with corn fields that stretched to the skyline, and all along the water's edge were little sandy coves and beaches where slim cottonwoods and willow saplings flickered.

The turbulence of the river in springtime discouraged milling, and, beyond keeping the old red bridge in repair, the busy farmers did not concern themselves with the stream; so the Sandtown boys were left in undisputed possession. In the autumn we hunted quail through the miles of stubble and fodder land along the flat shore, and, after the winter skating season was over and the ice had gone out, the spring freshets and flooded bottoms gave us our great excitement of the year. The channel was never the same for two successive seasons. Every spring the swollen stream undermined a bluff to the east, or bit out a few acres of corn field to the west and whirled the soil away to deposit it in spumy mud banks somewhere else. When the water fell low in midsummer, new sand bars were thus exposed to dry and whiten in the August sun. Sometimes these were banked so firmly that the fury of the next freshet failed to unseat them; the little willow seedlings emerged triumphantly from the yellow froth, broke into spring leaf, shot up into summer growth, and with their mesh of roots bound together the moist sand beneath them against the batterings of another April. Here and there a cottonwood soon glittered among them, quivering in the low current of air that, even on breathless days when the dust hung like smoke above the wagon road, trembled along the face of the water.

It was on such an island, in the third summer of its yellow green, that we built our watch fire; not in the thicket of dancing willow wands, but on the level terrace of fine sand which had been added that spring; a little new bit of world, beautifully ridged with ripple marks, and strewn with the tiny skeletons of turtles and fish, all as white and dry as if they had been expertly cured. We had been careful not to mar the freshness of the place, although we often swam to it on summer evenings and lay on the sand to rest.

This was our last watch fire of the year, and there were reasons why I should remember it better than any of the others. Next week the other boys were to file back to their old places in the Sandtown High School, but I was to go up to the Divide to teach my first country school in the Norwegian district. I was already homesick at the thought of quitting the boys with whom I had always played; of leaving the river, and going up into a windy plain that was all windmills and corn fields and big pastures; where there was nothing wilful or unmanageable in the landscape, no new islands, and no chance of unfamiliar birds – such as often followed the watercourses.

Other boys came and went and used the river for fishing or skating, but we six were sworn to the spirit of the stream, and we were friends mainly because of the river. There were the two Hassler boys, Fritz and Otto, sons of the little German tailor. They were the youngest of us; ragged boys of ten and twelve, with sunburned hair, weather-stained faces, and pale blue eyes. Otto, the elder, was the best mathematician in school, and clever at his books, but he always dropped out in the spring term as if the river could not get on without him. He and Fritz caught the fat, horned catfish and sold them about the town, and they lived so much in the water that they were as brown and sandy as the river itself.

There was Percy Pound, a fat, freckled boy with chubby cheeks, who took half a dozen boys' story-papers and was always being kept in for reading detectives stories behind his desk. There was Tip Smith, destined by his freckles and red hair to be the buffoon in all our games, though he walked like a timid little old man and had a funny, cracked laugh. Tip worked hard in his father's grocery store every afternoon, and swept it out before school in the morning. Even his recreations were laborious. He collected cigarette cards and tin tobacco-tags indefatigably, and would sit for hours humped up over a snarling little scroll-saw which he kept in his attic. His dearest possessions were some little pill bottles that purported to contain grains of wheat from the Holy Land, water from the Jordan and the Dead Sea, and earth from the Mount of Olives. His father had bought these dull things from a Baptist missionary who peddled them, and Tip seemed to derive great satisfaction from their remote origin.

The tall boy was Arthur Adams. He had fine hazel eyes that were almost too reflective and sympathetic for a boy, and such a pleasant voice that we all loved to hear him read aloud. Even when he had to read poetry aloud at school, no one ever thought of laughing. To be sure, he was not at school very much of the time. He was seventeen and should have finished the High School the year before, but he was always off somewhere with his gun. Arthur's mother was dead, and his father, who was feverishly absorbed in promoting schemes, wanted to send the boy away to school and get him off his hands; but Arthur always begged off for another year and promised to study. I remember him as a tall, brown boy with an intelligent face, always lounging among a lot of us little fellows, laughing at us oftener than with us, but such a soft, satisfied laugh that we felt rather flattered when we provoked it. In after-years people said that Arthur had been given to evil ways even as a lad, and it is true that we often saw him with the gambler's sons and with old Spanish Fanny's boy, but if he learned anything ugly in their company he never betrayed it to us. We would have followed Arthur anywhere, and I am bound to say that he led us into no worse place than the cattail marshes and the stubble fields. These, then, were the boys who camped with me that summer night upon the sand bar.

After we finished our supper we beat the willow thicket for driftwood. By the time we had collected enough, night had fallen, and the pungent, weedy smell from the shore increased with the coolness. We threw ourselves down about the fire and made another futile effort to show Percy Pound the Little Dipper. We had tried it often before, but he could never be got past the big one.

'You see those three big stars just below the handle, with the bright one in the middle?' said Otto Hassler; 'that's Orion's belt, and the bright one is the clasp.' I crawled behind Otto's shoulder and sighted up his arm to the star that seemed perched upon the tip of his steady fore-finger. The Hassler boys did seine-fishing at night, and they knew a good many stars.

Percy gave up the Little Dipper and lay back on the sand, his hands clasped under his head. 'I can see the North Star,' he announced, contentedly, pointing toward it with his big toe. 'Anyone might get lost and need to know that.'

We all looked up at it.

'How do you suppose Columbus felt when his compass didn't point north any more?' Tip asked.

Otto shook his head. 'My father says that there was another North Star once, and that maybe this one won't last always. I wonder what would happen to us down here if anything went wrong with it?'

Arthur chuckled. 'I wouldn't worry, Ott. Nothing's apt to happen to it in your time. Look at the Milky Way! There must be lots of good dead Indians.'

We lay back and looked, meditating, at the dark cover of the world. The gurgle of the water had become heavier. We had often noticed a mutinous, complaining note in it at night, quite different from its cheerful daytime chuckle, and seeming like the voice of a much deeper and more powerful stream. Our water had always these two moods: the one of sunny complaisance, the other of inconsolable, passionate regret.

'Queer how the stars are all in sort of diagrams,' remarked Otto. 'You could do most any proposition in geometry with 'em. They always look as if they meant something. Some folks say everybody's fortune is all written out in the stars, don't they?'

'They believe so in the old country,' Fritz affirmed.

But Arthur only laughed at him. 'You're thinking of Napoleon, Fritzey. He had a star that went out when he began to lose battles. I guess the stars don't keep any close tally on Sandtown folks.'

We were speculating on how many times we could count a hundred before the evening star went down behind the corn fields, when someone cried, 'There comes the moon, and it's as big as a cart wheel!'

We all jumped up to greet it as it swam over the bluffs behind us. It came up like a galleon in full sail; an enormous, barbaric thing, red as an angry heathen god.

'When the moon came up red like that, the Aztecs used to sacrifice their prisoners on the temple top,' Percy announced.

'Go on, Perce. You got that out of *Golden Days*. Do you believe that, Arthur?' I appealed.

Arthur answered, quite seriously: 'Like as not. The moon was one of their gods. When my father was in Mexico City he saw the stone where they used to sacrifice their prisoners.'

As we dropped down by the fire again some one asked whether the Mound-Builders were older than the Aztecs. When we once got upon the Mound-Builders we never willingly got away from them, and we were still conjecturing when we heard a loud splash in the water.

'Must have been a big cat jumping,' said Fritz. 'They do sometimes. They must see bugs in the dark. Look what a track the moon makes!'

There was a long, silvery streak on the water, and where the current fretted over a big log it boiled up like gold pieces.

'Suppose there ever *was* any gold hid away in this old river?' Fritz asked. He lay like a little brown Indian, close to the fire, his chin on his hand and his bare feet in the air. His brother laughed at him, but Arthur took his suggestion seriously.

'Some of the Spaniards thought there was gold up here somewhere. Seven cities chuck full of gold, they had it, and Coronado and his men came up to hunt it. The Spaniards were all over this country once.'

Percy looked interested. 'Was that before the Mormons went through?'

We all laughed at this.

'Long enough before. Before the Pilgrim Fathers, Perce. Maybe they came along this very river. They always followed the watercourses.'

'I wonder where this river really does begin?' Tip mused. That was an old and a favorite mystery which the map did not clearly explain. On the map the little black line stopped somewhere in western Kansas; but since rivers generally rose in mountains, it was only reasonable to suppose that ours came from the Rockies. Its destination, we knew, was the Missouri, and the Hassler boys always maintained that we could embark at Sandtown in floodtime, follow our noses, and eventually arrive at New Orleans. Now they took up their old argument. 'If us boys had grit enough to try it, it wouldn't take no time to get to Kansas City and St. Joe.'

We began to talk about the places we wanted to go to. The Hassler boys wanted to see the stockyards in Kansas City, and Percy wanted to see a big store in Chicago. Arthur was interlocutor and did not betray himself.

'Now it's your turn, Tip.'

Tip rolled over on his elbow and poked the fire, and his eyes looked shyly out of his queer, tight little face. 'My place is awful far away. My Uncle Bill told me about it.'

Tip's Uncle Bill was a wanderer, bitten with mining fever, who had drifted into Sandtown with a broken arm, and when it was well had drifted out again.

'Where is it?'

'Aw, it's down in New Mexico somewheres. There aren't no railroads or anything. You have to go on mules, and you run out of water before you get there and have to drink canned tomatoes.'

'Well, go on, kid. What's it like when you do get there?'

Tip sat up and excitedly began his story.

'There's a big red rock there that goes right up out of the sand for about nine hundred feet. The country's flat all around it, and this here rock goes up all by itself, like a monument. They call it the Enchanted Bluff down there, because no white man has ever been on top of it. The sides are smooth rock, and straight up, like a wall. The Indians say that hundreds of years ago, before the Spaniards came, there was a village away up there in the air. The tribe that lived there had some sort of steps, made out of wood and bark, hung down over the face of the bluff, and the braves went down to hunt and carried water up in big jars swung on their backs. They kept a big supply of water and dried meat up there, and never went down except to hunt. They were a peaceful tribe that made cloth and pottery, and they went up there to get out of the wars. You see, they could pick off any war party that tried to get up their little steps. The Indians say they were a handsome people, and they had some sort of queer religion. Uncle Bill thinks they were Cliff-Dwellers who had got into trouble and left home. They weren't fighters, anyhow.

'One time the braves were down hunting and an awful storm came up – a kind of waterspout – and when they got back to their rock they found their little staircase had been all broken to pieces, and only a few steps were left hanging away up in the air. While they were camped at the foot of the rock, wondering what to do, a war party from the north came along and massacred 'em to a man, with all the old folks and women looking on from the rock. Then the war party went on south and left the village to get down the best way they could. Of course they never got down. They starved to death up there, and when the war party came back on their way north, they could hear the children crying from the edge of the bluff where they had crawled out, but they didn't see a sign of a grown Indian, and nobody has ever been up there since.'

We exclaimed at this dolorous legend and sat up.

'There couldn't have been many people up there,' Percy demurred. 'How big is the top, Tip?'

'Oh, pretty big. Big enough so that the rock doesn't look nearly as tall as it is. The top's bigger than the base. The bluff is sort of worn away for several hundred feet up. That's one reason it's so hard to climb.'

I asked how the Indians got up, in the first place.

'Nobody knows how they got up or when. A hunting party came along once and saw that there was a town up there, and that was all.'

Otto rubbed his chin and looked thoughtful. 'Of course there must be some way to get up there. Couldn't people get a rope over someway and pull a ladder up?'

Tip's little eyes were shining with excitement. 'I know a way. Me and Uncle Bill talked it all over. There's a kind of rocket that would take a rope over — life-savers use 'em — and then you could hoist a rope ladder and peg it down at the bottom and make it tight with guy ropes on the other side. I'm going to climb that there bluff, and I've got it all planned out.'

Fritz asked what he expected to find when he got up there.

'Bones, maybe, or the ruins of their town, or pottery, or some of their idols. There might be 'most anything up there. Anyhow, I want to see.'

'Sure nobody else has been up there, Tip?' Arthur asked.

'Dead sure. Hardly anybody ever goes down there. Some hunters tried to cut steps in the rock once, but they didn't get higher than a man can reach. The Bluff's all red granite, and Uncle Bill thinks it's a boulder the glaciers left. It's a queer place, anyhow. Nothing but cactus and desert for hundreds of miles, and yet right under the Bluff there's good water and plenty of grass. That's why the bison used to go down there.'

Suddenly we heard a scream above our fire, and jumped up to see a dark, slim bird floating southward far above us – a whooping crane, we knew by her cry and her long neck. We ran to the edge of the island, hoping we might see her alight, but she wavered southward along the rivercourse until we lost her. The Hassler boys declared that by the look of the heavens it must be after midnight, so we threw more wood on our fire, put on our jackets, and curled down in the warm sand. Several of us pretended to doze, but I fancy we were really thinking about Tip's Bluff and the extinct people. Over in the wood the ring doves were calling mournfully to one another, and once we heard a dog bark, far away. 'Somebody getting into old Tommy's melon patch,' Fritz murmured sleepily, but nobody answered him. By and by Percy spoke out of the shadows.

'Say, Tip, when you go down there will you take me with you?'

'Maybe.'

'Suppose one of us beats you down there, Tip?'

'Whoever gets to the Bluff first has got to promise to tell the rest of us exactly what he finds,' remarked one of the Hassler boys, and to this we all readily assented.

Somewhat reassured, I dropped off to sleep. I must have dreamed about a race for the Bluff, for I awoke in a kind of fear that other people were getting ahead of me and that I was losing my chance. I sat up in my damp clothes and looked at the other boys, who lay tumbled in uneasy attitudes about the dead fire. It was still dark, but the sky was blue with the last wonderful azure of night. The stars glistened like crystal globes, and trembled as if they shone through a depth of clear water. Even as I watched, they began to pale and the sky brightened. Day came suddenly, almost instantaneously. I turned for another look at the blue night, and it was gone. Everywhere the birds began to call, and all manner of little insects began to chirp and hop about in the willows. A breeze sprang up from the west and brought the heavy smell of ripened corn. The boys rolled over and shook themselves. We stripped and plunged into the river just as the sun came up over the windy bluffs.

When I came home to Sandtown at Christmas time, we skated out to our island and talked over the whole project of Enchanted Bluff, renewing our resolution to find it.

Although that was twenty years ago, none of us have ever climbed the Enchanted Bluff. Percy Pound is a stockbroker in Kansas City and will go nowhere that his red touring car cannot carry him. Otto Hassler went on the railroad and lost his foot braking; after which he and Fritz succeeded their father as the town tailors.

Arthur sat about the sleepy little town all his life – he died before he was twenty-five. The last time I saw him, when I was home on one of my college vacations, he was sitting in a steamer chair under a cottonwood tree in the little yard behind one of the two Sandtown saloons. He was very untidy and his hand was not steady, but when he rose, unabashed, to greet me, his eyes were as clear and warm as ever. When I had talked with him for an hour and heard him laugh again, I wondered how it was that when Nature had taken such pains with a man, from his hands to the arch of his long foot, she had ever lost him in Sandtown. He joked about Tip Smith's Bluff, and declared he was going down there just as soon as the weather got cooler; he thought the Grand Canyon might be worth while, too.

I was perfectly sure when I left him that he would never get beyond the high plank fence and the comfortable shade of the cottonwood. And, indeed, it was under that very tree that he died one summer morning.

Tip Smith still talks about going to New Mexico. He married a slatternly, unthrifty country girl, has been much tied to a perambulator, and has grown stooped and gray from irregular meals and broken sleep. But the worst of his difficulties are now over, and he has, as he says, come into easy water. When I was last in Sandtown I walked home with him late one moonlight night, after he had balanced his cash and shut up his store. We took the long way around and sat down on the schoolhouse steps, and between us we quite revived the romance of the lone red rock and the extinct people. Tip insists that he still means to go down there, but he thinks now he will wait until his boy Bert is old enough to go with him. Bert has been let into the story, and thinks of nothing but the Enchanted Bluff.

First published in *Harper's*, April 1909.

THE BOHEMIAN GIRL

*T*HE transcontinental express swung along the windings of
the Sand River Valley, and in the rear seat of the observation
car a young man sat greatly at his ease, not in the least
discomfited by the fierce sunlight which beat in upon his
brown face and neck and strong back. There was a look of
relaxation and of great passivity about his broad shoulders,
which seemed almost too heavy until he stood up and
squared them. He wore a pale flannel shirt and a blue silk
necktie with loose ends. His trousers were wide and belted at
the waist, and his short sack coat hung open. His heavy shoes
had seen good service. His reddish-brown hair, like his
clothes, had a foreign cut. He had deep-set, dark blue eyes
under heavy reddish eyebrows. His face was kept clean only
by close shaving, and even the sharpest razor left a glint of
yellow in the smooth brown of his skin. His teeth and the
palms of his hands were very white. His head, which looked
hard and stubborn, lay indolently in the green cushion of the
wicker chair, and as he looked out at the ripe summer
country a teasing, not unkindly smile played over his lips.
Once, as he basked thus comfortably, a quick light flashed in
his eyes, curiously dilating the pupils, and his mouth became
a hard, straight line, gradually relaxing into its former smile
of rather kindly mockery. He told himself, apparently, that
there was no point in getting excited; and he seemed a
master hand at taking his ease when he could. Neither the
sharp whistle of the locomotive nor the brakeman's call

disturbed him. It was not until after the train had stopped that he rose, put on a Panama hat, took from the rack a small valise and a flute case, and stepped deliberately to the station platform. The baggage was already unloaded, and the stranger presented a check for a battered sole-leather steamer trunk.

'Can you keep it here for a day or two?' he asked the agent. 'I may send for it, and I may not.'

'Depends on whether you like the country, I suppose?' demanded the agent in a challenging tone.

'Just so.'

The agent shrugged his shoulders, looked scornfully at the small trunk, which was marked 'N.E.,' and handed out a claim check without further comment. The stranger watched him as he caught one end of the trunk and dragged it into the express room. The agent's manner seemed to remind him of something amusing. 'Doesn't seem to be a very big place,' he remarked, looking about.

'It's big enough for us,' snapped the agent, as he banged the trunk into a corner.

That remark, apparently, was what Nils Ericson had wanted. He chuckled quietly as he took a leather strap from his pocket and swung his valise around his shoulder. Then he settled his Panama securely on his head, turned up his trousers, tucked the flute case under his arm, and started off across the fields. He gave the town, as he would have said, a wide berth, and cut through a great fenced pasture, emerging, when he rolled under the barbed wire at the farther corner, upon a white dusty road which ran straight up from the river valley to the high prairies, where the ripe wheat stood yellow and the tin roofs and weathercocks were twinkling in the fierce sunlight. By the time Nils had done three miles, the sun was sinking and the farm wagons on their way home from town came rattling by, covering him with dust and making him sneeze. When one of the farmers pulled up and offered to give him a lift, he clambered in willingly. The driver was a thin, grizzled old man with a long lean neck and a foolish sort of beard, like a goat's. 'How fur ye goin'?' he asked, as he clucked to his horses and started off.

'Do you go by the Ericson place?'

'Which Ericson?' The old man drew in his reins as if he expected to stop again.

'Preacher Ericson's.'

'Oh, the Old Lady Ericson's!' He turned and looked at Nils. 'La, me! If you're goin' out there you might 'a' rid out in the automobile. That's a pity, now. The Old Lady Ericson was in town with her auto. You might 'a' heard it snortin' anywhere about the post office er the butcher shop.'

'Has she a motor?' asked the stranger absently.

''Deed an' she has! She runs into town every night about this time for her mail and meat for supper. Some folks say she's afraid her auto won't get exercise enough, but I say that's jealousy.'

'Aren't there any other motors about here?'

'Oh, yes! we have fourteen in all. But nobody else gets around like the Old Lady Ericson. She's out, rain er shine, over the whole county, chargin' into town and out amongst her farms, an' up to her sons' places. Sure you ain't going to the wrong place?' He craned his neck and looked at Nils' flute case with eager curiosity. 'The old woman ain't got any piany that I knows on. Olaf, he has a grand. His wife's musical: took lessons in Chicago.'

'I'm going up there tomorrow,' said Nils imperturbably. He saw that the driver took him for a piano tuner.

'Oh, I see!' The old man screwed up his eyes mysteriously. He was a little dashed by the stranger's noncommunicativeness, but he soon broke out again.

'I'm one o' Mis' Ericson's tenants. Look after one of her places. I did own the place myself oncet, but I lost it a while back, in the bad years just after the World's Fair. Just as well, too, I say. Lets you out o' payin' taxes. The Ericsons do own most of the county now. I remember the old preacher's fav'rite text used to be, "To them that hath shall be given." They've spread something wonderful – run over this here country like bindweed. But I ain't one that begretches it to 'em. Folks is entitled to what they kin git; and they're hustlers. Olaf, he's in the Legislature now, and a likely man fur Congress. Listen, if that ain't the old woman comin' now. Want I should stop her?'

Nils shook his head. He heard the deep chug-chug of a motor vibrating steadily in the clear twilight behind them. The pale lights of the car swam over the hill, and the old man slapped his reins and turned clear out of the road, ducking his head at the first of three angry snorts from behind. The motor was running at a hot, even speed, and passed without turning an inch from its course. The driver was a stalwart woman who sat at ease in the front seat and drove her car bareheaded. She left a cloud of dust and a trail of gasoline behind her. Her tenant threw back his head and sneezed.

'Whew! I sometimes say I'd as lief be *before* Mrs Ericson as behind her. She does beat all! Nearly seventy, and never lets another soul touch that car. Puts it into commission herself every morning, and keeps it tuned up by the hitch-bar all day. I never stop work for a drink o' water that I don't hear her a-churnin' up the road. I reckon her darter-in-laws never sets down easy nowadays. Never know when she'll pop in. Mis' Otto, she says to me: "We're so afraid that thing'll blow up and do Ma some injury yet, she's so turrible venturesome." Says I: "I wouldn't stew, Mis' Otto; the old lady'll drive that car to the funeral of every darter-in-law she's got." That was after the old woman had jumped a turrible bad culvert.'

The stranger heard vaguely what the old man was saying. Just now he was experiencing something very much like homesickness, and he was wondering what had brought it about. The mention of a name or two, perhaps; the rattle of a wagon along a dusty road; the rank, resinous smell of sunflowers and ironweed, which the night damp brought up from the draws and low places; perhaps, more than all, the dancing lights of the motor that had plunged by. He squared his shoulders with a comfortable sense of strength.

The wagon, as it jolted westward, climbed a pretty steady upgrade. The country, receding from the rough river valley, swelled more and more gently, as if it had been smoothed out by the wind. On one of the last of the rugged ridges, at the end of a branch road, stood a grim square house with a tin roof and double porches. Behind the house stretched a row of broken, wind-racked poplars, and down the hill slope to the left straggled the shed and stables. The old man stopped his horses where the Ericsons' road branched across a dry sand creek that wound about the foot of the hill.

'That's the old lady's place. Want I should drive in?'

'No, thank you. I'll roll out here. Much obliged to you. Good night.'

His passenger stepped down over the front wheel, and the old man drove on reluctantly, looking back as if he would like to see how the stranger would be received.

As Nils was crossing the dry creek he heard the restive tramp of a horse coming toward him down the hill. Instantly he flashed out of the road and stood behind a thicket of wild plum bushes that grew in the sandy bed. Peering through the dusk, he saw a light horse, under tight rein, descending the hill at a sharp walk. The rider was a slender woman – barely visible against the dark hillside – wearing an old-fashioned derby hat and a long riding skirt. She sat lightly in the saddle, with her chin high, and seemed to be looking into the distance. As she passed the plum thicket her horse snuffed the air and shied. She struck him, pulling him in sharply, with an angry exclamation, '*Blázne!*' in Bohemian. Once in the main road, she let him out into a lope, and they soon emerged upon the crest of high land, where they moved along the skyline, silhouetted against the band of faint color that lingered in the west. This horse and rider, with their free, rhythmical gallop, were the only moving things to be seen on the face of the flat country. They seemed, in the last sad light of evening, not to be there accidentally, but as an inevitable detail of the landscape.

Nils watched them until they had shrunk to a mere moving speck against the sky, then he crossed the sand creek and climbed the hill. When he reached the gate the front of the house was dark, but a light was shining from the side windows. The pigs were squealing in the hog corral, and Nils could see a tall boy, who carried two big wooden buckets, moving about among them. Halfway between the barn and the house, the windmill wheezed lazily. Following the path that ran around to the back porch, Nils stopped to look through the screen door into the lamplit kitchen. The kitchen was the largest room in the house; Nils remembered that his older brothers used to give dances there when he was a boy. Beside the stove stood a little girl with two light yellow braids and a broad, flushed face, peering anxiously into a frying pan. In the dining room beyond, a large, broad-shouldered woman was moving about the table. She walked with an active, springy step. Her face was heavy and florid, almost without wrinkles, and her hair was black at seventy. Nils felt proud of her as he watched her deliberate activity; never a momentary hesitation, or a movement that did not tell. He waited until she came out into the kitchen and, brushing the child aside, took her place at the stove. Then he tapped on the screen door and entered.

'It's nobody but Nils, Mother. I expect you weren't looking for me.'

Mrs Ericson turned away from the stove and stood staring at him. 'Bring the lamp, Hilda, and let me look.'

Nils laughed and unslung his valise. 'What's the matter, Mother? Don't you know me?'

Mrs Ericson put down the lamp. 'You must be Nils. You don't look very different, anyway.'

'Nor you, Mother. You hold your own. Don't you wear glasses yet?'

'Only to read by. Where's your trunk, Nils?'

'Oh, I left that in town. I thought it might not be convenient for you to have company so near threshing-time.'

'Don't be foolish, Nils.' Mrs Ericson turned back to the stove. 'I don't thresh now. I hitched the wheat land onto the next farm and have a tenant. Hilda, take some hot water up to the company room, and go call little Eric.'

The tow-haired child, who had been standing in mute

amazement, took up the tea kettle and withdrew, giving Nils a long, admiring look from the door of the kitchen stairs.

'Who's the youngster?' Nils asked, dropping down on the bench behind the kitchen stove.

'One of your Cousin Henrik's.'

'How long has Cousin Henrik been dead?'

'Six years. There are two boys. One stays with Peter and one with Anders. Olaf is their guardeen.'

There was a clatter of pails on the porch, and a tall, lanky boy peered wonderingly in through the screen door. He had a fair, gentle face and big gray eyes, and wisps of soft yellow hair hung down under his cap. Nils sprang up and pulled him into the kitchen, hugging him and slapping him on the shoulders. 'Well, if it isn't my kid! Look at the size of him! Don't you know me, Eric?'

The boy reddened under his sunburn and freckles, and hung his head. 'I guess it's Nils,' he said shyly.

'You're a good guesser,' laughed Nils giving the lad's hand a swing. To himself he was thinking: 'That's why the little girl looked so friendly. He's taught her to like me. He was only six when I went away, and he's remembered for twelve years.'

Eric stood fumbling with his cap and smiling. 'You look just like I thought you would,' he ventured.

'Go wash your hands, Eric,' called Mrs Ericson. 'I've got cob corn for supper, Nils. You used to like it. I guess you don't get much of that in the old country. Here's Hilda; she'll take you up to your room. You'll want to get the dust off you before you eat.'

Mrs Ericson went into the dining room to lay another plate, and the little girl came up and nodded to Nils as if to let him know that his room was ready. He put out his hand and she took it, with a startled glance up at his face. Little Eric dropped his towel, threw an arm about Nils and one about Hilda, gave them a clumsy squeeze, and then stumbled out to the porch.

During supper Nils heard exactly how much land each of his eight grown brothers farmed, how their crops were coming on, and how much live stock they were feeding. His mother watched him narrowly as she talked. 'You've got better looking, Nils,' she remarked abruptly, whereupon he grinned and the children giggled. Eric, although he was eighteen and as tall as Nils, was always accounted a child, being the last of so many sons. His face seemed childlike, too, Nils thought, and he had the open, wandering eyes of a little boy. All the others had been men at his age.

After supper Nils went out to the front porch and sat down on the step to smoke a pipe. Mrs Ericson drew a rocking chair up near him and began to knit busily. It was one of the few Old World customs she had kept up, for she could not bear to sit with idle hands.

'Where's little Eric, Mother?'

'He's helping Hilda with the dishes. He does it of his own will; I don't like a boy to be too handy about the house.'

'He seems like a nice kid.'

'He's very obedient.'

Nils smiled a little in the dark. It was just as well to shift the line of conversation. 'What are you knitting there, Mother?'

'Baby stockings. The boys keep me busy.' Mrs Ericson chuckled and clicked her needles.

'How many grandchildren have you?'

'Only thirty-one now. Olaf lost his three. They were sickly, like their mother.'

'I supposed he had a second crop by this time!'

'His second wife has no children. She's too proud. She tears about on horseback all the time. But she'll get caught up with, yet. She sets herself very high, though nobody knows what for. They were low enough Bohemians she came of. I never thought much of Bohemians; always drinking.'

Nils puffed away at his pipe in silence, and Mrs Ericson knitted on. In a few moments she added grimly: 'She was down here tonight, just before you came. She'd like to quarrel with me and come between me and Olaf, but I don't give her the chance. I suppose you'll be bringing a wife home some day.'

'I don't know. I've never thought much about it.'

'Well, perhaps it's best as it is,' suggested Mrs Ericson hopefully. 'You'd never be contented tied down to the land. There was roving blood in your father's family, and it's come out in you. I expect your own way of life suits you best.' Mrs Ericson had dropped into a blandly agreeable tone which Nils well remembered. It seemed to amuse him a good deal and his white teeth flashed behind his pipe. His mother's strategies had always diverted him, even when he was a boy – they were so flimsy and patent, so illy proportioned to her vigor and force. 'They've been waiting to see which way I'd jump,' he reflected. He felt that Mrs Ericson was pondering his case deeply as she sat clicking her needles.

'I don't suppose you've ever got used to steady work,' she went on presently. 'Men ain't apt to if they roam around too long. It's a pity you didn't come back the year after the World's Fair. Your father picked up a good bit of land cheap then, in the hard times, and I expect maybe he'd have give you a farm. It's too bad you put off comin' back so long, for I always thought he meant to do something by you.'

Nils laughed and shook the ashes out of his pipe. 'I'd have missed a lot if I had come back then. But I'm sorry I didn't get back to see father.'

'Well, I suppose we have to miss things at one end or the other. Perhaps you are as well satisfied with your own doings, now, as you'd have been with a farm,' said Mrs Ericson reassuringly.

'Land's a good thing to have,' Nils commented, as he lit another match and sheltered it with his hand.

His mother looked sharply at his face until the match burned out. 'Only when you stay on it!' she hastened to say.

Eric came round the house by the path just then, and Nils rose, with a yawn. 'Mother, if you don't mind, Eric and I will take a little tramp before bedtime. It will make me sleep.'

'Very well; only don't stay long. I'll sit up and wait for you. I like to lock up myself.'

Nils put his hand on Eric's shoulder, and the two tramped

down the hill and across the sand creek into the dusty highroad beyond. Neither spoke. They swung along at an even gait, Nils pulling at his pipe. There was no moon, and the white road and the wide fields lay faint in the starlight. Over everything was darkness and thick silence, and the smell of dust and sunflowers. The brothers followed the road for a mile or more without finding a place to sit down. Finally, Nils perched on a stile over the wire fence, and Eric sat on the lower step.

'I began to think you never would come back, Nils,' said the boy softly.

'Didn't I promise you I would?'

'Yes; but people don't bother about promises they make to babies. Did you really know you were going away for good when you went to Chicago with the cattle that time?'

'I thought it very likely, if I could make my way.'

'I don't see how you did it, Nils. Not many fellows could.' Eric rubbed his shoulder against his brother's knee.

'The hard thing was leaving home – you and father. It was easy enough, once I got beyond Chicago. Of course I got awful homesick; used to cry myself to sleep. But I'd burned my bridges.'

'You had always wanted to go, hadn't you?'

'Always. Do you still sleep in our little room? Is that cottonwood still by the window?'

Eric nodded eagerly and smiled up at his brother in the gray darkness.

'You remember how we always said the leaves were whispering when they rustled at night? Well, they always whispered to me about the sea. Sometimes they said names out of the geography books. In a high wind they had a desperate sound, like something trying to tear loose.'

'How funny, Nils,' said Eric dreamily, resting his chin on his hand. 'That tree still talks like that, and 'most always it talks to me about you.'

They sat a while longer, watching the stars. At last Eric whispered anxiously: 'Hadn't we better go back now?

Mother will get tired waiting for us.' They rose and took a short cut home, through the pasture.

II

The next morning Nils woke with the first flood of light that came with dawn. The white-plastered walls of his room reflected the glare that shone through the thin window shades, and he found it impossible to sleep. He dressed hurriedly and slipped down the hall and up the back stairs to the half-story room which he used to share with his little brother. Eric, in a skimpy nightshirt, was sitting on the edge of the bed, rubbing his eyes, his pale yellow hair standing up in tufts all over his head. When he saw Nils, he murmured something confusedly and hustled his long legs into his trousers. 'I didn't expect you'd be up so early, Nils,' he said, as his head emerged from his blue shirt.

'Oh, you thought I was a dude, did you?' Nils gave him a playful tap which bent the tall boy up like a clasp knife. 'See here; I must teach you to box.' Nils thrust his hands into his pockets and walked about. 'You haven't changed things much up here. Got most of my old traps, haven't you?'

He took down a bent, withered piece of sapling that hung over the dresser. 'If this isn't the stick Lou Sandberg killed himself with!'

The boy looked up from his shoe-lacing.

'Yes; you never used to let me play with that. Just how did he do it, Nils? You were with father when he found Lou, weren't you?'

'Yes. Father was going off to preach somewhere, and, as we drove along, Lou's place looked sort of forlorn, and we thought we'd stop and cheer him up. When we found him father said he'd been dead a couple days. He'd tied a piece of binding twine round his neck, made a noose in each end, fixed the nooses over the ends of a bent stick, and let the stick spring straight; strangled himself.'

'What made him kill himself such a silly way?'

The simplicity of the boy's question set Nils laughing. He

clapped little Eric on the shoulder. 'What made him such a silly as to kill himself at all, I should say!'

'Oh, well! But his hogs had the cholera, and all up and died on him, didn't they?'

'Sure they did; but he didn't have cholera; and there was plenty of hogs left in the world, weren't there?'

'Well, but, if they weren't his, how could they do him any good?' Eric asked, in astonishment.

'Oh, scat! He could have had lots of fun with other people's hogs. He was a chump, Lou Sandberg. To kill yourself for a pig — think of that, now!' Nils laughed all the way downstairs, and quite embarrassed little Eric, who fell to scrubbing his face and hands at the tin basin. While he was parting his wet hair at the kitchen looking glass, a heavy tread sounded on the stairs. The boy dropped his comb. 'Gracious, there's Mother. We must have talked too long.' He hurried out to the shed, slipped on his overalls, and disappeared with the milking pails.

Mrs Ericson came in, wearing a clean white apron, her black hair shining from the application of a wet brush.

'Good morning, Mother. Can't I make the fire for you?'

'No, thank you, Nils. It's no trouble to make a cob fire, and I like to manage the kitchen stove myself.' Mrs Ericson paused with a shovel full of ashes in her hand. 'I expect you will be wanting to see your brothers as soon as possible. I'll take you up to Anders' place this morning. He's threshing, and most of our boys are over there.'

'Will Olaf be there?'

Mrs Ericson went on taking out the ashes, and spoke between shovels. 'No; Olaf's wheat is all in, put away in his new barn. He got six thousand bushel this year. He's going to town today to get men to finish roofing his barn.'

'So Olaf is building a new barn?' Nils asked absently.

'Biggest one in the county, and almost done. You'll likely be here for the barn-raising. He's going to have a supper and a dance as soon as everybody's done threshing. Says it keeps the voters in a good humor. I tell him that's all nonsense; but Olaf has a long head for politics.'

'Does Olaf farm all Cousin Henrik's land?'

Mrs Ericson frowned as she blew into the faint smoke curling up about the cobs. 'Yes; he holds it in trust for the children, Hilda and her brothers. He keeps strict account of everything he raises on it, and puts the proceeds out at compound interest for them.'

Nils smiled as he watched the little flames shoot up. The door of the back stairs opened, and Hilda emerged, her arms behind her, buttoning up her long gingham apron as she came. He nodded to her gaily, and she twinkled at him out of her little blue eyes, set far apart over her wide cheekbones.

'There, Hilda, you grind the coffee – and just put in an extra handful; I expect your Cousin Nils likes his strong,' said Mrs Ericson, as she went out to the shed.

Nils turned to look at the little girl, who gripped the coffee grinder between her knees and ground so hard that her two braids bobbed and her face flushed under its broad spattering of freckles. He noticed on her middle finger something that had not been there last night, and that had evidently been put on for company: a tiny gold ring with a clumsily set garnet stone. As her hand went round and round he touched the ring with the tip of his finger, smiling.

Hilda glanced toward the shed door through which Mrs Ericson had disappeared. 'My Cousin Clara gave me that,' she whispered bashfully. 'She's Cousin Olaf's wife.'

III

Mrs Olaf Ericson – Clara Vavrika, as many people still called her – was moving restlessly about her big bare house that morning. Her husband had left for the county town before his wife was out of bed – her lateness in rising was one of the many things the Ericson family had against her. Clara seldom came downstairs before eight o'clock, and this morning she was even later, for she had dressed with unusual care. She put on, however, only a tight-fitting black dress, which people thereabouts thought very plain. She was a tall, dark woman of thirty, with a rather sallow complexion and a touch of dull salmon red in her cheeks, where the blood seemed to burn under her brown skin. Her hair, parted evenly above her low forehead, was so black that there were distinctly blue lights in it. Her black eyebrows were delicate half-moons and her lashes were long and heavy. Her eyes slanted a little, as if she had a strain of Tartar or gypsy blood, and were sometimes full of fiery determination and sometimes dull and opaque. Her expression was never altogether amiable; was often, indeed, distinctly sullen, or, when she was animated, sarcastic. She was most attractive in profile, for then one saw to advantage her small, well-shaped head and delicate ears, and felt at once that here was a very positive, if not an altogether pleasing, personality.

The entire management of Mrs Olaf's household devolved upon her aunt, Johanna Vavrika, a superstitious, doting woman of fifty. When Clara was a little girl her mother died, and Johanna's life had been spent in ungrudging service to her niece. Clara, like many self-willed and discontented persons, was really very apt, without knowing it, to do as other people told her, and to let her destiny be decided for her by intelligences much below her own. It was her Aunt Johanna who had humored and spoiled her in her girlhood, who had got her off to Chicago to study piano, and who had finally persuaded her to marry Olaf Ericson as the best match she would be likely to make in that part of the country. Johanna Vavrika had been deeply scarred by smallpox in the old country. She was short and fat, homely and jolly and sentimental. She was so broad, and took such short steps when she walked, that her brother, Joe Vavrika, always called her his duck. She adored her niece because of her talent, because of her good looks and masterful ways, but most of all because of her selfishness.

Clara's marriage with Olaf Ericson was Johanna's particular triumph. She was inordinately proud of Olaf's position, and she found a sufficiently exciting career in managing Clara's house, in keeping it above the criticism of the Ericsons, in pampering Olaf to keep him from finding fault with his wife, and in concealing from every one Clara's domestic infelicities. While Clara slept of a morning, Johanna Vavrika was bustling about, seeing that Olaf and the men had their breakfast, and that the cleaning or the butter-making or the washing was properly begun by the two girls in the kitchen. Then, at about eight o'clock, she would take Clara's coffee up to her, and chat with her while she drank it, telling her what was going on in the house. Old Mrs Ericson frequently said that her daughter-in-law would not know what day of the week it was if Johanna did not tell her every morning. Mrs Ericson despised and pitied Johanna, but did not wholly dislike her. The one thing she hated in her daughter-in-law above everything else was the way in which Clara could come it over people. It enraged her that the affairs of her son's big, barnlike house went on as well as they did, and she used to feel that in this world we have to wait overlong to see the guilty punished. 'Suppose Johanna Vavrika died or got sick?' the old lady used to say to Olaf. 'Your wife wouldn't know where to look for her own dishcloth.' Olaf only shrugged his shoulders. The fact remained that Johanna did not die, and, although Mrs Ericson often told her she was looking poorly, she was never ill. She seldom left the house, and she slept in a little room off the kitchen. No Ericson, by night or day, could come prying about there to find fault without her knowing it. Her one weakness was that she was an incurable talker, and she sometimes made trouble without meaning to.

This morning Clara was tying a wine-coloured ribbon about her throat when Johanna appeared with her coffee. After putting the tray on a sewing table, she began to make Clara's bed, chattering the while in Bohemian.

'Well, Olaf got off early, and the girls are baking. I'm going down presently to make some poppy-seed bread for Olaf. He asked for prune preserves at breakfast, and I told him I was out of them, and to bring some prunes and honey and cloves from town.'

Clara poured her coffee. 'Ugh! I don't see how men can eat so much sweet stuff. In the morning, too!'

Her aunt chuckled knowingly. 'Bait a bear with honey, as we say in the old country.'

'Was he cross?' her niece asked indifferently.

'Olaf? Oh, no! He was in fine spirits. He's never cross if you know how to take him. I never knew a man to make so little fuss about bills. I gave him a list of things to get a yard long, and he didn't say a word; just folded it up and put it in his pocket.'

'I can well believe he didn't say a word,' Clara remarked with a shrug. 'Some day he'll forget how to talk.'

'Oh, but they say he's a grand speaker in the Legislature. He knows when to keep quiet. That's why he's got such influence in politics. The people have confidence in him.' Johanna beat up a pillow and held it under her fat chin while she slipped on the case. Her niece laughed.

'Maybe we could make people believe we were wise, Aunty, if we held our tongues. Why did you tell Mrs Ericson that Norman threw me again last Saturday and turned my foot? She's been talking to Olaf.'

Johanna fell into great confusion. 'Oh, but, my precious, the old lady asked for you, and she's always so angry if I can't give an excuse. Anyhow, she needn't talk; she's always tearing up something with that motor of hers.'

When her aunt clattered down to the kitchen, Clara went to dust the parlor. Since there was not much there to dust, this did not take very long. Olaf had built the house new for her before their marriage, but her interest in furnishing it had been short-lived. It went, indeed, little beyond a bathtub and her piano. They had disagreed about almost every other article of furniture, and Clara had said she would rather have her house empty than full of things she didn't want. The house was set in a hillside, and the west windows of the parlor looked out above the kitchen yard thirty feet below. The east windows opened directly into the front yard. At one of the latter, Clara, while she was dusting, heard a low whistle. She did not turn at once, but listened intently as she drew her cloth slowly along the round of a chair. Yes, there it was:

I dreamt that I dwelt in ma-a-arble halls.

She turned and saw Nils Ericson laughing in the sunlight,

his hat in his hand, just outside the window. As she crossed the room he leaned against the wire screen. 'Aren't you at all surprised to see me, Clara Vavrika?'

'No; I was expecting to see you. Mother Ericson telephoned Olaf last night that you were here.'

Nils squinted and gave a long whistle. 'Telephoned? That must have been while Eric and I were out walking. Isn't she enterprising? Lift this screen, won't you?'

Clara lifted the screen, and Nils swung his leg across the window sill. As he stepped into the room she said: 'You didn't think you were going to get ahead of your mother, did you?'

He threw his hat on the piano. 'Oh, I do sometimes. You see, I'm ahead of her now. I'm supposed to be in Anders' wheat field. But, as we were leaving, Mother ran her car into a soft place beside the road and sank up to the hubs. While they were going for horses to pull her out, I cut away behind the stacks and escaped.' Nils chuckled. Clara's dull eyes lit up as she looked at him admiringly.

'You've got them guessing already. I don't know what your mother said to Olaf over the telephone, but he came back looking as if he'd seen a ghost, and he didn't go to bed until a dreadful hour – ten o'clock, I should think. He sat out on the porch in the dark like a graven image. It had been one of his talkative days, too.' They both laughed, easily and lightly, like people who have laughed a great deal together; but they remained standing.

'Anders and Otto and Peter looked as if they had seen ghosts, too, over in the threshing field. What's the matter with them all?'

Clara gave him a quick, searching look. 'Well, for one thing, they've always been afraid you have the other will.'

Nils looked interested. 'The other will?'

'Yes. A later one. They knew your father made another, but they never knew what he did with it. They almost tore the old house to pieces looking for it. They always suspected that he carried on a clandestine correspondence with you, for the one thing he would do was to get his own mail himself. So they thought he might have sent the new will to you for safekeeping. The old one, leaving everything to your mother, was made long before you went away, and it's understood among them that it cuts you out – that she will leave all the property to the others. Your father made the second will to prevent that. I've been hoping you had it. It would be such fun to spring it on them.' Clara laughed mirthfully, a thing she did not often do now.

Nils shook his head reprovingly. 'Come, now, you're malicious.'

'No, I'm not. But I'd like something to happen to stir them all up, just for once.There never was such a family for having nothing ever happen to them but dinner and threshing. I'd almost be willing to die, just to have a funeral. *You* wouldn't stand it for three weeks.'

Nils bent over the piano and began pecking at the keys with the finger of one hand. 'I wouldn't? My dear young lady, how do you know what I can stand? *You* wouldn't wait to find out.'

Clara flushed darkly and frowned. 'I didn't believe you would ever come back –' she said defiantly.

'Eric believed I would, and he was only a baby when I went away. However, all's well that ends well, and I haven't come back to be a skeleton at the feast. We mustn't quarrel. Mother will be here with a search warrant pretty soon.' He swung round and faced her, thrusting his hands into his coat pockets. 'Come, you ought to be glad to see me, if you want something to happen. I'm something, even without a will. We can have a little fun, can't we? I think we can!'

She echoed him, 'I think we can!' They both laughed and their eyes sparkled. Clara Vavrika looked ten years younger than when she had put the velvet ribbon about her throat that morning.

'You know, I'm so tickled to see mother,' Nils went on. 'I didn't know I was so proud of her. A regular pile driver. How about little pigtails, down at the house? Is Olaf doing the square thing by those children?'

Clara frowned pensively. 'Olaf has to do something that

looks like the square thing, now that he's a public man!' She glanced drolly at Nils. 'But he makes a good commission out of it. On Sundays they all get together here and figure. He lets Peter and Anders put in big bills for the keep of the two boys, and he pays them out of the estate. They are always having what they call accountings. Olaf gets something out of it, too. I don't know just how they do it, but it's entirely a family matter, as they say. And when the Ericsons say that —' Clara lifted her eyebrows.

Just then the angry *honk-honk* of an approaching motor sounded from down the road. Their eyes met and they began to laugh. They laughed as children do when they can not contain themselves, and can not explain the cause of their mirth to grown people, but share it perfectly together. When Clara Vavrika sat down at the piano after he was gone, she felt that she had laughed away a dozen years. She practised as if the house were burning over her head.

When Nils greeted his mother and climbed into the front seat of the motor beside her, Mrs Ericson looked grim, but she made no comment upon his truancy until she had turned her car and was retracing her revolutions along the road that ran by Olaf's big pasture. Then she remarked dryly:

'If I were you I wouldn't see too much of Olaf's wife while you are here. She's the kind of woman who can't see much of men without getting herself talked about. She was a good deal talked about before he married her.'

'Hasn't Olaf tamed her?' Nils asked indifferently.

Mrs Ericson shrugged her massive shoulders. 'Olaf don't seem to have much luck, when it comes to wives. The first one was meek enough, but she was always ailing. And this one has her own way. He says if he quarreled with her she'd go back to her father, and then he'd lose the Bohemian vote. There are a great many Bohunks in this district. But when you find a man under his wife's thumb you can always be sure there's a soft spot in him somewhere.'

Nils thought of his own father, and smiled. 'She brought him a good deal of money, didn't she, besides the Bohemian vote?'

Mrs Ericson sniffed. 'Well, she has a fair half section in her own name, but I can't see as that does Olaf much good. She will have a good deal of property some day, if old Vavrika don't marry again. But I don't consider a saloonkeeper's money as good as other people's money.'

Nils laughed outright. 'Come, Mother, don't let your prejudices carry you that far. Money's money. Old Vavrika's a mighty decent sort of saloonkeeper. Nothing rowdy about him.'

Mrs Ericson spoke up angrily: 'Oh, I know you always stood up for them! But hanging around there when you were a boy never did you any good, Nils, nor any of the other boys who went there. There weren't so many after her when she married Olaf, let me tell you. She knew enough to grab her chance.'

Nils settled back in his seat. 'Of course I liked to go there, Mother, and you were always cross about it. You never took the trouble to find out that it was the one jolly house in this country for a boy to go to. All the rest of you were working yourselves to death, and the houses were mostly a mess, full of babies and washing and flies. Oh, it was all right – I understand that; but you are young only once, and I happened to be young then. Now, Vavrika's was always jolly. He played the violin, and I used to take my flute, and Clara played the piano, and Johanna used to sing Bohemian songs. She always had a big supper for us – herrings and pickles and poppy-seed bread, and lots of cake and preserves. Old Joe had been in the army in the old country, and he could tell lots of good stories. I can see him cutting bread, at the head of the table, now. I don't know what I'd have done when I was a kid if it hadn't been for the Vavrikas, really.'

'And all the time he was taking money that other people had worked hard in the fields for,' Mrs Ericson observed.

'So do the circuses, Mother, and they're a good thing. People ought to get fun for some of their money. Even father liked old Joe.'

'Your father,' Mrs Ericson said grimly, 'liked everybody.'

As they crossed the sand creek and turned into her own

place, Mrs Ericson observed, 'There's Olaf's buggy. He's stopped on his way from town.' Nils shook himself and prepared to greet his brother, who was waiting on the porch.

Olaf was a big, heavy Norwegian, slow of speech and movement. His head was large and square, like a block of wood. When Nils, at a distance, tried to remember what his brother looked like, he could recall only his heavy head, high forehead, large nostrils, and pale blue eyes, set far apart. Olaf's features were rudimentary: the thing one noticed was the face itself, wide and flat and pale, devoid of any expression, betraying his fifty years as little as it betrayed anything else, and powerful by reason of its very stolidness. When Olaf shook hands with Nils he looked at him from under his light eyebrows, but Nils felt that no one could ever say what that pale look might mean. The one thing he had always felt in Olaf was a heavy stubbornness, like the unyielding stickiness of wet loam against the plow. He had always found Olaf the most difficult of his brothers.

'How do you do, Nils? Expect to stay with us long?'

'Oh, I may stay forever,' Nils answered gaily. 'I like this country better than I used to.'

'There's been some work put into it since you left,' Olaf remarked.

'Exactly. I think it's about ready to live in now – and I'm about ready to settle down.' Nils saw his brother lower his big head. ('Exactly like a bull,' he thought.) 'Mother's been persuading me to slow down now, and go in for farming,' he went on lightly.

Olaf made a deep sound in his throat. 'Farming ain't learned in a day,' he brought out, still looking at the ground.

'Oh, I know! But I pick things up quickly.' Nils had not meant to antagonize his brother, and he did not know now why he was doing it. 'Of course,' he went on, 'I shouldn't expect to make a big success, as you fellows have done. But then, I'm not ambitious. I won't want much. A little land, and some cattle, maybe.'

Olaf still stared at the ground, his head down. He wanted to ask Nils what he had been doing all these years, that he

didn't have a business somewhere he couldn't afford to
leave; why he hadn't more pride than to come back with
only a little sole-leather trunk to show for himself, and to
present himself as the only failure in the family. He did not
ask one of these questions, but he made them all felt
distinctly.

'Humph!' Nils thought. 'No wonder the man never talks,
when he can butt his ideas into you like that without ever
saying a word. I suppose he uses that kind of smokeless
powder on his wife all the time. But I guess she has her
innings.' He chuckled, and Olaf looked up. 'Never mind me,
Olaf. I laugh without knowing why, like little Eric. He's
another cheerful dog.'

'Eric,' said Olaf slowly, 'is a spoiled kid. He's just let his
mother's best cow go dry because he don't milk her right. I
was hoping you'd take him away somewhere and put him
into business. If he don't do any good among strangers, he
never will.' This was a long speech for Olaf, and as he
finished it he climbed into his buggy.

Nils shrugged his shoulders. 'Same old tricks,' he thought.
'Hits from behind you every time. What a whale of a man!'
He turned and went round to the kitchen, where his mother
was scolding little Eric for letting the gasoline get low.

IV

Joe Vavrika's saloon was not in the county seat, where Olaf
and Mrs Ericson did their trading, but in a cheerfuller place, a
little Bohemian settlement which lay at the other end of the
county, ten level miles north of Olaf's farm. Clara rode up to
see her father almost ever day. Vavrika's house was, so to
speak, in the back yard of his saloon. The garden between the
two buildings was inclosed by a high board fence as tight as a
partition, and in summer Joe kept beer tables and wooden
benches among the gooseberry bushes under his little cherry
tree. At one of these tables Nils Ericson was seated in the late
afternoon, three days after his return home. Joe had gone in
to serve a customer, and Nils was lounging on his elbows,

looking rather mournfully into his half-emptied pitcher, when he heard a laugh across the little garden. Clara, in her riding habit, was standing at the back door of the house, under the grapevine trellis that old Joe had grown there long ago. Nils rose.

'Come out and keep your father and me company. We've been gossiping all afternoon. Nobody to bother us but the flies.'

She shook her head. 'No, I never come out here any more. Olaf doesn't like it. I must live up to my position, you know.'

'You mean to tell me you never come out and chat with the boys, as you used to? He *has* tamed you! Who keeps up these flower beds?'

'I come out on Sundays, when father is alone, and read the Bohemian papers to him. But I am never here when the bar is open. What have you two been doing?'

'Talking, as I told you. I've been telling him about my travels. I find I can't talk much at home, not even to Eric.'

Clara reached up and poked with her riding-whip at a white moth that was fluttering in the sunlight among the vine leaves. 'I suppose you will never tell me about all those things.'

'Where can I tell them? Not in Olaf's house, certainly. What's the matter with our talking here?' He pointed persuasively with his hat to the bushes and the green table, where the flies were singing lazily above the empty beer glasses.

Clara shook her head weakly. 'No, it wouldn't do. Besides, I am going now.'

'I'm on Eric's mare. Would you be angry if I overtook you?'

Clara looked back and laughed. 'You might try and see. I can leave you if I don't want you. Eric's mare can't keep up with Norman.'

Nils went into the bar and attempted to pay his score. Big Joe, six feet four, with curly yellow hair and mustache, clapped him on the shoulder. 'Not a God-damn a your money go in my drawer, you hear? Only next time you bring

your flute, te-te-te-te-te-ty.' Joe wagged his fingers in imitation of the flute player's position. 'My Clara, she come all-a-
time Sundays an' play for me. She not like to play at Ericson's
place.' He shook his yellow curls and laughed. 'Not a God-
damn a fun at Ericson's. You come a Sunday. You like-a fun.
No forget de flute.' Joe talked very rapidly and always
tumbled over his English. He seldom spoke it to his customers,
and had never learned much.

Nils swung himself into the saddle and trotted to the west
end of the village, where the houses and gardens scattered
into prairie land and the road turned south. Far ahead of him,
in the declining light, he saw Clara Vavrika's slender figure,
loitering on horseback. He touched his mare with the whip,
and shot along the white, level road, under the reddening sky.
When he overtook Olaf's wife he saw that she had been
crying. 'What's the matter, Clara Vavrika?' he asked kindly.

'Oh, I get blue sometimes. It was awfully jolly living there
with father. I wonder why I ever went away.'

Nils spoke in a low, kind tone that he sometimes used with
women: 'That's what I've been wondering these many years.
You were the last girl in the country I'd have picked for a wife
for Olaf. What made you do it, Clara?'

'I suppose I really did it to oblige the neighbors' — Clara
tossed her head. 'People were beginning to wonder.'

'To wonder?'

'Yes — why I didn't get married. I suppose I didn't like to
keep them in suspense. I've discovered that most girls marry
out of consideration for the neighborhood.'

Nils bent his head toward her and his white teeth flashed.
'I'd have gambled that one girl I knew would say, "Let the
neighborhood be damned."'

Clara shook her head mournfully. 'You see, they have it on
you, Nils; that is, if you're a woman. They say you're beginning to go off. That's what makes us get married: we can't
stand the laugh.'

Nils looked sidewise at her. He had never seen her head
droop before. Resignation was the last thing he would have
expected of her. 'In your case, there wasn't something else?'

'Something else?'

'I mean, you didn't do it to spite somebody? Somebody who didn't come back?'

Clara drew herself up. 'Oh, I never thought you'd come back. Not after I stopped writing to you, at least. *That* was all over, long before I married Olaf.'

'It never occurred to you, then, that the meanest thing you could do to me was to marry Olaf?'

Clara laughed. 'No; I didn't know you were so fond of Olaf.'

Nils smoothed his horse's man with his glove. 'You know, Clara Vavrika, you are never going to stick it out. You'll cut away some day, and I've been thinking you might as well cut away with me.'

Clara threw up her chin. 'Oh, you don't know me as well as you think. I won't cut away. Sometimes, when I'm with father, I feel like it. But I can hold out as long as the Ericsons can. They've never got the best of me yet, and one can live, so long as one isn't beaten. If I go back to father, it's all up with Olaf in politics. He knows that, and he never goes much beyond sulking. I've as much wit as the Ericsons. I'll never leave them unless I can show them a thing or two.'

'You mean unless you can come it over them?'

'Yes – unless I go away with a man who is cleverer than they are, and who has more money.'

Nils whistled. 'Dear me, you are demanding a good deal. The Ericsons, take the lot of them, are a bunch to beat. But I should think the excitement of tormenting them would have worn off by this time.'

'It has, I'm afraid,' Clara admitted mournfully.

'Then why don't you cut away? There are more amusing games than this in the world. When I came home I thought it might amuse me to bully a few quarter sections out of the Ericsons; but I've almost decided I can get more fun for my money somewhere else.'

Clara took in her breath sharply. 'Ah, you have got the other will! That was why you came home!'

'No, it wasn't. I came home to see how you were getting on with Olaf.'

Clara struck her horse with the whip, and in a bound she was far ahead of him. Nils dropped one word, 'Damn!' and whipped after her; but she leaned forward in her saddle and fairly cut the wind. Her long riding skirt rippled in the still air behind her. The sun was just sinking behind the stubble in a vast, clear sky, and the shadows drew across the fields so rapidly that Nils could scarcely keep in sight of the dark figure on the road. When he overtook her he caught her horse by the bridle. Norman reared, and Nils was frightened for her; but Clara kept her seat.

'Let me go, Nils Ericson!' she cried. 'I hate you more than any of them. You were created to torture me, the whole tribe of you – to make me suffer in every possible way.'

She struck her horse again and galloped away from him. Nils set his teeth and looked thoughtful. He rode slowly home along the deserted road, watching the stars come out in the clear violet sky. They flashed softly into the limpid heavens, like jewels let fall into clear water. They were a reproach, he felt, to a sordid world. As he turned across the sand creek, he looked up at the North Star and smiled, as if there were an understanding between them. His mother scolded him for being late for supper.

v

On Sunday afternoon Joe Vavrika, in his shirtsleeves and carpet slippers, was sitting in his garden, smoking a long-tasseled porcelain pipe with a hunting scene painted on the bowl. Clara sat under the cherry tree, reading aloud to him from the weekly Bohemian papers. She had worn a white muslin dress under her riding habit, and the leaves of the cherry tree threw a pattern of sharp shadows over her skirt. The black cat was dozing in the sunlight at her feet, and Joe's dachschund was scratching a hole under the scarlet geraniums and dreaming of badgers. Joe was filling his pipe for the third time since dinner, when he heard a knocking on the fence. He broke into a loud guffaw and unlatched the little door that led into the street. He did not call Nils by

name, but caught him by the hand and dragged him in.
Clara stiffened and the color deepened under her dark skin.
Nils, too, felt a little awkward. He had not seen her since
the night when she rode away from him and left him alone
on the level road between the fields. Joe dragged him to the
wooden bench beside the green table.

'You bring de flute,' he cried, tapping the leather case
under Nils' arm. 'Ah, das-a good! Now we have some liddle
fun like old times. I got some'ting good for you.' Joe shook
his finger at Nils and winked his blue eye, a bright clear eye,
full of fire, though the tiny bloodvessels on the ball were
always a little distended. 'I got somet'ing for you from' – he
paused and waved his hand – 'Hongarie. You know Hongarie? You wait!' He pushed Nils down on the bench, and
went through the back door of his saloon.

Nils looked at Clara, who sat frigidly with her white skirts
drawn tight about her. 'He didn't tell you he had asked me
to come, did he? He wanted a party and proceeded to
arrange it. Isn't he fun? Don't be cross; let's give him a good
time.'

Clara smiled and shook out her skirt. 'Isn't that like
father? And he has sat here so meekly all day. Well, I won't
pout. I'm glad you came. He doesn't have very many good
times now any more. There are so few of his kind left. The
second generation are a tame lot.'

Joe came back with a flask in one hand and three wine
glasses caught by the stems between the fingers of the
other. These he placed on the table with an air of ceremony, and, going behind Nils, held the flask between him
and the sun, squinting into it admiringly. 'You know dis,
Tokai? A great friend of mine, he bring dis to me, a present
out of Hongarie. You know how much it cost, dis wine?
Chust so much what it weigh in gold. Nobody but de nobles
drink him in Bohemie. Many, many years I save him up, dis
Tokai.' Joe whipped out his official corkscrew and delicately
removed the cork. 'De old man die what bring him to me,
an' dis wine he lay on his belly in my cellar an' sleep. An'
now,' carefully pouring out the heavy yellow wine, 'an'

now he wake up; and maybe he wake us up, too!' He carried one of the glasses to his daughter and presented it with great gallantry.

Clara shook her head, but, seeing her father's disappoint-ment, relented. 'You taste it first. I don't want so much.'

Joe sampled it with a beatific expression, and turned to Nils. 'You drink him slow, dis wine. He very soft, but he go down hot. You see!'

After a second glass Nils declared that he couldn't take any more without getting sleepy. 'Now get your fiddle, Vavrika,' he said as he opened his flute case.

But Joe settled back in his wooden rocker and wagged his big carpet slipper. 'No-no-no-no-no-no-no! No play fiddle now any more: too much ache in de finger,' waving them, 'all-a-time rheumatiz. You play de flute, te-tety-te-tety-te. Bohemie songs.'

'I've forgotten all the Bohemian songs I used to play with you and Johanna. But here's one that will make Clara pout. You remember how her eyes used to snap when we called her the Bohemian Girl?' Nils lifted his flute and began 'When Other Lips and Other Hearts,' and Joe hummed the air in a husky baritone, waving his carpet slipper. 'Oh-h-h, das-a fine music,' he cried, clapping his hands as Nils finished. 'Now "Marble Halls, Marble Halls"! Clara, you sing him.'

Clara smiled and leaned back in her chair, beginning softly:

'I dreamt that I dwelt in ma-a-arble halls,
With vassals and serfs at my knee,'

and Joe hummed like a big bumblebee.

'There's one more you always played,' Clara said quietly; 'I remember that best.' She locked her hands over her knee and began 'The Heart Bowed Down,' and sang it through without groping for the words. She was singing with a good deal of warmth when she came to the end of the old song:

For memory is the only friend
That grief can call its own.

Joe flashed out his red silk handkerchief and blew his nose, shaking his head. 'No-no-no-no-no-no-no! Too sad, too sad! I not like-a dat. Play quick somet'ing gay now.'

Nils put his lips to the instrument, and Joe lay back in his chair, laughing and singing, 'Oh, Evelina, Sweet Evelina!' Clara laughed, too. Long ago, when she and Nils went to high school, the model student of their class was a very homely girl in thick spectacles. Her name was Evelina Oleson; she had a long, swinging walk which somehow suggested the measure of that song, and they used mercilessly to sing it at her.

'Dat ugly Oleson girl, she teach in de school,' Joe gasped, 'an' she still walk chust like dat, yup-a, yup-a, yup-a, chust like a camel she go! Now, Nils, we have some more li'l drink. Oh, yes-yes-yes-yes-yes-yes-*yes!* Dis time you haf to drink, and Clara she haf to, so she show she not jealous. So, we all drink to your girl. You not tell her name, eh? No-no-no, I no make you tell. She pretty, eh? She make good sweetheart? I bet!' Joe winked and lifted his glass. 'How soon you get married?'

Nils screwed up his eyes. 'That I don't know. When she says.'

Joe threw out his chest. 'Das-a way boys talks. No way for mans. Mans say, "You come to de church, an' get a hurry on you." Das-a way mans talks.'

'Maybe Nils hasn't got enough to keep a wife,' put in Clara ironically. 'How about that, Nils?' she asked him frankly, as if she wanted to know.

Nils looked at her coolly, raising one eyebrow. 'Oh, I can keep her, all right.'

'The way she wants to be kept?'

'With my wife, I'll decide that,' replied Nils calmly. 'I'll give her what's good for her.'

Clara made a wry face. 'You'll give her the strap, I expect, like old Peter Oleson gave his wife.'

'When she needs it,' said Nils lazily, locking his hands behind his head and squinting up through the leaves of the cherry tree. 'Do you remember the time I squeezed the cherries all over your clean dress, and Aunt Johanna boxed my ears for me? My gracious, weren't you mad! You had both hands full of cherries, and I squeezed 'em and made the juice fly all over you. I liked to have fun with you; you'd get so mad.'

'We *did* have fun, didn't we? None of the other kids ever had so much fun. We knew how to play.'

Nils dropped his elbows on the table and looked steadily across at her. 'I've played with lots of girls since, but I haven't found one who was such good fun.'

Clara laughed. The late afternoon sun was shining full in her face, and deep in the back of her eyes there shone something fiery, like the yellow drops of Tokai in the brown glass bottle. 'Can you still play, or are you only pretending?'

'I can play better than I used to, and harder.'

'Don't you ever work, then?' She had not intended to say it. It slipped out because she was confused enough to say just the wrong thing.

'I work between times.' Nils' steady gaze still beat upon her. 'Don't you worry about my working, Mrs Ericson. You're getting like all the rest of them.' He reached his brown, warm hand across the table and dropped in on Clara's, which was cold as an icicle. 'Last call for play, Mrs Ericson!' Clara shivered, and suddenly her hands and cheeks grew warm. Her fingers lingered in his a moment, and they looked at each other earnestly. Joe Vavrika had put the mouth of the bottle to his lips and was swallowing the last drops of the Tokai, standing. The sun, just about to sink behind his shop, glistened on the bright glass, on his flushed face and curly yellow hair. 'Look,' Clara whispered; 'that's the way I want to grow old.'

VI

On the day of Olaf Ericson's barn-raising, his wife, for once in a way, rose early. Johanna Vavrika had been baking cakes and frying and boiling and spicing meats for a week before-hand, but it was not until the day before the party was to take place that Clara showed any interest in it. Then she was seized with one of her fitful spasms of energy, and took the wagon and little Eric and spent the day on Plum Creek, gathering vines and swamp goldenrod to decorate the barn.

By four o'clock in the afternoon buggies and wagons began to arrive at the big unpainted building in front of Olaf's house. When Nils and his mother came at five, there were more than fifty people in the barn, and a great drove of children. On the ground floor stood six long tables, set with the crockery of seven flourishing Ericson families, lent for the occasion. In the middle of each table was a big yellow pumpkin, hollowed out and filled with woodbine. In one corner of the barn, behind a pile of green-and-white-striped watermelons, was a circle of chairs for the old people; the younger guests sat on bushel measures or barbed-wire spools, and the children tumbled about in the haymow. The box stalls Clara had converted into booths. The framework was hidden by goldenrod and sheaves of wheat, and the partitions were covered with wild grapevines full of fruit. At one of these Johanna Vavrika watched over her cooked meats, enough to provision an army; and at the next her kitchen girls had ranged the ice-cream freezers, and Clara was already cutting pies and cakes against the hour of serving. At the third stall, little Hilda, in a bright pink lawn dress, dispensed lemonade throughout the afternoon. Olaf, as a public man, had thought it inadvisable to serve beer in his barn; but Joe Vavrika had come over with two demijohns concealed in his buggy, and after his arrival the wagon shed was much frequented by the men.

'Hasn't Cousin Clara fixed things lovely?' little Hilda whispered, when Nils went up to her stall and asked for lemonade.

Nils leaned against the booth, talking to the excited little girl and watching the people. The barn faced the west, and the sun, pouring in at the big doors, filled the whole interior with golden light, through which filtered fine particles of dust from the haymow, where the children were romping. There was a great chattering from the stall where Johanna

Vavrika exhibited to the admiring women her platters heaped with fried chicken, her roasts of beef, boiled tongues, and baked hams with cloves stuck in the crisp brown fat and garnished with tansy and parsley. The older women, having assured themselves that there were twenty kinds of cake, not counting cookies, and three dozen fat pies, repaired to the corner behind the pile of watermelons, put on their white aprons, and fell to their knitting and fancywork. They were a fine company of old women, and a Dutch painter would have loved to find them there together, where the sun made bright patches on the floor and sent long, quivering shafts of gold through the dusky shade up among the rafters. There were fat, rosy old women who looked hot in their best black dresses; spare, alert old women with brown, dark-veined hands; and several of almost heroic frame, not less massive than old Mrs Ericson herself. Few of them wore glasses, and old Mrs Svendsen, a Danish woman, who was quite bald, wore the only cap among them. Mrs Oleson, who had twelve big grandchildren, could still show two braids of yellow hair as thick as her own wrists. Among all these grandmothers there were more brown heads than white. They all had a pleased, prosperous air, as if they were more than satisfied with themselves and with life. Nils, leaning against Hilda's lemonade stand, watched them as they sat chattering in four languages, their fingers never lagging behind their tongues.

'Look at them over there,' he whispered, detaining Clara as she passed him. 'Aren't they the Old Guard? I've just counted thirty hands. I guess they've wrung many a chicken's neck and warmed many a boy's jacket for him in their time.'

In reality he fell into amazement when he thought of the Herculean labors those fifteen pairs of hand had performed: of the cows they had milked, the butter they had made, the gardens they had planted, the children and grandchildren they had tended, the brooms they had worn out, the mountains of food they had cooked. It made him dizzy. Clara Vavrika smiled a hard, enigmatical smile at him and walked rapidly away. Nils' eyes followed her white figure as she went toward the house. He watched her walking alone in the sunlight, looked at her slender, defiant shoulders and her little hard-set head with its coils of blue-black hair. 'No,' he reflected; 'she'd never be like them, not if she lived here a hundred years. She'd only grow more bitter. You can't tame a wild thing; you can only chain it. People aren't all alike. I mustn't lose my nerve.' He gave Hilda's pigtail a parting tweak and set out after Clara. 'Where to?' he asked, as he came upon her in the kitchen.

'I'm going to the cellar for preserves.'

'Let me go with you. I never get a moment alone with you. Why do you keep out of my way?'

Clara laughed. 'I don't usually get in anybody's way.'

Nils followed her down the stairs and to the far corner of the cellar, where a basement window let in a stream of light. From a swinging shelf Clara selected several glass jars, each labeled in Johanna's careful hand. Nils took up a brown flask. 'What's this? It looks good.'

'It is. It's some French brandy father gave me when I was married. Would you like some? Have you a corkscrew? I'll get glasses.'

When she brought them, Nils took them from her and put them down on the window sill. 'Clara Vavrika, do you remember how crazy I used to be about you?'

Clara shrugged her shoulders. 'Boys are always crazy about somebody or other. I dare say some silly has been crazy about Evelina Oleson. You got over it in a hurry.'

'Because I didn't come back, you mean? I had to get on, you know, and it was hard sledding at first. Then I heard you'd married Olaf.'

'And then you stayed away from a broken heart,' Clara laughed.

'And then I began to think about you more than I had since I first went away. I began to wonder if you were really as you had seemed to me when I was a boy. I thought I'd like to see. I've had lots of girls, but no one ever pulled me the same way. The more I thought about you, the more I remembered how it used to be – like hearing a wild tune you can't resist, calling you out at night. It had been a long while since anything had pulled me out of my boots, and I wondered whether anything ever could again.' Nils thrust his hands into his coat pockets and squared his shoulders, as his mother sometimes squared hers, as Olaf, in a clumsier manner, squared his. 'So I thought I'd come back and see. Of course the family have tried to do me, and I rather thought I'd bring out father's will and make a fuss. But they can have their old land; they've put enough sweat into it.' He took the flask and filled the two glasses carefully to the brim. 'I've found out what I want from the Ericsons. Drink *skoal*, Clara.' He lifted his glass, and Clara took hers with downcast eyes. 'Look at me, Clara Vavrika. *Skoal!*'

She raised her burning eyes and answered fiercely: '*Skoal!*

The barn supper began at six o'clock and lasted for two hilarious hours. Yense Nelson had made a wager that he could eat two whole fried chickens, and he did. Eli Swanson stowed away two whole custard pies, and Nick Hermanson ate a chocolate layer cake to the last crumb. There was even a cooky contest among the children, and one thin, slablike Bohemian boy consumed sixteen and won the prize, a gingerbread pig which Johanna Vavrika had carefully decorated with red candies and burnt sugar. Fritz Sweiheart, the German carpenter, won in the pickle contest, but he disappeared soon after supper and was not seen for the rest of the evening. Joe Vavrika said that Fritz could have managed the pickles all right, but he had sampled the demijohn in his buggy too often before sitting down to the table.

While the supper was being cleared away the two fiddlers began to tune up for the dance. Clara was to accompany them on her old upright piano, which had been brought down from her father's. By this time Nils had renewed old acquaintances. Since his interview with Clara in the cellar, he had been busy telling all the old women how young they looked, and all the young ones how pretty they were, and assuring the men that they had here the best farmland in the world. He had made himself so agreeable that old Mrs

Ericson's friends began to come up to her and tell how lucky she was to get her smart son back again, and please to get him to play his flute. Joe Vavrika, who could still play very well when he forgot that he had rheumatism, caught up a fiddle from Johnny Oleson and played a crazy Bohemian dance tune that set the wheels going. When he dropped the bow every one was ready to dance.

Olaf, in a frock coat and a solemn made-up necktie, led the grand march with his mother. Clara had kept well out of *that* by sticking to the piano. She played the march with a pompous solemnity which greatly amused the prodigal son, who went over and stood behind her.

'Oh, aren't you rubbing it into them, Clara Vavrika? And aren't you lucky to have me here, or all your wit would be thrown away.'

'I'm used to being witty for myself. It saves my life.'

The fiddles struck up a polka, and Nils convulsed Joe Vavrika by leading out Evelina Oleson, the homely schoolteacher. His next partner was a very fat Swedish girl, who, although she was an heiress, had not been asked for the first dance, but had stood against the wall in her tight, high-heeled shoes, nervously fingering a lace handkerchief. She was soon out of breath, so Nils led her, pleased and panting, to her seat, and went over to the piano, from which Clara had been watching his gallantry. 'Ask Olena Yenson,' she whispered. 'She waltzes beautifully.'

Olena, too, was rather inconveniently plump, handsome in a smooth, heavy way, with a fine color and good-natured, sleepy eyes. She was redolent of violet sachet powder, and had warm, soft, white hands, but she danced divinely, moving as smoothly as the tide coming in. 'There, that's something like,' Nils said as he released her. 'You'll give me the next waltz, won't you? Now I must go and dance with my little cousin.'

Hilda was greatly excited when Nils went up to her stall and held out his arm. Her little eyes sparkled, but she declared that she could not leave her lemonade. Old Mrs Ericson, who happened along at this moment, said she would attend to that, and Hilda came out, as pink as her pink dress. The dance was a schottische, and in a moment her yellow braids were fairly standing on end. 'Bravo!' Nils cried encouragingly. 'Where did you learn to dance so nicely?'

'My Cousin Clara taught me,' the little girl panted.

Nils found Eric sitting with a group of boys who were too awkward or too shy to dance, and told him that he must dance the next waltz with Hilda.

The boy screwed up his shoulders. 'Aw, Nils, I can't dance. My feet are too big; I look silly.'

'Don't be thinking about yourself. It doesn't matter how boys look.'

Nils had never spoken to him so sharply before, and Eric made haste to scramble out of his corner and brush the straw from his coat.

Clara nodded approvingly. 'Good for you, Nils. I've been trying to get hold of him. They dance very nicely together; I sometimes play for them.'

'I'm obliged to you for teaching him. There's no reason why he should grow up to be a lout.'

'He'll never be that. He's more like you than any of them. Only he hasn't your courage.' From her slanting eyes Clara shot forth one of those keen glances, admiring and at the same time challenging, which she seldom bestowed on any one, and which seemed to say, 'Yes, I admire you, but I am your equal.'

Clara was proving a much better host than Olaf, who, once the supper was over, seemed to feel no interest in anything but the lanterns. He had brought a locomotive headlight from town to light the revels, and he kept skulking about it as if he feared the mere light from it might set his new barn on fire. His wife, on the contrary, was cordial to every one, was animated and even gay. The deep salmon color in her cheeks burned vividly, and her eyes were full of life. She gave the piano over to the fat Swedish heiress, pulled her father away from the corner where he sat gossiping with his cronies, and made him dance a Bohemian dance with her. In his youth Joe had been a famous dancer, and his daughter got him so limbered up that every one sat round and applauded them. The old ladies were particularly delighted, and made them go through the dance again. From their corner where they watched and commented, the old woman kept time with their feet and hands, and whenever the fiddles struck up new air old Mrs Svendsen's white cap would begin to bob.

Clara was waltzing with little Eric when Nils came up to them, brushed his brother aside, and swung her out among the dancers. 'Remember how we used to waltz on rollers at the old skating rink in town? I suppose people don't do that any more. We used to keep it up for hours. You know, we never did moon around as other boys and girls did. It was dead serious with us from the beginning. When we were most in love with each other, we used to fight. You were always pinching people; your fingers were like little nippers. A regular snapping turtle, you were. Lord, how you'd like Stockholm! Sit out in the streets in front of cafés and talk all night in summer. Just like a reception – officers and ladies and funny English people. Jolliest people in the world, the Swedes, once you get them going. Always drinking things – champagne and stout mixed, half-and-half; serve it out of big pitchers, and serve plenty. Slow pulse, you know; they can stand a lot. Once they light up, they're glowworms, I can tell you.'

'All the same, you don't really like gay people.'

'*I* don't?'

'No; I could see that when you were looking at the old women there this afternoon. They're the kind you really admire, after all; women like your mother. And that's the kind you'll marry.'

'Is it, Miss Wisdom? You'll see who I'll marry, and she won't have a domestic virtue to bless herself with. She'll be a snapping turtle, and she'll be a match for me. All the same, they're a fine bunch of old dames over there. You admire them yourself.'

'No, I don't; I detest them.'

'You won't, when you look back on them from Stockholm or Budapest. Freedom settles all that. Oh, but you're the real

Bohemian Girl, Clara Vavrika!' Nils laughed down at her sullen frown and began mockingly to sing:

'Oh, how could a poor gypsy maiden like me
Expect the proud bride of a baron to be?'

Clara clutched his shoulder. 'Hush, Nils; every one is looking at you.'

'I don't care. They can't gossip. It's all in the family, as the Ericsons say when they divide up little Hilda's patrimony amongst them. Besides, we'll give them something to talk about when we hit the trail. Lord, it will be a godsend to them! They haven't had anything so interesting to chatter about since the grasshopper year. It'll give them a new lease of life. And Olaf won't lose the Bohemian vote, either. They'll have the laugh on him so that they'll vote two apiece. They'll send him to Congress. They'll never forget his barn party, or us. They'll always remember us as we're dancing together now. We're making a legend. Where's my waltz, boys?' he called as they whirled past the fiddlers.

The musicians grinned, looked at each other, hesitated, and began a new air; and Nils sang with them, as the couples fell from a quick waltz to a long, slow glide:

'When other lips and other hearts
Their tale of love shall tell,
In language whose excess imparts
The power they feel so well.'

The old women applauded vigorously. 'What a gay one he is, that Nils!' And old Mrs Svendsen's cap lurched dreamily from side to side to the flowing measure of the dance.

Of days that have as ha-a-p-p-y been,
And you'll remember me.

VII

The moonlight flooded that great, silent land. The reaped fields lay yellow in it. The straw stacks and poplar wind-breaks threw sharp black shadows. The roads were white rivers of dust. The sky was a deep, crystalline blue, and the stars were few and faint. Everything seemed to have sunk to sleep, under the great, golden, tender, midsummer moon. The splendor of it seemed to transcend human life and human fate. The senses were too feeble to take it in, and every time one looked up at the sky one felt unequal to it, as if one were sitting deaf under the waves of a great river of melody. Near the road, Nils Ericson was lying against a straw stack in Olaf's wheat field. His own life seemed strange and unfamiliar to him, as if it were something he had read about, or dreamed, and forgotten. He lay very still, watching the white road that ran in front of him, lost itself among the fields, and then, at a distance, reappeared over a little hill. At last, against this white band he saw something moving rapidly, and he got up and walked to the edge of the field. 'She is passing the row of poplars now,' he thought. He heard the padded beat of hoofs along the dusty road, and as she came into sight he stepped out and waved his arms. Then, for fear of frightening the horse, he drew back and waited. Clara had seen him, and she came up at a walk. Nils took the horse by the bit and stroked his neck.

'What are you doing out so late, Clara Vavrika? I went to the house, but Johanna told me you had gone to your father's.'

'Who can stay in the house on a night like this? Aren't you out yourself?'

'Ah, but that's another matter.'

Nils turned the horse into the field.

'What are you doing? Where are you taking Norman?'

'Not far, but I want to talk to you tonight; I have something to say to you. I can't talk to you at the house, with Olaf sitting there on the porch, weighing a thousand tons.'

Clara laughed. 'He won't be sitting there now. He's in bed by this time, and asleep – weighing a thousand tons.'

Nils plodded on across the stubble. 'Are you really going to spend the rest of your life like this, night after night, summer after summer? Haven't you anything better to do on a night like this than to wear yourself and Norman out tearing across the country to your father's and back? Besides, your father won't live forever, you know. His little place will be shut up or sold, and then you'll have nobody but the Ericsons. You'll have to fasten down the hatches for the winter then.'

Clara moved her head restlessly. 'Don't talk about that. I try never to think of it. If I lost father I'd lose everything, even my hold over the Ericsons.'

'Bah! You'd lose a good deal more than that. You'd lose your race, everything that makes you yourself. You've lost a good deal of it now.'

'Of what?'

'Of your love of life, your capacity for delight.'

Clara put her hands up to her face. 'I haven't, Nils Ericson, I haven't! Say anything to me but that. I won't have it!' she declared vehemently.

Nils led the horse up a straw stack, and turned to Clara, looking at her intently, as he had looked at her that Sunday afternoon at Vavrika's. 'But why do you fight for that so? What good is the power to enjoy, if you never enjoy? Your hands are cold again; what are you afraid of all the time? Ah, you're afraid of losing it; that's what's the matter with you! And you will, Clara Vavrika, you will! When I used to know you – listen; you've caught a wild bird in your hand, haven't you, and felt its heart beat so hard that you were afraid it would shatter its little body to pieces? Well, you used to be just like that, a slender, eager thing with a wild delight inside you. That is how I remembered you. And I come back and find you – a bitter woman. This is a perfect ferret fight here; you live by biting and being bitten. Can't you remember what life used to be? Can't you remember that old delight? I've never forgotten it, or known its like, on land or sea.'

He drew the horse under the shadow of the straw stack. Clara felt him take her foot out of the stirrup, and she slid softly down into his arms. He kissed her slowly. He was a deliberate man, but his nerves were steel when he wanted anything. Something flashed out from him like a knife out of a sheath. Clara felt everything slipping away from her; she was flooded by the summer night. He thrust his hand into his pocket, and then held it out at arm's length. 'Look,' he said. The shadow of the straw stack fell sharp across his wrist, and in the palm of his hand she saw a silver dollar shining. 'That's my pile,' he muttered; 'will you go with me?'

Clara nodded, and dropped her forehead on his shoulder.

Nils took a deep breath. 'Will you go with me tonight?'

'Where?' she whispered softly.

'To town, to catch the midnight flyer.'

Clara lifted her head and pulled herself together. 'Are you crazy, Nils? We couldn't go away like that.'

'That's the only way we ever will go. You can't sit on the bank and think about it. You have to plunge. That's the way I've always done, and it's the right way for people like you and me. There's nothing so dangerous as sitting still. You've only got one life, one youth, and you can let it slip through your fingers if you want to; nothing easier. Most people do that. You'd be better off tramping the roads with me than you are here.' Nils held back her head and looked into her eyes. 'But I'm not that kind of a tramp, Clara. You won't have to take in sewing. I'm with a Norwegian shipping line; came over on business with the New York offices, but now I'm going straight back to Bergen. I expect I've got as much money as the Ericsons. Father sent me a little to get started. They never knew about that. There, I hadn't meant to tell you; I wanted you to come on your own nerve.'

Clara looked off across the fields. 'It isn't that, Nils, but something seems to hold me. I'm afraid to pull against it. It comes out of the ground, I think.'

'I know all about that. One has to tear loose. You're not needed here. Your father will understand; he's made like us. As for Olaf, Johanna will take better care of him than ever you could. It's now or never, Clara Vavrika. My bag's at the station; I smuggled it there yesterday.'

Clara clung to him and hid her face against his shoulder. 'Not tonight,' she whispered. 'Sit here and talk to me tonight. I don't want to go anywhere tonight. I may never love you like this again.'

Nils laughed through his teeth. 'You can't come that on

me. That's not my way, Clara Vavrika. Eric's mare is over there behind the stacks, and I'm off on the midnight. It's goodbye, or off across the world with me. My carriage won't wait. I've written a letter to Olaf; I'll mail it in town. When he reads it he won't bother us – not if I know him. He'd rather have the land. Besides, I could demand an investigation of his administration of Cousin Henrik's estate, and that would be bad for a public man. You've no clothes, I know; but you can sit up tonight, and we can get everything on the way. Where's your old dash, Clara Vavrika? What's become of your Bohemian blood? I used to think you had courage enough for anything. Where's your nerve – what are you waiting for?'

Clara drew back her head, and he saw the slumberous fire in her eyes. 'For you to say one thing, Nils Ericson.'

'I never say that thing to any woman, Clara Vavrika.' He leaned back, lifted her gently from the ground, and whispered through his teeth: 'But I'll never, never let you go, not to any man on earth but me! Do you understand me? Now, wait here.'

Clara sank down on a sheaf of wheat and covered her face with her hands. She did not know what she was going to do – whether she would go or stay. The great, silent country seemed to lay a spell upon her. The ground seemed to hold her as if by roots. Her knees were soft under her. She felt as if she could not bear separation from her old sorrows, from her old discontent. They were dear to her, they had kept her alive, they were a part of her. There would be nothing left of her if she were wrenched away from them. Never could she pass beyond that skyline against which her restlessness had beat so many times. She felt as if her soul had built itself a nest there on that horizon at which she looked every morning and every evening, and it was dear to her, inexpressibly dear. She pressed her fingers against her eyeballs to shut it out. Beside her she heard the tramping of horses in the soft earth. Nils said nothing to her. He put his hands under her arms and lifted her lightly to her saddle. Then he swung himself into his own.

'We shall have to ride fast to catch the midnight train. A last gallop, Clara Vavrika. Forward!'

There was a start, a thud of hoofs along the moonlit road, two dark shadows going over the hill; and then the great, still land stretched untroubled under the azure night. Two shadows had passed.

VIII

A year after the flight of Olaf Ericson's wife, the night train was steaming across the plains of Iowa. The conductor was hurrying through one of the day coaches, his lantern on his arm, when a lank, fair-haired boy sat up in one of the plush seats and tweaked him by the coat.

'What is the next stop, please, sir?'

'Red Oak, Iowa. But you go through to Chicago, don't you?' He looked down, and noticed that the boy's eyes were red and his face was drawn, as if he were in trouble.

'Yes. But I was wondering whether I could get off at the next place and get a train back to Omaha.'

'Well, I suppose you could. Live in Omaha?'

'No. In the western part of the State. How soon do we get to Red Oak?'

'Forty minutes. You'd better make up your mind, so I can tell the baggageman to put your trunk off.'

'Oh, never mind about that! I mean, I haven't got any,' the boy added, blushing.

'Run away,' the conductor thought, as he slammed the coach door behind him.

Eric Ericson crumpled down in his seat and put his brown hand to his forehead. He had been crying, and he had had no supper, and his head was aching violently. 'Oh, what shall I do?' he thought, as he looked dully down at his big shoes. 'Nils will be ashamed of me; I haven't got any spunk.'

Ever since Nils had run away with his brother's wife, life at home had been hard for little Eric. His mother and Olaf both suspected him of complicity. Mrs Ericson was harsh and faultfinding, constantly wounding the boy's pride; and Olaf was always setting her against him.

Joe Vavrika heard often from his daughter. Clara had always been fond of her father, and happiness made her kinder. She wrote him long accounts of the voyage to Bergen, and of the trip she and Nils took through Bohemia to the little town where her father had grown up and where she herself was born. She visited all her kinsmen there, and sent her father news of his brother, who was a priest; of his sister, who had married a horsebreeder – of their big farm and their many children. These letters Joe always managed to read to little Eric. They contained messages for Eric and Hilda. Clara sent presents, too, which Eric never dared to take home and which poor little Hilda never even saw, though she loved to hear Eric tell about them when they were out getting the eggs together. But Olaf once saw Eric coming out of Vavrika's house – the old man had never asked the boy to come into his saloon – and Olaf went straight to his mother and told her. That night Mrs Ericson came to Eric's room after he was in bed and made a terrible scene. She could be very terrifying when she was really angry. She forbade him ever to speak to Vavrika again, and after that night she would not allow him to go to town alone. So it was a long while before Eric got any more news of his brother. But old Joe suspected what was going on, and he carried Clara's letters about in his pocket. One Sunday he drove out to see a German friend of his, and chanced to catch sight of Eric, sitting by the cattle pond in the big pasture. They went together in Fritz Oberlies' barn, and read the letters and talked things over. Eric admitted that things were getting hard for him at home. That very night old Joe sat down and laboriously penned a statement of the case to his daughter.

Things got no better for Eric. His mother and Olaf felt that, however closely he was watched, he still, as they said, 'heard.' Mrs Ericson could not admit neutrality. She had sent Johanna Vavrika packing back to her brother's, though Olaf would much rather have kept her than Anders' eldest daughter, whom Mrs Ericson installed in her place. He was not so highhanded as his mother, and he once sulkily told her that she might better have taught her granddaughter to cook before she sent Johanna away. Olaf could have borne a good deal for the sake of prunes spiced in honey, the secret of which Johanna had taken away with her.

At last two letters came to Joe Vavrika: one from Nils, inclosing a postal order for money to pay Eric's passage to Bergen, and one from Clara, saying that Nils had a place for Eric in the offices of his company, that he was to live with them, and that they were only waiting for him to come. He was to leave New York on one of the boats of Nils' own line; the captain was one of their friends, and Eric was to make himself known at once.

Nils' direction were so explicit that a baby could have followed them, Eric felt. And here he was, nearing Red Oak, Iowa, and rocking backward and forward in despair. Never had he loved his brother so much, and never had the big world called to him so hard. But there was a lump in his throat which would not go down. Ever since nightfall he had been tormented by the thought of his mother, alone in that big house that had sent forth so many men. Her unkindness now seemed so little, and her loneliness so great. He remembered everything she had ever done for him: how frightened she had been when he tore his hand in the cornsheller, and how she wouldn't let Olaf scold him.

When Nils went away he didn't leave his mother all alone, or he would never have gone. Eric felt sure of that.

The train whistled. The conductor came in, smiling not unkindly. 'Well, young man, what are you going to do? We stop at Red Oak in three minutes.'

'Yes, thank you. I'll let you know.' The conductor went out, and the boy doubled up with misery. He couldn't let his one chance go like this. He felt for his breast pocket and crackled Nils' kind letter to give him courage. He didn't want Nils to be ashamed of him. The train stopped. Suddenly he remembered his brother's kind, twinkling eyes, that always looked at you as if from far away. The lump in his throat softened. 'Ah, but Nils, Nils would *understand*!' he thought. 'That's just it about Nils; he always understands.'

A lank, pale boy with a canvas telescope stumbled off the train to the Red Oak siding, just as the conductor called, 'All aboard!'

The next night Mrs Ericson was sitting alone in her wooden rocking chair on the front porch. Little Hilda had been sent to bed and had cried herself to sleep. The old woman's knitting was in her lap, but her hands lay motionless on top of it. For more than an hour she had not moved a muscle. She simply sat, as only the Ericsons and the mountains can sit. The house was dark, and there was no sound but the croaking of the frogs down in the pond of the little pasture.

Eric did not come home by the road, but across the fields, where no one could see him. He set his telescope down softly in the kitchen shed, and slipped noiselessly along the path to the front porch. He sat down on the step without saying anything. Mrs Ericson made no sign, and the frogs croaked on. At last the boy spoke timidly.

'I've come back, Mother.'

'Very well,' said Mrs Ericson.

Eric leaned over and picked up a little stick out of the grass. 'How about the milking?' he faltered.

'That's been done, hours ago.'

'Who did you get?'

'Get? I did it myself. I can milk as good as any of you.'

Eric slid along the step nearer to her. 'Oh, Mother, why did you?' he asked sorrowfully. 'Why didn't you get one of Otto's boys?'

'I didn't want anybody to know I was in need of a boy,' said Mrs Ericson bitterly. She looked straight in front of her and her mouth tightened. 'I always meant to give you the home farm,' she added.

The boy started and slid closer. 'Oh, Mother,' he faltered, 'I don't care about the farm. I came back because I thought you might be needing me, maybe.' He hung his head and got no further.

'Very well,' said Mrs Ericson. Her hand went out from her suddenly and rested on his head. Her fingers twined themselves in his soft, pale hair. His tears spashed down on the boards; happiness filled his heart.

First published in *McClure's*, August 1912.

CONSEQUENCES

HENRY Eastman, a lawyer, aged forty, was standing beside the Flatiron Building in a driving November rainstorm, signaling frantically for a taxi. It was six-thirty, and everything on wheels was engaged. The streets were in confusion about him, the sky was in turmoil above him, and the Flatiron Building, which seemed about to blow down, threw water like a mill-shoot. Suddenly, out of the brutal struggle of men and cars and machines and people tilting at each other with umbrellas, a quiet, well-mannered limousine paused before him, at the curb, and an agreeable, ruddy countenance confronted him through the open window of the car.

'Don't you want me to pick you up, Mr Eastman? I'm running directly home now.'

Eastman recognized Kier Cavenaugh, a young man of pleasure, who lived in the house on Central Park South, where he himself had an apartment.

'Don't I?' he exclaimed, bolting into the car. 'I'll risk getting your cushions wet without compunction. I came up in a taxi, but I didn't hold it. Bad economy. I thought I saw your car down on Fourteenth Street about half an hour ago.'

The owner of the car smiled. He had a pleasant, round face and round eyes, and a fringe of smooth, yellow hair showed under the brim of his soft felt hat. 'With a lot of little broilers fluttering into it? You did. I know some girls

who work in the cheap shops down there. I happened to be
downtown and I stopped and took a load of them home. I
do sometimes. Saves their poor little clothes, you know.
Their shoes are never any good.'

Eastman looked at his rescuer. 'Aren't they notoriously
afraid of cars and smooth young men?' he inquired.

Cavenaugh shook his head. 'They know which cars are
safe and which are chancy. They put each other wise. You
have to take a bunch at a time, of course. The Italian girls
can never come along; their men shoot. The girls understand, all right; but their fathers don't. One gets to see
queer places, sometimes, taking them home.'

Eastman laughed drily. 'Every time I touch the circle of
your acquaintance, Cavenaugh, it's a little wider. You must
know New York pretty well by this time.'

'Yes, but I'm on my good behavior below Twenty-third
Street,' the young man replied with simplicity. 'My little
friends down there would give me a good character. They're
wise little girls. They have grand ways with each other, a
romantic code of loyalty. You can find a good many of the
lost virtues among them.'

The car was standing still in a traffic block at Fortieth
Street, when Cavenaugh suddenly drew his face away from
the window and touched Eastman's arm. 'Look, please. You
see that hansom with the bony gray horse – driver has a
broken hat and red flannel around his throat. Can you see
who is inside?'

Eastman peered out. The hansom was just cutting across
the line, and the driver was making a great fuss about it,
bobbing his head and waving his whip. He jerked his
dripping old horse into Fortieth Street and clattered off past
the Public Library grounds toward Sixth Avenue. 'No, I
couldn't see the passenger. Someone you know?'

'Could you see whether there was a passenger?' Cavenaugh asked.

'Why, yes. A man, I think. I saw his elbow on the apron.
No driver ever behaves like that unless he has a passenger.'

'Yes, I may have been mistaken,' Cavenaugh murmured

absent-mindedly. Ten minutes or so later, after Cavenaugh's car had turned off Fifth Avenue into Fifty-eighth
Street, Eastman exclaimed, 'There's your same cabby, and
his cart's empty. He's headed for a drink now, I suppose.'
The driver in the broken hat and the red flannel neck cloth
was still brandishing the whip over his old gray. He was
coming from the west now, and turned down Sixth
Avenue, under the elevated.

Cavenaugh's car stopped at the bachelor apartment house
between Sixth and Seventh Avenues where he and Eastman lived, and they went up in the elevator together. They
were still talking when the lift stopped at Cavenaugh's
floor, and Eastman stepped out with him and walked down
the hall, finishing his sentence while Cavenaugh found his
latch-key. When he opened the door, a wave of fresh
cigarette smoke greeted them. Cavenaugh stopped short
and stared into his hallway. 'Now how in the devil –!' he
exclaimed angrily.

'Someone waiting for you? Oh, no, thanks. I wasn't
coming in. I have to work tonight. Thank you, but I
couldn't.' Eastman nodded and went up the two flights to
his own rooms.

Though Eastman did not customarily keep a servant he
had this winter a man who had been lent to him by a friend
who was abroad. Rollins met him at the door and took his
coat and hat.

'Put out my dinner clothes, Rollins, and then get out of
here until ten o'clock. I've promised to go to a supper
tonight. I shan't be dining. I've had a late tea and I'm going
to work until ten. You may put out some kumiss and biscuit
for me.'

Rollins took himself off, and Eastman settled down at the
big table in his sitting-room. He had to read a lot of letters
submitted as evidence in a breach of contract case, and
before he got very far he found that long paragraphs in
some of the letters were written in German. He had a
German dictionary at his office, but none here. Rollins had
gone, and anyhow, the bookstores would be closed. He

remembered having seen a row of dictionaries on the lower shelf of one of Cavenaugh's bookcases. Cavenaugh had a lot of books, though he never read anything but new stuff. Eastman prudently turned down his student's lamp very low – the thing had an evil habit of smoking – and went down two flights to Cavenaugh's door.

The young man himself answered Eastman's ring. He was freshly dressed for the evening, except for a brown smoking jacket, and his yellow hair had been brushed until it shone. He hesitated as he confronted his caller, still holding the door knob, and his round eyes and smooth forehead made their best imitation of a frown. When Eastman began to apologize, Cavenaugh's manner suddenly changed. He caught his arm and jerked him into the narrow hall. 'Come in, come in. Right along!' he said excitedly. 'Right along,' he repeated as he pushed Eastman before him into his sitting-room. 'Well I'll –' he stopped short at the door and looked about his own room with an air of complete mystification. The back window was wide open and a strong wind was blowing in. Cavenaugh walked over to the window and stuck out his head, looking up and down the fire escape. When he pulled his head in, he drew down the sash.

'I had a visitor I wanted you to see,' he explained with a nervous smile. 'At least I thought I had. He must have gone out that way,' nodding toward the window.

'Call him back. I only came to borrow a German dictionary, if you have one. Can't stay. Call him back.'

Cavenaugh shook his head despondently. 'No use. He's beat it. Nowhere in sight.'

'He must be active. Has he left something?' Eastman pointed to a very dirty white glove that lay on the floor under the window.

'Yes, that's his.' Cavenaugh reached for his tongs, picked up the glove, and tossed it into the grate, where it quickly shriveled on the coals. Eastman felt that he had happened in upon something disagreeable, possibly something shady, and he wanted to get away at once. Cavenaugh stood staring at the fire and seemed stupid and dazed; so he repeated his request rather sternly, 'I think I've seen a German dictionary down there among your books. May I have it?'

Cavenaugh blinked at him. 'A German dictionary? Oh, possibly! Those were my father's. I scarcely know what there is.' He put down the tongs and began to wipe his hands nervously with his handkerchief.

Eastman went over to the bookcase behind the Chesterfield, opened the door, swooped upon the book he wanted and stuck it under his arm. He felt perfectly certain now that something shady had been going on in Cavenaugh's rooms, and he saw no reason why he should come in for any hang-over. 'Thanks. I'll send it back tomorrow,' he said curtly as he made for the door.

Cavenaugh followed him. 'Wait a moment. I wanted you to see him. You did see his glove,' glancing at the grate.

Eastman laughed disagreeably. 'I saw a glove. That's not evidence. Do your friends often use that means of exit? Somewhat inconvenient.'

Cavenaugh gave him a startled glance. 'Wouldn't you think so? For an old man, a very rickety old party? The ladders are steep, you know, and rusty.' He approached the window again and put it up softly. In a moment he drew his head back with a jerk. He caught Eastman's arm and shoved him toward the window. 'Hurry, please. Look! Down there.' He pointed to the little patch of paved court four flights down.

The square of pavement was so small and the walls about it were so high, that it was a good deal like looking down a well. Four tall buildings backed upon the same court and made a kind of shaft, with flagstones at the bottom, and at the top a square of dark blue with some stars in it. At the bottom of the shaft Eastman saw a black figure, a man in a caped coat and a tall hat stealing cautiously around, not across the square of pavement, keeping close to the dark wall and avoiding the streak of light that fell on the flagstones from a window in the opposite house. Seen from that height he was of course fore-shortened and probably looked more shambling and decrepit than he was. He picked his way along with exaggerated care and looked like a silly old cat crossing a wet street. When he reached the gate that led into an alleyway between two buildings, he felt about for the latch, opened the door a mere crack, and then shot out under the feeble lamp that burned in the brick arch over the gateway. The door closed after him.

'He'll get run in,' Eastman remarked curtly, turning away from the window. 'That door shouldn't be left unlocked. Any crook could come in. I'll speak to the janitor about it, if you don't mind,' he added sarcastically.

'Wish you would.' Cavenaugh stood brushing down the front of his jacket, first with his right hand and then with his left. 'You saw him, didn't you?'

'Enough of him. Seems eccentric. I have to see a lot of buggy people. They don't take me in any more. But I'm keeping you and I'm in a hurry myself. Good night.'

Cavenaugh put out his hand detainingly and started to say something; but Eastman rudely turned his back and went down the hall and out of the door. He had never felt anything shady about Cavenaugh before, and he was sorry he had gone down for the dictionary. In five minutes he was deep in his papers; but in the half hour when he was loafing before he dressed to go out, the young man's curious behavior came into his mind again.

Eastman had merely a neighborly acquaintance with Cavenaugh. He had been to a supper at the young man's rooms once, but he didn't particularly like Cavenaugh's friends; so the next time he was asked, he had another engagement. He liked Cavenaugh himself, if for nothing else than because he was so cheerful and trim and ruddy. A good complexion is always at a premium in New York, especially when it shines reassuringly on a man who does everything in the world to lose it. It encourages fellow mortals as to the inherent vigor of the human organism and the amount of bad treatment it will stand for. 'Footprints that perhaps another,' etc.

Cavenaugh, he knew, had plenty of money. He was the

son of a Pennsylvania preacher, who died soon after he discovered that his ancestral acres were full of petroleum, and Kier had come to New York to burn some of the oil. He was thirty-two and was still at it; spent his life, literally, among the breakers. His motor hit the Park every morning as if it were the first time ever. He took people out to supper every night. He went from restaurant to restaurant, sometimes to half-a-dozen in an evening. The head waiters were his hosts and their cordiality made him happy. They made a life-line for him up Broadway and down Fifth Avenue. Cavenaugh was still fresh and smooth, round and plump, with a lustre to his hair and white teeth and a clear look in his round eyes. He seemed absolutely unwearied and unimpaired; never bored and never carried away.

Eastman always smiled when he met Cavenaugh in the entrance hall, serenely going forth to or returning from gladiatorial combats with joy, or when he saw him rolling smoothly up to the door in his car in the morning after a restful night in one of the remarkable new roadhouses he was always finding. Eastman had seen a good many young men disappear on Cavenaugh's route, and he admired this young man's endurance.

Tonight, for the first time, he had got a whiff of something unwholesome about the fellow – bad nerves, bad company, something on hand that he was ashamed of, a visitor old and vicious, who must have had a key to Cavenaugh's apartment, for he was evidently there when Cavenaugh returned at seven o'clock. Probably it was the same man Cavenaugh had seen in the hansom. He must have been able to let himself in, for Cavenaugh kept no man but his chauffeur; or perhaps the janitor had been instructed to let him in. In either case, and whoever he was, it was clear enough that Cavenaugh was ashamed of him and was mixing up in questionable business of some kind.

Eastman sent Cavenaugh's book back by Rollins, and for the next few weeks he had no word with him beyond a casual greeting when they happened to meet in the hall or the elevator. One Sunday morning Cavenaugh telephoned up to him to ask if he could motor out to a roadhouse in Connecticut that afternoon and have supper; but when Eastman found there were to be other guests he declined.

On New Year's eve Eastman dined at the University Club at six o'clock and hurried home before the usual manifestations of insanity had begun in the streets. When Rollins brought his smoking coat, he asked him whether he wouldn't like to get off early.

'Yes, sir. But won't you be dressing, Mr Eastman?' he inquired.

'Not tonight.' Eastman handed him a bill. 'Bring some change in the morning. There'll be fees.'

Rollins lost no time in putting everything to rights for the night, and Eastman couldn't help wishing that he were in such a hurry to be off somewhere himself. When he heard the hall door close softly, he wondered if there were any place, after all, that he wanted to go. From his window he looked down at the long lines of motors and taxis waiting for a signal to cross Broadway. He thought of some of their probable destinations and decided that none of those places pulled him very hard. The night was warm and wet, the air was drizzly. Vapor hung in clouds about the *Times* Building, half hid the top of it, and made a luminous haze along Broadway. While he was looking down at the army of wet, black carriage-tops and their reflected headlights and tail-lights, Eastman heard a ring at his door. He deliberated. If it were a caller, the hall porter would have telephoned up. It must be the janitor. When he opened the door, there stood a rosy young man in a tuxedo, without a coat or hat.

'Pardon. Should I have telephoned? I half thought you wouldn't be in.'

Eastman laughed. 'Come in, Cavenaugh. You weren't sure whether you wanted company or not, eh, and you were trying to let chance decide it? That was exactly my state of mind. Let's accept the verdict.' When they emerged from the narrow hall into his sitting-room, he pointed out a seat by the fire to his guest. He brought a tray of decanters and soda bottles and placed it on his writing table.

Cavenaugh hesitated, standing by the fire. 'Sure you weren't starting for somewhere?'

'Do I look it? No, I was just making up my mind to stick it out alone when you rang. Have one?' he picked up a tall tumbler.

'Yes, thank you. I always do.'

Eastman chuckled. 'Lucky boy! So will I. I had a very early dinner. New York is the most arid place on holidays,' he continued as he rattled the ice in the glasses. 'When one gets too old to hit the rapids down there, and tired of gobbling food to heathenish dance music, there is absolutely no place where you can get a chop and some milk toast in peace, unless you have strong ties of blood brotherhood on upper Fifth Avenue. But you, why aren't you starting for somewhere?'

The young man sipped his soda and shook his head as he replied:

'Oh, I couldn't get a chop, either. I know only flashy people, of course.' He looked up at his host with such a grave and candid expression that Eastman decided there couldn't be anything very crooked about the fellow. His smooth cheeks were positively cherubic.

'Well, what's the matter with them? Aren't they flashing tonight?'

'Only the very new ones seem to flash on New Year's eve. The older ones fade away. Maybe they are hunting a chop, too.'

'Well' – Eastman sat down – 'holidays do dash one. I was just about to write a letter to a pair of maiden aunts in my old home town, up-state; old coasting hill, snow-covered pines, lights in the church windows. That's what you've saved me from.'

Cavenaugh shook himself. 'Oh, I'm sure that wouldn't have been good for you. Pardon me,' he rose and took a photograph from the bookcase, a handsome man in shooting clothes. 'Dudley, isn't it? Did you know him well?'

'Yes. An old friend. Terrible thing, wasn't it? I haven't got over the jolt yet.'

'His suicide? Yes, terrible! Did you know his wife?'

'Slightly. Well enough to admire her very much. She must be terribly broken up. I wonder Dudley didn't think of that.'

Cavenaugh replaced the photograph carefully, lit a cigarette, and standing before the fire began to smoke. 'Would you mind telling me about him? I never met him, but of course I'd read a lot about him, and I can't help feeling interested. It was a queer thing.'

Eastman took out his cigar case and leaned back in his deep chair. 'In the days when I knew him best he hadn't any story, like the happy nations. Everything was properly arranged for him before he was born. He came into the world happy, healthy, clever, straight, with the right sort of connections and the right kind of fortune, neither too large nor too small. He helped to make the world an agreeable place to live in until he was twenty-six. Then he married as he should have married. His wife was a Californian, educated abroad. Beautiful. You have seen her picture?'

Cavenaugh nodded. 'Oh, many of them.'

'She was interesting, too. Though she was distinctly a person of the world, she had retained something, just enough of the large Western manner. She had the habit of authority, of calling out a special train if she needed it, of using all our ingenious mechanical contrivances lightly and easily, without over-rating them. She and Dudley knew how to live better than most people. Their house was the most charming one I have ever known in New York. You felt freedom there, and a zest of life, and safety – absolute sanctuary – from everything sordid or petty. A whole society like that would justify the creation of man and would make our planet shine with a soft, peculiar radiance among the constellations. You think I'm putting it on thick?'

The young man sighed gently. 'Oh, no! One has always felt there must be people like that. I've never known any.'

'They had two children, beautiful ones. After they had been married for eight years, Rosina met this Spaniard. He must have amounted to something. She wasn't a flighty woman. She came home and told Dudley how matters stood. He persuaded her to stay at home for six months and try to pull up. They were both fair-minded people, and I'm sure as if I were the Almighty, that she did try. But at the end of the time, Rosina went quietly off to Spain, and Dudley went to hunt in the Canadian Rockies. I met his party out there. I didn't know his wife had left him and talked about her a good deal. I noticed that he never drank anything, and his light used to shine through the log chinks of his room until all hours, even after a hard day's hunting. When I got back to New York, rumors were creeping about. Dudley did not come back. He bought a ranch in Wyoming, built a big log house and kept splendid dogs and horses. One of his sisters went out to keep house for him, and the children were there when they were not in school. He had a great many visitors, and everyone who came back talked about how well Dudley kept things going.

'He put in two years out there. Then, last month, he had to come back on business. A trust fund had to be settled up, and he was administrator. I saw him at the club; same light, quick step, same gracious handshake. He was getting gray, and there was something softer in his manner; but he had a fine red tan on his face and said he found it delightful to be here in the season when everything is going hard. The Madison Avenue house had been closed since Rosina left it. He went there to get some things his sister wanted. That, of course, was the mistake. He went alone, in the afternoon, and didn't go out for dinner – found some sherry and tins of biscuits in the sideboard. He shot himself sometime that night. There were pistols in his smoking-room. They found burnt out candles beside him in the morning. The gas and electricity were shut off. I suppose there, in his own house, among his own things, it was too much for him. He left no letters.'

Cavenaugh blinked and brushed the lapel of his coat. 'I suppose,' he said slowly, 'that every suicide is logical and reasonable, if one knew all the facts.'

Eastman roused himself. 'No, I don't think so. I've known

too many fellows who went off like that – more than I
deserve, I think – and some of them were absolutely
inexplicable. I can understand Dudley; but I can't see why
healthy bachelors, with money enough, like ourselves, need
such a device. It reminds me of what Dr Johnson said, that
the most discouraging thing about life is the number of fads
and hobbies and fake religions it takes to put people through
a few years of it.'

'Dr Johnson? The specialist? Oh, the old fellow!' said
Cavenaugh imperturbably. 'Yes, that's interesting. Still, I
fancy if one knew the facts – Did you know about Wyatt?'

'I don't think so.'

'You wouldn't, probably. He was just a fellow about town
who spent money. He wasn't one of the *forestieri*, though.
Had connections here and owned a fine old place over on
Staten Island. He went in for botany, and had been all over,
hunting things; rusts, I believe. He had a yacht and used to
take a gay crowd down about the South Seas, botanizing. He
really did botanize, I believe. I never knew such a spender –
only not flashy. He helped a lot of fellows and he was awfully
good to girls, the kind who come down here to get a little
fun, who don't like to work and still aren't really tough, the
kind you see talking hard for their dinner. Nobody knows
what becomes of them, or what they get out of it, and there
are hundreds of new ones every year. He helped dozens of
'em; it was he who got me curious about the little shop girls.
Well, one afternoon when his tea was brought, he took
prussic acid instead. He didn't leave any letters, either;
people of any taste don't. They wouldn't leave any material
reminder if they could help it. His lawyers found that he had
just $314.72 above his debts when he died. He had planned
to spend all his money, and then take his tea; he had worked
it out carefully.'

Eastman reached for his pipe and pushed his chair away
from the fire. 'That looks like a considered case, but I don't
think philosophical suicides like that are common. I think
they usually come from stress of feeling and are really, as the
newspapers call them, desperate acts; done without a

motive. You remember when Anna Karenina was under the wheels, she kept saying, "Why am I here?"'

Cavenaugh rubbed his upper lip with his pink finger and made an effort to wrinkle his brows. 'May I, please?' reaching for the whiskey. 'But have you,' he asked, blinking as the soda flew at him, 'have you ever known, yourself, cases that were really inexplicable?'

'A few too many. I was in Washington just before Captain Jack Purden was married and I saw a good deal of him. Popular army man, fine record in the Philippines, married a charming girl with lots of money; mutual devotion. It was the gayest wedding of the winter, and they started for Japan. They stopped in San Francisco for a week and missed their boat because, as the bride wrote back to Washington, they were too happy to move. They took the next boat, were both good sailors, had exceptional weather. After they had been out for two weeks, Jack got up from his deck chair one afternoon, yawned, put down his book, and stood before his wife. "Stop reading for a moment and look at me." She laughed and asked him why. "Because you happen to be good to look at." He nodded to her, went back to the stern and was never seen again. Must have gone down to the lower deck and slipped overboard, behind the machinery. It was the luncheon hour, not many people about; steamer cutting through a soft green sea. That's one of the most baffling cases I know. His friends raked up his past, and it was as trim as a cottage garden. If he'd so much as dropped an ink spot on his fatigue uniform, they'd have found it. He wasn't emotional or moody; wasn't, indeed, very interesting; simply a good soldier, fond of all the pompous little formalities that make up a military man's life. What do you make of that, my boy?'

Cavenaugh stroked his chin. 'It's very puzzling, I admit. Still, if one knew everything—'

'But we do know everything. His friends wanted to find something to help them out, to help the girl out, to help the case of the human creature.'

'Oh, I don't mean things that people could unearth,' said

Cavenaugh uneasily. 'But possibly there were things that couldn't be found out.'

Eastman shrugged his shoulders. 'It's my experience that when there are "things" as you call them, they're very apt to be found. There is no such thing as a secret. To make any move at all one has to employ human agencies, employ at least one human agent. Even when the pirates killed the men who buried their gold for them, the bones told the story.'

Cavenaugh rubbed his hands together and smiled his sunny smile.

'I like that idea. It's reassuring. If we can have no secrets, it means that we can't, after all, go so far afield as we might,' he hesitated, 'yes, as we might.'

Eastman looked at him sourly. 'Cavenaugh, when you've practised law in New York for twelve years, you find that people can't go far in any direction, except—' He thrust his forefinger sharply at the floor. 'Even in that direction, few people can do anything out of the ordinary. Our range is limited. Skip a few baths, and we become personally objectionable. The slightest carelessness can rot a man's integrity or give him ptomaine poisoning. We keep up only by incessant cleansing operations, of mind and body. What we call character, is held together by all sorts of tacks and strings and glue.'

Cavenaugh looked startled. 'Come now, it's not so bad as that, is it? I've always thought that a serious man, like you, must know a lot of Launcelots.' When Eastman only laughed, the younger man squirmed about in his chair. He spoke again hastily, as if he were embarrassed. 'Your military friend may have had personal experiences, however, that his friends couldn't possibly get a line on. He may accidentally have come to a place where he saw himself in too unpleasant a light. I believe people can be chilled by a draft from outside, somewhere.'

'Outside?' Eastman echoed. 'Ah, you mean the far outside! Ghosts, delusions, eh?'

Cavenaugh winced. 'That's putting it strong. Why not say

tips from the outside? Delusions belong to a diseased mind, don't they? There are some of us who have no minds to speak of, who yet have had experiences. I've had a little something in that line myself and I don't look it, do I?'

Eastman looked at the bland countenance turned toward him. 'Not exactly. What's your delusion?'

'It's not a delusion. It's a haunt.'

The lawyer chuckled. 'Soul of a lost Casino girl?

'No; an old gentleman. A most unattractive old gentleman, who follows me about.'

'Does he want money?'

Cavenaugh sat up straight. 'No. I wish to God he wanted anything – but the pleasure of my society! I'd let him clean me out to be rid of him. He's a real article. You saw him yourself that night when you came to my rooms to borrow a dictionary, and he went down the fire escape. You saw him down in the court.'

'Well, I saw somebody down in the court, but I'm too cautious to take it for granted that I saw what you saw. Why, anyhow, should I see your haunt? If it was your friend I saw, he impressed me disagreeably. How did you pick him up?'

Cavenaugh looked gloomy. 'That was queer, too. Charley Burke and I had motored out to Long Beach, about a year ago, sometime in October, I think. We had supper and stayed until late. When we were coming home, my car broke down. We had a lot of girls along who had to get back for morning rehearsals and things; so I sent them all into town in Charley's car, and he was to send a man back to tow me home. I was driving myself, and didn't want to leave my machine. We had not taken a direct road back; so I was stuck in a lonesome, woody place, no houses about. I got chilly and made a fire, and was putting in the time comfortably enough, when this old party steps up. He was in shabby evening clothes and a top hat, and had on his usual white gloves. How he got there, at three o'clock in the morning, miles from any town or railway, I'll leave it to you to figure out. *He* surely had no car. When I saw him coming up to the fire, I disliked him. He had a silly, apologetic walk. His teeth were chattering, and I asked him to sit down. He got down like a clothes-horse folding up. I offered him a cigarette, and when he took off his gloves I couldn't help noticing how knotted and spotty his hands were. He was asthmatic, and took his breath with a wheeze. "Haven't you got anything – refreshing in there?" he asked, nodding at the car. When I told him I hadn't, he sighed. "Ah, you young fellows are greedy. You drink it all up. You drink it all up, all up – up!" he kept chewing it over.'

Cavenaugh paused and looked embarrassed again. 'The thing that was most unpleasant is difficult to explain. The old man sat there by the fire and leered at me with a silly sort of admiration that was – well, more than humiliating. "Gay boy, gay dog!" he would mutter, and when he grinned he showed his teeth, worn and yellow – shells. I remembered that it was better to talk casually to insane people; so I remarked carelessly that I had been out with a party and got stuck.

'"Oh yes, I remember," he said, "Flora and Lottie and Maybelle and Marcelline, and poor Kate."

'He had named them correctly; so I began to think I had been hitting the bright waters too hard.

'Things I drank never had seemed to make me woody; but you can never tell when trouble is going to hit you. I pulled my hat down and tried to look as uncommunicative as possible; but he kept croaking on from time to time, like this: "Poor Katie! Splendid arms, but dope got her. She took up with Eastern religions after she had her hair dyed. Got to going to a Swami's joint, and smoking opium. Temple of the Lotus, it was called, and the police raided it."

'This was nonsense, of course; the young woman was in the pink of condition. I let him rave, but I decided that if something didn't come out for me pretty soon, I'd foot it across Long Island. There wasn't room enough for the two of us. I got up and took another try at my car. He hopped right after me.

'"Good car," he wheezed, "better than the little Ford."

'I'd had a Ford before, but so has everybody; that was a safe guess.

'"Still," he went on, "that run in from Huntington Bay in the rain wasn't bad. Arrested for speeding, he-he."

'It was true I had made such a run, under rather unusual circumstances, and had been arrested. When at last I heard my life-boat snorting up the road, my visitor got up, sighed, and stepped back into the shadow of the trees. I didn't wait to see what became of him, you may believe. That was visitation number one. What do you think of it?'

Cavenaugh looked at his host defiantly. Eastman smiled.

'I think you'd better change your mode of life, Cavenaugh. Had many returns?' he inquired.

'Too many, by far.' The young man took a turn about the room and came back to the fire. Standing by the mantel he lit another cigarette before going on with his story:

'The second visitation happened in the street, early in the evening, about eight o'clock. I was held up in a traffic block before the Plaza. My chauffeur was driving. Old Nibbs steps up out of the crowd, opens the door of my car, gets in and sits down beside me. He had on wilted evening clothes, same as before, and there was some sort of heavy scent about him. Such an unpleasant old party! A thorough-going rotter; you knew it at once. This time he wasn't talkative, as he had been when I first saw him. He leaned back in the car as if he owned it, crossed his hands on his stick and looked out at the crowd – sort of hungrily.

'I own I really felt a loathing compassion for him. We got down the avenue slowly. I kept looking out at the mounted police. But what could I do? Have him pulled? I was afraid to. I was awfully afraid of getting him into the papers.

'"I'm going to the New Astor," I said at last. "Can I take you anywhere?"

'"No, thank you," says he. "I get out when you do. I'm due on West Forty-fourth. I'm dining tonight with Marcelline – all that is left of her!'

'He put his hand to his hat brim with a grewsome salute. Such a scandalous, foolish old face as he had! When we pulled up at the Astor, I stuck my hand in my pocket and asked him if he'd like a little loan.

'"No, thank you, but" – he leaned over and whispered,

ugh! – "but save a little, save a little. Forty years from now –
a little – comes in handy. Save a little."

'His eyes fairly glittered as he made his remark. I jumped
out. I'd have jumped into the North River. When he tripped
off, I asked my chauffeur if he'd noticed the man who got
into the car with me. He said he knew someone was with
me, but he hadn't noticed just when he got in. Want to hear
any more?'

Cavenaugh dropped into his chair again. His plump cheeks
were a trifle more flushed than usual, but he was perfectly
calm. Eastman felt that the young man believed what he was
telling him.

'Of course I do. It's very interesting. I don't see quite where
you are coming out though.'

Cavenaugh sniffed. 'No more do I. I really feel that I've
been put upon. I haven't deserved it any more than any
other fellow of my kind. Doesn't impress you disagreeably?'

'Well, rather so. Has anyone else seen your friend?'

'You saw him.'

'We won't count that. As I said, there's no certainty that
you and I saw the same person in the court that night. Has
anyone else had a look in?'

'People sense him rather than see him. He usually crops up
when I'm alone or in a crowd on the street. He never
approaches me when I'm with people I know, though I've
seen him hanging about the doors of theatres when I come
out with a party; loafing around the stage exit, under a wall;
or across the street, in a doorway. To be frank, I'm not
anxious to introduce him. The third time, it was I who came
upon him. In November my driver, Harry, had a sudden
attack of appendicitis. I took him to the Presbyterian Hospital
in the car, early in the evening. When I came home, I found
the old villain in my rooms. I offered him a drink, and he sat
down. It was the first time I had seen him in a steady light,
with his hat off.

'His face is lined like a railway map, and as to color – Lord,
what a liver! His scalp grows tight to his skull, and his hair is
dyed until it's perfectly dead, like a piece of black cloth.'

Cavenaugh ran his fingers through his own neatly trimmed thatch, and seemed to forget where he was for a moment.

'I had a twin brother, Brian, who died when we were sixteen. I have a photograph of him on my wall, an enlargement from a kodak of him, doing a high jump, rather good thing, full of action. It seemed to annoy the old gentleman. He kept looking at it and lifting his eyebrows, and finally he got up, tip-toed across the room, and turned the picture to the wall.

'"Poor Brian! Fine fellow, but died young," says he.

'Next morning, there was the picture, still reversed.'

'Did he stay long?' Eastman asked interestedly.

'Half an hour, by the clock.'

'Did he talk?'

'Well, he rambled.'

'What about?'

Cavenaugh rubbed his pale eyebrows before answering.

'About things that an old man ought to want to forget. His conversation is highly objectionable. Of course he knows me like a book; everything I've ever done or thought. But when he recalls them, he throws a bad light on them, somehow. Things that weren't much off color, look rotten. He doesn't leave one a shred of self-respect, he really doesn't. That's the amount of it.' The young man whipped out his handkerchief and wiped his face.

'You mean he really talks about things that none of your friends know?'

'Oh, dear, yes! Recalls things that happened in school. Anything disagreeable. Funny thing, he always turns Brian's picture to the wall.'

'Does he come often?'

'Yes, oftener, now. Of course I don't know how he gets in downstairs. The hall boys never see him. But he has a key to my door. I don't know how he got it, but I can hear him turn it in the lock.'

'Why don't you keep your driver with you, or telephone for me to come down?'

'He'd only grin and go down the fire escape as he did before. He's often done it when Harry's come in suddenly. Everybody has to be alone sometimes, you know. Besides, I don't want anybody to see him. He has me there.'

'But why not? Why do you feel responsible for him?'

Cavenaugh smiled wearily. 'That's rather the point, isn't it? Why do I? But I absolutely do. That identifies him, more than his knowing all about my life and my affairs.'

Eastman looked at Cavenaugh thoughtfully. 'Well, I should advise you to go in for something altogether different and new, and go in for it hard; business, engineering, metallurgy, something this old fellow wouldn't be interested in. See if you can make him remember logarithms.'

Cavenaugh sighed. 'No, he has me there, too. People never really change; they go on being themselves. But I would never make much trouble. Why can't they let me alone, damn it! I'd never hurt anybody, except perhaps —'

'Except your old gentleman, eh?' Eastman laughed. 'Seriously, Cavenaugh, if you want to shake him, I think a year on a ranch would do it. He would never be coaxed far from his favorite haunts. He would dread Montana.'

Cavenaugh pursed up his lips. 'So do I!'

'Oh, you think you do. Try it, and you'll find out. A gun and a horse beats all this sort of thing. Besides losing your haunt, you'd be putting ten years in the bank for yourself. I know a good ranch where they take people, if you want to try it.'

'Thank you. I'll consider. Do you think I'm batty?'

'No, but I think you've been doing one sort of thing too long. You need big horizons. Get out of this.'

Cavenaugh smiled meekly. He rose lazily and yawned behind his hand. 'It's late, and I've taken your whole evening.' He strolled over to the window and looked out. 'Queer place, New York; rough on the little fellows. Don't you feel sorry for them, the girls especially? I do. What a fight they put up for a little fun! Why, even that old goat is sorry for them, the only decent thing he kept.'

Eastman followed him to the door and stood in the hall,

while Cavenaugh waited for the elevator. When the car came up Cavenaugh extended his pink, warm hand. 'Good night.'

The cage sank and his rosy countenance disappeared, his round-eyed smile being the last thing to go.

Weeks passed before Eastman saw Cavenaugh again. One morning, just as he was starting for Washington to argue a case before the Supreme Court, Cavenaugh telephoned him at his office to ask him about the Montana ranch he had recommended; said he meant to take his advice and go out there for the spring and summer.

When Eastman got back from Washington, he saw dusty trunks, just up from the trunk room, before Cavenaugh's door. Next morning, when he stopped to see what the young man was about, he found Cavenaugh in his shirt sleeves, packing.

'I'm really going; off tomorrow night. You didn't think it of me, did you?' he asked gaily.

'Oh, I've always had hopes of you!' Eastman declared. 'But you are in a hurry, it seems to me.'

'Yes, I am in a hurry.' Cavenaugh shot a pair of leggings into one of the open trunks. 'I telegraphed your ranch people, used your name, and they said it would be all right. By the way, some of my crowd are giving a little dinner for me at Rector's tonight. Couldn't you be persuaded, as it's a farewell occasion?' Cavenaugh looked at him hopefully.

Eastman laughed and shook his head. 'Sorry, Cavenaugh, but that's too gay a world for me. I've got too much work lined up before me. I wish I had time to stop and look at your guns, though. You seem to know something about guns. You've more than you'll need, but nobody can have too many good ones.' He put down one of the revolvers regretfully. 'I'll drop in to see you in the morning, if you're up.'

'I shall be up, all right. I've warned my crowd that I'll cut away before midnight.'

'You won't, though,' Eastman called back over his shoulder as he hurried downstairs.

The next morning, while Eastman was dressing, Rollins came in greatly excited.

'I'm a little late, sir. I was stopped by Harry, Mr Cavenaugh's driver. Mr Cavenaugh shot himself last night, sir.'

Eastman dropped his vest and sat down on his shoe-box. 'You're drunk, Rollins,' he shouted. 'He's going away today!'

'Yes, sir. Harry found him this morning. Ah, he's quite dead, sir. Harry's telephoned for the coroner. Harry don't know what to do with the ticket.'

Eastman pulled on his coat and ran down the stairway. Cavenaugh's trunks were strapped and piled before the door. Harry was walking up and down the hall with a long green railroad ticket in his hand and a look of complete stupidity on his face.

'What shall I do about this ticket, Mr Eastman?' he whispered. 'And what about his trunks? He had me tell the transfer people to come early. They may be here any minute. Yes, sir. I brought him home in the car last night, before twelve, as cheerful as could be.'

'Be quiet, Harry. Where is he?'

'In his bed, sir.'

Eastman went into Cavenaugh's sleeping-room. When he came back to the sitting-room, he looked over the writing table; railway folders, time-tables, receipted bills, nothing else. He looked up for the photograph of Cavenaugh's twin brother. There it was, turned to the wall. Eastman took it down and looked at it; a boy in track clothes, half lying in the air, going over the string shoulders first, above the heads of a crowd of lads who were running and cheering. The face was somewhat blurred by the motion and the bright sunlight. Eastman put the picture back, as he found it. Had Cavenaugh entertained his visitor last night, and had the old man been more convincing than usual? 'Well, at any rate, he's seen to it that the old man can't establish identity. What a soft lot they are, fellows like poor Cavenaugh!' Eastman thought of his office as a delightful place.

First published in *McClure's*, November 1915.

ARDESSA

THE grand-mannered old man who sat at a desk in the reception-room of 'The Outcry' offices to receive visitors and incidentally to keep the time-book of the employees, looked up as Miss Devine entered at ten minutes past ten and condescendingly wished him good morning. He bowed profoundly as she minced past his desk, and with an indifferent air took her course down the corridor that led to the editorial offices. Mechanically he opened the flat, black book at his elbow and placed his finger on D, running his eye along the line of figures after the name Devine. 'It's banker's hours she keeps, indeed,' he muttered. What was the use of entering so capricious a record? Nevertheless, with his usual preliminary flourish he wrote 10:10 under this, the fourth day of May.

The employee who kept banker's hours rustled on down the corridor to her private room, hung up her lavender jacket and her trim spring hat, and readjusted her side combs by the mirror inside her closet door. Glancing at her desk, she rang for an office boy, and reproved him because he had not dusted more carefully and because there were lumps in her paste. When he disappeared with the paste-jar, she sat down to decide which of her employer's letters he should see and which he should not.

Ardessa was not young and she was certainly not handsome. The coquettish angle at which she carried her head was a mannerism surviving from a time when it was more becoming. She shuddered at the cold candor of the new business woman, and was insinuatingly feminine.

Ardessa's employer, like young Lochinvar, had come out of the West, and he had done a great many contradictory things before he became proprietor and editor of 'The Outcry.' Before he decided to go to New York and make the East take notice of him, O'Mally had acquired a punctual, reliable silver-mine in South Dakota. This silent friend in the background made his journalistic success comparatively easy. He had figured out, when he was a rich nobody in Nevada, that the quickest way to cut into the known world was through the printing-press. He arrived in New York, bought a highly respectable publication, and turned it into a red-hot magazine of protest, which he called 'The Outcry.' He knew what the West wanted, and it proved to be what everybody secretly wanted. In six years he had done the thing that had hitherto seemed impossible: built up a national weekly, out on the news-stands the same day in New York and San Francisco; a magazine the people howled for, a moving-picture of their real tastes and interests.

O'Mally bought 'The Outcry' to make a stir, not to make a career, but he had got built into the thing more than he ever intended. It had made him a public man and put him into politics. He found the publicity game diverting, and it held him longer than any other game had ever done. He had built up about him an organization of which he was somewhat afraid and with which he was vastly bored. On his staff there were five famous men, and he had made every one of them. At first it amused him to manufacture celebrities. He found he could take an average reporter from the daily press, giving him a 'line' to follow, a trust to fight, a vice to expose, – this was all in that good time when people were eager to read about their own wickedness, – and in two years the reporter would be recognized as an authority. Other people – Napoleon, Disraeli, Sarah Bernhardt – had discovered that advertising would go all the way – as far as you wished to pay its passage. Any human countenance, plastered in three-sheet posters from sea to sea, would be revered by the American people. The strangest thing was that the owners of these grave countenances, staring at their own faces on news-stands and billboards, fell to venerating themselves; and even he, O'Mally, was more or less constrained by these reputations that he had created out of cheap paper and cheap ink.

Constraint was the last thing O'Mally liked. The most engaging and unusual thing about the man was that he couldn't be fooled by the success of his own methods, and no amount of 'recognition' could make a stuffed shirt of him. No matter how much he was advertised as a great medicine-man in the councils of the nation, he knew that he was a born gambler and a soldier of fortune. He left his dignified office to take care of itself for a good many months of the year while he played about on the outskirts of social order. He liked being a great man from the East in rough-and-tumble Western cities where he had once been merely an unconsidered spender.

O'Mally's long absences constituted one of the supreme advantages of Ardessa Devine's position. When he was at his post her duties were not heavy, but when he was giving balls in Goldfield, Nevada, she lived an ideal life. She came to the office every day, indeed, to forward such of O'Mally's letters as she thought best, to attend to his club notices and tradesmen's bills, and to taste the sense of her high connec-tions. The great men of the staff were all about her, as contemplative as Buddhas in their private offices, each meditating upon the particular trust or form of vice confided to his care. Thus surrounded, Ardessa had a pleasant sense of being at the heart of things. It was like a mental massage, exercise without exertion. She read and she embroidered. Her room was pleasant, and she liked to be seen at ladylike tasks and to feel herself a graceful contrast to the crude girls in the advertising and circulation departments across the hall. The younger stenographers, who had to get through with the enormous office correspondence, and who rushed about from one editor to another with wire baskets full of letters, made faces as they passed Ardessa's door and saw her cool and cloistered, daintily plying her needle. But no matter how hard the other stenographers were driven, no one, not even one of the five oracles of the staff, dared dictate so much as a letter to Ardessa. Like a sultan's bride, she was inviolate in her lord's absence; she had to be kept for him.

Naturally the other young women employed in 'The Outcry' offices disliked Miss Devine. They were all competent girls, trained in the exacting methods of modern business, and they had to make good every day in the week, had to get through with a great deal of work or lose their position. O'Mally's private secretary was a mystery to them. Her exemptions and privileges, her patronizing remarks, formed an exhaustless subject of conversation at the lunch-hour. Ardessa had, indeed, as they knew she must have, a kind of 'purchase' on her employer.

When O'Mally first came to New York to break into publicity, he engaged Miss Devine upon the recommendation of the editor whose ailing publication he bought and rechristened. That editor was a conservative, scholarly gentleman of the old school, who was retiring because he felt out of place in the world of brighter, breezier magazines that had been flowering since the new century came in. He believed that in this vehement world young O'Mally would make himself heard and that Miss Devine's training in an editorial office would be of use to him.

When O'Mally first sat down at a desk to be an editor, all the cards that were brought in looked pretty much alike to him. Ardessa was at his elbow. She had long been steeped in literary distinctions and in the social distinctions which used to count for much more than they do now. She knew all the great men, all the nephews and clients of great men. She knew which must be seen, which must be made welcome, and which could safely be sent away. She could give O'Mally on the instant the former rating in magazine offices of nearly every name that was brought in to him. She could give him an idea of the man's connections, of the price his work commanded, and insinuate whether he ought to be met with the old punctiliousness or with the new joviality. She was useful in explaining to her employer the significance of various invitations, and the standing of clubs and associations. At first she was virtually the social mentor of the bullet-headed young Westerner who wanted to break into everything, the solitary person about the office of the humming new magazine who knew anything about the editorial traditions of the eighties and nineties which, antiquated as they now were, gave an editor, as O'Mally said, a background.

Despite her indolence, Ardessa was useful to O'Mally as a social reminder. She was the card catalogue of his ever-changing personal relations. O'Mally went in for everything and got tired of everything; that was why he made a good editor. After he was through with people, Ardessa was very skilful in covering his retreat. She read and answered the letters of admirers who had begun to bore him. When great authors, who had been dined and fêted the month before, were suddenly left to cool their heels in the reception-room, thrown upon the suave hospitality of the grand old man at the desk, it was Ardessa who went out and made soothing and plausible explanations as to why the editor could not see them. She was the brake that checked the too-eager neophyte, the emollient that eased the severing of relationships, the gentle extinguisher of the lights that failed. When there were no longer messages of hope and cheer to be sent to ardent young writers and reformers, Ardessa delivered, as sweetly as possible, whatever messages were left.

In handling these people with whom O'Mally was quite through, Ardessa had gradually developed an industry which was immensely gratifying to her own vanity. Not only did she not crush them; she even fostered them a little. She continued to advise them in the reception-room and 'personally' received their manuscripts long after O'Mally had declared that he would never read another line they wrote. She let them outline their plans for stories and articles to her, promising to bring these suggestions to the editor's attention. She denied herself to nobody, was gracious even to the Shakespere-Bacon man, the perpetual-motion man, the travel-article man, the ghosts which haunt every magazine office. The writers who had had their happy hour of O'Mally's favor kept feeling that Ardessa might reinstate them. She answered their letters of inquiry in her most polished and elegant style, and even gave them hints as to the subjects in which the restless editor was or was not interested at the moment: she feared it would be useless to send him an article on 'How to Trap Lions,' because he had just bought an article on 'Elephant-Shooting in Majuba Land,' etc.

So when O'Mally plunged into his office at 11:30 on this, the fourth day of May, having just got back from three-days' fishing, he found Ardessa in the reception-room, surrounded by a little court of discards. This was annoying, for he always wanted his stenographer at once. Telling the office boy to give her a hint that she was needed, he threw off his hat and top-coat and began to race through the pile of letters Ardessa had put on his desk. When she entered, he did not wait for her polite inquiries about his trip, but broke in at once.

'What is that fellow who writes about phossy jaw still hanging round here for? I don't want any articles on phossy jaw, and if I did, I wouldn't want his.'

'He has just sold an article on the match industry to "The New Age," Mr O'Mally,' Ardessa replied as she took her seat at the editor's right.

'Why does he have to come and tell us about it? We've nothing to do with "The New Age." And that prison-reform guy, what's he loafing about for?'

Ardessa bridled.

'You remember, Mr O'Mally, he brought letters of intro-duction from Governor Harper, the reform Governor of Mississippi.'

O'Mally jumped up, kicking over his waste-basket in his impatience.

'That was months ago. I went through his letters and went through him, too. He hasn't got anything we want. I've been through with Governor Harper a long while. We're asleep at the switch in here. And let me tell you, if I catch sight of that

causes-of-blindness-in-babies woman around here again, I'll
do something violent. Clear them out, Miss Devine! Clear
them out! We need a traffic policeman in this office. Have
you got that article on "Stealing Our National Water Power"
ready for me?'

'Mr Gerrard took it back to make modifications. He gave it
to me at noon on Saturday, just before the office closed. I will
have it ready for you tomorrow morning, Mr O'Mally, if you
have not too many letters for me this afternoon,' Ardessa
replied pointedly.

'Holy Mike!' muttered O'Mally, 'we need a traffic policeman for the staff, too. Gerrard's modified that thing half a
dozen times already. Why don't they get accurate information in the first place?'

He began to dictate his morning mail, walking briskly up
and down the floor by way of giving his stenographer an
energetic example. Her indolence and her ladylike deportment weighed on him. He wanted to take her by the elbows
and run her around the block. He didn't mind that she loafed
when he was away, but it was becoming harder and harder
to speed her up when he was on the spot. He knew his
correspondence was not enough to keep her busy, so when
he was in town he made her type his own breezy editorials
and various articles by members of his staff.

Transcribing editorial copy is always laborious, and the
only way to make it easy is to farm it out. This Ardessa was
usually clever enough to do. When she returned to her own
room after O'Mally had gone out to lunch, Ardessa rang for
an office boy and said languidly, 'James, call Becky, please.'

In a moment a thin, tense-faced Hebrew girl of eighteen or
nineteen came rushing in, carrying a wire basket full of
typewritten sheets. She was as gaunt as a plucked spring
chicken, and her cheap, gaudy clothes might have been
thrown on her. She looked as if she were running to catch a
train and in mortal dread of missing it. While Miss Devine
examined the pages in the basket, Becky stood with her
shoulders drawn up and her elbows drawn in, apparently
trying to hide herself in her insufficient open-work waist.

Her wild, black eyes followed Miss Devine's hands desperately. Ardessa sighed.

'This seems to be very smeary copy again, Becky. You don't keep your mind on your work, and so you have to erase continually.'

Becky spoke up in wailing self-vindication.

'It ain't that, Miss Devine. It's so many hard words he uses that I have to be at the dictionary all the time. Look! Look!' She produced a bunch of manuscript faintly scrawled in pencil, and thrust it under Ardessa's eyes. 'He don't write out the words at all. He just begins a word, and then makes waves for you to guess.'

'I see you haven't always guessed correctly, Becky,' said Ardessa, with a weary smile. 'There are a great many words here that would surprise Mr Gerrard, I am afraid.'

'And the inserts,' Becky persisted. 'How is anybody to tell where they go, Miss Devine? It's mostly inserts; see, all over the top and sides and back.'

Ardessa turned her head away.

'Don't claw the pages like that, Becky. You make me nervous. Mr Gerrard has not time to dot his i's and cross his t's. That is what we keep copyists for. I will correct these sheets for you, – it would be terrible if Mr O'Mally saw them, – and then you can copy them over again. It must be done by tomorrow morning, so you may have to work late. See that your hands are clean and dry, and then you will not smear it.'

'Yes, ma'am. Thank you, Miss Devine. Will you tell the janitor, please, it's all right if I have to stay? He was cross because I was here Saturday afternoon doing this. He said it was a holiday, and when everybody else was gone I ought to—'

'That will do, Becky. Yes, I will speak to the janitor for you. You may go to lunch now.'

Becky turned on one heel and then swung back.

'Miss Devine,' she said anxiously, 'will it be all right if I get white shoes for now?'

Ardessa gave her kind consideration.

'For office wear, you mean? No, Becky. With only one pair, you could not keep them properly clean; and black shoes are much less conspicuous. Tan, if you prefer.'

Becky looked down at her feet. They were too large, and her skirt was as much too short as her legs were too long.

'Nearly all the girls I know wear white shoes to business,' she pleaded.

'They are probably little girls who work in factories or department stores, and that is quite another matter. Since you raise the question, Becky, I ought to speak to you about your new waist. Don't wear it to the office again, please. Those cheap open-work waists are not appropriate in an office like this. They are all very well for little chorus girls.'

'But Miss Kalski wears expensive waists to business more open than this, and jewelry—'

Ardessa interrupted. Her face grew hard.

'Miss Kalski,' she said coldly, 'works for the business department. You are employed in the editorial offices. There is a great difference. You see, Becky, I might have to call you in here at any time when a scientist or a great writer or the president of a university is here talking over editorial matters, and such clothes as you have on today would make a bad impression. Nearly all our connections are with important people of that kind, and we ought to be well, but quietly, dressed.'

'Yes, Miss Devine. Thank you.' Becky gasped and disappeared. Heaven knew she had no need to be further impressed with the greatness of 'The Outcry' office. During the year and a half she had been there she had never ceased to tremble. She knew the prices all the authors got as well as Miss Devine did, and everything seemed to her to be done on a magnificent scale. She hadn't a good memory for long technical words, but she never forgot dates or prices or initials or telephone numbers.

Becky felt that her job depended on Miss Devine, and she was so glad to have it that she scarcely realized she was being bullied. Besides, she was grateful for all that she had learned from Ardessa; Ardessa had taught her to do most of the things that she was supposed to do herself. Becky wanted to learn, she had to learn; that was the train she was always running for. Her father, Isaac Tietelbaum, the tailor, who pressed Miss Devine's skirts and kept her ladylike suits in order, had come to his client two years ago and told her he had a bright girl just out of a commercial high school. He implored Ardessa to find some office position for his daughter. Ardessa told an appealing story to O'Mally, and brought Becky into the office, at a salary of six dollars a week, to help with the copying and to learn business routine. When Becky first came she was as ignorant as a young savage. She was rapid at her shorthand and typing, but a Kaffir girl would have known as much about the English language. Nobody ever wanted to learn more than Becky. She fairly wore the dictionary out. She dug up her old school grammar and worked over it at night. She faithfully mastered Miss Devine's fussy system of punctuation.

There were eight children at home, younger than Becky, and they were all eager to learn. They wanted to get their mother out of the three dark rooms behind the tailor shop and to move into a flat upstairs, where they could, as Becky said, 'live private.' The young Tietelbaums doubted their father's ability to bring this change about, for the more things he declared himself ready to do in his window placards, the fewer were brought to him to be done. 'Dyeing, Cleaning, Ladies' Furs Remodeled' – it did no good.

Rebecca was out to 'improve herself,' as her father had told her she must. Ardessa had easy way with her. It was one of those rare relationships from which both persons profit. The more Becky could learn from Ardessa, the happier she was; and the more Ardessa could unload on Becky, the greater was her contentment. She easily broke Becky of the gum-chewing habit, taught her to walk quietly, to efface herself at the proper moment, and to hold her tongue. Becky had been raised to eight dollars a week; but she didn't care half so much about that as she did about her own increasing efficiency. The more work Miss Devine handed over to her the happier she was, and the faster she was able to eat it up.

She tested and tried herself in every possible way. She now had full confidence that she would surely one day be a high-priced stenographer, a real 'business woman.'

Becky would have corrupted a really industrious person, but a bilious temperament like Ardessa's couldn't make even a feeble stand against such willingness. Ardessa had grown soft and had lost the knack of turning out work. Sometimes, in her importance and serenity, she shivered. What if O'Mally should die, and she were thrust out into the world to work in competition with the brazen, competent young women she saw about her everywhere? She believed herself indispensable, but she knew that in such a mischanceful world as this the very powers of darkness might rise to separate her from this pearl among jobs.

When Becky came in from lunch she went down the long hall to the wash-room, where all the little girls who worked in the advertising and circulation departments kept their hats and jackets. There were shelves and shelves of bright spring hats, piled on top of one another, all as stiff as sheet-iron and trimmed with gay flowers. At the marble wash-stand stood Rena Kalski, the right bower of the business manager, polishing her diamond rings with a nail-brush.

'Hello, kid,' she called over her shoulder to Becky. 'I've got a ticket for you for Thursday afternoon.'

Becky's black eyes glowed, but the strained look on her face drew tighter than ever.

'I'll never ask her, Miss Kalski,' she said rapidly. 'I don't dare. I have to stay late tonight again; and I know she'd be hard to please after, if I was to try to get off on a week-day. I thank you, Miss Kalski, but I'd better not.'

Miss Kalski laughed. She was a slender young Hebrew, handsome in an impudent, Tenderloin sort of way, with a small head, reddish-brown almond eyes, a trifle tilted, a rapacious mouth, and a beautiful chin.

'Ain't you under that woman's thumb, though! Call her bluff. She isn't half the prima donna she thinks she is. On my side of the hall we know who's who about this place.'

The business and editorial departments of 'The Outcry'

were separated by a long corridor and a great contempt. Miss Kalski dried her rings with tissue-paper and studied them with an appraising eye.

'Well, since you're such a "fraidy-calf,"' she went on, 'maybe I can get a rise out of her myself. Now I've got you a ticket out of that shirt front, I want you to go. I'll drop in on Devine this afternoon.'

When Miss Kalski went back to her desk in the business manager's private office, she turned to him familiarly, but not impertinently.

'Mr Henderson, I want to send a kid over in the editorial stenographers' to the Palace Thursday afternoon. She's a nice kid, only she's scared out of her skin all the time. Miss Devine's her boss, and she'll be just mean enough not to let the young one off. Would you say a word to her?'

The business manager lit a cigar.

'I'm not saying words to any of the high-brows over there. Try it out with Devine yourself. You're not bashful.'

Miss Kalski shrugged her shoulders and smiled.

'Oh, very well.' She serpentined out of the room and crossed the Rubicon into the editorial offices. She found Ardessa typing O'Mally's letters and wearing a pained expression.

'Good afternoon, Miss Devine,' she said carelessly. 'Can we borrow Becky over there for Thursday afternoon? We're short.'

Miss Devine looked piqued and tilted her head.

'I don't think it's customary, Miss Kalski, for the business department to use our people. We never have girls enough here to do the work. Of course if Mr Henderson feels justified—'

'Thanks awfully, Miss Devine,' – Miss Kalski interrupted her with the perfectly smooth, good-natured tone which never betrayed a hint of the scorn every line of her sinuous figure expressed, – 'I will tell Mr Henderson. Perhaps we can do something for you some day.' Whether this was a threat, a kind wish, or an insinuation, no mortal could have told. Miss Kalski's face as always suggesting insolence without being quite insolent. As she returned to her own domain she met the cashier's head clerk in the hall. 'That Devine woman's a crime,' she murmured. The head clerk laughed tolerantly.

That afternoon as Miss Kalski was leaving the office at 5:15, on her way down the corridor she heard a typewriter clicking away in the empty, echoing editorial offices. She looked in, and found Becky bending forward over the machine as if she were about to swallow it.

'Hello, kid. Do you sleep with that?' she called. She walked up to Becky and glanced at her copy. 'What do you let 'em keep you up nights over that stuff for?' she asked contemptuously. 'The world wouldn't suffer if that stuff never got printed.'

Rebecca looked up wildly. Not even Miss Kalski's French pansy hat or her ear-rings and landscape veil could loosen Becky's tenacious mind from Mr Gerrard's article on water power. She scarcely knew what Miss Kalski had said to her, certainly not what she meant.

'But I must make progress already, Miss Kalski,' she panted.

Miss Kalski gave a low, siren laugh.

'I should say you must!' she ejaculated.

Ardessa decided to take her vacation in June, and she arranged that Miss Milligan should do O'Mally's work while she was away. Miss Milligan was blunt and noisy, rapid and inaccurate. It would be just as well for O'Mally to work with a coarse instrument for a time; he would be more appreciative, perhaps, of certain qualities to which he had seemed insensible of late. Ardessa was to leave for East Hampton on Sunday, and she spent Saturday morning instructing her substitute as to the state of the correspondence. At noon O'Mally burst into her room. All the morning he had been closeted with a new writer of mystery-stories just over from England.

'Can you stay and take my letters this afternoon, Miss Devine? You're not leaving until tomorrow.'

Ardessa pouted, and tilted her head at the angle he was tired of.

'I'm sorry, Mr O'Mally, but I've left all my shopping for this afternoon. I think Becky Tietelbaum could do them for you. I will tell her to be careful.'

'Oh, all right.' O'Mally bounced out with a reflection of Ardessa's disdainful expression on his face. Saturday afternoon was always a half-holiday, to be sure, but since she had weeks of freedom when he was away — However —

At two o'clock Becky Tietelbaum appeared at his door, clad in the sober office suit which Miss Devine insisted she should wear, her note-book in her hand, and so frightened that her fingers were cold and her lips were pale. She had never taken dictation from the editor before. It was a great and terrifying occasion.

'Sit down,' he said encouragingly. He began dictating while he shook from his bag the manuscripts he had snatched away from the amazed English author that morning. Presently he looked up.

'Do I go too fast?'

'No, sir,' Becky found strength to say.

At the end of an hour he told her to go and type as many of the letters as she could while he went over the bunch of stuff he had torn from the Englishman. He was with the Hindu detective in an opium den in Shanghai when Becky returned and placed a pile of papers on his desk.

'How many?' he asked, without looking up.

'All you gave me, sir.'

'All, so soon? Wait a minute and let me see how many mistakes.' He went over the letters rapidly, signing them as he read. 'They seem to be all right. I thought you were the girl that made so many mistakes.'

Rebecca was never too frightened to vindicate herself.

'Mr O'Mally, sir, I don't make mistakes with letters. It's only copying the articles that have so many long words, and when the writing isn't plain, like Mr Gerrard's. I never make many mistakes with Mr Johnson's articles, or with yours I don't.'

O'Mally wheeled round in his chair, looked with curiosity at her long, tense face, her black eyes, and straight brows.

'Oh, so you sometimes copy articles, do you? How does that happen?'

'Yes, sir. Always Miss Devine gives me the articles to do. It's good practice for me.'

'I see.' O'Mally shrugged his shoulders. He was thinking that he could get a rise out of the whole American public any day easier than he could get a rise out of Ardessa. 'What editorials of mine have you copied lately, for instance?'

Rebecca blazed out at him, reciting rapidly:

'Oh, "A Word about the Rosenbaums," "Useless Navy-Yards," "Who Killed Cock Robin"—'

'Wait a minute.' O'Mally checked her flow. 'What was that one about – Cock Robin?'

'It was all about why the secretary of the interior dismissed—'

'All right, all right. Copy those letters, and put them down the chute as you go out. Come in here for a minute on Monday morning.'

Becky hurried home to tell her father that she had taken the editor's letters and had made no mistakes. On Monday she learned that she was to do O'Mally's work for a few days. He disliked Miss Milligan, and he was annoyed with Ardessa for trying to put her over on him when there was better material at hand. With Rebecca he got on very well; she was impersonal, unreproachful, and she fairly panted for work. Everything was done almost before he told her what he wanted. She raced ahead with him; it was like riding a good modern bicycle after pumping along on an old hard tire.

On the day before Miss Devine's return O'Mally strolled over for a chat with the business office.

'Henderson, your people are taking vacations now, I suppose? Could you use an extra girl?'

'If it's that thin black one, I can.'

O'Mally gave him a wise smile.

'It isn't. To be honest, I want to put one over on you. I want you to take Miss Devine over here for a while and speed her up. I can't do anything. She's got the upper hand of me. I don't want to fire her, you understand, but she makes my life too difficult. It's my fault, of course. I've pampered her. Give her a chance over here; maybe she'll come back. You can be firm with 'em, can't you?'

Henderson glanced toward the desk where Miss Kalski's lightning eye was skimming over the printing-house bills that he was supposed to verify himself.

'Well, if I can't, I know who can,' he replied, with a chuckle.

'Exactly,' O'Mally agreed. 'I'm counting on the force of Miss Kalski's example. Miss Devine's all right, Miss Kalski, but she needs regular exercise. She owes it to her complexion. I can't discipline people.'

Miss Kalski's only reply was a low, indulgent laugh.

O'Mally braced himself on the morning of Ardessa's return. He told the waiter at his club to bring him a second pot of coffee and to bring it hot. He was really afraid of her. When she presented herself at his office at 10:30 he complimented her upon her tan and asked about her vacation. Then he broke the news to her.

'We want to make a few temporary changes about here, Miss Devine, for the summer months. The business department is short of help. Henderson is going to put Miss Kalski on the books for a while to figure out some economies for him, and he is going to take you over. Meantime I'll get Becky broken in so that she could take your work if you were sick or anything.'

Ardessa drew herself up.

'I've not been accustomed to commercial work, Mr O'Mally. I've no interest in it, and I don't care to brush up in it.'

'Brushing up is just what we need, Miss Devine.' O'Mally began tramping about his room expansively. 'I'm going to brush everybody up. I'm going to brush a few people out; but I want you to stay with us, of course. You belong here. Don't be hasty now. Go to your room and think it over.'

Ardessa was beginning to cry, and O'Mally was afraid he would lose his nerve. He looked out of the window at a new skyscraper that was building, while she retired without a word.

At her own desk Ardessa sat down breathless and trembling. The one thing she had never doubted was her unique value to O'Mally. She had, as she told herself, taught him everything. She would say a few things to Becky Tietelbaum, and to that pigeon-breasted tailor, her father, too! The worst of it was that Ardessa had herself brought it all about; she could see that clearly now. She had carefully trained and qualified her successor. Why had she ever civilized Becky? Why had she taught her manners and deportment, broken her of the gum-chewing habit, and made her presentable? In her original state O'Mally would never have put up with her, no matter what her ability.

Ardessa told herself that O'Mally was notoriously fickle; Becky amused him, but he would soon find out her limitations. The wise thing, she knew, was to humor him; but it seemed to her that she could not swallow her pride. Ardessa grew yellower within the hour. Over and over in her mind she bade O'Mally a cold adieu and minced out past the grand old man at the desk for the last time. But each exit she rehearsed made her feel sorrier for herself. She thought over all the offices she knew, but she realized that she could never meet their inexorable standards of efficiency.

While she was bitterly deliberating, O'Mally himself wandered in, rattling his keys nervously in his pocket. He shut the door behind him.

'Now, you're going to come through with this all right, aren't you, Miss Devine? I want Henderson to get over the notion that my people over here are stuck up and think the business department are old shoes. That's where we get our money from, as he often reminds me. You'll be the best-paid girl over there; no reduction, of course. You don't want to go wandering off to some new office where personality doesn't count for anything.' He sat down confidentially on the edge of her desk. 'Do you, now, Miss Devine?'

Ardessa simpered tearfully as she replied.

'Mr O'Mally,' she brought out, 'you'll soon find that Becky is not the sort of girl to meet people for you when you are away. I don't see how you can think of letting her.'

'That's one thing I want to change, Miss Devine. You're too soft-handed with the has-beens and the never-was-ers. You're too much of a lady for this rough game. Nearly everybody who comes in here wants to sell us a gold-brick, and you treat them as if they were bringing in wedding presents. Becky is as rough as sandpaper, and she'll clear out a lot of dead wood.' O'Mally rose, and tapped Ardessa's shrinking shoulder. 'Now, be a sport and go through with it, Miss Devine. I'll see that you don't lose. Henderson thinks you'll refuse to do his work, so I want you to get moved in there before he comes back from lunch. I've had a desk put in his office for you. Miss Kalski is in the bookkeeper's room half the time now.'

Rena Kalski was amazed that afternoon when a line of office boys entered, carrying Miss Devine's effects, and when Ardessa herself coldly followed them. After Ardessa had arranged her desk, Miss Kalski went over to her and told her about some matters of routine very good-naturedly. Ardessa looked pretty badly shaken up, and Rena bore no grudges.

'When you want the dope on the correspondence with the paper men, don't bother to look it up. I've got it all in my head, and I can save time for you. If he wants you to go over the printing bills every week, you'd better let me help you with that for a while. I can stay almost any afternoon. It's quite a trick to figure out the plates and over-time charges till you get used to it. I've worked out a quick method that saves trouble.'

When Henderson came in at three he found Ardessa, chilly, but civil, awaiting his instructions. He knew she disapproved of his tastes and his manners, but he didn't mind. What interested and amused him was that Rena Kalski, whom he had always thought as cold-blooded as an adding-machine, seemed to be making a hair-mattress of herself to break Ardessa's fall.

At five o'clock, when Ardessa rose to go, the business manager said breezily:

'See you at nine in the morning, Miss Devine. We begin on the stroke.'

Ardessa faded out of the door, and Miss Kalski's slender back squirmed with amusement.

'I never thought to hear such words spoken,' she admitted; 'but I guess she'll limber up all right. The atmosphere is bad over there. They get moldy.'

After the next monthly luncheon of the heads of departments, O'Mally said to Henderson, as he feed the coat-boy:

'By the way, how are you making it with the bartered bride?'

Henderson smashed on his Panama as he said:

'Any time you want her back, don't be delicate.'

But O'Mally shook his red head and laughed.

'Oh, I'm no Indian giver!'

First published in *Century*, May 1918.

COMING, APHRODITE!

DON HEDGER had lived for four years on the top floor of an old house on the south side of Washington Square, and nobody had ever disturbed him. He occupied one big room with no outside exposure except on the north, where he had built in a many-paned studio window that looked upon a court and upon the roofs and walls of other buildings. His room was very cheerless, since he never got a ray of direct sunlight; the south corners were always in shadow. In one of the corners was a clothes closet, built against the partition, in another a wide divan, serving as a seat by day and a bed by night. In the front corner, the one farther from the window, was a sink, and a table with two gas burners where he sometimes cooked his food. There, too, in the perpetual dusk, was the dog's bed, and often a bone or two for his comfort.

The dog was a Boston bull terrier, and Hedger explained his surly disposition by the fact that he had been bred to the point where it told on his nerves. His name was Caesar III, and he had taken prizes at very exclusive dog shows. When he and his master went out to prowl about University Place or to promenade along West Street, Caesar III was invariably fresh and shining. His pink skin showed through his mottled coat, which glistened as if it had just been rubbed with olive oil, and he wore a brass-studded collar, bought at the smartest saddler's. Hedger, as often as not, was hunched up in an old striped blanket coat, with a shapeless felt hat pulled over his bushy hair, wearing black shoes that had become grey, or brown ones that had become black, and he never put on gloves unless the day was biting cold.

Early in May, Hedger learned that he was to have a new neighbour in the rear apartment – two rooms, one large and one small, that faced the west. His studio was shut off from the larger of these rooms by double doors, which, though they were fairly tight, left him a good deal at the mercy of the occupant. The rooms had been leased, long before he came there, by a trained nurse who considered herself knowing in old furniture. She went to auction sales and bought up mahogany and dirty brass and stored it away here, where she meant to live when she retired from nursing. Meanwhile, she sub-let her rooms, with their precious furniture, to young people who came to New York to 'write' or to 'paint' – who proposed to live by the sweat of the brow rather than of the hand, and who desired artistic surroundings. When Hedger first moved in, these rooms were occupied by a young man who tried to write plays, – and who kept on trying until a week ago, when the nurse had put him out for unpaid rent.

A few days after the playwright left, Hedger heard an ominous murmur of voices through the bolted double doors: the lady-like intonation of the nurse – doubtless exhibiting her treasures – and another voice, also a woman's, but very different; young, fresh, unguarded, confident. All the same, it would be very annoying to have a woman in there. The only bath-room on the floor was at the top of the stairs in the front hall, and he would always be running into her as he came or went from his bath. He would have to be more careful to see that Caesar didn't leave bones about the hall, too; and she might object when he cooked steak and onions on his gas burner.

As soon as the talking ceased and the women left, he forgot them. He was absorbed in a study of paradise fish at the Aquarium, staring out at people through the glass and green water of their tank. It was a highly gratifying idea; the incommunicability of one stratum of animal life with another, – though Hedger pretended it was only an experiment in unusual lighting. When he heard trunks knocking against the

sides of the narrow hall, then he realized that she was
moving in at once. Toward noon, groans and deep gasps and
the creaking of ropes, made him aware that a piano was
arriving. After the tramp of the movers died away down the
stairs, somebody touched off a few scales and chords on the
instrument, and then there was peace. Presently he heard
her lock her door and go down the hall humming something; going out to lunch, probably. He stuck his brushes in a
can of turpentine and put on his hat, not stopping to wash
his hands. Caesar was smelling along the crack under the
bolted doors; his bony tail stuck out hard as a hickory withe,
and the hair was standing up about his elegant collar.

Hedger encouraged him. 'Come along, Caesar. You'll soon
get used to a new smell.'

In the hall stood an enormous trunk, behind the ladder
that led to the roof, just opposite Hedger's door. The dog flew
at it with a growl of hurt amazement. They went down three
flights of stairs and out into the brilliant May afternoon.

Behind the Square, Hedger and his dog descended into a
basement oyster house where there were no tablecloths on
the tables and no handles on the coffee cups, and the floor
was covered with sawdust, and Caesar was always welcome,
– not that he needed any such precautionary flooring. All the
carpets of Persia would have been safe for him. Hedger
ordered steak and onions absentmindedly, not realizing why
he had an apprehension that this dish might be less readily at
hand hereafter. While he ate, Caesar sat beside his chair,
gravely disturbing the sawdust with his tail.

After lunch Hedger strolled about the Square for the dog's
health and watched the stages pull out; – that was almost the
very last summer of the old horse stages on Fifth Avenue.
The fountain had but lately begun operations for the season
and was throwing up a mist of rainbow water which now
and then blew south and sprayed a bunch of Italian babies
that were being supported on the outer rim by older, very
little older, brothers and sisters. Plump robins were hopping
about on the soil; the grass was newly cut and blindingly
green. Looking up the Avenue through the Arch, one could

see the young poplars with their bright, sticky leaves, and the Brevoort glistening in its spring coat of paint, and shining horses and carriages, – occasionally an automobile, mis-shapen and sullen, like an ugly threat in a stream of things that were bright and beautiful and alive.

While Caesar and his master were standing by the fountain, a girl approached them, crossing the Square. Hedger noticed her because she wore a lavender cloth suit and carried in her arms a big bunch of fresh lilacs. He saw that she was young and handsome, – beautiful, in fact, with a splendid figure and good action. She, too, paused by the fountain and looked back through the Arch up the Avenue. She smiled rather patronizingly as she looked, and at the same time seemed delighted. Her slowly curving upper lip and half-closed eyes seemed to say: 'You're gay, you're exciting, you are quite the right sort of thing; but you're none too fine for me!'

In the moment she tarried, Caesar stealthily approached her and sniffed at the hem of her lavender skirt, then, when she went south like an arrow, he ran back to his master and lifted a face full of emotion and alarm, his lower lip twitching under his sharp white teeth and his hazel eyes pointed with a very definite discovery. He stood thus, motionless, while Hedger watched the lavender girl go up the steps and through the door of the house in which he lived.

'You're right, my boy, it's she! She might be worse looking, you know.'

When they mounted to the studio, the new lodger's door, at the back of the hall, was a little ajar, and Hedger caught the warm perfume of lilacs just brought in out of the sun. He was used to the musty smell of the old hall carpet. (The nurse-lessee had once knocked at his studio door and complained that Caesar must be somewhat responsible for the particular flavour of that mustiness, and Hedger had never spoken to her since.) He was used to the old smell, and he preferred it to that of the lilacs, and so did his companion, whose nose was so much more discriminating. Hedger shut his door vehemently, and fell to work.

Most young men who dwell in obscure studios in New York have had a beginning, come out of something, have somewhere a home town, a family, a paternal roof. But Don Hedger had no such background. He was a foundling, and had grown up in a school for homeless boys, where book-learning was a negligible part of the curriculum. When he was sixteen, a Catholic priest took him to Greensburg, Pennsylvania, to keep house for him. The priest did something to fill in the large gaps in the boy's education, – taught him to like 'Don Quixote' and 'The Golden Legend,' and encouraged him to mess with paints and crayons in his room up under the slope of the mansard. When Don wanted to go to New York to study at the Art League, the priest got him a night job as packer in one of the big department stores. Since then, Hedger had taken care of himself; that was his only responsibility. He was singularly unencumbered; had no family duties, no social ties, no obligations toward any one but his landlord. Since he travelled light, he had travelled rather far. He had got over a good deal of the earth's surface, in spite of the fact that he never in his life had more than three hundred dollars ahead at any one time, and he had already outlived a succession of convictions and revelations about his art.

Though he was not but twenty-six years old, he had twice been on the verge of becoming a marketable product; once through some studies of New York streets he did for a magazine, and once through a collection of pastels he brought home from New Mexico, which Remington, then at the height of his popularity, happened to see, and generously tried to push. But on both occasions Hedger decided that this was something he didn't wish to carry further, – simply the old thing over again and got nowhere, – so he took enquiring dealers experiments in a 'later manner,' that made them put him out of the shop. When he ran short of money, he could always get any amount of commercial work; he was an expert draughtsman and worked with lightning speed. The rest of his time he spent in groping his way from one kind of painting into another, or travelling about without luggage, like a tramp, and he was chiefly occupied with getting rid of ideas he had once thought very fine.

Hedger's circumstances, since he had moved to Washington Square, were affluent compared to anything he had ever known before. He was now able to pay advance rent and turn the key on his studio when he went away for four months at a stretch. It didn't occur to him to wish to be richer than this. To be sure, he did without a great many things other people think necessary, but he didn't miss them, because he had never had them. He belonged to no clubs, visited no houses, had no studio friends, and he ate his dinner alone in some decent little restaurant, even on Christmas and New Year's. For days together he talked to nobody but his dog and the janitress and the lame oysterman.

After he shut the door and settled down to his paradise fish on that first Tuesday in May, Hedger forgot all about his new neighbour. When the light failed, he took Caesar out for a walk. On the way home he did his marketing on West Houston Street, with a one-eyed Italian woman who always cheated him. After he had cooked his beans and scallopini, and drunk half a bottle of Chianti, he put his dishes in the sink and went up on the roof to smoke. He was the only person in the house who ever went to the roof, and he had a secret understanding with the janitress about it. He was to have 'the privilege of the roof,' as she said, if he opened the heavy trapdoor on sunny days to air out the upper hall, and was watchful to close it when rain threatened. Mrs Foley was fat and dirty and hated to climb stairs, – besides, the roof was reached by a perpendicular iron ladder, definitely inaccessible to a woman of her bulk, and the iron door at the top of it was too heavy for any but Hedger's strong arm to lift. Hedger was not above medium height, but he practised with weights and dumb-bells, and in the shoulders he was as strong as a gorilla.

So Hedger had the roof to himself. He and Caesar often slept up there on hot nights, rolled in blankets he had brought home from Arizona. He mounted with Caesar under his left arm. The dog had never learned to climb a perpendicular ladder, and never did he feel so much his master's greatness and his own dependence upon him, as when he crept under his arm for this perilous ascent. Up there was even gravel to scratch in, and a dog could do whatever he liked, so long as he did not bark. It was a kind of Heaven, which no one was strong enough to reach but his great, paint-smelling master.

On this blue May night there was a slender, girlish looking young moon in the west, playing with a whole company of silver stars. Now and then one of them darted away from the group and shot off into the gauzy blue with a soft little trail of light, like laughter. Hedger and his dog were delighted when a star did this. They were quite lost in watching the glittering game, when they were suddenly diverted by a sound, – not from the stars, though it was music. It was not the Prologue to Pagliacci, which rose ever and anon on hot evenings from an Italian tenement on Thompson Street, with the gasps of the corpulent baritone who got behind it; nor was it the hurdy-gurdy man, who often played at the corner in the balmy twilight. No, this was a woman's voice, singing the tempestuous, over-lapping phrases of Signor Puccini, then comparatively new in the world, but already so popular that even Hedger recognized his unmistakable gusts of breath. He looked about over the roofs; all was blue and still, with the well-built chimneys that were never used now standing up dark and mournful. He moved softly toward the yellow quadrangle where the gas from the hall shone up through the half-lifted trapdoor. Oh yes! It came up through the hole like a strong draught, a big, beautiful voice, and it sounded rather like a professional's. A piano had arrived in the morning, Hedger remembered. This might be a very great nuisance. It would be pleasant enough to listen to, if you could turn it on and off as you wished; but you couldn't. Caesar, with the gas light shining on his collar and his ugly but sensitive face, panted and looked up for information. Hedger put down a reassuring hand.

'I don't know. We can't tell yet. It may not be so bad.'

He stayed on the roof until all was still below, and finally descended, with quite a new feeling about his neighbour. Her voice, like her figure, inspired respect, – if one did not choose to call it admiration. Her door was shut, the transom was dark; nothing remained of her but the obtrusive trunk, unrightfully taking up room in the narrow hall.

II

For two days Hedger didn't see her. He was painting eight hours a day just then, and only went out to hunt for food. He noticed that she practised scales and exercises for about an hour in the morning; then she locked her door, went humming down the hall, and left him in peace. He heard her getting her coffee ready at about the same time he got his. Earlier still, she passed his room on her way to her bath. In the evening she sometimes sang, but on the whole she didn't bother him. When he was working well he did not notice anything much. The morning paper lay before his door until he reached out for his milk bottle, then he kicked the sheet inside and it lay on the floor until evening. Sometimes he read it and sometimes he did not. He forgot there was anything of importance going on in the world outside of his third floor studio. Nobody had ever taught him that he ought to be interested in other people; in the Pittsburgh steel strike, in the Fresh Air Fund, in the scandal about the Babies' Hospital. A grey wolf, living in a Wyoming canyon, would hardly have been less concerned about these things than was Don Hedger.

One morning he was coming out of the bath-room at the front end of the hall, having just given Caesar his bath and rubbed him into a glow with a heavy towel. Before the door, lying in wait for him, as it were, stood a tall figure in a flowing blue silk dressing gown that fell away from her marble arms. In her arms she carried various accessories of the bath.

'I wish,' she said distinctly, standing in the way, 'I wish

you wouldn't wash your dog in the tub. I never heard of such a thing! I've found his hair in the tub, and I've smelled a doggy smell, and now I've caught you at it. It's an outrage!'

Hedger was badly frightened. She was so tall and positive, and was fairly blazing with beauty and anger. He stood blinking, holding on to his sponge and dog-soap, feeling that he ought to bow very low to her. But what he actually said was:

'Nobody has ever objected before. I always wash the tub, – and, anyhow, he's cleaner than most people.'

'Cleaner than me?' her eyebrows went up, her white arms and neck and her fragrant person seemed to scream at him like a band of outraged nymphs. Something flashed through his mind about a man who was turned into a dog, or was pursued by dogs, because he unwittingly intruded upon the bath of beauty.

'No, I didn't mean that,' he muttered, turning scarlet under the bluish stubble of his muscular jaws. 'But I know he's cleaner than I am.'

'That I don't doubt!' Her voice sounded like a soft shivering of crystal, and with a smile of pity she drew the folds of her voluminous blue robe close about her and allowed the wretched man to pass. Even Caesar was frightened; he darted like a streak down the hall, through the door and to his own bed in the corner among the bones.

Hedger stood still in the doorway, listening to indignant sniffs and coughs and a great swishing of water about the sides of the tub. He had washed it; but as he had washed it with Caesar's sponge, it was quite possible that a few bristles remained; the dog was shedding now. The playwright had never objected, nor had the jovial illustrator who occupied the front apartment, – but he, as he admitted, 'was usually pye-eyed, when he wasn't in Buffalo.' He went home to Buffalo sometimes to rest his nerves.

It had never occurred to Hedger that any one would mind using the tub after Caesar; – but then, he had never seen a beautiful girl caparisoned for the bath before. As soon as he beheld her standing there, he realized the unfitness of it. For that matter, she ought not to step into a tub that any other mortal had bathed in; the illustrator was sloppy and left cigarette ends on the moulding.

All morning as he worked he was gnawed by a spiteful desire to get back at her. It rankled that he had been so vanquished by her disdain. When he heard her locking her door to go out for lunch, he stepped quickly into the hall in his messy painting coat, and addressed her.

'I don't wish to be exigent, Miss,' – he had certain grand words that he used upon occasion – 'but if this is your trunk, it's rather in the way here.'

'Oh, very well!' she exclaimed carelessly, dropping her keys into her handbag. 'I'll have it moved when I can get a man to do it,' and she went down the hall with her free, roving stride.

Her name, Hedger discovered from her letters, which the postman left on the table in the lower hall, was Eden Bower.

III

In the closet that was built against the partition separating his room from Miss Bower's, Hedger kept all his wearing apparel, some of it on hooks and hangers, some of it on the floor. When he opened his closet door now-a-days, little dust-coloured insects flew out on downy wing, and he suspected that a brood of moths were hatching in his winter overcoat. Mrs Foley, the janitress, told him to bring down all his heavy clothes and she would give them a beating and hang them in the court. The closet was in such disorder that he shunned the encounter, but one hot afternoon he set himself to the task. First he threw out a pile of forgotten laundry and tied it up in a sheet. The bundle stood as high as his middle when he had knotted the corners. Then he got his shoes and overshoes together. When he took his overcoat from its place against the partition, a long ray of yellow light shot across the dark enclosure, – a knot hole, evidently, in the high wainscoting of the west room. He had never noticed it before, and without realizing what he was doing, he stooped and squinted through it.

Yonder, in a pool of sunlight, stood his new neighbour, wholly unclad, doing exercises of some sort before a long gilt mirror. Hedger did not happen to think how unpardonable it was of him to watch her. Nudity was not improper to any one who had worked so much from the figure, and he continued to look, simply because he had never seen a woman's body so beautiful as this one, – positively glorious in action. As she swung her arms and changed from one pivot of motion to another, muscular energy seemed to flow through her from her toes to her finger-tips. The soft flush of exercise and the gold of afternoon sun played over her flesh together, enveloped her in a luminous mist which, as she turned and twisted, made now an arm, now a shoulder, now a thigh, dissolve in pure light and instantly recover its outline with the next gesture. Hedger's fingers curved as if he were holding a crayon; mentally he was doing the whole figure in a single running line, and the charcoal seemed to explode in his hand at the point where the energy of each gesture was discharged into the whirling disc of light, from a foot or shoulder, from the up-thrust chin or the lifted breasts.

He could not have told whether he watched her for six minutes or sixteen. When her gymnastics were over, she paused to catch up a lock of hair that had come down, and examined with solicitude a little reddish mole that grew under her left arm-pit. Then, with her hand on her hip, she walked unconcernedly across the room and disappeared through the door into her bedchamber.

Disappeared – Don Hedger was crouching on his knees, staring at the golden shower which poured in through the west windows, at the lake of gold sleeping on the faded Turkish carpet. The spot was enchanted; a vision out of Alexandria, out of the remote pagan past, had bathed itself there in Helianthine fire.

When he crawled out of his closet, he stood blinking at the grey sheet stuffed with laundry, not knowing what had happened to him. He felt a little sick as he contemplated the bundle. Everything here was different; he hated the disorder of the place, the grey prison light, his old shoes and himself and all his slovenly habits. The black calico curtains that ran on wires over his big window were white with dust. There were three greasy frying pans in the sink, and the sink itself – He felt desperate. He couldn't stand this another minute. He took up an armful of winter clothes and ran down four flights into the basement.

'Mrs Foley,' he began, 'I want my room cleaned this afternoon, thoroughly cleaned. Can you get a woman for me right away?'

'Is it company you're having?' the fat, dirty janitress enquired. Mrs Foley was the widow of a useful Tammany man, and she owned real estate in Flatbush. She was huge and soft as a feather bed. Her face and arms were permanently coated with dust, grained like wood where the sweat had trickled.

'Yes, company. That's it.'

'Well, this is a queer time of the day to be asking for a cleaning woman. It's likely I can get old Lizzie, if she's not drunk. I'll send Willy round to see.'

Willy, the son of fourteen, roused from the stupor and stain of his fifth box of cigarettes by the gleam of a quarter, went out. In five minutes he returned with old Lizzie, – she smelling strong of spirits and wearing several jackets which she had put on one over the other, and a number of skirts, long and short, which made her resemble an animated dish-clout. She had, of course, to borrow her equipment from Mrs Foley, and toiled up the long flights, dragging mop and pail and broom. She told Hedger to be of good cheer, for he had got the right woman for the job, and showed him a great leather strap she wore about her wrist to prevent dislocation of tendons. She swished about the place, scattering dust and splashing soapsuds, while he watched her in nervous despair. He stood over Lizzie and made her scour the sink, directing her roughly, then paid her and got rid of her. Shutting the door on his failure, he hurried off with his dog to lose himself among the stevedores and dock labourers on West Street.

A strange chapter began for Don Hedger. Day after day, at that hour in the afternoon, the hour before his neighbour dressed for dinner, he crouched down in his closet to watch her go through her mysterious exercises. It did not occur to him that his conduct was detestable; there was nothing shy or retreating about this unclad girl, – a bold body, studying itself quite coolly and evidently well pleased with itself, doing all this for a purpose. Hedger scarcely regarded his action as conduct at all; it was something that had happened to him. More than once he went out and tried to stay away for the whole afternoon, but at about five o'clock he was sure to find himself among his old shoes in the dark. The pull of that aperture was stronger than his will, – and he had always considered his will the strongest thing about him. When she threw herself upon the divan and lay resting, he still stared, holding his breath. His nerves were so on edge that a sudden noise made him start and brought out the sweat on his forehead. The dog would come and tug at his sleeve, knowing that something was wrong with his master. If he attempted a mournful whine, those strong hands closed about his throat.

When Hedger came slinking out of his closet, he sat down on the edge of the couch, sat for hours without moving. He was not painting at all now. This thing, whatever it was, drank him up as ideas had sometimes done, and he sank into a stupor of idleness as deep and dark as the stupor of work. He could not understand it; he was no boy, he had worked from models for years, and a woman's body was no mystery to him. Yet now he did nothing but sit and think about one. He slept very little, and with the first light of morning he awoke as completely possessed by this woman as if he had been with her all the night before. The unconscious operations of life went on in him only to perpetuate this excitement. His brain held but one image now – vibrated, burned with it. It was a heathenish feeling; without friendliness, almost without tenderness.

Women had come and gone in Hedger's life. Not having had a mother to begin with, his relations with them, whether amorous or friendly, had been casual. He got on well with janitresses and wash-women, with Indians and with the peasant women of foreign countries. He had friends among the silk-skirt factory girls who came to eat their lunch in Washington Square, and he sometimes took a model for a day in the country. He felt an unreasoning antipathy toward the well-dressed women he saw coming out of big shops, or driving in the Park. If, on his way to the Art Museum, he noticed a pretty girl standing on the steps of one of the houses on upper Fifth Avenue, he frowned at her and went by with his shoulders hunched up as if he were cold. He had never known such girls, or heard them talk, or seen the inside of the houses in which they lived; but he believed them all to be artificial and, in an aesthetic sense, perverted. He saw them enslaved by desire of merchandise and manu- factured articles, effective only in making life complicated and insincere and in embroidering it with ugly and meaning- less trivialities. They were enough, he thought, to make one almost forget woman as she existed in art, in thought, and in the universe.

He had no desire to know the woman who had, for the time at least, so broken up his life, – no curiosity about her every-day personality. He shunned any revelation of it, and he listened for Miss Bower's coming and going, not to encounter, but to avoid her. He wished that the girl who wore shirt-waists and got letters from Chicago would keep out of his way, that she did not exist. With her he had naught to make. But in a room full of sun, before an old mirror, on a little enchanted rug of sleeping colours, he had seen a woman who emerged naked through a door, and disap- peared naked. He thought of that body as never having been clad, or as having worn the stuffs and dyes of all the centuries but his own. And for him she had no geographical associa- tions; unless with Crete, or Alexandria, or Veronese's Venice. She was the immortal conception, the perennial theme.

The first break in Hedger's lethargy occurred one after- noon when two young men came to take Eden Bower out to dine. They went into her music room, laughed and talked for a few minutes, and then took her away with them. They were gone a long while, but he did not go out for food himself; he waited for them to come back. At last he heard them coming down the hall, gayer and more talkative than when they left. One of them sat down at the piano, and they all began to sing. This Hedger found absolutely unendurable. He snatched up his hat and went running down the stairs. Caesar leaped beside him, hoping that old times were coming back. They had supper in the oysterman's basement and then sat down in front of their own doorway. The moon stood full over the Square, a thing of regal glory; but Hedger did not see the moon; he was looking, murderously, for men. Presently two, wearing straw hats and white trousers and carrying canes, came down the steps from his house. He rose and dogged them across the Square. They were laughing and seemed very much elated about something. As one stopped to light a cigarette, Hedger caught from the other:

'Don't you think she has a beautiful talent?'

His companion threw away his match. 'She has a beautiful figure.' They both ran to catch the stage.

Hedger went back to his studio. The light was shining from her transom. For the first time he violated her privacy at night, and peered through that fatal aperture. She was sitting, fully dressed, in the window, smoking a cigarette and looking out over the housetops. He watched her until she rose, looked about her with a disdainful, crafty smile, and turned out the light.

The next morning, when Miss Bower went out, Hedger followed her. Her white skirt gleamed ahead of him as she sauntered about the Square. She sat down behind the Garibaldi statue and opened a music book she carried. She turned the leaves carelessly, and several times glanced in his direction. He was on the point of going over to her, when she rose quickly and looked up at the sky. A flock of pigeons had risen from somewhere in the crowded Italian quarter to the south, and were wheeling rapidly up through the morning air, soaring and dropping, scattering and coming together, now grey, now white as silver, as they caught or intercepted the sunlight. She put up her hand to shade her eyes and followed them with a kind of defiant delight in her face.

Hedger came and stood beside her. 'You've surely seen them before?'

'Oh, yes,' she replied, still looking up. 'I see them every day from my windows. They always come home about five o'clock. Where do they live?'

'I don't know. Probably some Italian raises them for the market. They were here long before I came, and I've been here four years.'

'In that same gloomy room? Why didn't you take mine when it was vacant?'

'It isn't gloomy. That's the best light for painting.'

'Oh, is it? I don't know anything about painting. I'd like to see your pictures sometime. You have such a lot in there. Don't they get dusty, piled up against the wall like that?'

'Not very. I'd be glad to show them to you. Is your name really Eden Bower? I've seen your letters on the table.'

'Well, it's the name I'm going to sing under. My father's name is Bowers, but my friend Mr Jones, a Chicago newspaper man who writes about music, told me to drop the "s." He's crazy about my voice.'

Miss Bower didn't usually tell the whole story, – about anything. Her first name, when she lived in Huntington, Illinois, was Edna, but Mr Jones had persuaded her to change it to one which he felt would be worthy of her future. She was quick to take suggestions, though she told him she 'didn't see what was the matter with "Edna."'

She explained to Hedger that she was going to Paris to study. She was waiting in New York for Chicago friends who were to take her over, but who had been detained. 'Did you study in Paris?' she asked.

'No, I've never been in Paris. But I was in the south of France all last summer, studying with C——. He's the biggest man among the moderns, – at least I think so.'

Miss Bower sat down and made room for him on the

bench. 'Do tell me about it. I expected to be there by this time, and I can't wait to find out what it's like.'

Hedger began to relate how he had seen some of this Frenchman's work in an exhibition, and deciding at once that this was the man for him, he had taken a boat for Marseilles the next week, going over steerage. He proceeded at once to the little town on the coast where his painter lived, and presented himself. The man never took pupils, but because Hedger had come so far, he let him stay. Hedger lived at the master's house and every day they went out together to paint, sometimes on the blazing rocks down by the sea. They wrapped themselves in light woollen blankets and didn't feel the heat. Being there and working with C— was being in Paradise, Hedger concluded; he learned more in three months than in all his life before.

Eden Bower laughed. 'You're a funny fellow. Didn't you do anything but work? Are the women very beautiful? Did you have awfully good things to eat and drink?'

Hedger said some of the women were fine looking, especially one girl who went about selling fish and lobsters. About the food there was nothing remarkable, – except the ripe figs, he liked those. They drank sour wine, and used goat-butter, which was strong and full of hair, as it was churned in a goat skin.

'But don't they have parties or banquets? Aren't there any fine hotels down there?'

'Yes, but they are all closed in summer, and the country people are poor. It's a beautiful country, though.'

'How, beautiful?' she persisted.

'If you want to go in, I'll show you some sketches, and you'll see.'

Miss Bower rose. 'All right. I won't go to my fencing lesson this morning. Do you fence? Here comes your dog. You can't move but he's after you. He always makes a face at me when I meet him in the hall, and shows his nasty little teeth as if he wanted to bite me.'

In the studio Hedger got out his sketches, but to Miss Bower, whose favourite pictures were Christ Before Pilate and a redhaired Magdalen of Henner, these landscapes were not at all beautiful, and they gave her no idea of any country whatsoever. She was careful not to commit herself, however. Her vocal teacher had already convinced her that she had a great deal to learn about many things.

'Why don't we go out to lunch somewhere?' Hedger asked, and began to dust his fingers with a handkerchief – which he got out of sight as swiftly as possible.

'All right, the Brevoort,' she said carelessly. 'I think that's a good place, and they have good wine. I don't care for cocktails.'

Hedger felt his chin uneasily. 'I'm afraid I haven't shaved this morning. If you could wait for me in the Square? It won't take me ten minutes.'

Left alone, he found a clean collar and handkerchief, brushed his coat and blacked his shoes, and last of all dug up ten dollars from the bottom of an old copper kettle he had brought from Spain. His winter hat was of such a complexion that the Brevoort hall boy winked at the porter as he took it and placed it on the rack in a row of fresh straw ones.

IV

That afternoon Eden Bower was lying on the couch in her music room, her face turned to the window, watching the pigeons. Reclining thus she could see none of the neighbouring roofs, only the sky itself and the birds that crossed and recrossed her field of vision, white as scraps of paper blowing in the wind. She was thinking that she was young and handsome and had had a good lunch, that a very easy-going, light-hearted city lay in the streets below her; and she was wondering why she found this queer painter chap, with his lean, bluish cheeks and heavy black eyebrows, more interesting than the smart young men she met at her teacher's studio.

Eden Bower was, at twenty, very much the same person that we all know her to be at forty, except that she knew a great deal less. But one thing she knew: that she was to be Eden Bower. She was like some one standing before a great show window full of beautiful and costly things, deciding which she will order. She understands that they will not all be delivered immediately, but one by one they will arrive at her door. She already knew some of the many things that were to happen to her; for instance, that the Chicago millionaire who was going to take her abroad with his sister as chaperone, would eventually press his claim in quite another manner. He was the most circumspect of bachelors, afraid of everything obvious, even of women who were too flagrantly handsome. He was a nervous collector of pictures and furniture, a nervous patron of music, and a nervous host; very cautious about his health, and about any course of conduct that might make him ridiculous. But she knew that he would at last throw all his precautions to the winds.

People like Eden Bower are inexplicable. Her father sold farming machinery in Huntington, Illinois, and she had grown up with no acquaintances or experiences outside of that prairie town. Yet from her earliest childhood she had not one conviction or opinion in common with the people about her, – the only people she knew. Before she was out of short dresses she had made up her mind that she was going to be an actress, that she would live far away in great cities, that she would be much admired by men and would have everything she wanted. When she was thirteen, and was already singing and reciting for church entertainments, she read in some illustrated magazine a long article about the late Czar of Russia, then just come to the throne or about to come to it. After that, lying in the hammock on the front porch on summer evenings, or sitting through a long sermon in the family pew, she amused herself by trying to make up her mind whether she would or would not be the Czar's mistress when she played in his Capital. Now Edna had met this fascinating word only in the novels of Ouida, – her hard-worked little mother kept a long row of them in the upstairs storeroom, behind the linen chest. In Huntington, women who bore that relation to men were called by a very different name, and their lot was not an enviable one; of all the shabby and poor, they were the shabbiest. But then, Edna had never lived in Huntington, not even before she began to find books like 'Sapho' and 'Mademoiselle de Maupin,' secretly sold in paper covers throughout Illinois. It was as if she had come into Huntington, into the Bowers family, on one of the trains that puffed over the marshes behind their back fence all day long, and was waiting for another train to take her out.

As she grew older and handsomer, she had many beaux, but these small-town boys didn't interest her. If a lad kissed her when he brought her home from a dance, she was indulgent and she rather liked it. But if he pressed her further, she slipped away from him, laughing. After she began to sing in Chicago, she was consistently discreet. She stayed as a guest in rich people's houses, and she knew that she was being watched like a rabbit in a laboratory. Covered up in bed, with the lights out, she thought her own thoughts, and laughed.

This summer in New York was her first taste of freedom. The Chicago capitalist, after all his arrangements were made for sailing, had been compelled to go to Mexico to look after oil interests. His sister knew an excellent singing master in New York. Why should not a discreet, well-balanced girl like Miss Bower spend the summer there, studying quietly? The capitalist suggested that his sister might enjoy a summer on Long Island; he would rent the Griffith's place for her, with all the servants, and Eden could stay there. But his sister met this proposal with a cold stare. So it fell out, that between selfishness and greed, Eden got a summer all her own, – which really did a great deal toward making her an artist and whatever else she was afterward to become. She had time to look about, to watch without being watched; to select diamonds in one window and furs in another, to select shoulders and moustaches in the big hotels where she went to lunch. She had the easy freedom of obscurity and the consciousness of power. She enjoyed both. She was in no hurry.

While Eden Bower watched the pigeons, Don Hedger sat on the other side of the bolted doors, looking into a pool of dark turpentine, at his idle brushes, wondering why a woman could do this to him. He, too, was sure of his future and knew that he was a chosen man. He could not know, of course, that he was merely the first to fall under a fascination which was to be disastrous to a few men and pleasantly stimulating to many thousands. Each of these two young people sensed the future, but not completely. Don Hedger knew that nothing much would ever happen to him. Eden Bower understood that to her a great deal would happen. But she did not guess that her neighbour would have more tempestuous adventures sitting in his dark studio than she would find in all the capitals of Europe, or in all the latitude of conduct she was prepared to permit herself.

V

One Sunday morning Eden was crossing the Square with a spruce young man in a white flannel suit and a panama hat. They had been breakfasting at the Brevoort and he was coaxing her to let him come up to her rooms and sing for an hour.

'No, I've got to write letters. You must run along now. I see a friend of mine over there, and I want to ask him about something before I go up.'

'That fellow with the dog? Where did you pick him up?' the young man glanced toward the seat under a sycamore where Hedger was reading the morning paper.

'Oh, he's an old friend from the West,' said Eden easily. 'I won't introduce you, because he doesn't like people. He's a recluse. Good-bye. I can't be sure about Tuesday. I'll go with you if I have time after my lesson.' She nodded, left him, and went over to the seat littered with newspapers. The young man went up the Avenue without looking back.

'Well, what are you going to do today? Shampoo this animal all morning?' Eden enquired teasingly.

Hedger made room for her on the seat. 'No, at twelve o'clock I'm going out to Coney Island. One of my models is going up in a balloon this afternoon. I've often promised to go and see her, and now I'm going.'

Eden asked if models usually did such stunts. No, Hedger told her, but Molly Welch added to her earnings in that way. 'I believe,' he added, 'she likes the excitement of it. She's got a good deal of spirit. That's why I like to paint her. So many models have flaccid bodies.'

'And she hasn't, eh? Is she the one who comes to see you? I can't help hearing her, she talks so loud.'

'Yes, she has a rough voice, but she's a fine girl. I don't suppose you'd be interested in going?'

'I don't know,' Eden sat tracing patterns on the asphalt with the end of her parasol. 'Is it any fun? I got up feeling I'd like to do something different today. It's the first Sunday I've not had to sing in church. I had that engagement for breakfast at the Brevoort, but it wasn't very exciting. That chap can't talk about anything but himself.'

Hedger warmed a little. 'If you've never been to Coney Island, you ought to go. It's nice to see all the people; tailors and bar-tenders and prize-fighters with their best girls, and all sorts of folks taking a holiday.'

Eden looked sidewise at him. So one ought to be interested in people of that kind, ought one? He was certainly a funny fellow. Yet he was never, somehow, tiresome. She had seen a good deal of him lately, but she kept wanting to know him better, to find out what made him different from men like the one she had just left – whether he really was as different as he seemed. 'I'll go with you,' she said at last, 'if you'll leave that at home.' She pointed to Caesar's flickering ears with her sunshade.

'But he's half the fun. You'd like to hear him bark at the waves when they come in.'

'No, I wouldn't. He's jealous and disagreeable if he sees you talking to any one else. Look at him now.'

'Of course, if you make a face at him. He knows what that means, and he makes a worse face. He likes Molly Welch, and she'll be disappointed if I don't bring him.'

Eden said decidedly that he couldn't take both of them. So at twelve o'clock when she and Hedger got on the boat at Desbrosses street, Caesar was lying on his pallet, with a bone.

Eden enjoyed the boat-ride. It was the first time she had been on the water, and she felt as if she were embarking for France. The light warm breeze and the plunge of the waves made her very wide awake, and she liked crowds of any kind. They went to the balcony of a big, noisy restaurant and had a shore dinner, with tall steins of beer. Hedger had got a big advance from his advertising firm since he first lunched with Miss Bower ten days ago, and he was ready for anything.

After dinner they went to the tent behind the bathing beach, where the tops of two balloons bulged out over the canvas. A red-faced man in a linen suit stood in front of the tent, shouting in a hoarse voice and telling the people that if the crowd was good for five dollars more, a beautiful young woman would risk her life for their entertainment. Four little boys in dirty red uniforms ran about taking contributions in their pill-box hats. One of the balloons was bobbing up and down in its tether and people were shoving forward to get nearer the tent.

'Is it dangerous, as he pretends?' Eden asked.

'Molly says it's simple enough if nothing goes wrong with the balloon. Then it would be all over, I suppose.'

'Wouldn't you like to go up with her?'

'I? Of course not. I'm not fond of taking foolish risks.'

Eden sniffed. 'I shouldn't think sensible risks would be very much fun.'

Hedger did not answer, for just then every one began to shove the other way and shout, 'Look out. There she goes!' and a band of six pieces commenced playing furiously.

As the balloon rose from its tent enclosure, they saw a girl in green tights standing in the basket, holding carelessly to one of the ropes with one hand and with the other waving to the spectators. A long rope trailed behind to keep the balloon from blowing out to sea.

As it soared, the figure in green tights in the basket diminished to a mere spot, and the balloon itself, in the brilliant light, looked like a big silver-grey bat, with its wings folded. When it began to sink, the girl stepped through the hole in the basket to a trapeze that hung below, and gracefully descended through the air, holding to the rod with both hands, keeping her body taut and her feet close together. The crowd, which had grown very large by this time, cheered vociferously. The men took off their hats and waved, little boys shouted, and fat old women, shining with the heat and a beer lunch, murmured admiring comments upon the balloonist's figure. 'Beautiful legs, she has!'

'That's so,' Hedger whispered. 'Not many girls would look well in that position.' Then, for some reason, he blushed a slow, dark, painful crimson.

The balloon descended slowly, a little way from the tent, and the red-faced man in the linen suit caught Molly Welch before her feet touched the ground, and pulled her to one side. The band struck up 'Blue Bell' by way of welcome, and one of the sweaty pages ran forward and presented the balloonist with a large bouquet of artificial flowers. She smiled and thanked him, and ran back across the sand to the tent.

'Can't we go inside and see her?' Eden asked. 'You can explain to the door man. I want to meet her.' Edging forward, she herself addressed the man in the linen suit and slipped something from her purse into his hand.

They found Molly seated before a trunk that had a mirror in the lid and a 'make-up' outfit spread upon the tray. She was wiping the cold cream and powder from her neck with a discarded chemise.

'Hello, Don,' she said cordially. 'Brought a friend?'

Eden liked her. She had an easy, friendly manner, and there was something boyish and devil-may-care about her.

'Yes, it's fun. I'm mad about it,' she said in reply to Eden's questions. 'I always want to let go, when I come down on the bar. You don't feel your weight at all, as you would on a stationary trapeze.'

The big drum boomed outside, and the publicity man began shouting to newly arrived boatloads. Miss Welch took a last pull at her cigarette. 'Now you'll have to get out, Don. I change for the next act. This time I go up in a black evening dress, and lose the skirt in the basket before I start down.'

'Yes, go along,' said Eden. 'Wait for me outside the door. I'll stay and help her dress.'

Hedger waited and waited, while women of every build bumped into him and begged his pardon, and the red pages ran about holding out their caps for coins, and the people ate and perspired and shifted parasols against the sun. When the band began to play a two-step, all the bathers ran up out of the surf to watch the ascent. The second balloon bumped and rose, and the crowd began shouting to the girl in a black evening dress who stood leaning against the ropes and smiling. 'It's a new girl,' they called. 'It ain't the Countess this time. You're a peach, girlie!'

The balloonist acknowledged these compliments, bowing and looking down over the sea of upturned faces, – but Hedger was determined she should not see him, and he darted behind the tent-fly. He was suddenly dripping with cold sweat, his mouth was full of the bitter taste of anger and his tongue felt stiff behind his teeth. Molly Welch, in a shirt-waist and a white tam-o'-shanter cap, slipped out from the tent under his arm and laughed up in his face. 'She's a crazy one you brought along. She'll get what she wants!'

'Oh, I'll settle with you, all right!' Hedger brought out with difficulty.

'It's not my fault, Donnie. I couldn't do anything with her. She bought me off. What's the matter with you? Are you soft on her? She's safe enough. It's as easy as rolling off a log, if you keep cool.' Molly Welch was rather excited herself, and she was chewing gum at a high speed as she stood beside him, looking up at the floating silver cone. 'Now watch,' she exclaimed suddenly. 'She's coming down on the bar. I advised her to cut that out, but you see she does it first-rate.

And she got rid of the skirt, too. Those black tights show off her legs very well. She keeps her feet together like I told her, and makes a good line along the back. See the light on those silver slippers, – that was a good idea I had. Come along to meet her. Don't be a grouch; she's done it fine!'

Molly tweaked his elbow, and then left him standing like a stump, while she ran down the beach with the crowd.

Though Hedger was sulking, his eye could not help seeing the low blue welter of the sea, the arrested bathers, standing in the surf, their arms and legs stained red by the dropping sun, all shading their eyes and gazing upward at the slowly falling silver star.

Molly Welch and the manager caught Eden under the arms and lifted her aside, a red page dashed up with a bouquet, and the band struck up 'Blue Bell.' Eden laughed and bowed, took Molly's arm, and ran up the sand in her black tights and silver slippers, dodging the friendly old women, and the gallant sports who wanted to offer their homage on the spot.

When she emerged from the tent, dressed in her own clothes, that part of the beach was almost deserted. She stepped to her companion's side and said carelessly: 'Hadn't we better try to catch this boat? I hope you're not sore at me. Really, it was lots of fun.'

Hedger looked at his watch. 'Yes, we have fifteen minutes to get to the boat,' he said politely.

As they walked toward the pier, one of the pages ran up panting. 'Lady, you're carrying off the bouquet,' he said, aggrievedly.

Eden stopped and looked at the bunch of spotty cotton roses in her hand. 'Of course. I want them for a souvenir. You gave them to me yourself.'

'I give 'em to you for looks, but you can't take 'em away. They belong to the show.'

'Oh, you always use the same bunch?'

'Sure we do. There ain't too much money in this business.'

She laughed and tossed them back to him. 'Why are you angry?' she asked Hedger. 'I wouldn't have done it if I'd been with some fellows, but I thought you were the sort who wouldn't mind. Molly didn't for a minute think you would.'

'What possessed you to do such a fool thing?' he asked roughly.

'I don't know. When I saw her coming down, I wanted to try it. It looked exciting. Didn't I hold myself as well as she did?'

Hedger shrugged his shoulders, but in his heart he forgave her.

The return boat was not crowded, though the boats that passed them, going out, were packed to the rails. The sun was setting. Boys and girls sat on the long benches with their arms about each other, singing. Eden felt a strong wish to propitiate her companion, to be alone with him. She had been curiously wrought up by her balloon trip; it was a lark, but not very satisfying unless one came back to something after the flight. She wanted to be admired and adored. Though Eden said nothing, and sat with her arms limp on the rail in front of her, looking languidly at the rising silhouette of the city and the bright path of the sun, Hedger felt a strange drawing near to her. If he but brushed her white skirt with his knee, there was instant communication between them, such as there had never been before. They did not talk at all, but when they went over the gang-plank she took his arm and kept her shoulder close to his. He felt as if they were enveloped in a highly charged atmosphere, an invisible network of subtle, almost painful sensibility. They had somehow taken hold of each other.

An hour later, they were dining in the back garden of a little French hotel on Ninth Street, long since passed away. It was cool and leafy there, and the mosquitoes were not very numerous. A party of South Americans at another table were drinking champagne, and Eden murmured that she thought she would like some, if it were not too expensive. 'Perhaps it will make me think I am in the balloon again. That was a very nice feeling. You've forgiven me, haven't you?'

Hedger gave her a quick straight look from under his black eyebrows, and something went over her that was like a chill, except that it was warm and feathery. She drank most of the wine; her companion was indifferent to it. He was talking more to her tonight than he had ever done before. She asked him about a new picture she had seen in his room; a queer thing full of stiff, supplicating female figures. 'It's Indian, isn't it?'

'Yes. I call it Rain Spirits, or maybe, Indian Rain. In the Southwest, where I've been a good deal, the Indian traditions make women have to do with the rain-fall. They were supposed to control it, somehow, and to be able to find springs, and make moisture come out of the earth. You see I'm trying to learn to paint what people think and feel; to get away from all that photographic stuff. When I look at you, I don't see what a camera would see, do I?'

'How can I tell?'

'Well, if I should paint you, I could make you understand what I see.' For the second time that day Hedger crimsoned unexpectedly, and his eyes fell and steadily contemplated a dish of little radishes. 'That particular picture I got from a story a Mexican priest told me; he said he found it in an old manuscript book in a monastery down there, written by some Spanish Missionary, who got his stories from the Aztecs. This one he called "The Forty Lovers of the Queen," and it was more or less about rain-making.'

'Aren't you going to tell it to me?' Eden asked.

Hedger fumbled among the radishes. 'I don't know if it's the proper kind of story to tell a girl.'

She smiled; 'Oh, forget about that! I've been balloon riding today. I like to hear you talk.'

Her low voice was flattering. She had seemed like clay in his hands ever since they got on the boat to come home. He leaned back in his chair, forgot his food, and, looking at her intently, began to tell his story, the theme of which he somehow felt was dangerous tonight.

The tale began, he said, somewhere in Ancient Mexico, and concerned the daughter of a king. The birth of this Princess was preceded by unusual portents. Three times her mother dreamed that she was delivered of serpents, which betokened that the child she carried would have power with the rain gods. The serpent was the symbol of water. The Princess grew up dedicated to the gods, and wise men taught her the rain-making mysteries. She was with difficulty restrained from men and was guarded at all times, for it was the law of the Thunder that she be maiden until her marriage. In the years of her adolescence, rain was abundant with her people. The oldest man could not remember such fertility. When the Princess had counted eighteen summers, her father went to drive out a war party that harried his borders on the north and troubled his prosperity. The King destroyed the invaders and brought home many prisoners. Among the prisoners was a young chief, taller than any of his captors, of such strength and ferocity that the King's people came a day's journey to look at him. When the Princess beheld his great stature, and saw that his arms and breast were covered with the figures of wild animals, bitten into the skin and coloured, she begged his life from her father. She desired that he should practise his art upon her, and prick upon her skin the signs of Rain and Lightning and Thunder, and stain the wounds with herb-juices, as they were upon his own body. For many days, upon the roof of the King's house, the Princess submitted herself to the bone needle, and the women with her marvelled at her fortitude. But the Princess was without shame before the Captive, and it came about that he threw from him his needles and his stains, and fell upon the Princess to violate her honour; and her women ran down from the roof screaming, to call the guard which stood at the gateway of the King's house, and none stayed to protect their mistress. When the guard came, the Captive was thrown into bonds, and he was gelded, and his tongue was torn out, and he was given for a slave to the Rain Princess.

The country of the Aztecs to the east was tormented by thirst, and their king, hearing much of the rain-making arts of the Princess, sent an embassy to her father, with presents and an offer of marriage. So the Princess went from her father to be the Queen of the Aztecs, and she took with her the Captive, who served her in everything with entire fidelity and slept upon a mat before her door.

The King gave his bride a fortress on the outskirts of the city, whither she retired to entreat the rain gods. This fortress was called the Queen's House, and on the night of the new moon the Queen came to it from the palace. But when the moon waxed and grew toward the round, because the god of Thunder had had his will of her, then the Queen returned to the King. Drought abated in the country and rain fell abundantly by reason of the Queen's power with the stars.

When the Queen went to her own house she took with her no servant but the Captive, and he slept outside her door and brought her food after she had fasted. The Queen had a jewel of great value, a turquoise that had fallen from the sun, and had the image of the sun upon it. And when she desired a young man whom she had seen in the army or among the slaves, she sent the Captive to him with the jewel, for a sign that he should come to her secretly at the Queen's House upon business concerning the welfare of all. And some, after she had talked with them, she sent away with rewards; and some she took into her chamber and kept them by her for one night or two. Afterward she called the Captive and bade him conduct the youth by the secret way he had come, underneath the chambers of the fortress. But for the going away of the Queen's lovers the Captive took out the bar that was beneath a stone in the floor of the passage, and put in its stead a rush-reed, and the youth stepped upon it and fell through into a cavern that was the bed of an underground river, and whatever was thrown into it was not seen again. In this service nor in any other did the Captive fail the Queen.

But when the Queen sent for the Captain of the Archers, she detained him four days in her chamber, calling often for food and wine, and was greatly content with him. On the fourth day she went to the Captive outside her door and said: 'Tomorrow take this man up by the sure way, by which the King comes, and let him live.'

In the Queen's door were arrows, purple and white. When

she desired the King to come to her publicly, with his guard, she sent him a white arrow; but when she sent the purple, he came secretly, and covered himself with his mantle to be hidden from the stone gods at the gate. On the fifth night that the Queen was with her lover, the Captive took a purple arrow to the King, and the King came secretly and found them together. He killed the Captain with his own hand, but the Queen he brought to public trial. The Captive, when he was put to the question, told on his fingers forty men that he had let through the underground passage into the river. The Captive and the Queen were put to death by fire, both on the same day, and afterward there was scarcity of rain.

Eden Bower sat shivering a little as she listened. Hedger was not trying to please her, she thought, but to antagonize and frighten her by his brutal story. She had often told herself that his lean, big-boned lower jaw was like his bull-dog's, but tonight his face made Caesar's most savage and determined expression seem an affectation. Now she was looking at the man he really was. Nobody's eyes had ever defied her like this. They were searching her and seeing everything; all she had concealed from Livingston, and from the millionaire and his friends, and from the newspaper men. He was testing her, trying her out, and she was more ill at ease than she wished to show.

'That's quite a thrilling story,' she said at last, rising and winding her scarf about her throat. 'It must be getting late. Almost every one has gone.'

They walked down the Avenue like people who have quarrelled, or who wish to get rid of each other. Hedger did not take her arm at the street crossings, and they did not linger in the Square. At her door he tried none of the old devices of the Livingston boys. He stood like a post, having forgotten to take off his hat, gave her a harsh, threatening glance, muttered 'goodnight,' and shut his own door noisily.

There was no question of sleep for Eden Bower. Her brain was working like a machine that would never stop. After she undressed, she tried to calm her nerves by smoking a cigarette, lying on the divan by the open window. But she grew wider and wider awake, combating the challenge that had flamed all evening in Hedger's eyes. The balloon had been one kind of excitement, the wine another; but the thing that had roused her, as a blow rouses a proud man, was the doubt, the contempt, the sneering hostility with which the painter had looked at her when he told his savage story. Crowds and balloons were all very well, she reflected, but woman's chief adventure is man. With a mind over active and a sense of life over strong, she wanted to walk across the roofs in the starlight, to sail over the sea and face at once a world of which she had never been afraid.

Hedger must be asleep; his dog had stopped sniffing under the double doors. Eden put on her wrapper and slippers and stole softly down the hall over the old carpet; one loose board creaked just as she reached the ladder. The trapdoor was open, as always on hot nights. When she stepped out on the roof she drew a long breath and walked across it, looking up at the sky. Her foot touched something soft; she heard a low growl, and on the instant Caesar's sharp little teeth caught her ankle and waited. His breath was like steam on her leg. Nobody had ever intruded upon his roof before, and he panted for the movement or the word that would let him spring his jaw. Instead, Hedger's hand seized his throat.

'Wait a minute. I'll settle with him,' he said grimly. He dragged the dog toward the manhole and disappeared. When he came back, he found Eden standing over by the dark chimney, looking away in an offended attitude.

'I caned him unmercifully,' he panted. 'Of course you didn't hear anything; he never whines when I beat him. He didn't nip you, did he?'

'I don't know whether he broke the skin or not,' she answered aggrievedly, still looking off into the west.

'If I were one of your friends in white pants, I'd strike a match to find whether you were hurt, though I know you are not, and then I'd see your ankle, wouldn't I?'

'I suppose so.'

He shook his head and stood with his hands in the pockets

of his old painting jacket. 'I'm not up to such boy-tricks. If you want the place to yourself, I'll clear out. There are plenty of places where I can spend the night, what's left of it. But if you stay here and I stay here –' He shrugged his shoulders.

Eden did not stir, and she made no reply. Her head drooped slightly, as if she were considering. But the moment he put his arms about her they began to talk, both at once, as people do in an opera. The instant avowal brought out a flood of trivial admissions. Hedger confessed his crime, was reproached and forgiven, and now Eden knew what it was in his look that she had found so disturbing of late.

Standing against the black chimney, with the sky behind and blue shadows before, they looked like one of Hedger's own paintings of that period; two figures, one white and one dark, and nothing whatever distinguishable about them but that they were male and female. The faces were lost, the contours blurred in shadow, but the figures were a man and a woman, and that was their whole concern and their mysterious beauty, – it was the rhythm in which they moved, at last, along the roof and down into the dark hole; he first, drawing her gently after him. She came down very slowly. The excitement and bravado and uncertainty of that long day and night seemed all at once to tell upon her. When his feet were on the carpet and he reached up to lift her down, she twined her arms about his neck as after a long separation, and turned her face to him, and her lips, with their perfume of youth and passion.

One Saturday afternoon Hedger was sitting in the window of Eden's music room. They had been watching the pigeons come wheeling over the roofs from their unknown feeding grounds.

'Why,' said Eden suddenly, 'don't we fix those big doors into your studio so they will open? Then, if I want you, I won't have to go through the hall. That illustrator is loafing about a good deal of late.'

'I'll open them, if you wish. The bolt is on your side.'

'Isn't there one on yours, too?'

'No. I believe a man lived there for years before I came in, and the nurse used to have these rooms herself. Naturally, the lock was on the lady's side.'

Eden laughed and began to examine the bolt. 'It's all stuck up with paint.' Looking about, her eye lighted upon a bronze Buddha which was one of the nurse's treasures. Taking him by his head, she struck the bolt a blow with his squatting posteriors. The two doors creaked, sagged, and swung weakly inward a little way, as if they were too old for such escapades. Eden tossed the heavy idol into a stuffed chair. 'That's better,' she exclaimed exultantly. 'So the bolts are always on the lady's side? What a lot society takes for granted!'

Hedger laughed, sprang up and caught her arms roughly. 'Whoever takes you for granted – Did anybody, ever?'

'Everybody does. That's why I'm here. You are the only one who knows anything about me. Now I'll have to dress if we're going out for dinner.'

He lingered, keeping his hold on her. 'But I won't always be the only one, Eden Bower. I won't be the last.'

'No, I suppose not,' she said carelessly. 'But what does that matter? You are the first.'

As a long, despairing whine broke in the warm stillness, they drew apart. Caesar, lying on his bed in the dark corner, had lifted his head at this invasion of sunlight, and realized that the side of his room was broken open, and his whole world shattered by change. There stood his master and this woman, laughing at him! The woman was pulling the long black hair of this mightiest of men, who bowed his head and permitted it.

VI

In time they quarrelled, of course, and about an abstraction, – as young people often do, as mature people almost never do. Eden came in late one afternoon. She had been with some of her musical friends to lunch at Burton Ives' studio, and she began telling Hedger about its splendours. He listened a moment and then threw down his brushes. 'I know exactly what it's like,' he said impatiently. 'A very good department-store conception of a studio. It's one of the show places.'

'Well, it's gorgeous, and he said I could bring you to see him. The boys tell me he's awfully kind about giving people a lift, and you might get something out of it.'

Hedger started up and pushed his canvas out of the way. 'What could I possibly get from Burton Ives? He's almost the worst painter in the world; the stupidest, I mean.'

Eden was annoyed. Burton Ives had been very nice to her and had begged her to sit for him. 'You must admit that he's a very successful one,' she said coldly.

'Of course he is! Anybody can be successful who will do that sort of thing. I wouldn't paint his pictures for all the money in New York.'

'Well, I saw a lot of them, and I think they are beautiful.'

Hedger bowed stiffly.

'What's the use of being a great painter if nobody knows about you?' Eden went on persuasively. 'Why don't you paint the kind of pictures people can understand, and then, after you're successful, do whatever you like?'

'As I look at it,' said Hedger brusquely, 'I am successful.'

Eden glanced about. 'Well, I don't see any evidences of it,' she said, biting her lip. 'He has a Japanese servant and a wine cellar, and keeps a riding horse.'

Hedger melted a little. 'My dear, I have the most expensive luxury in the world, and I am much more extravagant than Burton Ives, for I work to please nobody but myself.'

'You mean you could make money and don't? That you don't try to get a public?'

'Exactly. A public only wants what has been done over and over. I'm painting for painters, – who haven't been born.'

'What would you do if I brought Mr Ives down here to see your things?'

'Well, for God's sake, don't! Before he left I'd probably tell him what I thought of him.'

Eden rose. 'I give you up. You know very well there's only one kind of success that's real.'

'Yes, but it's not the kind you mean. So you've been thinking me a scrub painter, who needs a helping hand from some fashionable studio man? What the devil have you had anything to do with me for, then?'

'There's no use talking to you,' said Eden walking slowly toward the door. 'I've been trying to pull wires for you all afternoon, and this is what it comes to.' She had expected that the tidings of a prospective call from the great man would be received very differently, and had been thinking as she came home in the stage how, as with a magic wand, she might gild Hedger's future, float him out of his dark hole on a tide of prosperity, see his name in the papers and his pictures in the windows on Fifth Avenue.

Hedger mechanically snapped the midsummer leash on Caesar's collar and they ran downstairs and hurried through Sullivan Street off toward the river. He wanted to be among rough, honest people, to get down where the big drays bumped over stone paving blocks and the men wore corduroy trousers and kept their shirts open at the neck. He stopped for a drink in one of the sagging bar-rooms on the water front. He had never in his life been so deeply wounded; he did not know he could be so hurt. He had told this girl all his secrets. On the roof, in these warm, heavy summer nights, with her hands locked in his, he had been able to explain all his misty ideas about an unborn art the world was waiting for; had been able to explain them better than he had ever done to himself. And she had looked away to the chattels of this uptown studio and coveted them for him! To her he was only an unsuccessful Burton Ives.

Then why, as he had put it to her, did she take up with him? Young, beautiful, talented as she was, why had she wasted herself on a scrub? Pity? Hardly; she wasn't sentimental. There was no explaining her. But in this passion that had seemed so fearless and so fated to be, his own position now looked to him ridiculous; a poor dauber without money or fame, – it was her caprice to load him with favours. Hedger ground his teeth so loud that his dog, trotting beside him, heard him and looked up.

While they were having supper at the oysterman's, he planned his escape. Whenever he saw her again, everything he had told her, that he should never have told any one, would come back to him; ideas he had never whispered even to the painter whom he worshipped and had gone all the way to France to see. To her they must seem his apology for not having horses and a valet, or merely the puerile boastfulness of a weak man. Yet if she slipped the bolt tonight and came through the doors and said, 'Oh, weak man, I belong to you!' what could he do? That was the danger. He would catch the train out to Long Beach tonight, and tomorrow he would go on to the north end of Long Island, where an old friend of his had a summer studio among the sand dunes. He would stay until things came right in his mind. And she could find a smart painter, or take her punishment.

When he went home, Eden's room was dark; she was dining out somewhere. He threw his things into a holdall he had carried about the world with him, strapped up some colours and canvases, and ran downstairs.

VII

Five days later Hedger was a restless passenger on a dirty, crowded Sunday train, coming back to town. Of course he saw now how unreasonable he had been in expecting a Huntington girl to know anything about pictures; here was a whole continent full of people who knew nothing about pictures and he didn't hold it against them. What had such things to do with him and Eden Bower? When he lay out on the dunes, watching the moon come up out of the sea, it had seemed to him that there was no wonder in the world like the wonder of Eden Bower. He was going back to her because she was older than art, because she was the most overwhelming thing that had ever come into his life.

He had written her yesterday, begging her to be at home this evening, telling her that he was contrite, and wretched enough.

Now that he was on his way to her, his stronger feeling unaccountably changed to a mood that was playful and tender. He wanted to share everything with her, even the most trivial things. He wanted to tell her about the people on the train, coming back tired from their holiday with bunches of wilted flowers and dirty daisies; to tell her that the fish-man, to whom she had often sent him for lobsters, was among the passengers, disguised in a silk shirt and a spotted tie, and how his wife looked exactly like a fish, even to her eyes, on which cataracts were forming. He could tell her too, that he hadn't as much as unstrapped his canvases, – that ought to convince her.

In those days passengers from Long Island came into New York by ferry. Hedger had to be quick about getting his dog out of the express car in order to catch the first boat. The East River, and the bridges, and the city to the west, were burning in the conflagration of the sunset; there was that great home-coming reach of evening in the air.

The car changes from Thirty-fourth Street were too many and too perplexing; for the first time in his life Hedger took a hansom cab for Washington Square. Caesar sat bolt upright on the worn leather cushion beside him, and they jogged off, looking down on the rest of the world.

It was twilight when they drove down lower Fifth Avenue into the Square, and through the Arch behind them were the two long rows of pale violet lights that used to bloom so beautifully against the grey stone and asphalt. Here and yonder about the Square hung globes that shed a radiance not unlike the blue mists of evening, emerging softly when daylight died, as the stars emerged in the thin blue sky. Under them the sharp shadows of the trees fell on the cracked pavement and the sleeping grass. The first stars and the first lights were growing silver against the gradual darkening, when Hedger paid his driver and went into the house, – which, thank God, was still there! On the hall table lay his letter of yesterday, unopened.

He went upstairs with every sort of fear and every sort of hope clutching at his heart; it was as if tigers were tearing him. Why was there no gas burning in the top hall? He found matches and the gas bracket. He knocked, but got no answer; nobody was there. Before his own door were exactly five bottles of milk, standing in a row. The milk-boy had taken spiteful pleasure in thus reminding him that he forgot to stop his order.

Hedger went down to the basement; it, too, was dark. The janitress was taking her evening airing on the basement steps. She sat waving a palm-leaf fan majestically, her dirty calico dress open at the neck. She told him at once that there had been 'changes.' Miss Bower's room was to let again, and the piano would go tomorrow. Yes, she left yesterday, she sailed for Europe with friends from Chicago. They arrived on Friday, heralded by many telegrams. Very rich people they were said to be, though the man had refused to pay the nurse a month's rent in lieu of notice, – which would have been only right, as the young lady had agreed to take the rooms until October. Mrs Foley had observed, too, that he didn't overpay her or Willy for their trouble, and a great deal of trouble they had been put to, certainly. Yes, the young lady was very pleasant, but the nurse said there were rings on the mahogany table where she had put tumblers and wine glasses. It was just as well she was gone. The Chicago man was uppish in his ways, but not much to look at. She supposed he had poor health, for there was nothing to him inside his clothes.

Hedger went slowly up the stairs – never had they seemed so long, or his legs so heavy. The upper floor was emptiness and silence. He unlocked his room, lit the gas, and opened the windows. When he went to put his coat in the closet, he found, hanging among his clothes, a pale, flesh-tinted dressing gown he had liked to see her wear, with a perfume – oh, a perfume that was still Eden Bower! He shut the door behind him and there, in the dark, for a moment he lost his manliness. It was when he held this garment to him that he found a letter in the pocket.

The note was written with a lead pencil, in haste: She was sorry that he was angry, but she still didn't know just what she had done. She had thought Mr Ives would be useful to him; she guessed he was too proud. She wanted awfully to see him again, but Fate came knocking at her door after he had left her. She believed in Fate. She would never forget him, and she knew he would become the greatest painter in the world. Now she must pack. She hoped he wouldn't mind her leaving the dressing gown; somehow, she could never wear it again.

After Hedger read this, standing under the gas, he went back into the closet and knelt down before the wall; the knot hole had been plugged up with a ball of wet paper, – the same blue note-paper on which her letter was written.

He was hard hit. Tonight he had to bear the loneliness of a whole lifetime. Knowing himself so well, he could hardly believe that such a thing had ever happened to him, that such a woman had lain happy and contented in his arms. And now it was over. He turned out the light and sat down on his painter's stool before the big window. Caesar, on the floor beside him, rested his head on his master's knee. We must leave Hedger thus, sitting in his tank with his dog, looking up at the stars.

COMING, APHRODITE! This legend, in electric lights over the Lexington Opera House, had long announced the return of Eden Bower to New York after years of spectacular success in Paris. She came at last, under the management of an American Opera Company, but bringing her own *chef d'orchestre*.

One bright December afternoon Eden Bower was going down Fifth Avenue in her car, on the way to her broker, in Williams Street. Her thoughts were entirely upon stocks, – Cerro de Pasco, and how much she should buy of it, – when she suddenly looked up and realized that she was skirting

Washington Square. She had not seen the place since she rolled out of it in an old-fashioned four-wheeler to seek her fortune, eighteen years ago.

'*Arrêtez, Alphonse. Attendez moi,*' she called, and opened the door before he could reach it. The children who were streaking over the asphalt on roller skates saw a lady in a long fur coat, and short, high-heeled shoes, alight from a French car and pace slowly about the Square, holding her muff to her chin. This spot, at least, had changed very little, she reflected; the same trees, the same fountain, the white arch, and over yonder, Garibaldi, drawing the sword for freedom. There, just opposite her, was the old red brick house.

'Yes, that is the place,' she was thinking. 'I can smell the carpets now, and the dog, – what was his name? That grubby bathroom at the end of the hall, and that dreadful Hedger – still, there was something about him, you know –' She glanced up and blinked against the sun. From somewhere in the crowded quarter south of the Square a flock of pigeons rose, wheeling quickly upward into the brilliant blue sky. She threw back her head, pressed her muff closer to her chin, and watched them with a smile of amazement and delight. So they still rose, out of all that dirt and noise and squalor, fleet and silvery, just as they used to rise that summer when she was twenty and went up in a balloon on Coney Island!

Alphonse opened the door and tucked her robes about her. All the way down town her mind wandered from Cerro de Pasco, and she kept smiling and looking up at the sky.

When she had finished her business with the broker, she asked him to look in the telephone book for the address of M. Gaston Jules, the picture dealer, and slipped the paper on which he wrote it into her glove. It was five o'clock when she reached the French Galleries, as they were called. On entering she gave the attendant her card, asking him to take it to M. Jules. The dealer appeared very promptly and begged her to come into his private office, where he pushed a great chair toward his desk for her and signalled his secretary to leave the room.

'How good your lighting is in here,' she observed, glancing about. 'I met you at Simon's studio, didn't I? Oh, no! I never forget anybody who interests me.' She threw her muff on his writing table and sank into the deep chair. 'I have come to you for some information that's not in my line. Do you know anything about an American painter named Hedger?'

He took the seat opposite her. 'Don Hedger? But, certainly! There are some very interesting things of his in an exhibition at V—'s. If you would care to –'

She held up her hand.'No, no. I've no time to go to exhibitions. Is he a man of any importance?'

'Certainly. He is one of the first men among the moderns. That is to say, among the very moderns. He is always coming up with something different. He often exhibits in Paris, you must have seen –'

'No, I tell you I don't go to exhibitions. Has he had great success? That is what I want to know.'

M. Jules pulled at his short grey moustache. 'But, Madame, there are many kinds of success,' he began cautiously.

Madame gave a dry laugh. 'Yes, so he used to say. We once quarrelled on that issue. And how would you define his particular kind?'

M. Jules grew thoughtful. 'He is a great name with all the young men, and he is decidedly an influence in art. But one can't definitely place a man who is original, erratic, and who is changing all the time.'

She cut him short. 'Is he much talked about at home? In Paris, I mean? Thanks. That's all I want to know.' She rose and began buttoning her coat. 'One doesn't like to have been an utter fool, even at twenty.'

'*Mais, non!*' M. Jules handed her her muff with a quick, sympathetic glance. He followed her out through the carpeted show-room, now closed to the public and draped in cheesecloth, and put her into her car with words appreciative of the honour she had done him in calling.

Leaning back in the cushions, Eden Bower closed her eyes, and her face, as the street lamps flashed their ugly orange light upon it, became hard and settled, like a plaster cast; so a sail, that has been filled by a strong breeze, behaves when the wind suddenly dies. Tomorrow night the wind would blow again, and this mask would be the golden face of Aphrodite. But a 'big' career takes its toll, even with the best of luck.

First published in *Smart Set*, August 1920.

UNCLE VALENTINE
(ADAGIO NON TROPPO)

ONE morning not long ago I heard Louise Ireland give a singing lesson to a young countrywoman of mine, in her studio in Paris. Ireland must be quite sixty now, but there is not a break in the proud profile; she is still beautiful, still the joy of men, young and old. To hear her give a lesson is to hear a fine performance. The pupil was a girl of exceptional talent, handsome and intelligent, but she had the characteristic deficiency of her generation – she found nothing remarkable. She realized that she was fortunate to get in a few lessons with Ireland, but good fortune was what she expected, and she probably thought Ireland didn't every day find such good material to work with.

When the vocal lesson was over the girl said, 'May I try that song you told me to look at?'

'If you wish. Have you done anything with it?'

'I've worked on it a little.' The young woman unstrapped a roll of music. 'I've tried over most of the songs in this book. I'm crazy about them. I never heard of Valentine Ramsay before.'

'Sad for him,' murmured the teacher.

'Was he English?'

'No, American, like you,' sarcastically.

'I went back to the shop for more of his things, but they had only this one collection. Didn't he do any others?'

'A few. But these are the best.'

'But I don't understand. If he could do things like these, why didn't he keep it up? What prevented him?'

'Oh, the things that always prevent one: marriage, money, friends, the general social order. Finally a motor truck prevented him, one of the first in Paris. He was struck and killed one night, just out of the window there, as he was going on to the Pont Royal. He was barely thirty.'

The girl said 'Oh!' in a subdued voice, and actually crossed the room to look out of the window.

'If you wish to know anything further about him, this American lady can tell you. She knew him in his own country. Now I'll see what you've done with that.' Ireland shook her loose sleeves back from her white arms and began to play the song:

I know a wall where red roses grow . . .

I

Yes, I had known Valentine Ramsay. I knew him in a lovely place, at a lovely time, in a bygone period of American life; just at the incoming of this century which has made all the world so different.

I was a girl of sixteen, living with my aunt and uncle at Fox Hill, in Greenacre. My mother and father had died young, leaving me and my little sister, Betty Jane, with scant provision for our future. Aunt Charlotte and Uncle Harry Waterford took us to live with them, and brought us up with their own four little daughters. Harriet, their oldest girl, was two years younger than I, and Elizabeth, the youngest, was just the age of Betty Jane. When cousins agree at all, they agree better than sisters, and we were all extraordinarily happy. The Ramsays were our nearest neighbors; their place, Bonnie Brae, sat on the same hilltop as ours – a houseful of lonely men (and such strange ones!) tyrannized over by a Swedish woman who was housekeeper.

Greenacre was a little railway station where every evening dogcarts and carriages drew up and waited for the express that brought the business men down from the City, and then rolled them along smooth roads to their dwellings, scattered about on the fine line of hills, clad with forest, that rose above a historic American river.

The City up the river it is scarcely necessary to name; a big inland American manufacturing city, older and richer and gloomier than most, also more powerful and important. Greenacre was not a suburb in the modern sense. It was as old as the City, and there were no small holdings. The people who lived there had been born there, and inherited their land from fathers and grandfathers. Every householder had his own stables and pasture land, and hay meadows and orchard. There were plenty of servants in those days.

My Aunt Charlotte lived in the house where she was born, and ever since her marriage she had been playing with it and enlarging it, as if she had foreseen that she was one day to have a large family on her hands. She loved that house and she loved to work on it, making it always more and more just as she wanted it to be, and yet keeping it what it always had been – a big, rambling, hospitable old country house. As one drove up the hill from the station, Fox Hill, under its tall oaks and sycamores, looked like several old farmhouses pieced together; uneven roofs with odd gables and dormer windows sticking out, porches on different levels connected by sagging steps. It was all in the dull tone of scaling brown paint and old brown wood – though often, as we came up the hill in the late afternoon, the sunset flamed wonderfully on the diamond-paned windows that were so gray and inconspicuous by day.

The house kept its rusty outer shell, like an old turtle's, all the while that it was growing richer in color and deeper in comfort within. These changes were made very cautiously, very delicately. Though my aunt was constantly making changes, she was terribly afraid of them. When she brought things back from Spain or Italy for her house, they used to stay in the barn, in their packing cases, for months before she would even try them. Then some day, when we children were all at school and she was alone, they would be smuggled in one at a time – sometimes to vanish forever after a day or two. There was something she wanted to get, in this corner or that, but there was something she was even more afraid of losing. The boldest enterprise she ever undertook was the construction of the new music-room, on the north side of the house, towards the Ramsays'. Even that was done very quietly, by the village workmen. The piano was moved out into the big square hall, and the door between the hall and the scene of the carpenters' activities was closed up. When, after a month or so, it was opened again, there was the new music-room, a proper room for chamber music, such as the petty kings and grand dukes of old Germany had in their castles; finished and empty, as it was to remain; nothing to be seen but a long room of satisfying proportions, with many wax candles flickering in the polish of the dark wooden walls and floor.

It was into this music-room that Aunt Charlotte called Harriet and me one November afternoon to tell us that Valentine Ramsay was coming home. She was sitting at the piano with a book of Debussy's piano pieces open before her. His music was little known in America then, but when she was alone she played it a great deal. She took a letter from between the leaves of the book. There was a flutter of excitement in her voice and in her features as she told us: 'He says he will take the next fast steamer after his letter. He must be on the water now.'

'Oh, aren't you happy, Aunt Charlotte!' I cried, knowing well how fond she was of him.

'Very, Marjorie. And a little troubled too. I'm not quite sure that people will be nice to him. The Oglethorpes are very influential, and now that Janet is living here – '

'But she's married again.'

'Nevertheless, people feel that Valentine behaved very badly. He'll be here for Christmas, and I've been thinking what we can do for him. We must work very hard on our part songs. Good singing pleases him more than anything. I've been hoping he may fall into the way of composing again while he's with us. His life has been so distracted for the last few years that he's almost given up writing songs.

Go to the playroom, Harriet, and tell the little girls to get their school work done early. We'll have a long rehearsal tonight. I suppose they scarcely remember him.'

Three years before Valentine Ramsay had been at home for several weeks before his brother Horace died. Even at that sad time his being there was like a holiday for us children, and all the Greenacre people seemed glad to have him back again. But much had happened since then. Valentine had deserted his wife for a singer, notorious for her beauty and misconduct; had, as my friends at school often told me, utterly disgraced himself. His wife, Janet Oglethorpe, was now living in her house in the City. I had seen her twice at Saturday matinées, and I didn't wonder that Valentine had run away with a beautiful woman. The second time I saw her very well – it was a charity performance, and she was sitting in a box with her new husband, a young man who was the perfection of good tailoring, who was reputed handsome, who appeared so, indeed, until you looked closely into his vain, apprehensive face. He was immensely conceited, but not sure of himself, and kept arranging his features as he talked to the women in the box. As for Janet, I thought her an unattractive red-faced woman, very ordinary, as we said. Aunt Charlotte murmured in my ear that she had once been better looking, but that after her marriage with Valentine she had grown stouter and 'coarsened' – my aunt hurried over the word.

Aunt Charlotte had never, I knew, approved of the marriage. When he was a little boy Valentine had been her squire and had loved her devotedly. After his mother died, leaving him in a houseful of grown men, she had looked out for him and tried to direct his studies. She was ten years older than Valentine, and, in the years when Uncle Harry came a-courting, the spoiled neighbor boy was always hanging about and demanding attention. He had a pretty talent for the piano, and for composition; but he wouldn't work regularly at anything, and there was no one to make him. He drifted along until he was a young fellow of twenty, and then he met Janet Oglethorpe.

Valentine had a habit of running up to the City to dawdle about the Steinerts' music store and practice on their pianos. The two young Steinert lads were musical and were great friends of his. It was there, when she went in to buy tickets for a concert, that Janet Oglethorpe first saw Valentine and heard him play. He was a strikingly handsome boy, and picturesque – certainly very different from the canny Oglethorpe men and their friends. Janet took to him at once, began inviting him to the house and asking musicians there to meet him. The Ramsays were greatly pleased; the Oglethorpes were the richest family in a whole cityful of rich people. They owned mines and mills and oil wells and gas works and farms and banks. Unlike some of our great Scotch families, they didn't become idlers and coupon-clippers in the third generation. They held their edge – kept their keenness for money as if they were just beginning, must sink or swim, and hadn't millions behind them. Janet was one of the third generation, and it was well known that she was as shrewd in business as old Duncan himself, the founder of the Oglethorpe fortune, who was still living, having buried three wives, and spry enough to attend directors' meetings and make plenty of trouble for the young men.

Janet was older than Valentine in years, and much older in experience and judgment. Even after she had announced her engagement to him, Aunt Charlotte prevailed upon him to go abroad to study for a little. He was happily settled in Paris, under Saint-Saëns, but before the year was out Janet followed him up and married him. They lived abroad. Aunt Charlotte visited them in Rome, but she never said much about them.

Later, when the scandal came, and everyone in the City, and in Greenacre as well, fell upon Valentine for a worthless scamp, Uncle Harry and Aunt Charlotte always stood up for him, and said that when Janet married a flighty student she took the chance with her eyes open. Some of our friends insisted that he had shattered himself with drink, like so many of the Ramsay men; others hinted that he must 'take something', meaning drugs. No one could believe that a man entirely in his right mind would run away from so much money – toss it overboard, mills and mines, stocks and bonds; and that when he had none himself, and Bonnie Brae was plastered with mortgages, and old Uncle Jonathan had already two helpless men to take care of.

II

For ten days after his letter came we waited and waited for Valentine. Everyone was restless – except Uncle Jonathan, who often told us that he enjoyed anticipation as much as realization. Uncle Morton, Valentine's much older brother, used to stumble in of an evening, when we were all gathered in the big hall after dinner, to announce the same news about boats that he had given us the evening before, wave his long thin hands a little, and boast in a husky voice about his gifted brother. Aunt Charlotte put her impatience to some account by rehearsing us industriously in the part songs we were working up for Valentine. She called us her sextette, and she trained us very well. Several of us were said to have good voices. My aunt used to declare that she liked us better when we were singing than at any other time, and that drilling us was the chief pleasure she got out of having such a large family.

Aunt Charlotte was the person who felt all that went on about her – and all that did not go on – and understood it. I find that I did not know her very well then. It was not until years afterwards, not until after her death, indeed, that I began really to know her. Recalling her quickly, I see a dark, full-figured woman, dressed in dark, rich materials; I remember certain velvet dresses, brown, claret-colored, deep violet, which especially became her, and certain fur hats and capes and coats. Though she was a little over-weight, she seemed often to be withdrawing into her clothes, not shrinking, but retiring behind the folds of her heavy cloaks and gowns and soft barricades of fur. She had to do with people constantly, and her house was often overflowing with guests, but she was by nature very shy. I now believe that she suffered all her life from a really painful timidity, and had to keep taking herself in hand. I have said that she was dark; her skin and hair and eyes were all brown. Even when she was out in the garden her face seemed always in shadow.

As a child I understood that my aunt had what we call a strong nature; still, deep and, on the whole, happy. Whatever it is that enables us to make our peace with life, she had found it. She cared more for music than for anything else in the world, and after that for her family and her house and her friends. She was very intelligent, but she had entirely too much respect for the opinions of others. Even in music she was often dominated by people who were much less discerning than she, but more aggressive. If her preference was disputed or challenged, she easily gave up. She knew what she liked, but she was apt to be apologetic about it. When she mentioned a composition or an artist she admired, or spoke the name of a person or place she loved, I remember a dark, rich color used to come into her voice, and sometimes she uttered the name with a curious little intake of the breath.

Aunt Charlotte's real life went on very deep within her, I suspect, though she seemed so open and cordial, and not especially profound. No one ever thought of her as intellectual, though people often spoke of her wonderful taste; of how, without effort, she was able to make her garden and house exactly right. Our old friends considered taste as something quite apart from intelligence, instead of the flower of it. She read little, it is true; what other people learned from books she learned from music, – all she needed to give her a rich enjoyment of art and life. She played the piano extremely well; it was not an accomplishment with her, but a way of living. The rearing of six little girls did not seem to strain her patience much. She allowed us a great deal of liberty and demanded her own in return. We were permitted to have our own thoughts and feelings, and even Elizabeth and Betty Jane understood that it is a great happiness to be permitted to be glad or sorry in one's own way.

III

On the night of Valentine's return, our household went in a body over to Bonnie Brae to make a short call. It was delightful to see the old house looking so festive, with lights streaming from all the windows. We found the family in the long, pale parlor; the men of the house, and half a dozen Ramsay cousins with their wives and children.

Valentine was standing near the fireplace when we entered, beside his father's armchair. The little girls at once tripped down the long room toward him, Uncle Harry following. But Aunt Charlotte stopped short in the doorway and stood there in the shadow of the curtains, watching Valentine across the heads of the company, as if she wished to remain an outsider. Through the buzz and flutter of greetings, his eyes found her there. He left the others, crossed the room in a flash, and, giving her a quick, sidewise look, put down his head to be kissed, like a little boy. As he stood there for a moment, so close to us, he struck me at once as altogether too young to have had so much history, as very hardy and high-colored and unsubdued. His thick, seal-brown hair grew on his head exactly like fur, there was no part in it anywhere. His short mustache and eyebrows had the same furry look. His red lips and white teeth gave him a striking freshness – there was something very roguish and wayward, very individual about his mouth. He seldom looked at one when he talked to one – he had a habit of frowning at the floor or looking fixedly at some object when he was speaking, but one felt his eyes through the lowered lids – felt his pleasure or his annoyance, his affection or impatience.

Since gay Uncle Horace died the Ramsay men did not often give parties, and that night they roamed about somewhat uneasily, all but Uncle Jonathan, who was always superbly at his ease. He kept his armchair, with a cape about his shoulders to protect him from drafts. The old man's hair and beard were just the color of dirty white snow, and he was averse to having them trimmed. He was a gracious host, having the air of one to whom many congratulations are due. Roland had put on a frock coat and was doing his duty, making himself quite agreeable to everyone. His handsome silver-gray head and fine physique would have added to the distinction of any company. Uncle Morton was wandering about from group to group, jerking his hands this way and that – a curiously individual gesture from the wrist, as if he were making signals from a world too remote for speech. He fastened himself upon me, as he was very likely to do (finding me out in the little corner sofa to which I had retreated), sat down beside me and began talking about his brother in disconnected sentences, trying to focus his almost insensible eyes upon me.

'My brother is very devoted to your aunt. She must help me with his studio. We are going to make a studio for him off in the wing, for the quiet. Something very nice. I think I shall have the walls upholstered, like cushions, to keep the noise out. It will be handsome, you understand. We can give parties there – receptions. My brother is a fine musician. Could play anything when he was eleven – classical music – the most difficult compositions.' In the same expansive spirit Uncle Morton had once planned a sunken garden for my aunt, and a ballroom for Harriet and me.

Molla Carlsen brought in cake and port and sherry. She had been at the door to admit us, and had since been intermittently in the background, disappearing and reappearing as if she were much occupied. She had always this air of moving quietly and efficiently in her own province. Molla was very correct in deportment, was there and not too much there. She was fair, and good looking, very. The only fault Aunt Charlotte had to find with her appearance was the way she wore her hair. It was yellow enough to be showy in any case, and she made it more so by parting it very low on one side, just over her left ear, indeed, so that it lay across her head in a long curly wave, making her low forehead lower still and giving her an air that, as some of our neighbors declared, was little short of 'tough'.

After we had sipped our wine the cousins began to gather up their babies for departure, and we younger ones had all to go up to Uncle Jonathan and kiss him good night. It was a rite we shrank from, he was always so strong of tobacco and snuff, but he liked to kiss us, and there was no escape.

When we left, Uncle Valentine put his arm through Aunt Charlotte's and walked with us as far as the summerhouse, looking about him and up overhead through the trees. I heard him say suddenly, as if it had just struck him:

'Isn't it funny, Charlotte; no matter how much things or people ought to be different, what we love them for is for being just the same!'

IV

The next afternoon when Harriet and I got home from Miss Demming's school, we heard two pianos going, and knew that Uncle Valentine was there. The door between the big hall and the music-room was open, and Aunt Charlotte called to us:

'Harriet and Marjorie? Run upstairs and make yourselves neat. You may have tea with us presently.'

When we came down, the music had ceased, and the hall was empty. Black John, coming through with a plate of toast, told us he had taken tea into the study.

My uncle's study was my favorite spot in that house full of lovely places. It was a little room just off the library, very quiet, like a little pond off the main currents of the house. There was but one door, and no one ever passed through it on the way to another room. As it had formerly been a conservatory for winter flowers, it was all glass on two sides, with heavy curtains one could draw at night to shut out the chill. There was always a little coal fire in the grate, Uncle Harry's favorite books on the shelves, and the new ones he was reading arranged on the table, along with his

pipes and tobacco jars. Sitting beside the red coals one could
look out into the great forking sycamore limbs, with their
mottled bark of white and olive green, and off across the bare
tops of the winter trees that grew down the hill slopes – until
finally one looked into nothingness, into the great stretch of
open sky above the river, where the early sunsets burned or
brooded over our valley. It was with delight I heard we were to
have our tea there.

We found my aunt and Valentine before the grate, the
steaming samovar between them, the glass room full of gray
light, a little warmed by the glowing coals.

'Aren't you surprised to find us here?' There was just a
shade of embarrassment in my aunt's voice. 'This was Uncle
Valentine's choice.' Curious; though she always looked so at
ease, so calm in her matronly figure, a little thing like having
tea in an unusual room could make her a trifle self-conscious
and apologetic.

Valentine, in brown corduroy with a soft shirt and a
Chinese-red necktie, was sitting in Uncle Harry's big chair,
one foot tucked under him. He told us he had been all over the
hills that morning, clear up to Flint Ridge. 'I came home by the
near side of Blinker's Hill, past the Wakeley place. I wish Belle
wouldn't stay abroad so long; it's a shame to keep that jolly old
house shut up.' He said he liked having tea in the study
because the outlook was the same as from his upstairs room at
home. 'I was always supposed to be doing lessons there as
evening came on. I'm sure I don't know what I was doing –
writing serenades for you, probably, Charlotte.'

Aunt Charlotte was nursing the samovar along – it never
worked very well. 'I've been hoping,' she murmured, 'that
you would bring me home some new serenades – or songs of
some kind.'

'Songs? Oh, hell, Charlotte!' He jerked his foot from under
him and sat up straight. 'Sorry I swore, but you evidently
don't know what I've been up against these last four years.
You'll have to know, and so will your maidens fair. Anyhow, if
you're to have a rake next door to a houseful of daughters,
you'd better look into it.'

Aunt Charlotte caught her breath painfully, glanced at Harriet and me and then at the door. Valentine sprang up, went to the door and closed it. 'Oh, don't look so frightened!' he exclaimed irritably, 'and don't send the girls away. Do you suppose they've heard nothing? What to you think girls whisper about at school, anyway? You'd better let me explain a little.'

'I think it unnecessary,' she murmured entreatingly.

'You mean they'll think what you tell them to — stay where you put them, like china shepherdesses. Well, they won't!'

We were almost as much frightened as Aunt Charlotte. He was standing before us, his brow wrinkled in a heavy frown, his shoulders lowered, his red lips thrust out petulantly. I am sure I was hoping that he wouldn't quite explain away the legend of his awful wickedness. As he addressed us he looked not at us but at the floor.

'You've heard, haven't you, Harriet and Marjorie, that I deserted a noble wife and ran away with a wicked woman? Well, she wasn't a wicked woman. She is kind and generous, and she ran away with me out of charity, to get me out of the awful mess I was in. The mess, you understand, was just being married to this noble wife. Janey is all right for her own kind, for Oglethorpes in general, but she was all wrong for me.'

Here he stopped and made a wry face, as if his pedagogical tone put a bad taste in his mouth. He glanced at my aunt for help, but she was looking steadfastly at the samovar.

'Hang it, Charlotte,' he broke out, 'these girls are not in the nursery! They must hear what they hear and think what they think. It's got to come out. You know well enough what dear Janey is; you've known ever since you stayed with us in Rome. She's a common, energetic, close-fisted little tradeswoman, who ought to be keeping a shop and doing people out of their eyeteeth. She thinks, day and night, about common, trivial, worthless things. And what's worse, she talks about them day and night. She bargains in her sleep. It's what she can get out of this dressmaker or that porter; it's getting the royal suite in a hotel for the price of some other suite. We left you in Rome and dashed off to Venice that fall because she could get a palazzo at a bargain. Some English people had to go home on account of a grandmother dying and had to sub-let in a hurry. That was her only reason for going to Venice. And when we got there she did nothing but beat the house servants down to lower wages, and get herself burned red as a lobster staying out in boats all day to get her money's worth. I was dragged about the world for five years in an atmosphere of commonness and meanness and coarseness. I tell you I was paralyzed by the flood of the trivial, vulgar nagging that poured over me and never stopped. Even Dickie – I might have had some fun with the little chap, but she never let me. She never let me have any but the most painful relations with him. With two nurses sitting idle, she'd make me chase off in a cab to demand his linen from special laundresses, or scurry around a whole day to find some silly kind of milk – all utter nonsense. The child was never sick and could take any decent milk. But she likes to make a fuss; calls it "managing".

'Sometimes I used to try to get off by myself long enough to return to consciousness, to find whether I had any consciousness left to return to – but she always came pelting after. I got off to Bayreuth one time. Thought I'd covered my tracks so well. She arrived in the middle of the Ring. My God, the agony of having to sit through music with that woman!' Valentine sat down and wiped his forehead. It glistened with perspiration; the roots of his furry hair were quite wet.

After a moment he said doggedly, 'I give you my word, Charlotte, there was nothing for it but to make a scandal; to hurt her pride so openly that she'd have to take action. I don't know that she'd have done it then, if Seymour Towne hadn't turned up to sympathize with her. You can't hurt anybody as beefy as that without being a butcher!' He shuddered.

'Louise Ireland offered to be the sacrifice. She hadn't

much to lose in the way of – well, of the proprieties, of course. But she's a glorious creature. I couldn't have done it with a horrid woman. Don't think anything nasty of her, any of you, I won't have it. Everything she does is lovely, somehow or other, just as every song she sings is more beautiful than it ever was before. She's been more or less irregular in behavior – as you've doubtless heard with augmentation. She had certainly run away with desperate men before. But behavior, I find, is more or less accidental, Charlotte. Oh, don't look so scared! Your dovelets will have to face facts some day. Aesthetics come back to predestination, if theology doesn't. A woman's behavior may be irreproachable and she herself may be gross – just gross. She may do her duty, and defile everything she touches. And another woman may be erratic, imprudent, self-indulgent if you like, and all the while be – what is it the Bible says? Pure in heart. People are as they are, and that's all there is to life. And now –' Valentine got up and went toward the door to open it.

Aunt Charlotte came out of her lethargy and held up her finger. 'Valentine,' she said with a deep breath, 'I wasn't afraid of letting the girls hear what you had to say – not exactly afraid. But I thought it unnecessary. I understood everything as soon as I looked at you last night. One hasn't watched people from their childhood for nothing.'

He wheeled round to her. 'Of course *you* would know! But these girls aren't you, my dear! I doubt if they ever will be, even with luck!' The tone in which he said this, the proud, sidelong glance he flashed upon her, made this a rich and beautiful compliment – so violent a one that it seemed almost to hurt that timid woman. Slowly, slowly, the red burned up in her dark cheeks, and it was a long while dying down.

'Now we've finished with this – what a relief!' Valentine knelt down on the window seat between Harriet and me and put an arm lightly around each of us. 'There's a fine sunset coming on, come and look at it, Charlotte.'

We huddled together, looking out over the descending

knolls of bare tree tops into the open space over the river, where the smoky gray atmosphere was taking on a purple tinge, like some thick liquid changing color. The sun, which had all day been a shallow white ring, emerged and swelled into an orange-red globe. It hung there without changing, as if the density of the atmosphere supported it and would not let it sink. We sat hushed and still, living in some strong wave of feeling or memory that came up in our visitor. Valentine had that power of throwing a mood over people. There was nothing imaginary about it; it was as real as any form of pain or pleasure. One had only to look at Aunt Charlotte's face, which had become beautiful, to know that.

It was Uncle Harry who brought us back into the present again. He had caught an early train down from the City, hoping to come upon us just like this, he said. He was almost pathetically eager for anything of this sort he could get, and was glad to come in for cold toast and tea.

'Awfully happy I got here before Valentine got away,' he said, as he turned on the light. 'And, Charlotte, how rosy you are! It takes you to do that to her, Val.' She still had the dusky color which had been her unwilling response to Valentine's compliment.

V

Within a few days Uncle Valentine ran over to beg my aunt to go shopping with him. Something had reminded him that Christmas was very near.

'It's awfully embarrassing,' he said. 'Nobody in Paris was saying anything about Christmas before I sailed. Here I've come home with empty trunks, and Paris full of things that everybody wants.'

Aunt Charlotte laughed at him and said she thought they would find plenty of things from Paris up in the City.

The next morning Valentine appeared before we left for school. He was in a very businesslike mood, and his check book was sticking out from the breast pocket of his fur coat. They were to catch the eight-thirty train. The day was dark and gray, I remember, though our valley was white, for there had been a snowfall the day before. Standing on the porch with my school satchel, I watched them get into the carriage and go down the hill as the train whistled for the station below ours – they would just have time to catch it. Aunt Charlotte looked so happy. She didn't often have Valentine to herself for a whole day. Well, she deserved it.

I could follow them in my mind: Valentine with his brilliant necktie and foreign-cut clothes, hurrying about the shops, so lightning-quick, when all the men they passed in the street were so slow and ponderous or, when they weren't ponderous, stiff – stiff because they were wooden, or because they weren't wooden and were in constant dread of betraying it. Everybody would be trying not to look at bright-colored, foreign-living, disgracefully divorced Valentine Ramsay; some in contempt – some in secret envy, because everything about him told how free he was. And up there, nobody was free. They were imprisoned in their harsh Calvinism, or in their merciless business grind, or in mere apathy – a mortal dullness.

Oh, I could see those two, walking about the narrow streets of the grim, raw, dark gray old city, cold with its river damp, and severe by reason of the brooding frown of huge stone churches that loomed up even in the most congested part of the shopping district. There were old graveyards round those churches, with gravestones sunken and tilted and blackened – covered this morning with dirty snow – and jangling car lines all about them. The street lamps would be burning all day, on account of the fog, full of black smoke from the furnace chimneys. Hidden away in the grime and damp and noise were the half dozen special shops which imported splendors for the owners of those mills that made the city so dark and so powerful.

Their shopping over, Valentine was going to take Aunt Charlotte to lunch at a hotel where they could get a very fine French wine she loved. What a day they would have! There was only one thing to be feared. They might easily chance to meet one of the Oglethorpe men, there were so

many of them, or Janet herself, face to face, or her new
husband, Seymour Towne, who had been the idle son of an
industrious family, and by idling abroad had stepped into
such a good thing that now his hard-working brothers
found life bitter in their mouths.

But they didn't meet with anything disagreeable. They
came home on the four-thirty train, before the rush, bringing their spoils with them (no motor truck deliveries down
the valley in those days), and their faces shone like the
righteous in his Heavenly Father's house. Aunt Charlotte
admitted that she was tired and went upstairs to lie down
directly after tea. Valentine took me down into the music-
room to show me where to put the blossoming mimosa tree
he had found for Aunt Charlotte, when it came down on
the express tomorrow. The little girls followed us, and when
he told them to be still they crept into the corners.

Valentine sat down at the piano and began to play very
softly; something dark and rich and shadowy, but not
somber, with a silvery air flowing through its mysterious-
ness. It might, I thought, be something of Debussy's that I
had never heard . . . but no, I was sure it was not.

Presently he rose abruptly to go without taking leave, but
one of the little girls ran up to him – Helen, probably, she
was the most musical – and asked him what he had been
playing, please.

'Oh, some old thing, I guess. I wasn't thinking,' he
muttered vaguely, and escaped through the glass doors that
led directly into the garden between our house and his. I
felt very sure that it was nothing old, but something new –
just beginning, indeed. That would be a pleasant thing to
tell Aunt Charlotte. I ran upstairs; the door of her room was
ajar, but all was dark within. I entered on tiptoe and
listened; she was sound asleep. What a day she had had!

VI

Aunt Charlotte planned a musical party for Christmas eve
and invited a dozen or more of her old friends. They were

coming home with her after the evening church service; we were to sing carols, and Uncle Valentine was to play. She telephoned the invitations, and made it very clear that Valentine Ramsay was going to be there. Whoever didn't want to meet him could decline. Nobody declined; some even said it would be a pleasure to hear him play again.

On Christmas eve, after dinner, Uncle Harry and I were left alone in the house. All the children went to the church with Aunt Charlotte; she left me to help Black John arrange the table for a late supper after the music. After I had seen to everything, I had an hour or so alone upstairs in my own room.

I well remember how beautiful our valley looked from my window that winter night. Through the creaking, shaggy limbs of the great sycamores I could look off at the white, white landscape; the deep folds of the snow-covered hills, the high drifts over the bushes, the gleaming ice on the broken road, and the thin, gauzy clouds driving across the crystal-clear, star-spangled sky.

Across the garden was Bonnie Bray, with so many windows lighted; the parlor, the library, Uncle Jonathan's room, Morton's room, a yellow patch on the snow from Roland's window, which I could not see; off there, at the end of the long, dark, sagging wing, Valentine's study, lit up like a lantern. I often looked over at our neighbors' house and thought about how much life had gone on in it, and about the muted, mysterious lives that still went on there. In the garret were chests full of old letters; all the highly descriptive letters that Uncle Jonathan had written his wife when he was traveling abroad; family letters, love letters, every letter the boys had written home when they were away at school. And in all these letters were tender references to the garden, the old trees, the house itself. And now so many of those who had loved the old place and danced in the long parlor were dead. I wondered, as young people often do, how my elders had managed to bear life at all, either its killing happiness or its despair.

I heard wheels on the drive, and laughter. Looking out I

saw guests alighting on one side of the house, and on the other side Uncle Valentine running across the garden, bareheaded in the snow. I started downstairs with a little faintness at heart – I knew how much my aunt had counted on bringing Valentine again into the circle of her friends, under her own roof. I found him in the big hall, surrounded by the ladies – they hadn't yet taken off their wraps – and I surveyed them from the second landing where the stairway turned. They were doing their best, I thought. Some of the younger women kept timidly at the outer edge of the group, but all the ones who counted most were emphatic in their cordiality. Deaf old Mrs Hungerford, who rather directed public opinion in Greenacre, patted him on the back, shouted that now the naughty boy had come home to be good, and thrust out her ear trumpet at him. Julia Knewstubb, who for some reason, I never discovered why, was an important person, stood beside him in a brassy, patronizing way, and Ida Milholland, the intellectual light of the valley, began speaking slow, crusty French at him. In short, all was well.

Salutations over, Aunt Charlotte led the way to the music-room and signaled to her six girls. We sang one carol after another, and a fragment of John Bennett's we had especially practiced for Uncle Valentine – a song about a bluebird flying over a gray landscape and making it all blue; a pretty thing for high voices. But when we finished this and looked about to see whether it had pleased him, Valentine was nowhere to be found. Aunt Charlotte drew me aside while the others went out to supper and told me I must search all through the house, go to Bonnie Brae if necessary, and fetch him. It would never do for him to behave thus, when they had unbent so far as to come and greet him.

I looked out of the window and saw a light in his study at the end of the wing. The rooms between his study and the main house were unused, filled with old furniture. He avoided that chain of dusty, echoing chambers and came and went by a back door that opened into the old apple orchard. I dashed across the garden and ran in upon him without knocking.

There he was, lounging before the fire in his slippers and wine-colored velvet jacket, a pipe in his mouth and a yellow French book on his knee. I gasped and explained to him that he must come at once; the company was waiting for him.

He shrugged and waved his pipe. 'I'm not going back at all. Pouf, what's the use? I'd only behave badly if I did. I don't want to lose my temper on Christmas eve.'

'But you promised Aunt Charlotte, and she's told them you'd play,' I pleaded.

He flung down his book wrathfully. 'Oh, I can't stand them! I didn't know who Charlotte was going to ask . . . seems to me she's got together all the most objectionable old birds in the valley. There's Julia Knewstubb, with her nippers hanging on her nose, looking more like a horse than ever. Old Mrs Hungerford, poking her ear trumpet at me and stroking me on the back – I can't talk into an ear trumpet – can't think of anything important enough to say! And that bump of intellect, Ida Milholland, creaking at every joint and practicing her French grammar on me. Charlotte knows that I hate ugly women – what did she get such a bunch together for? Not much, I'm not going back. Sit down and I'll read you something. I've got a new collection of all the legends about Tristan and Iseult. You can understand French?'

I said I would be dreadfully scolded if I did such a thing. 'And you will hurt Aunt Charlotte's feelings, terribly!'

He laughed and poked out his red lower lip at me. 'Shall I? Oh, but I can mend them again! Listen, I've got a new song for her, a good one. You sit down, and we'll work a spell on her; we'll wish and wish, and she'll come running over. While we wait I'll play it for you.'

He put his pipe on the mantel, went to the piano, and commenced to play the Ballad of the Young Knight, which begins:

'From the Ancient Kingdoms,
Through the wood of dreaming . . .'

It was the same thing I had heard him trying out the afternoon he and Aunt Charlotte got home from the City.

'Now, you try it over with me, Margie. It's meant for high voice, you see. By the time she comes, we can give her a good performance.'

'But she won't come, Uncle Valentine! She can't leave her guests.'

'Oh, they'll soon be gone! Old tabbies always get sleepy after supper – you said they were at supper. She'll come.'

I was so excited, so distressed and delighted, that I made a poor showing at reading the manuscript, and was well scolded. Valentine always wrote the words of his songs, as well as the music, like the old troubadours, and the words of this one were beautiful. 'And what wood do you suppose it is?' He played the dark music with his left hand.

I said it made me think of the wood on the other side of Blinker's Hill.

'I guess so,' he muttered. 'But of course it will be different woods to different people. Don't tell Charlotte, but I'm doing a lot of songs. I think of a new one almost every morning, when I waken up. Our woods are full of them, but they're terribly, terribly coy. You can't trap them, they're too wild . . . No, you can't catch them . . . sometimes one comes and lights on your shoulder; I always wonder why.'

It did not seem very long until Aunt Charlotte entered, bareheaded, her long black cape over he shoulders, a look of distress and anxiety on her face. Valentine sprang up and caught her hand.

'Not a word, Charlotte, don't scold, look before you leap! I kept Margie because I knew you'd come to hunt her, and I didn't just know any other way of getting you here. Now don't be angry, because when you get angry your face puffs up just a little, and I have reason to hate women whose faces swell. Sit down by the fire. We've had a rehearsal, and now we'll sing my new song for you. Don't glare at the child, or she can't sing. Why haven't you taught her to follow manuscript better?'

Aunt Charlotte didn't have a chance to speak until we had gone through with the song. But though my eyes were glued to the page, I knew her face was going through many changes.

'Now,' he said exultantly as we finished, 'with a song like that under my shirt, did I have to sit over there and let old Ida wise-bump practice her French on me – period of Bossuet, I guess!'

Aunt Charlotte laughed softly and asked us to sing it again. The second time we did better; Valentine hadn't much voice, but of course he knew how. As we finished we heard a queer sound, something like a snore and something like a groan, in the wall behind us. Valentine held up his finger sharply, tiptoed to the door behind the fireplace that led into the old wing, put down his head and listened for a moment. Then he wrenched open the door.

There stood Roland, holding himself steady by an old chest of drawers, his eyes looking blind, tears shining on his white face. He did not say a word; put his hands to his forehead as if to collect himself, and went away through the dark rooms, swaying slightly and groping along the floor with his feet.

'Poor old chap, perfectly soaked! I thought it was Molla Carlsen, spooking round.' Valentine threw himself into a chair. 'Do you suppose that's the way I'll be keeping Christmas ten years from now, Charlotte? What else is there for us to do, I ask you? Sons of an easy-going, self-satisfied American family, never taught anything until we are too old to learn. What could Roland do when he came home from Germany fifteen years ago? . . . Lord, it's more than that now . . . it's nineteen! Nineteen years!' Valentine dropped his head into his hands and rumpled his hair as if he were washing it, which was a sign with him that a situation was too hopeless for discussion. 'Well, what could he have done, Charlotte? What could he do now? Teach piano, take the bread out of somebody's mouth? My son

Dickie, he'll be an Oglethorpe! He'll get on, and won't carry this damned business any farther.'

On Christmas morning Molla Carlsen came over and reported with evident satisfaction that Roland and Valentine had made a night of it, and were both keeping their rooms in consequence. Aunt Charlotte was sad and downcast all day long.

VII

Molla Carlsen loved to give my aunt the worst possible account of the men she kept house for, though in talking to outsiders I think she was discreet and loyal. She was a strange woman, then about forty years old, and she had been in the Ramsay household for more than twelve years. She managed everything over there, and was paid very high wages. She was grasping, but as honest as she was heartless. The house was well conducted, though it was managed, as Valentine said, somewhat like an institution. No matter how many thousand roses were blooming in the garden, it never occurred to Molla to cut any and put them in the bare, faded parlor. The men who lived there got no coddling; they were terribly afraid of her. When a wave of red went over Molla's white skin, poor Uncle Morton's shaky hands trembled more than ever, and his faraway eyes shrank to mere pin-points. He was the one who most often angered her, because he dropped things. Once when Aunt Charlotte remonstrated with her about her severity, she replied that a woman who managed a houseful of alcoholics must be a tyrant, or the place would be a sty.

This made us all indignant. Morton, we thought, was the only one who could justly be thus defined. He was the oldest of Uncle Jonathan's sons; tall, narrow, utterly spare, with a long, thin face, a shriveled scalp with a little dry hair on it, parted in the middle, eyes that never looked at you because the pupils were always shrunk so small. Morton was awfully proud of the fact that he was a business man; he alone of that household went up on the business men's train in the morning. He went to an office in the City, climbed upon a high stool, and fastened his distant eyes upon a ledger. (It was a coal business, in which his father owned a good deal of stock, and every night an accountant went over Morton's books and corrected his mistakes). On his way to the office, he stopped at the bar of a most respectable hotel. He stopped there again before lunch at noon, and on his way to the station in the late afternoon. He often told Uncle Harry that he never took anything during business hours. Nobody ever saw Morton thoroughly intoxicated, but nobody ever saw him quite himself. He had good manners, a kind voice, though husky, and he was usually very quiet.

Uncle Jonathan, to be sure, took a good deal of whisky during the day – but then he ate almost nothing. Whisky and tobacco were his nourishment. He was frail, but he had been so even as a young man, and he outlived all his sons except Morton – lived on until the six little girls at Fox Hill were all grown women. No, I don't think it was alcohol that preserved him; I think it was his fortunate nature, his happy form of self-esteem. He was perfectly satisfied with himself and his family – with whatever they had done and whatever they had not done. He was glad that Roland had declined the nervous strain of an artistic career, and that Morton was in business; in each generation some of the Ramsays had been business men. Uncle Jonathan had loved his wife dearly and he must have missed her, but he was pleased with the verses he had written about her since her death, verses in the manner of Tom Moore, whom he considered an absolutely satisfactory poet. He had, of course, been proud of Valentine's brilliant marriage. The divorce he certainly regretted. But whatever pill life handed out to him he managed to swallow with equanimity.

Uncle Jonathan spent his days in the library, across the hall from the parlor, where he was writing a romance of the French and Indian wars. The room was lined with his father's old brown theological books, and everything one touched there felt dusty. There was always a scattering of tobacco crumbs over the hearth, the floor, the desk, and over Uncle Jonathan's waistcoat and whiskers. It wasn't in Molla Carlsen's contract to keep the tobacco dust off her master.

Roland Ramsay was Uncle Jonathan's much younger brother. When he was a boy of twelve and fourteen, he had been a musical prodigy, had played to large and astonished audiences in New York and Boston and Philadelphia. Later he was sent to Germany to study under Liszt and D'Albert. At twenty-eight he returned to Bonnie Brae – and he had been there ever since. He was a big, handsome man, never ill, but something had happened to his nervous system. He could not play in public, not even in his own city. Ever since Valentine was a little boy, Uncle Roland and his piano had lived upstairs at Bonnie Brae. There were several stories: that he had been broken by a love affair with a German singer; that Wagner had hurt his feelings so cruelly he could never get over it; that at his debut in Paris he had forgotten in the middle of his sonata in what key the next movement was written, and had labored through the rest of his program like a man stupefied by drugs.

At any rate, Roland had broken nerves, just a some people have a weak heart, and he lived in solitude and silence. Occasionally when some fine orchestra or a new artist played in the City up the river, Roland's waxy, frozen face was to be seen in the audience; but not often. Five or six times a year he went on a long spree. Then he would shut himself up in his room and play the piano – it couldn't be called practicing – for eight or ten hours a day. Sometimes in the evening Aunt Charlotte would put on a cloak and go out into the garden to listen to him. 'Harry,' she said once when she came back into the house, 'I was walking under Roland's window. Really, he is playing like a god tonight.'

Inert and inactive as he was, Roland kept his good physique. He used to sit all afternoon beside his window with a book; as we came up the hill we could see his fine head and shoulders there, motionless as if in a frame. I never liked to look at his face, for his strong, well-cut features never moved. His eyes were large and uncomfortable-looking, under heavy lids with deep hollows beneath — curiously like the eyes of the tired American business men whose pictures appear in the papers when they are getting a divorce.

I had heard it whispered at school that Uncle Jonathan was 'in Molla Carlsen's power,' because Horace, the wild son, had made vehement advances to her long ago when she first came into the house, and that his bad behavior had hastened his mother's end. However it came about, in her power the lonely men at Bonnie Brae certainly were. When Molla was dressed to go up to the city, she walked down the front steps and got into the carriage with the air of mistress of the place. And her furs, we knew, had cost more than Aunt Charlotte's.

VIII

All that winter Valentine was tremendously busy. He was not only writing ever so many new songs, but was hunting up beautiful old ones for our sextette, and he trained us so industriously that the little girls fell behind in their lessons, and Aunt Charlotte had to limit rehearsals to three nights a week. I remember he made us an arrangement for voices of the minuet in the third movement of Brahms' second symphony, and wrote words to it.

We were not allowed to sing any of Valentine's songs in company, not even for Aunt Charlotte's old friends. He was rather proud and sulky with most of the neighbors, and wouldn't have it. When we tried out his new songs for the home circle, as he said, Uncle Morton was allowed to come over, and Uncle Jonathan in his black cape. Roland came too, and sat off in a corner by himself. Uncle Jonathan thought very well of his own judgment in music. He liked all Valentine's songs, but warned him against writing things without a sufficient 'climax', mildly bidding him beware of a too modern manner.

I remember he used to repeat for his son's guidance two lines from one of his favorite poets, accenting the measure with the stogie he held in his fingers – a particularly noxious kind of cigar which he not only smoked but, on occasion, ate!

'Avoid eccentricity, Val,' he would say, beaming softly at his son. 'Remember this admirable rule for poets and composers:

> Be not the first by whom the new is tried,
> Nor yet the last to lay the old aside.'

That year the spring began early. I remember March and April as a succession of long walks and climbs with Valentine. Sometimes Aunt Charlotte went with us, but she was not a nimble walker, and Valentine liked climb and dash and short-cut. We would plunge into the wooded course of Blue Run or Powhatan Creek, and get to the top of Flint Ridge by a quicker route than any path. That long, windy ridge lay behind Blinker's Hill and Fox Hill; the top was a bare expanse, except for a few bleached boulders and twisted oaks. From there we could look off over all the great wrinkles of hills, catch glimpses of the river, and see the black pillar of cloud to the north where the City lay. This dark cloud, as evening came on, took deep rich colors from the sunset; and after the sun was gone it sent out all night an orange glow from the furnace fires that burned there. But that smoke did not come down to us; our evenings were pure and silvery – soft blue skies seen through the budding trees above us, or over the folds and folds of lavender forest below us.

One Saturday afternoon we took Aunt Charlotte along and got to the top of Flint Ridge by the winding roadway. As we were walking upon the crest, curtains of mist began to rise from the river and from between the lines of hills. Soon the darkening sky was full of fleecy clouds, and the countryside below us disappeared into nothingness.

Suddenly, in the low cut between the hills across the river, we saw a luminousness, throbbing and phosphorescent, a ghostly brightness with mists streaming about it and enfolding it, struggling to quench it. We knew it was the moon, but we could see no form, no solid image; it was a flowing, surging, liquid gleaming; now stronger, now softer.

'The Rhinegold!' murmured Valentine and Aunt Charlotte in one breath. The little girls were silent; Betty Jane felt for my hand. They were awed, not so much by the light, as by something in the two voices that had spoken together. Presently we dropped into the dark winding road along Blue Run and got home late for dinner.

While we were at dessert, Uncle Valentine went into the music-room and began to play the Rhine music. He played on as if he would never stop; Siegmund's love song and the Valhalla music and back to the Rhine journey and the Rhine maidens. The cycle was like a plaything in his hands. Presently a shadow fell in the patch of moonlight on the floor, and looking out I saw Roland, without a hat, standing just outside the open window. He often appeared at the window or the doorway when we were singing with Valentine, but if we noticed him, or addressed him, he faded quickly away.

As Valentine stopped for a moment, his uncle tapped on the window glass.

'Going over now, Valentine? It's getting late.'

'Yes, I suppose it is. I say, Charlotte, do you remember how we used to play the Ring to each other hours on end, long ago, when Damrosch first brought the German opera over? Why can't people stay young forever?'

'Maybe you will, Val,' said Aunt Charlotte, musing. 'What a difference Wagner made in the world, after all!'

'It's not a good thing to play Wagner at night,' said the gray voice outside the window. 'It brings on sleeplessness.'

'I'll come along presently, Roland,' the nephew called. 'I'm warm now; I'll take cold if I go out.'

The large figure went slowly away.

'Poor old Roland, isn't he just a coffin of a man!' Valentine got up and lit the fagots in the fireplace. 'I feel shivery. I've had him on my hands a good deal this winter. He'll come drifting in through the wing and settle himself in my study and sit there half the night without opening his head.'

'Doesn't he talk to you, even?' I asked.

'Hardly, though I get fidgety and talk to him. Sometimes he plays. He's always interesting at the piano. It's remarkable that he plays as well as he does, when he's so irregular.'

'Does he really read? We so often see him sitting by his upstairs window with a book.'

'He reads too much, German philosophy and things that aren't good for him. Did you know, Charlotte, that he keeps a diary. At least he writes often in a big ledger Morton brought him from town. Sometimes he's at it for hours. Lord, I'd like to know what he puts down in it!' Valentine plunged his head in his hands and began rumpling his hair. 'Can you remember him much before he went abroad, Charlotte?'

'When I was little I was taken to hear him play in Steinway Hall, just before he went to Germany. From what I can remember, it was very brilliant. He had splendid hands, and a wonderful memory. When he came back he was much more musical, but he couldn't play in public.'

'Queer! How he supports the years as they come and go . . . Of course, he loves the place, just as I do; that's something. By the way, when I was home three years ago I was let into a family secret; it was Roland who was Molla Carlsen's suitor and made all the row, not poor Horace at all! Oh, shouldn't I have said that before the sextette? They'll forget it. They forget most things. What haunts me about Roland is the feeling of kinship. So often it flashes into my mind: "Yes, I might be struck dumb some day, just like that." Oh, don't laugh! It *was* like that, for months and months, while I was trying to live with Janet. My skin would get yellow, and I'd feel a perfect loathing of speech. My jaws would set together so that I couldn't open them. I'd walk along the quais in Paris and go without a newspaper because I couldn't bring myself to say good-morning to the old woman and buy one. I'd wander about awfully hungry because I couldn't bear the sound of talk in a restaurant. I dodged everybody I knew, or cut them.'

There was something funny about his self-commiseration, and I wanted to hear more; but just at this point we were told that we must go instantly to bed.

'And I?' Valentine asked, 'must I go too?'

'No. You may stay a little longer.'

Aunt Charlotte must have thought he needed a serious talking-to, for she almost never saw him alone. Her life was hedged about by very subtle but sure conventionalities, and that was only one of many things she did not permit herself.

IX

Fox Hill was soon besieged on all sides by spring. The first attack came by way of the old apple orchard that ran irregularly behind our carriage house and Uncle Valentine's studio. The foaming, flowery trees were a beautiful sight from his doorstep. Aunt Charlotte and Morton were carrying on a hot rivalry in tulips. Uncle Jonathan now came out to sun himself on the front porch, in a broad-rimmed felt hat and a green plaid shawl which his father used to wear on horseback trips over the hills.

Though spring first attacked us through the orchard, the great assault, for which we children waited, came on the side of the hill next the river; it was violent, blood-red, long drawn-out, and when it was over, our hill belonged to summer. The vivid event of our year was the blooming of the wall.

Along the front of Fox Hill, where the lawn ended in a steep descent, Uncle Harry had put in a stone retaining wall to keep the ground from washing out. This wall, he said, he intended to manage himself, and when he first announced that he was going to cover it with red rambler roses, his wife laughed at him and told him he would spoil the whole hill. But in the event she was converted. Nowhere in the valley did ramblers thrive so well and bloom so gorgeously. From the railway station our home-coming business men could see that crimson wall, running along high on the green hillside.

One Sunday morning when the ramblers were at their height, we all went with Uncle Harry and Valentine down the driveway to admire them. Aunt Charlotte admitted that they were very showy, very decorative, but she added under her breath that she couldn't feel much enthusiasm for scentless roses.

'But they are quite another sort of thing,' Uncle Harry expostulated. 'They go right about their business and bloom. I like their being without an odor; it gives them a kind of frankness and innocence.'

In the bright sunlight I could see her dark skin flush a little. 'Innocence?' she murmured, 'I shouldn't call it just that.'

I was wondering what she would call it, when our stableman Bill came up from the post office with his leather bag and emptied the contents on the grass. He always brought the Ramsays' mail with ours, and we often teased Uncle Valentine about certain bright purple letters from Paris, addressed to him in a woman's hand. Because of the curious ways of mail steamers they sometimes came in pairs, and that morning there were actually five of these purple punctuations in the pile of white letters. The children laughed immoderately. Betty Jane and Elizabeth shouted for joy as they fished them out. 'Poor Uncle Val! When will you ever get time to answer them all?'

'Ah, that's it!' he said as he began stuffing them away in his pockets.

The next afternoon Aunt Charlotte and I were sewing, seated in the little covered balcony out of her room, with honeysuckle vines all about us. We saw Valentine, hatless, in his striped blazer, come around the corner of the house and seat himself at the tea-table under one of the big sycamores, just below us. We were about to call to him, when he took out those five purple envelopes and spread them on the table before him as if he were going to play a game with them. My aunt looked at me with a sparkle in her eye and put her finger to her lips to keep me quiet. Elizabeth came running across from the summerhouse with her kitten. He called to her.

'Just a moment, Elizabeth. I want you to choose one of these.'

'But how? What for?' she asked, much astonished.

'Oh, just choose one, any one,' he said carelessly. 'Put your finger down.' He took out a lead pencil. 'Now, we'll mark that 1. Choose again; very well, that's number 2; another, another. Thank you. Now the one that's left will necessarily be 5, won't it?'

'But, Uncle Val, aren't those the ones that came yesterday? And you haven't read them yet?'

'Hush, not so loud, dear.' He took up his half-burned cigarette. 'You see, when so many come at once, it's not easy to know which should be read first. But you've settled that difficulty for me.' He swept them lightly into the two side pockets of his blazer and sprang up. 'Where are the others? Can't we go off for a tramp somewhere? Up Blue Run, to see the wild azaleas?'

Elizabeth came into the house calling for us, and Aunt Charlotte and I went down to him.

'We're going up Blue Run to see the azaleas, Charlotte, won't you come?'

She looked wistful. 'It's very hot. I'm afraid I ought not to climb, and you'll want to go the steep way.'

She waited, hoping to be urged, but he said no more about it. He was sometimes quite heartless.

That evening we came home tired, and the little girls were sent to bed soon after dinner. It was the most glorious of summer nights; I couldn't think of giving it up and going to sleep. Our valley was still, breathlessly still, and full of white moonlight. The garden gave off a heavy perfume, the lawn and house were mottled with intense black and intense white, a mosaic so perplexing that I could hardly find my way along the familiar paths. There was a languorous spirit of beauty abroad – warm, sensuous, oppressive, like the pressure of a warm, clinging body. I felt vaguely afraid to be alone.

I looked for Aunt Charlotte, and found her in the little balcony off her bedroom, where we had been sitting that morning. She spoke to me impatiently, in a way that quite hurt my feelings.

'You must go to bed, Marjorie. I have a headache and I can't be with anyone tonight.'

I could feel that she did not want me near her, that my intrusion was most unwelcome. I went downstairs. Uncle Harry was in his study, doing accounts.

'Fine night, isn't it?' he said cheerfully. 'I'm going out to see a little of it presently. Almost done my figures.' His accounts must have troubled him sometimes; his household cost a great deal of money.

I retreated to the apple orchard. Seeing that the door of Valentine's study was open, I approached cautiously and looked in. He was on his divan, which he had pulled up into the moonlight, lying on his back with his arms under his head.

'Run away, Margie, I'm busy,' he muttered, not looking at me but staring past me.

I walked alone about the garden, smelling the stocks until I could smell them no more. I noticed how many moonflowers had come out on the Japanese summerhouse that stood on the line between our ground and the Ramsays'. As I drew near it I heard a groan, not loud, but long, long, as if the unhappiness of a whole lifetime were coming out in one despairing breath. I looked in through the vines. There sat Roland, his head in his hands, the moonlight on his silver hair. I stole softly away through the grass. It seemed that tonight everyone wanted to be alone with his ghost.

Going home through the garden I heard a low call; 'Wait, wait a minute!' Uncle Morton came out of the darkness of the vine-covered side porch and beckoned me to follow him. He led me to the plot where his finest roses were in bloom and stopped before a bush that had a great many buds on it, but only one open flower – a great white rose, almost as big as a moonflower, its petals beautifully curled.

'Wait a minute,' he whispered again. He took out his pocket knife, and with great care and considerable difficulty managed to cut the rose with a long stem. He held it out to me in his shaking hand. 'There,' he said proudly. 'That's my best one, the Queen of Savoy. I've been waiting for someone to give it to!'

This was a bold adventure for Morton. I saw that he meant it as a high compliment, and that he was greatly pleased with himself as he wavered back along the white path and disappeared into the darkness under the honeysuckle vines.

X

The next morning Valentine went up to town with Morton on the early train, and at six o'clock that evening Morton came back without him. Aunt Charlotte, who was watching in the garden, went quickly across the Ramsays' lawn.

'Morton, where is Valentine?'

Morton stood holding his straw hat before him in both hands, telling her vaguely that Valentine was going to spend the night in town, at a hotel. 'He has to be near the cable office – been sending messages all day – something very important.'

Valentine remained in the City for several days. We did not see him again until he joined us one afternoon when we were having tea in the garden. He looked fresh and happy, in new white flannels and one of his gayest neckties.

'Oh, it's delightful to be back, Charlotte!' he exclaimed as he sank into a chair near her.

'We've missed you, Valentine.' She, too, looked radiantly happy.

'I should hope so! Because you're probably going to have a great deal of me. Likely I'm here forever, like Roland and the oak trees. I've been staying up in the City, on neutral ground for a few days, to find out what I really want. Do you know, Betty Jane and Elizabeth, that's a sure test; the place you wish for the first moment you're awake in the morning, is the place where you most want to be. I often want to do two things at once, be in two places at once, but this time I don't think I had a moment's indecision.' He did not say about what, but presently he drew off a seal ring he wore on his little finger and began playing with it. I knew it was Louise Ireland's ring, he had told me so once. It was an intaglio, a three-masted ship under full sail, and over it, in old English letters, *Telle est la Vie*.

He sat playing with the ring, tossing it up into the sunlight and catching it in his palm, while he addressed my aunt.

'Ireland's leaving Paris. Off for a long tour in South Africa and Australia. She's like a sea gull or a swallow, that woman, forever crossing water. I'm sorry I can't be with her. She's the best friend I've ever had – except you, Charlotte.' He did not look at my aunt, but the drop in his voice was a look. 'I do seem to be tied to you.'

'It's the valley you're tied to. The place is necessary to you, Valentine.'

'Yes, it's the place, and it's you and the children – it's even Morton and Roland, God knows why!'

Aunt Charlotte was right. It was the place. The people were secondary. Indeed, I have often wondered, had he been left to his own will, how long he would have been content there. A man under thirty does not settle down to live with old men and children. But the place was vocal to him. During the year that he was with us he wrote all of the thirty-odd songs by which he lives. Some artists profit by exile. He was one of those who do not. And his country was not a continent, but a few wooded hills in a river valley, a few old houses and gardens that were home.

XI

The summer passed joyously. Valentine went on making new songs for us and we went on singing them. I expected life to be like that forever. The golden year, Aunt Charlotte called it, when I visited her at Fox Hill years afterward. September came and went, and then a cold wind blew down upon us.

Uncle Harry and Morton came home one night with

disturbing news. It was said in the City that the old Wakeley estate had been sold. Miss Belle Wakeley, the sole heir, had lived in Italy for several years; her big house on the unwooded side of Blinker's Hill had been shut up, her many acres rented out or lying idle.

Very soon after Uncle Harry startled us with this news, Valentine came over to ask us whether such a thing were possible. No large tract of land had changed hands in Greenacre for many years.

'I rather think it's true,' said Uncle Harry. 'I'm going to the agent tomorrow to find out any particulars I can. It seems to be a very guarded transaction. I suppose this means that Belle has decided to live abroad for good. I'm sorry.'

'It's very wrong of her,' said Aunt Charlotte, 'and I think she'll regret it. If she hasn't any feeling for her property now, she will have some day. Why, her grandfather was born there!'

'Yes, I'm disappointed. I thought Belle had a great deal of sentiment underneath.' Uncle Harry had always been Miss Wakeley's champion, liked her independent ways, and was amused by her brusque manners.

Valentine was standing by the fireplace, abstracted and deeply concerned.

'Just how much does the Wakeley property take in, Harry? I've never known exactly.'

'A great deal. It covers the courses of both creeks, Blue Run and Powhatan Creek, and runs clear back to the top of Flint Ridge. It's our biggest estate, by long odds.'

Valentine began pacing the floor. 'Did you know she wanted to sell? Couldn't the neighbors have clubbed together and bought it, rather than let strangers in?'

Uncle Harry laughed and shook his head. 'I'm afraid we're not rich enough, Val. It's worth a tremendous lot of money. Most of us have all the land we can take care of.'

'I suppose so,' he muttered. 'Father's pretty well mortgaged up, isn't he?'

'Pretty well,' Uncle Harry admitted. 'Don't worry. I'll see

what I can find out tomorrow. I can't think Belle would sell to a speculator, and let her estate be parceled out. She'd have too much consideration for the rest of us. She was the finest kind of neighbor. I wish we had her back.'

'It never occurred to me, Harry, that the actual country-side could be sold; the creeks and woods and hills. That shouldn't be permitted. They ought to be kept just as they are, since they give the place its character.'

Uncle Harry said he was afraid the only way of keeping a place the same, in this country, was to own it.

'But there are some things one doesn't think of in terms of money,' Valentine persisted. 'If I'd had bushels of money when I came home last winter, it would never have occur-red to me to try to buy Blinker's Hill, any more than the sky over it. I didn't know that the Wakeleys or anybody else owned the creeks, and the forest up toward the Ridge.'

Aunt Charlotte rose and went up to Uncle Harry's chair. 'Is it really too late to do anything? Too late to cable Belle and ask her to give her neighbors a chance to buy it in first?'

'My dear, you never do realize much about the cost of things. But remember, Belle is a shrewd business woman. She knows well enough that no dozen of her neighbors could raise so much ready money. I understand it's a cash transaction.'

Aunt Charlotte looked hurt. 'Well, I can only say it was faithless of her. People have some responsibility toward the place where they were born, and toward their old friends.'

Dinner was announced, and Valentine was urged to stay, but he refused.

'I don't want any dinner, I'm too nervous. I'm awfully fussed by this affair, Charlotte.' He stood beside my aunt at the door for a moment, hanging his head despondently, and went away.

That evening my aunt and uncle could talk of nothing but the sale of the Wakeley property. Uncle Harry said sadly that he had never before so wished that he were a rich man. 'Though even if I were, I don't know that I'd have thought of making Belle an offer. I'm as impractical as Valentine. But if I'd had money, I do believe Belle would have given me the first chance. We're her nearest neighbors, and whoever buys Blinker's Hill has to be part of our landscape, and to come into our life more or less.'

'Have you any suspicion who it may be?' She spoke very low.

Uncle Harry was standing beside her, his back to the hall fire, smoking his church-warden pipe. 'The purchaser? Not the slightest. Have you?'

'Yes.' She spoke lower still. 'A suspicion that tortures me. It flashed into my mind the moment you told us. I don't know why.'

'Then keep it to yourself, my dear,' he said resolutely, as if he had all he cared to shoulder. I heard a snap, and saw that he had broken the long stem of his pipe. 'There,' he said, throwing it into the fire, 'you and Valentine have got me worked up with your fussing. I'm as shaky as poor Morton tonight.'

XII

The next day Uncle Harry telephoned my aunt from his office in town; Miss Wakeley's agent was not at liberty to disclose the purchaser's name, but assured him that the estate was not sold to a speculator, but an old resident of the City who would preserve the property very much as it was and would respect the feelings of the community.

I was sent over to Bonnie Brae with the good tidings. We all felt so much encouraged that we decided to spend the afternoon in the woods that had been restored to us. It was a yellow October day, and our country had never looked more beautiful. We had tea beside Powhatan Creek, where it curved wide and shallow through green bottom land. A plantation of sycamores grew there, their old white roots bursting out of the low banks and forking into the stream itself. The bark of those sycamores was always peculiarly white, and the sunlight played on the silvery interlacing of the great boughs. Dry ledges of slate rock stood out of the cold green water here and there, and on the up-stream side of each ledge lay a little trembling island of yellow leaves, unable to pass the barrier. The meadow in which we lingered was smooth turf, of that intense green of autumn grass that has been already a little touched by frost.

As we sat on the warm slate rocks, we looked up at the wooded side of Blinker's Hill — like a mellow old tapestry. The fiercest autumn colors had burned themselves out; the gold on the smoke-colored beeches was thin and pale, so that through their horizontal branches one could see the colored carpet of leaves on the ground. Only the young oaks held all their ruby leaves, the deepest tone in the whole scale of reds — and they would still be there, a little duller, when the snow was flying.

I remember my aunt's voice, a tone not quite natural, when she said suddenly, 'Valentine, how beautiful the Tuileries gardens are on an afternoon like this — down about the second fountain. The color lasts in the sky so long after dusk comes on, — behind the Eiffel tower.'

He was lying on his back. He sat up and looked at her sharply. 'Oh, yes!'

'Aren't you beginning to be a little homesick for it?' she asked bashfully.

'A little. But it's rather nice to sit safe and lazy on Fox Hill and be a trifle homesick for far-away places. Even Roland gets homesick for Bavaria in the spring, he tells me. He takes a drink or two and recovers. Are you trying to shove me off somewhere?'

She sighed. 'Oh, no! No, indeed, I'm not.'

But she had, in some way, broken the magical contentment of the afternoon. The little girls began to seem restless, so we gathered them up and started home.

We followed the road round the foot of Blinker's Hill, to the cleared side on which stood the old Wakeley house. There we saw a man and woman coming down the drive-way from the house itself. The man stopped and hesitated, but the woman quickened her pace and came toward us.

Aunt Charlotte became very pale. She had recognized them at a distance, and so had I; Janet Oglethorpe and her second husband. I remember exactly how she looked. She was wearing a black and white check out-of-door coat and a hard black turban. Her face, always high-colored, was red and shiny from exercise. She waved to us cordially as she came up, but did not offer to shake hands. Her husband took off his hat and smiled scornfully. He stood well behind her, looking very ill at ease, with his elbows out and his chin high, and as the conversation went on his haughty smile became a nervous grin.

'How do you do, Mrs Waterford, and how do you do, Valentine,' Mrs Towne began effusively. She spoke very fast, and her lips seemed not to keep up with her enunciation; they were heavy and soft, and made her speech slushy. Her mouth was her bad feature – her teeth were too far apart, there was something crude and inelegant about them. 'We are going to be neighbors, Mrs Waterford. I don't want it noised abroad yet, but I've just bought the Wakeley place. I'm going to do the house over and live down here. I hope you won't mind our coming.'

Aunt Charlotte made some reply. Valentine did not utter a sound. He took off his hat, replaced it, and stood with his hands in his jacket pockets, looking at the ground.

'I've always had my eye on this property,' Mrs Towne went on, 'but it took Belle a long while to make up her mind. It's too fine a place to be left going to waste. It will be nice for Valentine's boy to grow up here where he did, and to be near his Grandfather Ramsay. I want him to know his Ramsay kin.'

Valentine behaved very badly. He addressed her without lifting his eyes from the ground or taking his hands out of his pockets; merely kicked a dead leaf out of the road and said: 'He's not my boy, and the less he sees of the Ramsays, the better. You've got him, it's your affair to make an Oglethorpe of him and see that he stays one. What do you want to make the kid miserable for?'

Mrs Towne grew as much redder as it was possible to be,

but she spoke indulgently. 'Now, Valentine, why can't you be sensible? Certainly, on Mrs Waterford's account –'

'Oh, yes!' he muttered. 'That's the Oglethorpe notion of good manners, before people!'

'I'm sorry, Mrs Waterford. I had no idea he would be so naughty, or I wouldn't have stopped you. But I did want you to be the first person to know.' Mrs Towne turned to my aunt with great self-command and a ready flow of speech. Her alarmingly high color and a slight swelling of the face, a puffing-up about her eyes and nose, betrayed her state of feeling.

The women talked politely for a few moments, while the two men stood sulking, each in his own way. When the conference was over, Mrs Towne crossed the road resolutely and took the path to the station. Towne again took off his hat, looking nowhere, and followed her. Valentine did not return the salute.

As our meek band went on around the foot of the hill, he merely pulled his hat lower over his eyes and said, 'She's Scotch; she couldn't let anything get away – not even me. All damned bunk about wanting to get Dickie down here. Everything about her's bunk, except her damned money. That's a fact, and it's got me – it's got me.'

Aunt Charlotte's breathing was so irregular that she could scarcely speak. 'Valentine, I've had a presentiment of that, from the beginning. I scarcely slept at all last night. I can't have it so. Harry must find some way out.'

'No way out, Charlotte,' he went along swinging his shoulders and speaking in a dull sing-song voice. 'That was her creek we were playing along this afternoon; Blue Run, Powhatan Creek, the big woods, Flint Ridge, Blinker's Hill. I can't get in or out. What does it say on the rat-bane bottle; *put the poison along all his runways.* That's the right idea!'

He did not stop with us, but cut back through the orchard to his study. After dinner we waited for him, sitting solemnly about the fire. At last Aunt Charlotte started up as if she could bear it no longer.

'Come on, Harry,' she said firmly. 'We must see about Valentine.'

He looked up at her pathetically. 'Take Marjorie, won't you? I really don't want to see the poor chap tonight, Charlotte.'

We hurried across the garden. The studio was dark, the fire had gone out. He was lying on the couch, but he did not answer us. I found a box of matches and lit a candle.

One of Uncle Jonathan's rye bottles stood half empty on the mantelpiece. He had had no dinner, had drunk off nearly a pint of whisky and dropped on the couch. He was deathly white, and his eyes were rolled up in his head.

Aunt Charlotte knelt down beside him and covered him with her cloak. 'Run for your Uncle Harry, as fast as you can,' she said.

XIII

The end? That was the end for us. Within the week workmen were pulling down the wing of the Wakeley house, in order to get as much work as possible done before the cold weather came. The sound of the stone masons' tools rang out clear across the cut between the two hills; even in Valentine's study one could not escape it. We wished that Morton had carried out his happy idea of making a padded cell of it!

Valentine lingered on at Bonnie Brae for a month, though he never went off his father's place again. He did not sail until the end of November, stayed out his year with us, but he had become a different man. All of us, except Aunt Charlotte, were eager to have him go. He had tonsillitis, I remember, and lay on the couch in his study ill and feverish for two weeks. He seemed not to be working, yet he must have been, for when he went away he left between the leaves of one of my aunt's music books the manuscript of the most beautiful and heart-breaking of all his songs:

I know a wall where red roses grow . . .

He deferred his departure from date to date, changed his

passage several times. The night before he went we were sitting by the hall fire, and he said he wished that all the trains and all the boats in the world would stop moving, stop forever.

When his trunks had gone, and his bags were piled up ready to be put into the carriage, he took a latchkey from his pocket and gave it to Aunt Charlotte.

'That's the key to my study. Keep it for me. I don't know that I'll ever need it again, but I'd like to think that you have it.'

Less than two years afterwards, Valentine was accidentally killed, struck by a motor truck one night at the Pont Royal, just as he was leaving Louise Ireland's apartment on the quai.

Aunt Charlotte survived him by eleven years, but after her death we found his latchkey in her jewel box. I have it still. There is now no door for it to open. Bonnie Brae was pulled down during the war. The wave of industrial expansion swept down that valley, and roaring mills belch their black smoke up to the heights where those lovely houses used to stand. Fox Hill is gone, and our wall is gone. *I know a wall where red roses grow;* youngsters sing it still. The roses of song and the roses of memory, they are the only ones that last.

First published in *Woman's Home Companion*, February, March 1925

NEIGHBOUR ROSICKY

WHEN Doctor Burleigh told neighbour Rosicky he had a bad heart, Rosicky protested.

'So? No, I guess my heart was always pretty good. I got a little asthma, maybe. Just a awful short breath when I was pitchin' hay last summer, dat's all.'

'Well now, Rosicky, if you know more about it than I do, what did you come to me for? It's your heart that makes you short of breath, I tell you. You're sixty-five years old, and you've always worked hard, and your heart's tired. You've got to be careful from now on, and you can't do heavy work any more. You've got five boys at home to do it for you.'

The old farmer looked up at the Doctor with a gleam of amusement in his queer triangular-shaped eyes. His eyes were large and lively, but the lids were caught up in the middle in a curious way, so that they formed a triangle. He did not look like a sick man. His brown face was creased but not wrinkled, he had a ruddy colour in his smooth-shaven cheeks and in his lips, under his long brown moustache. His hair was thin and ragged around his ears, but very little grey. His forehead, naturally high and crossed by deep parallel lines, now ran all the way up to his pointed crown. Rosicky's face had the habit of looking interested, – suggested a contented disposition and a reflective quality that was gay rather than grave. This gave him a certain detachment, the easy manner of an onlooker and observer.

'Well, I guess you ain't got no pills fur a bad heart, Doctor Ed. I guess the only thing is fur me to git me a new one.'

Doctor Burleigh swung round in his desk-chair and frowned at the old farmer. 'I think if I were you I'd take a little care of the old one, Rosicky.'

Rosicky shrugged. 'Maybe I don't know how. I expect you mean fur me not to drink my coffee no more.'

'I wouldn't, in your place. But you'll do as you choose about that. I've never yet been able to separate a Bohemian from his coffee or his pipe. I've quit trying. But the sure thing is you've got to cut out farm work. You can feed the stock and do chores about the barn, but you can't do anything in the fields that makes you short of breath.'

'How about shelling corn?'

'Of course not!'

Rosicky considered with puckered brows.

'I can't make my heart go no longer'n it wants to, can I, Doctor Ed?'

'I think it's good for five or six years yet, maybe more, if you'll take the strain off it. Sit around the house and help Mary. If I had a good wife like yours, I'd want to stay around the house.'

His patient chuckled. 'It ain't no place fur a man. I don't like no old man hanging round the kitchen too much. An' my wife, she's a awful hard worker her own self.'

'That's it; you can help her a little. My Lord, Rosicky, you are one of the few men I know who has a family he can get some comfort out of; happy dispositions, never quarrel among themselves, and they treat you right. I want to see you live a few years and enjoy them.'

'Oh, they're good kids, all right,' Rosicky assented.

The Doctor wrote him a prescription and asked him how his oldest son, Rudolph, who had married in the spring, was getting on. Rudolph had struck out for himself, on rented land. 'And how's Polly? I was afraid Mary mightn't like an American daughter-in-law, but it seems to be working out all right.'

'Yes, she's a fine girl. Dat widder woman bring her

daughters up very nice. Polly got lots of spunk, an' she got some style, too. Da's nice, for young folks to have some style.' Rosicky included his head gallantly. His voice and his twinkly smile were an affectionate compliment to his daughter-in-law.

'It looks like a storm, and you'd better be getting home before it comes. In town in the car?' Doctor Burleigh rose.

'No, I'm in de wagon. When you got five boys, you ain't got much chance to ride round in de Ford. I ain't much for cars, noway.'

'Well, it's a good road out to your place; but I don't want you bumping around in a wagon much. And never again on a hay-rake, remember!'

Rosicky placed the Doctor's fee delicately behind the desk-telephone, looking the other way, as if this were an absent-minded gesture. He put on his plush cap and his corduroy jacket with a sheepskin collar, and went out.

The Doctor picked up his stethoscope and frowned at it as if he were seriously annoyed with the instrument. He wished it had been telling tales about some other man's heart, some old man who didn't look the Doctor in the eye so knowingly, or hold out such a warm brown hand when he said good-bye. Doctor Burleigh had been a poor boy in the country before he went away to medical school; he had known Rosicky almost ever since he could remember, and he had a deep affection for Mrs Rosicky.

Only last winter he had had such a good breakfast at Rosicky's, and that when he needed it. He had been out all night on a long, hard confinement case at Tom Marshall's, – a big rich farm where there was plenty of stock and plenty of feed and a great deal of expensive farm machinery of the newest model, and no comfort whatever. The woman had too many children and too much work, and she was no manager. When the baby was born at last, and handed over to the assisting neighbour woman, and the mother was properly attended to, Burleigh refused any breakfast in that slovenly house, and drove his buggy – the snow was too deep for a car – eight miles to Anton Rosicky's place. He didn't know another farm-house where a man could get such a warm welcome, and such good strong coffee with rich cream. No wonder the old chap didn't want to give up his coffee!

He had driven in just when the boys had come back from the barn and were washing up for breakfast. The long table, covered with a bright oilcloth, was set out with dishes waiting for them, and the warm kitchen was full of the smell of coffee and hot biscuit and sausage. Five big handsome boys, running from twenty to twelve, all with what Burleigh called natural good manners, – they hadn't a bit of the painful self-consciousness he himself had to struggle with when he was a lad. One ran to put his horse away, another helped him off with his fur coat and hung it up, and Josephine, the youngest child and the only daughter, quickly set another place under her mother's direction.

With Mary, to feed creatures was the natural expression of affection, – her chickens, the calves, her big hungry boys. It was a rare pleasure to feed a young man whom she seldom saw and of whom she was as proud as if he belonged to her. Some country housekeepers would have stopped to spread a white cloth over the oilcloth, to change the thick cups and plates for their best china, and the wooden-handled knives for plated ones. But not Mary.

'You must take us as you find us, Doctor Ed. I'd be glad to put out my good things for you if you was expected, but I'm glad to get you any way at all.'

He knew she was glad, – she threw back her head and spoke out as if she were announcing him to the whole prairie. Rosicky hadn't said anything at all; he merely smiled his twinkling smile, put some more coal on the fire, and went into his own room to pour the Doctor a little drink in a medicine glass. When they were all seated, he watched his wife's face from his end of the table and spoke to her in Czech. Then, with the instinct of politeness which seldom failed him, he turned to the Doctor and said shyly; 'I was just tellin' her not to ask you no questions about Mrs Marshall till you eat some breakfast. My wife, she's terrible fur to ask questions.'

The boys laughed, and so did Mary. She watched the Doctor devour her biscuit and sausage, too much excited to eat anything herself. She drank her coffee and sat taking in everything about her visitor. She had known him when he was a poor country boy, and was boastfully proud of his success, always saying: 'What do people go to Omaha for, to see a doctor, when we got the best one in the State right here?' If Mary liked people at all, she felt physical pleasure in the sight of them, personal exultation in any good fortune that came to them. Burleigh didn't know many women like that, but he knew she was like that.

When his hunger was satisfied, he did, of course, have to tell them about Mrs Marshall, and he noticed what a friendly interest the boys took in the matter.

Rudolph, the oldest son (he was still living at home then), said: 'The last time I was over there, she was lifting them big heavy milkcans, and I knew she oughtn't to be doing it.'

'Yes, Rudolph told me about that when he come home, and I said it wasn't right,' Mary put in warmly. 'It was all right for me to do them things up to the last, for I was terrible strong, but that woman's weakly. And do you think she'll be able to nurse it, Ed?' She sometimes forgot to give him the title she was so proud of. 'And to think of your being up all night and then not able to get a decent breakfast! I don't know what's the matter with such people.'

'Why, Mother,' said one of the boys, 'if Doctor Ed had got breakfast there, we wouldn't have him here. So you ought to be glad.'

'He knows I'm glad to have him, John, any time. But I'm sorry for that poor woman, how bad she'll feel the Doctor had to go away in the cold without his breakfast.'

'I wish I'd been in practice when these were getting born.' The doctor looked down the row of close-clipped heads. 'I missed some good breakfasts by not being.'

The boys began to laugh at their mother because she flushed so red, but she stood her ground and threw up her head. 'I don't care, you wouldn't have got away from this

house without breakfast. No doctor ever did. I'd have had
something ready fixed that Anton could warm up for you.'

The boys laughed harder than ever, and exclaimed at her:
'I'll bet you would!' 'She would, that!'

'Father, did you get breakfast for the doctor when we
were born?'

'Yes, and he used to bring me my breakfast too, mighty
nice. I was always awful hungry!' Mary admitted with a
guilty laugh.

While the boys were getting the Doctor's horse, he went
to the window to examine the house plants. 'What do you
do to your geraniums to keep them blooming all winter,
Mary? I never pass this house that from the road I don't see
your window full of flowers.'

She snapped off a dark red one, and a ruffled new green
leaf, and put them in his buttonhole. 'There, that looks
better. You look too solemn for a young man, Ed. Why
don't you git married? I'm worried about you. Settin' at
breakfast, I looked at you real hard, and I seen you've got
some grey hairs already.'

'Oh, yes! They're coming. Maybe they'd come faster if I
married.'

'Don't talk so. You'll ruin your health eating at the hotel.
I could send your wife a nice loaf of nut bread, if you only
had one. I don't like to see a young man getting grey. I'll
tell you something, Ed; you make some strong black tea
and keep it handy in a bowl, and every morning just brush
it into your hair, an' it'll keep the grey from showin' much.
That's the way I do!'

Sometimes the Doctor heard the gossipers in the drug-store
wondering why Rosicky didn't get on faster. He was
industrious, and so were his boys, but they were rather free
and easy, weren't pushers, and they didn't always show
good judgment. They were comfortable, they were out of
debt, but they didn't get much ahead. Maybe, Doctor
Burleigh reflected, people as generous and warm-hearted
and affectionate as the Rosickys never got ahead much;

maybe you couldn't enjoy your life and put it into the bank, too.

II

When Rosicky left Doctor Burleigh's office he went into the farm-implement store to light his pipe and put on his glasses and read over the list Mary had given him. Then he went into the general merchandise place next door and stood about until the pretty girl with the plucked eyebrows, who always waited on him, was free. Those eyebrows, two thin India-ink strokes, amused him, because he remembered how they used to be. Rosicky always prolonged his shopping by a little joking; the girl knew the old fellow admired her, and she liked to chaff with him.

'Seems to me about every other week you buy ticking, Mr Rosicky, and always the best quality,' she remarked as she measured off the heavy bolt with red stripes.

'You see, my wife is always makin' goose-fedder pillows, an' de thin stuff don't hold in dem little down-fedders.'

'You must have lots of pillows at your house.'

'Sure. She makes quilts of dem, too. We sleeps easy. Now she's makin' a fedder quilt for my son's wife. You know Polly, that married my Rudolph. How much my bill, Miss Pearl?'

'Eight eighty-five.'

'Chust make it nine, and put in some candy fur de women.'

'As usual. I never did see a man buy so much candy for his wife. First thing you know, she'll be getting too fat.'

'I'd like that. I ain't much fur all dem slim women like what de style is now.'

'That's one for me, I suppose, Mr Bohunk!' Pearl sniffed and elevated her India-ink strokes.

When Rosicky went out to his wagon, it was beginning to snow, – the first snow of the season, and he was glad to see it. He rattled out of town and along the highway through a wonderfully rich stretch of country, the finest farms in the county. He admired this High Prairie, as it was called, and always liked to drive through it. His own place lay in a rougher territory, where there was some clay in the soil and it was not so productive. When he bought his land, he hadn't the money to buy on High Prairie; so he told his boys, when they grumbled, that if their land hadn't some clay in it, they wouldn't own it at all. All the same, he enjoyed looking at these fine farms, as he enjoyed looking at a prize bull.

After he had gone eight miles, he came to the graveyard, which lay just at the edge of his own hay-land. There he stopped his horses and sat still on his wagon seat, looking about at the snowfall. Over yonder on the hill he could see his own house, crouching low, with the clump of orchard behind and the windmill before, and all down the gentle hill-slope the rows of pale gold cornstalks stood out against the white field. The snow was falling over the cornfield and the pasture and the hay-land, steadily, with very little wind, – a nice dry snow. The graveyard had only a light wire fence about it and was all overgrown with long red grass. The fine snow, settling into this red grass and upon the few little evergreens and the headstones, looked very pretty.

It was a nice graveyard, Rosicky reflected, sort of snug and homelike, not cramped or mournful, – a big sweep all round it. A man could lie down in the long grass and see the complete arch of the sky over him, hear the wagons go by; in summer the mowing-machine rattled right up to the wire fence. And it was so near home. Over there across the cornstalks his own roof and windmill looked so good to him that he promised himself to mind the Doctor and take care of himself. He was awful fond of his place, he admitted. He wasn't anxious to leave it. And it was a comfort to think that he would never have to go further than the edge of his own hayfield. The snow, falling over his barnyard and the graveyard, seemed to draw things together like. And they were all old neighbours in the graveyard, most of them friends; there was nothing to feel awkward or embarrassed about. Embarrassment was the most disagreeable feeling Rosicky knew. He didn't often have it, – only with certain people whom he didn't understand at all.

Well, it was a nice snowstorm; a fine sight to see the snow falling so quietly and graciously over so much open country. On his cap and shoulders, on the horses' backs and manes, light, delicate, mysterious it fell; and with it a dry cool fragrance was released into the air. It meant rest for vegetation and men and beasts, for the ground itself; a season of long nights for sleep, leisurely breakfasts, peace by the fire. This and much more went through Rosicky's mind, but he merely told himself that winter was coming, clucked to his horses, and drove on.

When he reached home, John, the youngest boy, ran out to put away his team for him, and he met Mary coming up from the outside cellar with her apron full of carrots. They went into the house together. On the table, covered with oilcloth figured with clusters of blue grapes, a place was set, and he smelled hot coffee-cake of some kind. Anton never lunched in town; he thought that extravagant, and anyhow he didn't like the food. So Mary always had something ready for him when he got home.

After he was settled in his chair, stirring his coffee in a big cup, Mary took out of the oven a pan of *kolache* stuffed with apricots, examined them anxiously to see whether they had got too dry, put them beside his plate, and then sat down opposite him.

Rosicky asked her in Czech if she wasn't going to have any coffee.

She replied in English, as being somehow the right language for transacting business: 'Now what did Doctor Ed say, Anton? You tell me just what.'

'He said I was to tell you some compliments, but I forgot 'em.' Rosicky's eyes twinkled.

'About you, I mean. What did he say about your asthma?'

'He says I ain't got no asthma.' Rosicky took one of the little rolls in his broad brown fingers. The thickened nail of his right thumb told the story of his past.

'Well, what is the matter? And don't try to put me off.'

'He don't say nothing much, only I'm a little older, and my heart ain't so good like it used to be.'

Mary started and brushed her hair back from her temples with both hands as if she were a little out of her mind. From the way she glared, she might have been in a rage with him. 'He says there's something the matter with your heart? Doctor Ed says so?'

'Now don't yell at me like I was a hog in de garden, Mary. You know I always did like to hear a woman talk soft. He didn't say anything de matter wid my heart, only it ain't so young like it used to be, an' he tell me not to pitch hay or run de corn-sheller.'

Mary wanted to jump up, but she sat still. She admired the way he never under any circumstances raised his voice or spoke roughly. He was city-bred, and she was country-bred; she often said she wanted her boys to have their papa's nice ways.

'You never have no pain there, do you? It's your breathing and your stomach that's been wrong. I wouldn't believe nobody but Doctor Ed about it. I guess I'll go see him myself. Didn't he give you no advice?'

'Chust to take it easy like, an' stay round de house dis winter. I guess you got some carpenter work for me to do. I kin make some new shelves for you, and I want dis long time to build a closet in de boys' room and make dem two little fellers keep dere clo'es hung up.'

Rosicky drank his coffee from time to time, while he considered. His moustache was of the soft long variety and came down over his mouth like the teeth of a buggy-rake over a bundle of hay. Each time he put down his cup, he ran his blue handkerchief over his lips. When he took a drink of water, he managed very neatly with the back of his hand.

Mary sat watching him intently, trying to find any change in his face. It is hard to see anyone who has become like your own body to you. Yes, his hair had got thin, and his high forehead had deep lines running from left to right. But his neck, always clean shaved except in the busiest seasons, was not loose or baggy. It was burned a dark reddish brown, and there were deep creases in it, but it looked firm and full of blood. His cheeks had a good colour. On either side of his mouth there was a half-moon down the length of his cheek, not wrinkles, but two lines that had come there from his habitual expression. He was shorter and broader than when she married him; his back had grown broad and curved, a good deal like the shell of an old turtle, and his arms and legs were short.

He was fifteen years older than Mary, but she had hardly ever thought about it before. He was her man, and the kind of man she liked. She was rough, and he was gentle, — city-bred, as she always said. They had been shipmates on a rough voyage and had stood by each other in trying times. Life had gone well with them because, at bottom, they had the same ideas about life. They agreed, without discussion, as to what was most important and what was secondary. They didn't often exchange opinions, even in Czech, – it was as if they had thought the same thought together. A good deal had to be sacrificed and thrown overboard in a hard life like theirs, and they had never disagreed as to the things that could go. It had been a hard life, and a soft life, too. There wasn't anything brutal in the short, broad-backed man with the three-cornered eyes and the forehead that went on to the top of his skull. He was a city man, a gentle man, and though he had married a rough farm girl, he had never touched her without gentleness.

They had been at one accord not to hurry through life, not to be always skimping and saving. They saw their neighbours buy more land and feed more stock than they did, without discontent. Once when the creamery agent came to the Rosickys to persuade them to sell him their cream, he told them how much money the Fasslers, their nearest neighbours, had made on their cream last year.

'Yes,' said Mary, 'and look at them Fassler children! Pale, pinched little things, they look like skimmed milk. I'd rather put some colour into my children's faces than put money into the bank.'

The agent shrugged and turned to Anton.

'I guess we'll do like she says,' said Rosicky.

III

Mary very soon got into town to see Doctor Ed, and then she had a talk with her boys and set a guard over Rosicky. Even John, the youngest, had his father on his mind. If Rosicky went to throw hay down from the loft, one of the boys ran up the ladder and took the fork from him. He sometimes complained that though he was getting to be an old man, he wasn't an old woman yet.

That winter he stayed in the house in the afternoons and carpentered, or sat in the chair between the window full of plants and the wooden bench where the two pails of drinking-water stood. This spot was called 'Father's corner,' though it was not a corner at all. He had a shelf there, where he kept his Bohemian papers and his pipes and tobacco, and his shears and needles and thread and tailor's thimble. Having been a tailor in his youth, he couldn't bear to see a woman patching at his clothes, or at the boys'. He liked tailoring, and always patched all the overalls and jackets and work shirts. Occasionally he made over a pair of pants one of the older boys had outgrown, for the little fellow.

While he sewed, he let his mind run back over his life. He had a good deal to remember, really; life in three countries. The only part of his youth he didn't like to remember was the two years he had spent in London, in Cheapside, working for a German tailor who was wretchedly poor. Those days, when he was nearly always hungry, when his clothes were dropping off him for dirt, and the sound of a strange language kept him in continual bewilderment, had left a sore spot in his mind that wouldn't bear touching.

He was twenty when he landed at Castle Garden in New York, and he had a protector who got him work in a tailor shop in Vesey Street, down near the Washington Market. He looked upon that part of his life as very happy. He became a good workman, he was industrious, and his wages were increased from time to time. He minded his own business and envied nobody's good fortune. He went to night school and learned to read English. He often did overtime work and was well paid for it, but somehow he never saved anything. He couldn't refuse a loan to a friend, and he was self-indulgent. He liked a good dinner, and a little went for beer, a little for tobacco; a good deal went to the girls. He often stood through an opera on Saturday nights; he could get standing-room for a dollar. Those were the great days of opera in New York, and it gave a fellow something to think about for the rest of the week. Rosicky had a quick ear, and a childish love of all the stage splendour; the scenery, the costumes, the ballet. He usually went with a chum, and after the performance they had beer and maybe some oysters somewhere. It was a fine life; for the first five years or so it satisfied him completely. He was never hungry or cold or dirty, and everything amused him: a fire, a dog fight, a parade, a storm, a ferry ride. He thought New York the finest, richest, friendliest city in the world.

Moreover, he had what he called a happy home life. Very near the tailor shop was a small furniture-factory, where an old Austrian, Loeffler, employed a few skilled men and made unusual furniture, most of it to order, for the rich German housewives up-town. The top floor of Loeffler's five-storey factory was a loft, where he kept his choice lumber and stored the odd pieces of furniture left on his hands. One of the young workmen he employed was a Czech, and he and Rosicky became fast friends. They persuaded Loeffler to let them have a sleeping-room in one corner of the loft. They bought good beds and bedding and had their pick of the furniture kept up there. The loft was low-pitched, but light and airy, full of windows, and good-smelling by reason of the fine lumber put up there to season. Old Loeffler used to go down to the docks and buy wood from South America and the East from the sea captains. The young men were as foolish about their house as a bridal pair. Zichec, the young cabinet-maker, devised every sort of convenience, and Rosicky kept their clothes in order. At night and on Sundays, when the quiver of machinery underneath was still, it was the quietest place in the world, and on summer nights all the sea winds blew in. Zichec often practised on his flute in the evening. They were both fond of music and went to the opera together. Rosicky thought he wanted to live like that for ever.

But as the years passed, all alike, he began to get a little restless. When spring came round, he would begin to feel fretted, and he got to drinking. He was likely to drink too much of a Saturday night. On Sunday he was languid and heavy, getting over his spree. On Monday he plunged into work again. So he never had time to figure out what ailed him, though he knew something did. When the grass turned green in Park Place, and the lilac hedge at the back of Trinity churchyard put out its blossoms, he was tormented by a longing to run away. That was why he drank too much; to get a temporary illusion of freedom and wide horizons.

Rosicky, the old Rosicky, could remember as if it were yesterday the day when the young Rosicky found out what was the matter with him. It was on a Fourth of July afternoon, and he was sitting in Park Place in the sun. The lower part of New York was empty. Wall Street, Liberty Street, Broadway, all empty. So much stone and asphalt with nothing going on, so many empty windows. The emptiness was intense, like the stillness in a great factory when the machinery stops and the belts and bands cease running. It was too great a change, it took all the strength out of one. Those blank buildings, without the stream of life pouring through them, were like empty jails. It struck young Rosicky that this was the trouble with big cities; they built you in from the earth itself, cemented you away from any contact with the ground. You lived in an unnatural world, like the fish in an aquarium, who were probably much more comfortable than they ever were in the sea.

On that very day he began to think seriously about the articles he had read in the Bohemian papers, describing prosperous Czech farming communities in the West. He believed he would like to go out there as a farm hand; it was hardly possible that he could ever have land of his own. His people had always been workmen; his father and grandfather had worked in shops. His mother's parents had lived in the country, but they rented their farm and had a hard time to get along. Nobody in his family had ever owned any land, – that belonged to a different station of life altogether. Anton's mother died when he was little, and he was sent into the country to her parents. He stayed with them until he was twelve, and formed those ties with the earth and the farm animals and growing things which are never made at all unless they are made early. After his grandfather died, he went back to live with his father and stepmother, but she was very hard on him, and his father helped him to get passage to London.

After that Fourth of July day in Park Place, the desire to return to the country never left him. To work on another man's farm would be all he asked; to see the sun rise and set and to plant things and watch them grow. He was a very simple man. He was like a tree that has not many roots, but one tap-root that goes down deep. He subscribed for a Bohemian paper printed in Chicago, then for one printed in Omaha. His mind got farther and farther west. He began to save a little money to buy his liberty. When he was thirty-five, there was a great meeting in New York of Bohemian athletic societies, and Rosicky left the tailor shop and went home with the Omaha delegates to try his fortune in another part of the world.

IV

Perhaps the fact that his own youth was well over before he began to have a family was one reason why Rosicky was so fond of his boys. He had almost a grandfather's indulgence for them. He had never had to worry about any of them – except, just now, a little about Rudolph.

On Saturday night the boys always piled into the Ford, took little Josephine, and went to town to the moving-picture show. One Saturday morning they were talking at the breakfast table about starting early that evening, so that they would have an hour or so to see the Christmas things in the stores before the show began. Rosicky looked down the table.

'I hope you boys ain't disappointed, but I want you to let me have de car tonight. Maybe some of you can go in with de neighbours.'

Their faces fell. They worked hard all week, and they were still like children. A new jack-knife or a box of candy pleased the older ones as much as the little fellow.

'If you and Mother are going to town,' Frank said, 'maybe you could take a couple of us along with you, anyway.'

'No, I want to take de car down to Rudolph's, and let him an' Polly go in to de show. She don't git into town enough, an' I'm afraid she's gettin' lonesome, an' he can't afford no car yet.'

That settled it. The boys were a good deal dashed. Their father took another piece of apple-cake and went on: 'Maybe next Saturday night de two little fellers can go along wid dem.'

'Oh, is Rudolph going to have the car every Saturday night?'

Rosicky did not reply at once; then he began to speak seriously: 'Listen, boys; Polly ain't lookin' so good. I don't like to see nobody lookin' sad. It comes hard fur a town girl to be a farmer's wife. I don't want no trouble to start in Rudolph's family. When it starts, it ain't so easy to stop. An American girl don't git used to our ways all at once. I like to tell Polly she and Rudolph can have the car every Saturday night till after New Year's, if it's all right with you boys.'

'Sure it's all right, Papa,' Mary cut in. 'And it's good you thought about that. Town girls is used to more than country girls. I lay awake nights, scared she'll make Rudolph discontented with the farm.'

The boys put as good a face on it as they could. They surely looked forward to their Saturday nights in town. That evening Rosicky drove the car the half-mile down to Rudolph's new, bare little house.

Polly was in a short-sleeved gingham dress, clearing away the supper dishes. She was a trim, slim little thing, with blue eyes and shingled yellow hair, and her eyebrows were reduced to a mere brush-stroke, like Miss Pearl's.

'Good evening, Mr Rosicky. Rudolph's at the barn, I guess.' She never called him father, or Mary mother. She was sensitive about having married a foreigner. She never in the world would have done it if Rudolph hadn't been such a handsome, persuasive fellow and such a gallant lover. He had graduated in her class in the high school in town, and their friendship began in the ninth grade.

Rosicky went in, though he wasn't exactly asked. 'My boys ain't goin' to town tonight, an' I brought de car over fur you two to go in to de picture show.'

Polly, carrying dishes to the sink, looked over her shoulder to him. 'Thank you. But I'm late with my work tonight, and pretty tired. Maybe Rudolph would like to go in with you.'

'Oh, I don't go to the shows! I'm too old-fashioned. You won't feel so tired after you ride in de air a ways. It's a nice clear night, an' it ain't cold. You go an' fix yourself up, Polly, an' I'll wash de dishes an' leave everything nice fur you.'

Polly blushed and tossed her bob. 'I couldn't let you do that, Mr Rosicky. I wouldn't think of it.'

Rosicky said nothing. He found a bib apron on a nail behind the kitchen door. He slipped it over his head and then took Polly by her two elbows and pushed her gently toward the door of her own room. 'I washed up de kitchen many times for my wife, when de babies was sick or somethin'. You go an' make yourself look nice. I like you to look prettier'n any of dem town girls when you go in. De young folks must have some fun, an' I'm goin' to look out fur you, Polly.'

That kind, reassuring grip on her elbows, the old man's funny bright eyes, made Polly want to drop her head on his shoulder for a second. She restrained herself, but she lingered in his grasp at the door of her room, murmuring tearfully: 'You always lived in the city when you were young, didn't you? Don't you ever get lonesome out here?'

As she turned round to him, her hand fell naturally into his, and he stood holding it and smiling into her face with his peculiar, knowing, indulgent smile without a shadow of reproach in it. 'Dem big cities is all right fur de rich, but dey is terrible hard fur de poor.'

'I don't know. Sometimes I think I'd like to take a chance. You lived in New York, didn't you?'

'An' London. Da's bigger still. I learned my trade dere. Here's Rudolph comin', you better hurry.'

'Will you tell me about London some time?'

'Maybe. Only I ain't no talker, Polly. Run an' dress yourself up.'

The bedroom door closed behind her, and Rudolph came in from the outside, looking anxious. He had seen the car and was sorry any of his family should come just then. Supper hadn't been a very pleasant occasion. Halting in the doorway, he saw his father in a kitchen apron, carrying dishes to the sink. He flushed crimson and something flashed in his eyes. Rosicky held up a warning finger.

'I brought de car over fur you an' Polly to go to de picture show, an' I made her let me finish here so you won't be late. You go put on a clean shirt, quick!'

'But don't the boys want the car, Father?'

'Not tonight dey don't.' Rosicky fumbled under his apron and found his pants pocket. He took out a silver dollar and said in a hurried whisper: 'You go an' buy dat girl some ice cream an' candy tonight, like you was courtin'. She's awful good friends wid me.'

Rudolph was very short of cash, but he took the money as if it hurt him. There had been a crop failure all over the county. He had more than once been sorry he'd married this year.

In a few minutes the young people came out, looking clean and a little stiff. Rosicky hurried them off, and then he took his own time with the dishes. He scoured the pots and pans and put away the milk and swept the kitchen. He put some coal in the stove and shut off the draughts, so the place would be warm for them when they got home late at night. Then he sat down and had a pipe and listened to the clock tick.

Generally speaking, marrying an American girl was certainly a risk. A Czech should marry a Czech. It was lucky that Polly was the daughter of a poor widow woman; Rudolph was proud, and if she had a prosperous family to throw up at him, they could never make it go. Polly was one of four sisters, and they all worked; one was book-keeper in the bank, one taught music, and Polly and her younger sister had been clerks, like Miss Pearl. All four of them were musical, had pretty voices, and sang in the Methodist choir, which the eldest sister directed.

Polly missed the sociability of a store position. She missed the choir, and the company of her sisters. She didn't dislike housework, but she disliked so much of it. Rosicky was a little anxious about this pair. He was afraid Polly would grow so discontented that Rudy would quit the farm and take a factory job in Omaha. He had worked for a winter up there, two years ago, to get money to marry on. He had done very well, and they would always take him back at the stockyards. But to Rosicky that meant the end of everything for his son. To be a landless man was to be a wage-earner, a slave, all your life; to have nothing, to be nothing.

Rosicky thought he would come over and do a little carpentering for Polly after the New Year. He guessed she needed jollying. Rudolph was a serious sort of chap, serious in love and serious about his work.

Rosicky shook out his pipe and walked home across the fields. Ahead of him the lamplight shone from his kitchen windows. Suppose he were still in a tailor shop on Vesey Street, with a bunch of pale, narrow-chested sons working on machines, all coming home tired and sullen to eat supper in a kitchen that was a parlour also; with another crowded, angry family quarrelling just across the dumb-waiter shaft, and squeaking pulleys at the windows where dirty washings hung on dirty lines above a court full of old brooms and mops and ash-cans. . . .

He stopped by the windmill to look up at the frosty winter stars and draw a long breath before he went inside. The kitchen with the shining windows was dear to him; but the sleeping fields and bright stars and the noble darkness were dearer still.

V

On the day before Christmas the weather set in very cold; no snow, but a bitter, biting wind that whistled and sang over the flat land and lashed one's face like fine wires. There was baking going on in the Rosicky kitchen all day, and Rosicky sat inside, making over a coat that Albert had outgrown into an overcoat for John. Mary had a big red geranium in bloom for Christmas, and a row of Jerusalem cherry trees, full of berries. It was the first year she had ever grown these; Doctor Ed brought her the seeds from Omaha when he went to some medical convention. They reminded Rosicky of plants he had seen in England; and all afternoon, as he stitched, he sat thinking about those two years in London, which his mind usually shrank from even after all this while.

He was a lad of eighteen when he dropped down into London, with no money and no connexions except the address of a cousin who was supposed to be working at a confectioner's. When he went to the pastry shop, however, he found that the cousin had gone to America. Anton tramped the streets for several days, sleeping in doorways and on the Embankment, until he was in utter despair. He knew no English, and the sound of the strange language all about him confused him. By chance he met a poor German tailor who had learned his trade in Vienna, and could speak a little Czech. This tailor, Lifschnitz, kept a repair shop in a Cheapside basement, underneath a cobbler. He didn't much need an apprentice, but he was sorry for the boy and took him in for no wages but his keep and what he could pick up. The pickings were supposed to be coppers given you when you took work home to a customer. But most of the customers called for their clothes themselves, and the coppers that came Anton's way were very few. He had, however, a place to sleep. The tailor's family lived upstairs in three rooms; a kitchen, a bedroom, where Lifschnitz and his wife and five children slept, and a living-room. Two corners of this living-room were curtained off for lodgers; in one Rosicky slept on an old horsehair sofa, with a feather quilt to wrap himself in. The other corner was rented to a wretched, dirty boy, who was studying the violin. He actually practised there. Rosicky was dirty, too. There was no way to be anything else. Mrs Lifschnitz got the water she cooked and washed with from a pump in a brick court, four flights down. There were bugs in the place, and multitudes of fleas, though the poor woman did the best she could. Rosicky knew she often went empty to give another potato or a spoonful of dripping to the two hungry, sad-eyed boys who lodged with her. He used to think he would never get out of there, never get a clean shirt to his back again. What would he do, he wondered, when his clothes actually dropped to pieces and the worn cloth wouldn't hold patches any longer?

It was still early when the old farmer put aside his sewing and his recollections. The sky had been a dark grey all day, with not a gleam of sun, and the light failed at four o'clock. He went to shave and change his shirt while the turkey was roasting. Rudolph and Polly were coming over for supper.

After supper they sat round in the kitchen, and the younger boys were saying how sorry they were it hadn't snowed. Everybody was sorry. They wanted a deep snow that would lie long and keep the wheat warm, and leave the ground soaked when it melted.

'Yes, sir!' Rudolph broke out fiercely; 'if we have another dry year like last year, there's going to be hard times in this country.'

Rosicky filled his pipe. 'You boys don't know what hard times is. You don't owe nobody, you got plenty to eat an' keep warm, an' plenty water to keep clean. When you got them, you can't have it very hard.'

Rudolph frowned, opened and shut his big right hand, and dropped it clenched upon his knee. 'I've got to have a good deal more than that, Father, or I'll quit this farming gamble. I can always make good wages railroading, or at the packing house, and be sure of my money.'

'Maybe so,' his father answered dryly.

Mary, who had just come in from the pantry and was

wiping her hands on the roller towel, thought Rudy and his
father were getting too serious. She brought her darning-
basket and sat down in the middle of the group.

'I ain't much afraid of hard times, Rudy,' she said heartily.
'We've had a plenty, but we've always come through. Your
father wouldn't never take nothing very hard, not even hard
times. I got a mind to tell you a story on him. Maybe you
boys can't hardly remember the year we had that terrible hot
wind, that burned everything up on the Fourth of July? All
the corn an' the gardens. An' that was in the days when we
didn't have alfalfa yet, – I guess it wasn't invented.

'Well, that very day your father was out cultivatin' corn,
and I was here in the kitchen makin' plum preserves. We had
bushels of plums that year. I noticed it was terrible hot, but
it's always hot in the kitchen when you're preservin', an' I
was too busy with my plums to mind. Anton come in from
the field about three o'clock, an' I asked him what was the
matter.

'"Nothin'," he says, "but it's pretty hot, an' I think I won't
work no more today." He stood round for a few minutes, an'
then he says: "Ain't you near through? I want you should git
up a nice supper for us tonight. It's Fourth of July."

'I told him to git along, that I was right in the middle of
preservin', but the plums would taste good on hot biscuit.
"I'm goin' to have fried chicken, too," he says, and he went
off an' killed a couple. You three oldest boys was little fellers,
playin' round outside, real hot an' sweaty, an' your father
took you to the horse tank down by the windmill an' took off
your clothes an' put you in. Them two box-elder trees was
little then, but they made shade over the tank. Then he took
off all his own clothes, an' got in with you. While he was
playin' in the water with you, the Methodist preacher drove
into our place to say how all the neighbours was goin' to
meet at the schoolhouse that night, to pray for rain. He drove
right to the windmill, of course, and there was your father
and you three with no clothes on. I was in the kitchen door,
an' I had to laugh, for the preacher acted like he ain't never
seen a naked man before. He surely was embarrassed, an'

your father couldn't git to his clothes; they was all hangin' up on the windmill to let the sweat dry out of 'em. So he laid in the tank where he was, an' put one of you boys on top of him to cover him up a little, an' talked to the preacher.

'When you got through playin' in the water, he put clean clothes on you and a clean shirt on himself, an' by that time I'd begun to get supper. He says: "It's too hot in here to eat comfortable. Let's have a picnic in the orchard. We'll eat our supper behind the mulberry hedge, under them linden trees."

'So he carried our supper down, an' a bottle of my wild-grape wine, an' everything tasted good, I can tell you. The wind got cooler as the sun was goin' down, and it turned out pleasant, only I noticed how the leaves was curled up on the linden trees. That made me think, an' I asked your father if that hot wind all day hadn't been terrible hard on the gardens an' the corn.

'"Corn," he says, "there ain't no corn."

'"What you talkin' about?" I said. "Ain't we got forty acres?"

'"We ain't got an ear," he says, "nor nobody else ain't got none. All the corn in this country was cooked by three o'clock today, like you'd roasted it in an oven."

'"You mean you won't get no crop at all?" I asked him. I couldn't believe it, after he'd worked so hard.

'"No crop this year," he says. "That's why we're havin' a picnic. We might as well enjoy what we got."

'An' that's how your father behaved, when all the neigh-bours was so discouraged they couldn't look you in the face. An' we enjoyed ourselves that year, poor as we was, an' our neighbours wasn't a bit better off for bein' miserable. Some of 'em grieved till they got poor digestions and couldn't relish what they did have.'

The younger boys said they thought their father had the best of it. But Rudolph was thinking that, all the same, the neighbours had managed to get ahead more, in the fifteen years since that time. There must be something wrong about his father's way of doing things. He wished he knew what was going on in the back of Polly's mind. He knew she liked his father, but he knew, too, that she was afraid of something. When his mother sent over coffee-cake or prune tarts or a loaf of fresh bread Polly seemed to regard them with a certain suspicion. When she observed to him that his brothers had nice manners, her tone implied that it was remarkable they should have. With his mother she was stiff and on her guard. Mary's hearty frankness and gusts of good humour irritated her. Polly was afraid of being unusual or conspicuous in anyway, of being 'ordinary,' as she said!

When Mary had finished her story, Rosicky laid aside his pipe.

'You boys like me to tell you about some of dem hard times I been through in London?' Warmly encouraged, he sat rubbing his forehead along the deep creases. It was bothersome to tell a long story in English (he nearly always talked to the boys in Czech), but he wanted Polly to hear this one.

'Well, you know about dat tailor shop I worked in in London? I had one Christmas dere I ain't never forgot. Times was awful bad before Christmas; de boss ain't got much work, an' have it awful hard to pay his rent. It ain't so much fun, bein' poor in a big city like London, I'll say! All de windows is full of good t'ings to eat, an' all de pushcarts in de streets is full, an' you smell 'em all de time, an' you ain't got no money, – not a damn bit. I didn't mind de cold so much, though I didn't have no overcoat, chust a short jacket I'd outgrowed so it wouldn't meet on me, an' my hands was chapped raw. But I always had a good appetite, like you all know, an' de sight of dem pork pies in de windows was awful fur me!

'Day before Christmas was terrible foggy dat year, an' dat fog gits into your bones and makes you all damp like. Mrs Lifschnitz didn't give us nothin' but a little bread an' drippin' for supper, because she was savin' to try for to give us a good dinner on Christmas Day. After supper de boss say I can go an' enjoy myself, so I went into de streets to listen to de Christmas singers. Dey sing old songs an' make very nice music, an' I run round after dem a good ways, till I got awful hungry. I t'ink maybe if I go home, I can sleep till morning an' forgit my belly.

'I went into my corner real quiet, and roll up in my fedder quilt. But I ain't got my head down, till I smell somet'ing good. Seem like it git stronger an' stronger, an' I can't git to sleep noway. I can't understand dat smell. Dere was a gas light in a hall across de court, dat always shine in at my window a little. I got up an' look round. I got a little wooden box in my corner fur a stool, 'cause I ain't got no chair. I picks up dat box, and under it dere is a roast goose on a platter! I can't believe my eyes. I carry it to de window where de light comes in, an' touch it and smell it to find out, an' den I taste it to be sure. I say, I will eat chust one little bit of dat goose, so I can go to sleep, and tomorrow I won't eat none at all. But I tell you, boys, when I stop, one half of dat goose was gone!'

The narrator bowed his head, and the boys shouted. But little Josephine slipped behind his chair and kissed him on the neck beneath his ear.

'Poor little Papa, I don't want him to be hungry!'

'Da's long ago, child. I ain't never been hungry since I had your mudder to cook fur me.'

'Go on and tell us the rest, please,' said Polly.

'Well, when I come to realize what I done, of course, I felt terrible. I felt better in de stomach, but very bad in de heart. I set on my bed wid dat platter on my knees, an' it all come to me; how hard dat woman save to buy dat goose, and how she get some neighbour to cook it dat got more fire, an' how she put it in my corner to keep it away from dem hungry children. Dey was a old carpet hung up to shut my corner off, an' de children wasn't allowed to go in dere. An' I know she put it in my corner because she trust me more'n she did de violin boy. I can't stand it to face her after I spoil de Christmas. So I put on my shoes and go out into de city. I tell myself I better throw myself in de river; but I guess I ain't dat kind of a boy.

'It was after twelve o'clock, an' terrible cold, an' I start out to walk about London all night. I walk along de river awhile, but dey was lots of drunks all along; men and women too. I chust move along to keep away from de police. I git onto de Strand, an' den over to New Oxford Street, where dere was a big German restaurant on de ground floor, wid big windows all fixed up fine, an' I could see de people havin' parties inside. While I was lookin' in, two men and two ladies come out, laughin' and talkin' and feelin' happy about all dey been eatin' an' drinkin', and dey was speakin' Czech, – not like de Austrians, but like de home folks talk it.

'I guess I went crazy, an' I done what I ain't never done before nor since. I went right up to dem gay people an' begun to beg dem: "Fellow-countrymen, for God's sake give me money enough to buy a goose!"

'Dey laugh, of course, but de ladies speak awful kind to me, an' dey take me back into de restaurant and give me hot coffee and cakes, an' make me tell all about how I happened to come to London, an' what I was doin' dere. Dey take my name and where I work down on paper, an' both of dem ladies give me ten shillings.

'De big market at Covent Garden ain't very far away, an' by dat time it was open. I go dere an' buy a big goose an' some pork pies, an' potatoes and onions, an' cakes an' oranges fur de children, – all I could carry! When I git home, everybody is still asleep. I pile all I bought on de kitchen table, an' go in an' lay down on my bed, an' I ain't waken up till I hear dat woman scream when she come out into her kitchen. My goodness, but she was surprise! She laugh an' cry at de same time, an' hug me and waken all de children. She ain't stop fur no breakfast; she git de Christmas dinner ready dat morning, and we all sit down an' eat all we can hold. I ain't never seen dat violin boy have all he can hold before.

'Two three days after dat, de two men come to hunt me up, an' dey ask my boss, and he give me a good report an' tell dem I was a steady boy all right. One of dem Bohemians was very smart an' run a Bohemian newspaper in New York, an' de odder was a rich man, in de importing business, an' dey been travelling togedder. Dey told me how t'ings was easier in New York, an' offered to pay my passage when dey was going' home soon on a boat. My boss say to me: "You go. You ain't got no chance here, an' I like to see you git ahead, fur you always been a good boy to my woman, and fur dat fine Christmas dinner you give us all." An' da's how I got to New York.'

That night when Rudolph and Polly, arm in arm, were running home across the fields with the bitter wind at their backs, his heart leaped for joy when she said she thought they might have his family come over for supper on New Year's Eve. 'Let's get up a nice supper, and not let your mother help at all; make her be company for once.'

'That would be lovely of you, Polly,' he said humbly. He was a very simple, modest boy, and he, too, felt vaguely that Polly and her sisters were more experienced and worldly than his people.

VI

The winter turned out badly for farmers. It was bitterly cold, and after the first light snows before Christmas there was no snow at all, – and no rain. March was as bitter as February. On those days when the wind fairly punished the country, Rosicky sat by his window. In the fall he and the boys had put in a big wheat planting, and now the seed had frozen in the ground. All that land would have to be ploughed up and planted over again, planted in corn. It had happened before, but he was younger then, and he never worried about what had to be. He was sure of himself and of Mary; he knew they could bear what they had to bear, that they would always pull through somehow. But he was not so sure about the young ones, and he felt troubled because Rudolph and Polly were having such a hard start.

Sitting beside his flowering window while the panes rattled and the wind blew in under the door, Rosicky gave himself to reflection as he had not done since those Sundays in the loft of the furniture-factory in New York, long ago. Then he was trying to find what he wanted in life for himself; now he was trying to find what he wanted for his boys, and why it was he so hungered to feel sure they would be here, working this very land, after he was gone.

They would have to work hard on the farm, and probably they would never do much more than make a living. But if he could think of them as staying here on the land, he wouldn't have to fear any great unkindness for them. Hardships, certainly; it was a hardship to have the wheat freeze in the ground when seed was so high; and to have to sell your stock because you had no feed. But there would be other years when everything came along right, and you caught up. And what you had was your own. You didn't have to choose between bosses and strikers, and go wrong either way. You didn't have to do with dishonest and cruel people. They were the only things in his experience he had found terrifying and horrible; the look in the eyes of a dishonest and crafty man, of a scheming and rapacious woman.

In the country, if you had a mean neighbour, you could keep off his land and make him keep off yours. But in the city, all the foulness and misery and brutality of your neighbours was part of your life. The worst things he had come upon in his journey through the world were human, – depraved and poisonous specimens of man. To this day he could recall certain terrible faces in the London streets. There were mean people everywhere, to be sure, even in their own country town here. But they weren't tempered, hardened, sharpened, like the treacherous people in cities who live by grinding or cheating or poisoning their fellow-men. He had helped to bury two of his fellow-workmen in the tailoring trade, and he was distrustful of the organized industries that see one out of the world in big cities. Here, if you were sick, you had Doctor Ed to look after you; and if you died, fat Mr Haycock, the kindest man in the world, buried you.

It seemed to Rosicky that for good, honest boys like his, the worst they could do on the farm was better than the best they would be likely to do in the city. If he'd had a mean boy, now, one who was crooked and sharp and tried to put anything over on his brothers, then town would be the place for him. But he had no such boy. As for Rudolph, the discontented one, he would give the shirt off his back to anyone who touched his heart. What Rosicky really hoped for his boys was that they could get through the world without ever knowing much about the cruelty of human beings. 'Their mother and me ain't prepared them for that,' he sometimes said to himself.

These thoughts brought him back to a grateful consideration of his own case. What an escape he had had, to be sure! He, too, in his time, had had to take money for repair work from the hand of a hungry child who let it go so wistfully; because it was money due his boss. And now, in all these years, he had never had to take a cent from anyone in bitter need, – never had to look at the face of a woman become like a wolf's from struggle and famine. When he thought of these things, Rosicky would put on his cap and jacket and slip down to the barn and give his work-horses a little extra oats, letting them eat it out of his hand in their slobbery fashion. It was his way of expressing what he felt, and made him chuckle with pleasure.

The spring came warm, with blue skies, – but dry, dry as a bone. The boys began ploughing up the wheat-fields to plant them over in corn. Rosicky would stand at the fence corner and watch them, and the earth was so dry it blew up in clouds of brown dust that hid the horses and the sulky plough and the driver. It was a bad outlook.

The big alfalfa-field that lay between the home place and Rudolph's came up green, but Rosicky was worried because during that open windy winter a great many Russian thistle plants had blown in there and lodged. He kept asking the boys to rake them out; he was afraid their seed would root and 'take the alfalfa.' Rudolph said that was nonsense. The boys were working so hard planting corn, their father felt he couldn't insist about the thistles, but he set great store by that big alfalfa field. It was a feed you could depend on, – and there was some deeper reason, vague, but strong. The peculiar green of that clover woke early memories in old Rosicky, went back to something in his childhood in the old world. When he was a little boy, he had played in fields of that strong blue-green colour.

One morning, when Rudolph had gone to town in the car, leaving a work-team idle in his barn, Rosicky went over to his son's place, put the horses to the buggy-rake, and set about quietly raking up those thistles. He behaved with guilty caution, and rather enjoyed stealing a march on Doctor Ed, who was just then taking his first vacation in seven years of practice and was attending a clinic in Chicago. Rosicky got the thistles raked up, but did not stop to burn them. That would take some time, and his breath was pretty short, so he thought he had better get the horses back to the barn.

He got them into the barn and to their stalls, but the pain had come on so sharp in his chest that he didn't try to take the harness off. He started for the house, bending lower with every step. The cramp in his chest was shutting him up like a jack-knife. When he reached the windmill, he swayed and caught at the ladder. He saw Polly coming down the hill, running with the swiftness of a slim greyhound. In a flash she had her shoulder under his armpit.

'Lean on me, Father, hard! Don't be afraid. We can get to the house all right.'

Somehow they did, though Rosicky became blind with pain; he could keep on his legs, but he couldn't steer his course. The next thing he was conscious of was lying on Polly's bed, and Polly bending over him wringing out bath towels in hot water and putting them on his chest. She stopped only to throw coal into the stove, and she kept the tea-kettle and the black pot going. She put these hot applications on him for nearly an hour, she told him afterwards, and all that time he was drawn up stiff and blue, with the sweat pouring off him.

As the pain gradually loosed its grip, the stiffness went out of his jaws, the black circles round his eyes disappeared, and a little of his natural colour came back. When his daughter-in-law buttoned his shirt over his chest at last, he sighed.

'Da's fine, de way I feel now, Polly. It was a awful bad spell, an' I was so sorry it all come on you like it did.'

Polly was flushed and excited. 'Is the pain really gone? Can I leave you long enough to telephone over to your place?'

Rosicky's eyelids fluttered. 'Don't telephone, Polly. It ain't no use to scare my wife. It's nice and quiet here, an' if I ain't too much trouble to you, just let me lay still till I feel like myself. I ain't got no pain now. It's nice here.'

Polly bent over him and wiped the moisture from his face. 'Oh, I'm so glad it's over!' she broke out impulsively. 'It just broke my heart to see you suffer so, Father.'

Rosicky motioned her to sit down on the chair where the tea-kettle had been, and looked up at her with that lively affectionate gleam in his eyes. 'You was awful good to me, I won't never forgit dat. I hate it to be sick on you like dis. Down at de barn I say to myself, dat young girl ain't had much experience in sickness, I don't want to scare her, an' maybe she's got a baby comin' or somet'ing.'

Polly took his hand. He was looking at her so intently and affectionately and confidingly; his eyes seemed to caress her face, to regard it with pleasure. She frowned with her funny streaks of eyebrows, and then smiled back at him.

'I guess maybe there is something of that kind going to happen. But I haven't told anyone yet, not my mother or Rudolph. You'll be the first to know.'

His hand pressed hers. She noticed that it was warm again. The twinkle in his yellow-brown eyes seemed to come nearer.

'I like mighty well to see dat little child, Polly,' was all he said. Then he closed his eyes and lay half-smiling. But Polly sat still, thinking hard. She had a sudden feeling that nobody in the world, not her mother, not Rudolph, or anyone, really loved her as much as old Rosicky did. It perplexed her. She sat frowning and trying to puzzle it out. It was as if Rosicky had a special gift for loving people, something that was like an ear for music or an eye for colour. It was quiet, unobtrusive; it was merely there. You saw it in his eyes, – perhaps that was why they were merry. You felt it in his hands, too. After he dropped off to sleep, she sat holding his warm, broad, flexible brown hand. She had never seen another in the least like it. She wondered if it wasn't a kind of gypsy hand, it was so alive and quick and light in its communications, – very strange in a farmer. Nearly all the farmers she knew had huge lumps of fists, like mauls, or they were knotty and bony and uncomfortable-looking, with stiff fingers. But Rosicky's was like quicksilver, flexible, muscular, about the colour of a pale cigar, with deep, deep creases across the palm. It wasn't nervous, it wasn't a stupid lump; it was a warm brown human hand, with some cleverness in it, a great deal of generosity, and something else which Polly could only call 'gypsy-like,' – something nimble and lively and sure, in the way that animals are.

Polly remembered that hour long afterwards; it had been like an awakening to her. It seemed to her that she had never learned so much about life from anything as from old Rosicky's hand. It brought her to herself; it communicated some direct and untranslatable message.

When she heard Rudolph coming in the car, she ran out to meet him.

'Oh, Rudy, your father's been awful sick! He raked up those thistles he's been worrying about, and afterwards he could hardly get to the house. He suffered so I was afraid he was going to die.'

Rudolph jumped to the ground. 'Where is he now?'

'On the bed. He's asleep. I was terribly scared, because, you know, I'm so fond of your father.' She slipped her arm through his and they went into the house. That afternoon they took Rosicky home and put him to bed, though he protested that he was quite well again.

The next morning he got up and dressed and sat down to breakfast with his family. He told Mary that his coffee tasted better than usual to him, and he warned the boys not to bear any tales to Doctor Ed when he got home. After breakfast he sat down by his window to do some patching and asked Mary to thread several needles for him before she went to feed her chickens, – her eyes were better than his, and her hands steadier. He lit his pipe and took up John's overalls. Mary had been watching him anxiously all morning, and as she went out of the door with her bucket of scraps, she saw that he was smiling. He was thinking, indeed, about Polly, and how he might never have known what a tender heart she had if he hadn't got sick over there. Girls nowadays didn't wear their heart on their sleeve. But now he knew Polly would make a fine woman after the foolishness wore off. Either a woman had that sweetness at her heart or she hadn't. You couldn't always tell by the look of them; but if they had that, everything came out right in the end.

After he had taken a few stitches, the cramp began in his chest, like yesterday. He put his pipe cautiously down on the window-sill and bent over to ease the pull. No use, – he had better try to get to his bed if he could. He rose and groped his way across the familiar floor, which was rising and falling like the deck of a ship. At the door he fell. When Mary came in, she found him lying there, and the moment she touched him she knew that he was gone.

Doctor Ed was away when Rosicky died, and for the first few weeks after he got home he was hard driven. Every day he said to himself that he must get out to see that family that had lost their father. One soft, warm moonlit night in early summer he started for the farm. His mind was on other things, and not until his road ran by the graveyard did he realize that Rosicky wasn't over there on the hill where the red lamplight shone, but here, in the moonlight. He stopped his car, shut off the engine, and sat there for a while.

A sudden hush had fallen on his soul. Everything here seemed strangely moving and significant, though signifying what, he did not know. Close by the wire fence stood Rosicky's mowing-machine, where one of the boys had been cutting hay that afternoon; his own work-horses had been going up and down there. The new-cut hay perfumed all the night air. The moonlight silvered the long, billowy grass that grew over the graves and hid the fence; the few little evergreens stood out black in it, like shadows in a pool. The sky was very blue and soft, the stars rather faint because the moon was full.

For the first time it struck Doctor Ed that this was really a beautiful graveyard. He thought of city cemeteries; acres of shrubbery and heavy stone, so arranged and lonely and unlike anything in the living world. Cities of the dead, indeed; cities of the forgotten, of the 'put away.' But this was open and free, this little square of long grass which the wind for ever stirred. Nothing but the sky overhead, and the many-coloured fields running on until they met that sky. The horses worked here in summer; the neighbours passed on their way to town; and over yonder, in the cornfield, Rosicky's own cattle would be eating fodder as winter came on. Nothing could be more undeathlike than this place; nothing could be more right for a man who had helped to do the work of great cities and had always longed for the open country and had got to it at last. Rosicky's life seemed to him complete and beautiful.

First published in *Woman's Home Companion*, April, May 1930

TWO FRIENDS

I

*E*VEN in early youth, when the mind is so eager for the new and untried, while it is still a stranger to faltering and fear, we yet like to think that there are certain unalterable realities, somewhere at the bottom of things. These anchors may be ideas; but more often they are merely pictures, vivid memories, which in some unaccountable and very personal way give us courage. The sea-gulls, that seem so much creatures of the free wind and waves, that are as homeless as the sea (able to rest upon the tides and ride the storm, needing nothing but water and sky), at certain seasons even they go back to something they have known before; to remote islands and lonely ledges that are their breeding-grounds. The restlessness of youth has such retreats, even though it may be ashamed of them.

Long ago, before the invention of the motorcar (which has made more changes in the world than the War, which indeed produced the particular kind of war that happened just a hundred years after Waterloo), in a little wooden town in a shallow Kansas river valley, there lived two friends. They were 'business men,' the two most prosperous and influential men in our community, the two men whose affairs took them out into the world to big cities, who had 'connections' in St Joseph and Chicago. In my childhood they represented to me success and power.

R.E. Dillon was of Irish extraction, one of the dark Irish, with glistening jet-black hair and moustache, and thick eyebrows. His skin was very white, bluish on his shaven cheeks and chin. Shaving must have been a difficult process for him, because there were no smooth expanses for the razor to glide over. The bony structure of his face was prominent and unusual; high cheek-bones, a bold Roman nose, a chin cut by deep lines, with a hard dimple at the tip, a jutting ridge over his eyes where his curly black eyebrows grew and met. It was a face in many planes, as if the carver had whittled and modelled and indented to see how far he could go. Yet on meeting him what you saw was an imperious head on a rather small, wiry man, a head held conspicuously and proudly erect, with a carriage unmistakably arrogant and consciously superior. Dillon had a musical, vibrating voice, and the changeable grey eye that is peculiarly Irish. His full name, which he never used, was Robert Emmet Dillon, so there must have been a certain feeling somewhere back in his family.

He was the principal banker in our town, and proprietor of the large general store next the bank; he owned farms up in the grass country, and a fine ranch in the green timbered valley of the Caw. He was, according to our standards, a rich man.

His friend, J.H. Trueman, was what we called a big cattleman. Trueman was from Buffalo; his family were old residents there, and he had come West as a young man because he was restless and unconventional in his tastes. He was fully ten years older than Dillon, – in his early fifties, when I knew him; large, heavy, very slow in his movements, not given to exercise. His countenance was as unmistakably American as Dillon's was not, – but American of that period, not of this. He did not belong to the time of efficiency and advertising and progressive methods. For any form of pushing or boosting he had a cold, unqualified contempt. All this was in his face, – heavy, immobile, rather melancholy, not remarkable in any particular. But the moment one looked at him one felt solidity, an entire absence of anything mean or small, easy carelessness, courage, a high sense of honour.

These two men had been friends for ten years before I

knew them, and I knew them from the time I was ten until I was thirteen. I saw them as often as I could, because they led more varied lives than the other men in our town; one could look up to them. Dillon, I believe, was the more intelligent. Trueman had, perhaps, a better tradition, more background.

Dillon's bank and general store stood at the corner of Main Street and a cross-street, and on this cross-street, two short blocks away, my family lived. On my way to and from school, and going on the countless errands that I was sent upon day and night, I always passed Dillon's store. Its long, red brick wall, with no windows except high overhead, ran possibly a hundred feet along the sidewalk of the cross-street. The front door and show windows were on Main Street, and the bank was next door. The board sidewalk along that red brick wall was wider than any other piece of walk in town, smoother, better laid, kept in perfect repair; very good to walk on in a community where most things were flimsy. I liked the store and the brick wall and the sidewalk because they were solid and well built, and possibly I admired Dillon and Trueman for much the same reason. They were secure and established. So many of our citizens were nervous little hopper men, trying to get on. Dillon and Trueman had got on; they stood with easy assurance on a deck that was their own.

In the daytime one did not often see them together – each went about his own affairs. But every evening they were both to be found at Dillon's store. The bank, of course, was locked and dark before the sun went down, but the store was always open until ten o'clock; the clerks put in a long day. So did Dillon. He and his store were one. He never acted as salesman, and he kept a cashier in the wire-screened office at the back end of the store; but he was there to be called on. The thrifty Swedes to the north, who were his best customers, usually came to town and did their shopping after dark – they didn't squander daylight hours in farming season. In these evening visits with his customers, and on his drives in his buckboard among the farms, Dillon learned all he needed to know about how much money it was safe to advance a farmer who wanted to feed cattle, or to buy a steam thrasher or build a new barn.

Every evening in winter, when I went to the post-office after supper, I passed through Dillon's store instead of going round it, – for the warmth and cheerfulness, and to catch sight of Mr Dillon and Mr Trueman playing checkers in the office behind the wire screening; both seated on high accountant's stools, with the checker-board on the cashier's desk before them. I knew all Dillon's clerks, and if they were not busy, I often lingered about to talk to them; sat on one of the grocery counters and watched the checker-players from a distance. I remember Mr Dillon's hand used to linger in the air above the board before he made a move; a well-kept hand, white, marked with blue veins and streaks of strong black hair. Trueman's hands rested on his knees under the desk while he considered; he took a checker, set it down, then dropped his hand on his knee again. He seldom made an unnecessary movement with his hands or feet. Each of the men wore a ring on his little finger. Mr Dillon's was a large diamond solitaire set in a gold claw, Trueman's the head of a Roman soldier cut in onyx and set in pale twisted gold; it had been his father's, I believe.

Exactly at ten o'clock the store closed. Mr Dillon went home to his wife and family, to his roomy, comfortable house with a garden and orchard and big stables. Mr Trueman, who had long been a widower, went to his office to begin the day over. He led a double life, and until one or two o'clock in the morning entertained the poker-players of our town. After everything was shut for the night, a queer crowd drifted into Trueman's back office. The company was seldom the same on two successive evenings, but there were three tireless poker-players who always came: the billiard-hall proprietor, with green-gold moustache and eyebrows, and big white teeth; the horse-trader, who smelled of horses; the dandified cashier of the bank that rivalled Dillon's. The gamblers met in Trueman's place because a game that went on there was respectable, was a social game, no matter how much money changed hands. If the horse-trader or the crooked money-lender got over-heated and broke loose a little, a look or a remark from Mr Trueman would freeze them up. And his remark was always the same:

'Careful of the language around here.'

It was never 'your' language, but 'the' language, – though he certainly intended no pleasantry. Trueman himself was not a lucky poker man; he was never ahead of the game on the whole. He played because he liked it, and he was willing to pay for his amusement. In general he was large and indifferent about money-matters, – always carried a few hundred-dollar bills in his inside coat-pocket, and left his coat hanging anywhere, – in his office, in the bank, in the barber shop, in the cattlesheds behind the freight yard.

Now, R.E. Dillon detested gambling, often dropped a contemptuous word about 'poker bugs' before the horse-trader and the billiard-hall man and the cashier of the other bank. But he never made remarks of that sort in Trueman's presence. He was a man who voiced his prejudices fearlessly and cuttingly, but on this and other matters he held his peace before Trueman. His regard for him must have been very strong.

During the winter, usually in March, the two friends always took a trip together, to Kansas City and St Joseph. When they got ready, they packed their bags and stepped aboard a fast Santa Fé train and went; the Limited was often signalled to stop for them. Their excursions made some of the rest of us feel less shut away and small-townish, just as their fur overcoats and silk shirts did. They were the only men in Singleton who wore silk shirts. The other business men wore white shirts with detachable collars, high and stiff or low and sprawling, which were changed much oftener than the shirts. Neither of my heroes was afraid of laundry bills. They did not wear waistcoats; their suspenders were chosen with as much care as their neckties and handkerchiefs. Once when a bee stung my hand in the store (a few of them had got into the brown-sugar barrel), Mr Dillon himself moistened the sting, put baking soda on it, and bound my hand up with his pocket handkerchief. It was of the smoothest linen, and in one corner was a violet square bearing his initials, R.E.D., in white. There were never any handkerchiefs like that in my family. I cherished it until it was laundered, and I returned it with regret.

It was in the spring and summer that one saw Mr Dillon and Mr Trueman at their best. Spring began early with us, – often the first week of April was hot. Every evening when he came back to the store after supper, Dillon had one of his clerks bring two arm-chairs out to the wide sidewalk that ran beside the red brick wall, – office chairs of the old-fashioned sort, with a low round back which formed a half-circle to enclose the sitter, and spreading legs, the front ones slightly higher. In those chairs the two friends would spend the evening. Dillon would sit down and light a good cigar. In a few moments Mr Trueman would come across from Main Street, walking slowly, spaciously, as if he were used to a great deal of room. As he approached, Mr Dillon would call out to him:

'Good evening, J.H. Fine weather.'

J.H. would take his place in the empty chair.

'Spring in the air,' he might remark, if it were April. Then he would relight a dead cigar which was always in his hand, – seemed to belong there, like a thumb or finger.

'I drove up north today to see what the Swedes are doing,' Mr Dillon might begin. 'They're the boys to get the early worm. They never let the ground go to sleep. Whatever moisture there is, they get the benefit of it.'

'The Swedes are good farmers. I don't sympathize with the way they work their women.'

'The women like it, J.H. It's the old-country way; they're accustomed to it, and they like it.'

'Maybe. I don't like it,' Trueman would reply with something like a grunt.

They talked very much like this all evening; or, rather, Mr Dillon talked, and Mr Trueman made an occasional observation. No one could tell just how much Mr Trueman knew about anything, because he was so consistently silent. Not from diffidence, but from superiority; from a contempt for chatter, and a liking for silence, a taste for it. After they had exchanged a few remarks, he and Dillon often sat in an easy quiet for a long time, watching the passers-by, watching the wagons on the road, watching the stars. Sometimes, very rarely, Mr Trueman told a long story, and it was sure to be an interesting and unusual one.

But on the whole it was Mr Dillon who did the talking; he had a wide-awake voice with much variety in it. Trueman's was thick and low, – his speech was rather indistinct and never changed in pitch or tempo. Even when he swore wickedly at the hands who were loading his cattle into freight cars, it was a mutter, a low, even growl. There was a curious attitude in men of his class and time, that of being rather above speech, as they were above any kind of fussiness or eagerness. But I knew he liked to hear Mr Dillon talk, – anyone did. Dillon had such a crisp, clear enunciation, and he could say things so neatly. People would take a reprimand from him they wouldn't have taken from anyone else, because he put it so well. His voice was never warm or soft – it had a cool, sparkling quality; but it could be very humorous, very kind and considerate, very teasing and stimulating. Every sentence he uttered was alive, never languid, perfunctory, slovenly, unaccented. When he made a remark, it not only meant something, but sounded like something, – sounded like the thing he meant.

When Mr Dillon was closeted with a depositor in his private room in the bank, and you could not hear his words through the closed door, his voice told you exactly the degree of esteem in which he held that customer. It was interested, encouraging, deliberative, humorous, satisfied, admiring, cold, critical, haughty, contemptuous, according to the deserts and pretentions of his listener. And one could tell when the person closeted with him was a woman; a farmer's wife, or a woman who was trying to run a little business, or a country girl hunting a situation. There was a difference; something peculiarly kind and encouraging. But if it were a foolish, extravagant woman, or a girl he didn't approve of, oh, then one knew it well enough! The tone was courteous, but cold; relentless as the multiplication table.

All these possibilities of voice made his evening talk in the spring dusk very interesting; interesting for Trueman and for me. I found many pretexts for lingering near them, and they never seemed to mind my hanging about. I was very quiet. I often sat on the edge of the sidewalk with my feet hanging down and played jacks by the hour when there was moonlight. On dark nights I sometimes perched on top of one of the big goods-boxes – we called them 'store boxes,' – there were usually several of these standing empty on the sidewalk against the red brick wall.

I liked to listen to those two because theirs was the only 'conversation' one could hear about the streets. The older men talked of nothing but politics and their business, and the very young men's talk was entirely what they called 'josh'; very personal, supposed to be funny, and really not funny at all. It was scarcely speech, but noises, snorts, giggles, yawns, sneezes, with a few abbreviated words and slang expressions which stood for a hundred things. The original Indians of the Kansas plains had more to do with articulate speech than had our promising young men.

To be sure my two aristrocrats sometimes discussed politics, and joked each other about the policies and pretentions of their respective parties. Mr Dillon, of course, was a Democrat, – it was in the very frosty sparkle of his speech, – and Mr Trueman was a Republican; his rear, as he walked about the town, looked a little like the walking elephant labelled 'G.O.P.' in *Puck*. But each man seemed to enjoy hearing his party ridiculed, took it as a compliment.

In the spring their talk was usually about weather and planting and pasture and cattle. Mr Dillon went about the country in his light buckboard a great deal at that season, and he knew what every farmer was doing and what his chances were, just how much he was falling behind or getting ahead.

'I happened to drive by Oscar Ericson's place today, and I saw as nice a lot of calves as you could find anywhere,' he would begin, and Ericson's history and his family would be pretty thoroughly discussed before they changed the subject.

Or he might come out with something sharp: 'By the way, J.H., I saw an amusing sight today. I turned in at Sandy Bright's place to get water for my horse, and he had a photographer out there taking pictures of his house and barn. It would be more to the point if he had a picture taken of the mortgages he's put on that farm.'

Trueman would give a short, mirthless response, more like a cough than a laugh.

Those April nights, when the darkness itself tasted dusty (or, by the special mercy of God, cool and damp), when the smell of burning grass was in the air, and a sudden breeze brought the scent of wild plum blossoms, – those evenings were only a restless preparation for the summer nights, – nights of full liberty and perfect idleness. Then there was no school, and one's family never bothered about where one was. My parents were young and full of life, glad to have the children out of the way. All day long there had been the excitement that intense heat produces in some people, – a mild drunkenness made of sharp contrasts; thirst and cold water, the blazing stretch of Main Street and the cool of the brick stores when one dived into them. By nightfall one was ready to be quiet. My two friends were always in their best form on those moonlit summer nights, and their talk covered a wide range.

I suppose there were moonless nights, and dark ones with but a silver shaving and pale stars in the sky, just as in the spring. But I remember them all as flooded by the rich indolence of a full moon, or a half-moon set in uncertain blue. Then Trueman and Dillon would sit with their coats off and have a supply of fresh handkerchiefs to mop their faces; they were more largely and positively themselves. One could distinguish their features, the stripes on their shirts, the flash of Mr Dillon's diamond; but their shadows made two dark masses on the white sidewalk. The brick wall behind them, faded almost pink by the burning of successive summers, took on a carnelian hue at night. Across the street, which was merely a dusty road, lay an open space, with a few stunted box-elder trees, where the farmers left their wagons and teams when they came to town. Beyond this space stood a row of frail wooden buildings, due to be pulled down any day; tilted, crazy, with outside stairs going up to rickety second-storey porches that sagged in the middle. They had once been white, but were now grey, with faded blue doors along the wavy upper porches. These abandoned buildings, an eyesore by day, melted together into a curious pile in the moonlight, became an immaterial structure of velvet-white and glossy blackness, with here and there a faint smear of blue door, or a tilted patch of sage-green that had once been a shutter.

The road, just in front of the sidewalk where I sat and played jacks, would be ankle-deep in dust, and seemed to drink up the moonlight like folds of velvet. It drank up sound, too; muffled the wagon-wheels and hoof-beats; lay soft and meek like the last residuum of material things, – the soft bottom resting-place. Nothing in the world, not snow mountains or blue seas, is so beautiful in moonlight as the soft, dry summer roads in a farming country, roads where the white dust falls back from the slow wagon-wheel.

Wonderful things do happen even in the dullest places – in the cornfields and the wheat-fields. Sitting there on the edge of the sidewalk one summer night, my feet hanging in the warm dust, I saw a transit of Venus. Only the three of us were there. It was a hot night, and the clerks had closed the store and gone home. Mr Dillon and Mr Trueman waited on a little while to watch. It was a very blue night, breathless and clear, not the smallest cloud from horizon to horizon. Everything up there overheard seemed as usual, it was the familiar face of a summer-night sky. But presently we saw one bright star moving. Mr Dillon called to me; told me to watch what was going to happen, as I might never chance to see it again in my lifetime.

That big star certainly got nearer and nearer the moon, – very rapidly, too, until there was not the width of your hand between them – now the width of two fingers – then it passed directly into the moon at about the middle of its girth; absolutely disappeared. The star we had been watching was gone. We waited, I do not know how long, but it seemed to me about fifteen minutes. Then we saw a bright wart on the other edge of the moon, but for a second only, – the machinery up there worked fast. While the two men were exclaiming and telling me to look, the planet swung clear of the golden disk, a rift of blue came between them and widened very fast. The planet did not seem to move, but that inky blue space between it and the moon seemed to spread. The thing was over.

My friends stayed on long past their usual time and talked about eclipses and such matters.

'Let me see,' Mr Trueman remarked slowly, 'they reckon the moon's about two hundred and fifty thousand miles away from us. I wonder how far that star is.'

'I don't know, J.H., and I really don't much care. When we can get the tramps off the railroad, and manage to run this town with one fancy house instead of two, and have a Federal Government that is as honest as a good banking business, then it will be plenty of time to turn our attention to the stars.'

Mr Trueman chuckled and took his cigar from between his teeth. 'Maybe the stars will throw some light on all that, if we get the run of them,' he said humorously. Then he added: 'Mustn't be a reformer, R.E. Nothing in it. That's the only time you ever get off on the wrong foot. Life is what it always has been, always will be. No use to make a fuss.' He got up, said: 'Good-night, R.E.,' said good-night to me, too, because this had been an unusual occasion, and went down the sidewalk with his wide, sailor-like tread, as if he were walking the deck of his own ship.

When Dillon and Trueman went to St Joseph, or, as we called it, St Joe, they stopped at the same hotel, but their diversions were very dissimilar. Mr Dillon was a family man and a good Catholic; he behaved in St Joe very much as if he were at home. His sister was Mother Superior of a convent there, and he went to see her often. The nuns made much of him, and he enjoyed their admiration and all the ceremony with which they entertained him. When his two daughters were going to the convent school, he used to give theatre parties for them, inviting all their friends.

Mr Trueman's way of amusing himself must have tried his

friend's patience – Dillon liked to regulate other people's affairs if they needed it. Mr Trueman had a lot of poker-playing friends among the commission men in St Joe, and he sometimes dropped a good deal of money. He was supposed to have rather questionable women friends there, too. The grasshopper men of our town used to say that Trueman was financial adviser to a woman who ran a celebrated sporting house. Mary Trent, her name was. She must have been a very unusual woman; she had credit with all the banks, and never got into any sort of trouble. She had formerly been head mistress of a girls' finishing school and knew how to manage young women. It was probably a fact that Trueman knew her and found her interesting, as did many another sound business man of that time. Mr Dillon must have shut his ears to these rumours, – a measure of the great value he put on Trueman's companionship.

Though they did not see much of each other on these trips, they immensely enjoyed taking them together. They often dined together at the end of the day, and afterwards went to the theatre. They both loved the theatre; not this play or that actor, but the theatre, – whether they saw *Hamlet* or *Pinafore*. It was an age of good acting, and the drama held a more dignified position in the world than it holds today.

After Dillon and Trueman had come home from the city, they used sometimes to talk over the plays they had seen, recalling the great scenes and fine effects. Occasionally an item in the Kansas City *Star* would turn their talk to the stage.

'J.H., I see by the paper that Edwin Booth is very sick,' Mr Dillon announced one evening as Trueman came up to take the empty chair.

'Yes, I noticed.' Trueman sat down and lit his dead cigar. 'He's not a young man any more.' A long pause. Dillon always seemed to know when the pause would be followed by a remark, and waited for it. 'The first time I saw Edwin Booth was in Buffalo. It was in *Richard the Second*, and it made a great impression on me at the time.' Another pause. 'I don't know that I'd care to see him in that play again. I like tragedy, but that play's a little too tragic. Something very black about it. I think I prefer *Hamlet*.'

They had seen Mary Anderson in St Louis once, and talked of it for years afterwards. Mr Dillon was very proud of her because she was a Catholic girl, and called her 'our Mary.' It was curious that a third person, who had never seen these actors or read the plays, could get so much of the essence of both from the comments of two business men who used none of the language in which such things are usually discussed, who merely reminded each other of moments here and there in the action. But they saw the play over again as they talked of it, and perhaps whatever is seen by the narrator as he speaks is sensed by the listener, quite irrespective of words. This transference of experience went further: in some way the lives of those two men came across to me as they talked, the strong, bracing reality of successful, large-minded men who had made their way in the world when business was still a personal adventure.

II

Mr Dillon went to Chicago once a year to buy goods for his store. Trueman would usually accompany him as far as St Joe, but no farther. He dismissed Chicago as 'too big.' He didn't like to be one of the crowd, didn't feel at home in a city where he wasn't recognized as J.H. Trueman.

It was one of these trips to Chicago that brought about the end – for me and for them; a stupid, senseless, commonplace end.

Being a Democrat, already somewhat 'tainted' by the free-silver agitation, one spring Dillon delayed his visit to Chicago in order to be there for the Democratic Convention – it was the Convention that first nominated Bryan.

On the night after his return from Chicago, Mr Dillon was seated in his chair on the sidewalk, surrounded by a group of men who wanted to hear all about the nomination of a man from a neighbour State. Mr Trueman came across the street in his leisurely way, greeted Dillon, and asked him how he had found Chicago, – whether he had had a good trip.

Mr Dillon must have been annoyed because Trueman didn't mention the Convention. He threw back his head haughtily. 'Well, J.H., since I saw you last, we've found a great leader in this country, and a great orator.' There was a frosty sparkle in his voice that presupposed opposition, – like the feint of a boxer getting ready.

'Great windbag!' muttered Trueman. He sat down in his chair, but I noticed that he did not settle himself and cross his legs as usual.

Mr Dillon gave an artificial laugh. 'It's nothing against a man to be a fine orator. All the great leaders have been eloquent. This Convention was a memorable occasion; it gave the Democratic party a rebirth.'

'Gave it a black eye, and a blind spot, I'd say!' commented Trueman. He didn't raise his voice, but he spoke with more heat than I had ever heard from him. After a moment he added: 'I guess Grover Cleveland must be a sick man; must feel like he'd taken a lot of trouble for nothing.'

Mr Dillon ignored these thrusts and went on telling the group around him about the Convention, but there was a special nimbleness and exactness in his tongue, a chill politeness in his voice that meant anger. Presently he turned again to Mr Trueman, as if he could now trust himself:

'It was one of the great speeches of history, J.H.; our grandchildren will have to study it in school, as we did Patrick Henry's.'

'Glad I haven't got any grandchildren, if they'd be brought up on that sort of tall talk,' said Mr Trueman. 'Sounds like a schoolboy had written it. Absolutely nothing back of it but an unsound theory.'

Mr Dillon's laugh made me shiver; it was like a thin glitter of danger. He arched his curly eyebrows provokingly.

'We'll have four years of currency reform, anyhow. By the end of that time, you old dyed-in-the-wool Republicans will be thinking differently. The under dog is going to have a chance.'

Mr Trueman shifted in his chair. 'That's no way for a banker to talk.' He spoke very low. 'The Democrats will have a long time to be sorry they ever turned Pops. No use talking to you while your Irish is up. I'll wait till you cool off.' He rose and walked away, less deliberately than usual, and Mr Dillon, watching his retreating figure, laughed haughtily and disagreeably. He asked the grain-elevator man to take the vacated chair. The group about him grew, and he sat expounding the reforms proposed by the Democratic candidate until a late hour.

For the first time in my life I listened with breathless interest to a political discussion. Whoever Mr Dillon failed to convince, he convinced me. I grasped it at once: that gold had been responsible for most of the miseries and inequalities of the world; that it had always been the club the rich and cunning held over the poor; and that 'the free and unlimited coinage of silver' would remedy all this. Dillon declared that young Mr Bryan had looked like the patriots of old when he faced and challenged high finance with: 'You shall not press this crown of thorns upon the brow of labour; you shall not crucify mankind upon a cross of gold.' I thought that magnificent; I thought the cornfields would show them a thing or two, back there!

R.E. Dillon had never taken an aggressive part in politics. But from that night on, the Democratic candidate and the free-silver plank were the subject of his talks with his customers and depositors. He drove about the country convincing the farmers, went to the neighbouring towns to use his influence with the merchants, organized the Bryan Club and the Bryan Ladies' Quartette in our county, contributed largely to the campaign fund. This was all a new line of conduct for Mr Dillon, and it sat unsteadily on him. Even his voice became unnatural; there was a sting of comeback in it. His new character made him more like other people and took away from his special personal quality. I wonder whether it was not Trueman, more than Bryan, who put such an edge on him.

While all these things were going on, Trueman kept to his

own office. He came to Dillon's bank on business, but he did
not 'come back to the sidewalk,' as I put it to myself. He waited
and said nothing, but he looked grim. After a month or so,
when he saw that this thing was not going to blow over, when
he heard how Dillon had been talking to representative men
all over the county, and saw the figure he had put down for
the campaign fund, then Trueman remarked to some of his
friends that a banker had no business to commit himself to a
scatter-brained financial policy which would destroy credit.

The next morning Mr Trueman went to the bank across the
street, the rival of Dillon's, and wrote a check on Dillon's bank
'for the amount of my balance.' He wasn't the sort of man who
would ever know what his balance was, he merely kept it big
enough to cover emergencies. That afternoon the Merchants'
National took the check over to Dillon on its collecting rounds,
and by night the word was all over town that Trueman had
changed his bank. After this there would be no going back,
people said. To change your bank was one of the most final
things you could do. The little, unsuccessful men were
pleased, as they always are at the destruction of anything
strong and fine.

All through the summer and the autumn of that campaign
Mr Dillon was away a great deal. When he was at home, he
took his evening airing on the sidewalk, and there was always
a group of men about him, talking of the coming election; that
was the most exciting presidential campaign people could
remember. I often passed this group of my way to the post-
office, but there was no temptation to linger now. Mr Dillon
seemed like another man, and my zeal to free humanity from
the cross of gold had cooled. Mr Trueman I seldom saw. When
he passed me on the street, he nodded kindly.

The election and Bryan's defeat did nothing to soften
Dillon. He had been sure of a Democratic victory. I believe he
felt almost as if Trueman were responsible for the triumph of
Hanna and McKinley. At least he knew that Trueman was
exceedingly well satisfied, and that was bitter to him. He
seemed to me sarcastic and sharp all the time now.

I don't believe self-interest would ever have made a breach

between Dillon and Trueman. Neither would have taken advantage of the other. If a combination of circumstances had made it necessary that one or the other should take a loss in money or prestige, I think Trueman would have pocketed the loss. That was his way. It was his code, moreover. A gentleman pocketed his gains mechanically, in the day's routine; but he pocketed losses punctiliously, with a sharp, if bitter, relish. I believe now, as I believed then, that this was a quarrel of 'principle.' Trueman looked down on anyone who could take the reasoning of the Populist party seriously. He was a perfectly direct man, and he showed his contempt. That was enough. It lost me my special pleasure of summer nights: the old stories of the early West that sometimes came to the surface; the minute biographies of the farming people; the clear, detailed, illuminating accounts of all that went on in the great crop-growing, cattle-feeding world; and the silence, – the strong, rich, outflowing silence between two friends, that was as full and satisfying as the moonlight. I was never to know its like again.

After that rupture nothing went well with either of my two great men. Things were out of true, the equilibrium was gone. Formerly, when they used to sit in their old places on the sidewalk, two black figures with patches of shadow below, they seemed like two bodies held steady by some law of balance, an unconscious relation like that between the earth and the moon. It was this mathematical harmony which gave a third person pleasure.

Before the next presidential campaign came round, Mr Dillon died (a young man still) very suddenly, of pneumonia. We didn't know that he was seriously ill until one of his clerks came running to our house to tell us he was dead. The same clerk, half out of his wits – it looked like the end of the world to him – ran on to tell Mr Trueman.

Mr Trueman thanked him. He called his confidential man, and told him to order flowers from Kansas City. Then he went to his house, informed his housekeeper that he was going away on business, and packed his bag. That same night he boarded the Santa Fé Limited and didn't stop until he was in San Francisco. He was gone all spring. His confidential clerk wrote him letters every week about the business and the new calves, and got telegrams in reply. Trueman never wrote letters.

When Mr Trueman at last came home, he stayed only a few months. He sold out everything he owned to a stranger from Kansas City; his feeding ranch, his barns and sheds, his house and town lots. It was a terrible blow to me; now only the common, everyday people would be left. I used to walk mournfully up and down before his office while all these deeds were being signed, – there were usually lawyers and notaries inside. But once, when he happened to be alone, he called me in, asked me how old I was now, and how far along I had got in school. His face and voice were more than kind, but he seemed absent-minded, as if he were trying to recall something. Presently he took from his watch-chain a red seal I had always admired, reached for my hand, and dropped the piece of carnelian into my palm.

'For a keepsake,' he said evasively.

When the transfer of his property was completed, Mr Trueman left us for good. He spent the rest of his life among the golden hills of San Francisco. He moved into the Saint Francis Hotel when it was first built, and had an office in a high building at the top of what is now Powell Street. There he read his letters in the morning and played poker at night. I've heard a man whose offices were next his tell how Trueman used to sit tilted back in his desk chair, a half-consumed cigar in his mouth, morning after morning, apparently doing nothing, watching the Bay and the ferry-boats, across a line of wind-racked eucalyptus trees. He died at the Saint Francis about nine years after he left our part of the world.

The breaking-up of that friendship between two men who scarcely noticed my existence was a real loss to me, and has ever since been a regret. More than once, in Southern countries where there is a smell of dust and dryness in the air and the nights are intense, I have come upon a stretch of dusty white road drinking up the moonlight beside a blind wall, and have felt a sudden sadness. Perhaps it was not until the next morning that I knew why, – and then only because I had dreamed of Mr Dillon or Mr Trueman in my sleep. When that old scar is occasionally touched by chance, it rouses the old uneasiness; the feeling of something broken that could so easily have been mended; of something delightful that was senselessly wasted, of a truth that was accidentally distorted – one of the truths we want to keep.

First published in *Woman's Home Companion*, July 1932.

OLD MRS HARRIS

I

MRS David Rosen, cross-stitch in hand, sat looking out of the window across her own green lawn to the ragged, sunburned back yard of her neighbours on the right. Occasionally she glanced anxiously over her shoulder toward her shining kitchen, with a black and white linoleum floor in big squares, like a marble pavement.

'Will dat woman never go?' she muttered impatiently, just under her breath. She spoke with a light accent − it affected only her *th's*, and, occasionally, the letter *v*. But people in Skyline thought this unfortunate, in a woman whose superiority they recognized.

Mrs Rosen ran out to move the sprinkler to another spot on the lawn, and in doing so she saw what she had been waiting to see. From the house next door a tall, handsome woman emerged, dressed in white broadcloth and a hat with white lilacs; she carried a sunshade and walked with a free, energetic step, as if she were going out on a pleasant errand.

Mrs Rosen darted quickly back into the house, lest her neighbour should hail her and stop to talk. She herself was in her kitchen housework dress, a crisp blue chambray which fitted smoothly over her tightly corseted figure, and her lustrous black hair was done in two smooth braids, wound flat at the back of her head, like a braided rug. She did not stop for a hat − her dark, ruddy, salmon-tinted skin had little to fear from the sun. She opened the half-closed oven door and took out a symmetrically plaited coffee-cake, beautifully browned, delicately peppered over with poppy seeds, with sugary margins about the twists. On the kitchen table a tray stood ready with cups and saucers. She wrapped the cake in a napkin, snatched up a little French coffee-pot with a black wooden handle, and ran across her green lawn, through the alley-way and the sandy, unkept yard next door, and entered her neighbour's house by the kitchen.

The kitchen was hot and empty, full of the untempered afternoon sun. A door stood open into the next room; a cluttered, hideous room, yet somehow homely. There, beside a goods-box covered with figured oilcloth, stood an old woman in a brown calico dress, washing her hot face and neck at a tin basin. She stood with her feet wide apart, in an attitude of profound weariness. She started guiltily as the visitor entered.

'Don't let me disturb you, Grandma,' called Mrs Rosen. 'I always have my coffee at dis hour in the afternoon. I was just about to sit down to it when I thought: "I will run over and see if Grandma Harris won't take a cup with me." I hate to drink my coffee alone.'

Grandma looked troubled, – at a loss. She folded her towel and concealed it behind a curtain hung across the corner of the room to make a poor sort of closet. The old lady was always composed in manner, but it was clear that she felt embarrassment.

'Thank you, Mrs Rosen. What a pity Victoria just this minute went down town!'

'But dis time I came to see you yourself, Grandma. Don't let me disturb you. Sit down there in your own rocker, and I will put my tray in this little chair between us, so!'

Mrs Harris sat down in her black wooden rocking-chair with curved arms and a faded cretonne pillow on the wooden seat. It stood in the corner beside a narrow spindle-frame lounge. She looked on silently while Mrs Rosen uncovered the cake and delicately broke it with her plump, smooth, dusky-red hands. The old lady did not seem pleased – seemed uncertain and apprehensive, indeed. But she was not fussy or fidgety. She had the kind of quiet, intensely quiet, dignity that comes from complete resignation to the chances of life. She watched Mrs Rosen's deft hands out of grave, steady brown eyes.

'Dis is Mr Rosen's favourite coffee-cake. Grandma, and I want you to try it. You are such a good cook yourself, I would like your opinion of my cake.'

'It's very nice, ma'am,' said Mrs Harris politely, but without enthusiasm.

'And you aren't drinking your coffee; do you like more cream in it?'

'No, thank you. I'm letting it cool a little. I generally drink it that way.'

'Of course she does,' thought Mrs Rosen, 'since she never has her coffee until all the family are done breakfast!'

Mrs Rosen had brought Grandma Harris coffee-cake time and again, but she knew that Grandma merely tasted it and saved it for her daughter Victoria, who was as fond of sweets as her own children, and jealous about them, moreover, – couldn't bear that special dainties should come into the house for anyone but herself. Mrs Rosen, vexed at her failures, had determined that just once she would take a cake to 'de old lady Harris,' and with her own eyes see her eat it. The result was not all she had hoped. Receiving a visitor alone, unsupervised by her daughter, having cake and coffee that should properly be saved for Victoria, was all so irregular that Mrs Harris could not enjoy it. Mrs Rosen doubted if she tasted the cake as she swallowed it, – certainly she ate it without relish, as a hollow form. But Mrs Rosen enjoyed her own cake, at any rate, and she was glad of an opportunity to sit quietly and look at Grandmother, who was more interesting to her than the handsome Victoria.

It was a queer place to be having coffee, when Mrs Rosen liked order and comeliness so much: a hideous, cluttered room, furnished with a rocking-horse, a sewing-machine, an empty baby-buggy. A walnut table stood against a blind window, piled high with old magazines and tattered books, and children's caps and coats. There was a wash-stand (two wash-stands, if you counted the oilcloth-covered box as one). A corner of the room was curtained off with some black-and-red-striped cotton goods, for a clothes closet. In another corner was the wooden lounge with a thin mattress and a red calico spread which was Grandma's bed. Beside it was her wooden rocking-chair, and the little splint-bottom chair with the legs sawed short on which her darning-basket usually stood, but which Mrs Rosen was now using for a tea-table.

The old lady was always impressive, Mrs Rosen was thinking, – one could not say why. Perhaps it was the way she held her head, – so simply, unprotesting and unprotec-ted; or the gravity of her large, deep-set brown eyes, a warm, reddish-brown, though their look, always direct, seemed to ask nothing and hope for nothing. They were not cold, but inscrutable, with no kindling gleam of intercourse in them. There was the kind of nobility about her head that there is about an old lion's: an absence of self-conscious-ness, vanity, preoccupation – something absolute. Her grey hair was parted in the middle, wound in two little horns over her ears, and done in a little flat knot behind. Her mouth was large and composed, – resigned, the corners drooping. Mrs Rosen had very seldom heard her laugh (and then it was a gentle, polite laugh which meant only polite-ness). But she had observed that whenever Mrs Harris's grandchildren were about, tumbling all over her, asking for cookies, teasing her to read to them, the old lady looked happy.

As she drank her coffee, Mrs Rosen tried one subject after another to engage Mrs Harris's attention.

'Do you feel this hot weather, Grandma? I am afraid you are over the stove too much. Let those naughty children have a cold lunch occasionally.'

'No'm, I don't mind the heat. It's apt to come on like this for a spell in May. I don't feel the stove. I'm accustomed to it.'

'Oh, so am I! But I get very impatient with my cooking in hot weather. Do you miss your old home in Tennessee very much, Grandma?'

'No'm, I can't say I do. Mr Templeton thought Colorado was a better place to bring up the children.'

'But you had things much more comfortable down there, I'm sure. These little wooden houses are too hot in summer.'

'Yes'm, we were comfortable. We had more room.'

'And a flower-garden, and beautiful old trees, Mrs Templeton told me.'

'Yes'm, we had a great deal of shade.'

Mrs Rosen felt that she was not getting anywhere. She almost believed that Grandma thought she had come on an equivocal errand, to spy out something in Victoria's absence. Well, perhaps she had! Just for once she would like to get past the others to the real grandmother, – and the real grandmother was on her guard, as always. At this moment she heard a faint miaow. Mrs Harris rose, lifting herself by the wooden arms of her chair, said: 'Excuse me,' went into the kitchen, and opened the screen door.

In walked a large, handsome, thickly furred Maltese cat, with long whiskers and yellow eyes and a white star on his breast. He preceded Grandmother, waited until she sat down. Then he sprang up into her lap and settled himself comfortably in the folds of her full-gathered calico skirt. He rested his chin in his deep bluish fur and regarded Mrs Rosen. It struck her that he held his head in just the way Grandmother held hers. And Grandmother now became more alive, as if some missing part of herself were restored.

'This is Blue Boy,' she said, stroking him. 'In winter, when the screen door ain't on, he lets himself in. He stands up on his hind legs and presses the thumb-latch with his paw, and just walks in like anybody.'

'He's your cat, isn't he, Grandma?' Mrs Rosen couldn't help prying just a little; if she could find but a single thing that was Grandma's own!

'He's our cat,' replied Mrs Harris 'We're all very fond of him. I expect he's Vickie's more'n anybody's.'

'Of course!' groaned Mrs Rosen to herself. 'Dat Vickie is her mother over again.'

Here Mrs Harris made her first unsolicited remark. 'If you was to be troubled with mice at any time, Mrs Rosen, ask one of the boys to bring Blue Boy over to you, and he'll clear them out. He's a master mouser.' She scratched the thick blue fur at the back of his neck, and he began a deep purring. Mrs Harris smiled. 'We call that spinning, back with us. Our children still say: "Listen to Blue Boy spin", though none of 'em is ever heard a spinning-wheel – except maybe Vickie remembers.'

'Did you have a spinning-wheel in your own house, Grandma Harris?'

'Yes'm. Miss Sadie Crummer used to come and spin for us. She was left with no home of her own, and it was to give her something to do, as much as anything, that we had her. I spun a good deal myself, in my young days.' Grandmother stopped and put her hands on the arms of her chair, as if to rise. 'Did you hear a door open? It might be Victoria.'

'No, it was the wind shaking the screen door. Mrs Templeton won't be home yet. She is probably in my husband's store this minute, ordering him about. All the merchants down town will take anything from your daughter. She is very popular wid de gentlemen, Grandma.'

Mrs Harris smiled complacently, 'Yes'm. Victoria was always much admired.'

At this moment a chorus of laughter broke in upon the warm silence, and a host of children, as it seemed to Mrs Rosen, ran through the yard. The hand-pump on the back porch, outside the kitchen door, began to scrape and gurgle.

'It's the children, back from school,' said Grandma. 'They are getting a cool drink.'

'But where is the baby, Grandma?'

'Vickie took Hughie in his cart over to Mr Holliday's yard, where she studies. She's right good about minding him.'

Mrs Rosen was glad to hear that Vickie was good for something.

Three little boys came running in through the kitchen; the

twins, aged ten, and Ronald, aged six, who went to kindergarten. They snatched off their caps and threw their jackets
and school bags on the table, the sewing-machine, the
rocking-horse.

'Howdy do, Mrs Rosen.' They spoke to her nicely. They
had nice voices, nice faces, and were always courteous, like
their father. 'We are going to play in our back yard with
some of the boys, Gram'ma', said one of the twins respectfully, and they ran out to join a troop of schoolmates who
were already shouting and racing over that poor trampled
back yard, strewn with velocipedes and croquet mallets and
toy wagons, which was such an eyesore to Mrs Rosen.

Mrs Rosen got up and took her tray.

'Can't you stay a little, ma'am? Victoria will be here any
minute.'

But her tone let Mrs Rosen know that Grandma really
wished her to leave before Victoria returned.

A few moments after Mrs Rosen had put the tray down in
her own kitchen, Victoria Templeton came up the wooden
sidewalk, attended by Mr Rosen, who had quitted his store
half an hour earlier than usual for the pleasure of walking
home with her. Mrs Templeton stopped by the picket fence
to smile at the children playing in the back yard, – and it
was a real smile, she was glad to see them. She called
Ronald over to the fence to give him a kiss. He was hot and
sticky.

'Was your teacher nice today? Now run in and ask
Grandma to wash your face and put a clean waist on you.'

II

That night Mrs Harris got supper with an effort – had to
drive herself harder than usual. Mandy, the bound girl they
had brought with them from the South, noticed that the old
lady was uncertain and short of breath. The hours from two
to four, when Mrs Harris usually rested, had not been at all
restful this afternoon. There was an understood rule that
Grandmother was not to receive visitors alone. Mrs Rosen's

call, and her cake and coffee, were too much out of the accepted order. Nervousness had prevented the old lady from getting any repose during her visit.

After the rest of the family had left the supper table, she went into the dining-room and took her place, but she ate very little. She put away the food that was left, and then, while Mandy washed the dishes, Grandma sat down in her rocking chair in the dark and dozed.

The three little boys came in from playing under the electric light (arc lights had been but lately installed in Skyline) and began begging Mrs Harris to read *Tom Sawyer* to them. Grandmother loved to read, anything at all, the Bible or the continued story in the Chicago weekly paper. She roused herself, lit her brass 'safety-lamp,' and pulled her black rocker out of its corner to the wash-stand (the table was too far away from her corner, and anyhow it was completely covered with coats and school satchels). She put on her old-fasioned silver-rimmed spectacles and began to read. Ronald lay down on Grandmother's lounge bed, and the twins, Albert and Adelbert, called Bert and Del, sat down against the wall, one on a low box covered with felt, and the other on the little sawed-off chair upon which Mrs Rosen had served coffee. They looked intently at Mrs Harris, and she looked intently at the book.

Presently Vickie, the oldest grandchild, came in. She was fifteen. Her mother was entertaining callers in the parlour, callers who didn't interest Vickie, so she was on her way up to her own room by the kitchen stairway.

Mrs Harris looked up over her glasses. 'Vickie, maybe you'd take the book awhile, and I can do my darning.'

'All right,' said Vickie. Reading aloud was one of the things she would always do toward the general comfort. She sat down by the wash-stand and went on with the story. Grandmother got her darning-basket and began to drive her needle across great knee-holes in the boys' stockings. Sometimes she nodded for a moment, and her hands fell into her lap. After a while the little boy on the lounge went to sleep. But the twins sat upright, their hands on their knees, their round brown eyes fastened upon Vickie, and when there was anything funny, they giggled. They were chubby, dark-skinned little boys, with round jolly faces, white teeth, and yellow-brown eyes that were always bubbling with fun unless they were sad, – even then their eyes never got red or weepy. Their tears sparkled and fell; left no trace but a streak on the cheeks, perhaps.

Presently old Mrs Harris gave out a long snore of utter defeat. She had been overcome at last. Vickie put down the book. 'That's enough for tonight. Grandmother's sleepy, and Ronald's fast asleep. What'll we do with him?'

'Bert and me'll get him undressed,' said Adelbert. The twins roused the sleepy little boy and prodded him up the back stairway to the bare room without window blinds, where he was put into his cot beside their double bed. Vickie's room was across the narrow hallway; not much bigger than a closet, but, anyway, it was her own. She had a chair and an old dresser and beside her bed was a high stool which she used as a lamp-table, – she always read in bed.

After Vickie went upstairs, the house was quiet. Hughie, the baby, was asleep in his mother's room, and Victoria herself, who still treated her husband as if he were her 'beau', had persuaded him to take her down to the ice-cream parlour. Grandmother's room, between the kitchen and the dining-room, was rather like a passage-way; but now that the children were upstairs and Victoria was off enjoying herself somewhere, Mrs Harris could be sure of enough privacy to undress. She took off the calico cover from her lounge bed and folded it up, put on her nightgown and white nightcap.

Mandy, the bound girl, appeared at the kitchen door.

'Miz' Harris,' she said in a guarded tone, ducking her head, 'you want me to rub your feet for you?'

For the first time in the long day the old woman's low composure broke a little. 'Oh, Mandy, I would take it kindly of you!' she breathed gratefully.

That had to be done in the kitchen; Victoria didn't like anybody slopping about. Mrs Harris put an old checked shawl round her shoulders and followed Mandy. Beside the kitchen stove Mandy had a little wooden tub full of warm water. She knelt down and untied Mrs Harris's garter strings and took off her flat cloth slippers and stockings.

'Oh, Miz' Harris, your feet an' legs is swelled turrible tonight!'

'I expect they air, Mandy. They feel like it.'

'Pore soul!' murmured Mandy. She put Grandma's feet in the tub and, crouching beside it, slowly, slowly rubbed her swollen legs. Mandy was tired, too. Mrs Harris sat in her nightcap and shawl, her hands crossed in her lap. She never asked for this greatest solace of the day; it was something that Mandy gave, who had nothing else to give. If there could be a comparison in absolutes, Mandy was the needier of the two, – but she was younger. The kitchen was quiet and full of shadow, with only the light from an old lantern. Neither spoke. Mrs Harris dozed from comfort, and Mandy herself was half asleep as she performed one of the oldest rites of compassion.

Although Mrs Harris's lounge had no springs, only a thin cotton mattress between her and the wooden slats, she usually went to sleep as soon as she was in bed. To be off her feet, to lie flat, to say over the psalm beginning: '*The Lord is my shepherd*,' was comfort enough. About four o'clock in the morning, however, she would begin to feel the hard slats under her, and the heaviness of the old home-made quilts, with weight but little warmth, on top of her. Then she would reach under her pillow for her little comforter (she called it that to herself) that Mrs Rosen had given her. It was a tan sweater of very soft brushed wool, with one sleeve torn and ragged. A young nephew from Chicago had spent a fortnight with Mrs Rosen last summer and had left this behind him. One morning, when Mrs Harris went out to the stable at the back of the yard to pat Buttercup, the cow, Mrs Rosen ran across the alley-way.

'Grandma Harris,' she said, coming into the shelter of the stable, 'I wonder if you could make use of this sweater Sammy left? The yarn might be good for your darning.'

Mrs Harris felt of the article gravely. Mrs Rosen thought her face brightened, 'Yes'm, indeed I could use it. I thank you kindly.'

She slipped it under her apron, carried it into the house with her, and concealed it under her mattress. There she had kept it ever since. She knew Mrs Rosen understood how it was; that Victoria couldn't bear to have anything come into the house that was not for her to dispose of.

On winter nights, and even on summer nights after the cocks began to crow, Mrs Harris often felt cold and lonely about the chest. Sometimes her cat, Blue Boy, would creep in beside her and warm that aching spot. But on spring and summer nights he was likely to be abroad skylarking, and this little sweater had become the dearest of Grandmother's few possessions. It was kinder to her, she used to think, as she wrapped it about her middle, than any of her own children had been. She had married at eighteen and had had eight children; but some had died, and some were, as she said, scattered.

After she was warm in that tender spot under her ribs, the old woman could lie patiently on the slats, waiting for daybreak; thinking about the comfortable rambling old house in Tennessee, its feather beds and handwoven rag carpets and splint-bottom chairs, the mahogany sideboard, and the marble-top parlour table; all that she had left behind to follow Victoria's fortunes.

She did not regret her decison; indeed, there had been no decison. Victoria had never once thought it possible that Ma should not go wherever she and the children went, and Mrs Harris had never thought it possible. Of course she regretted Tennessee, though she would never admit it to Mrs Rosen: – the old neighbours, the yard and garden she had worked in all her life, the apple trees she had planted, the lilac arbour, tall enough to walk in, which she had clipped and shaped so many years. Especially she missed her lemon tree, in a tub on the front porch, which bore little lemons almost every summer, and folks would come for miles to see it.

But the road had led westward, and Mrs Harris didn't believe that women, especially old women, could say when or where they would stop. They were tied to the chariot of young life, and had to go where it went, because they were needed. Mrs Harris had gathered from Mrs Rosen's manner, and from comments she occasionally dropped, that the Jewish people had an altogether different attitude toward their old folks; therefore her friendship with this kind neighbour was almost as disturbing as it was pleasant. She didn't want Mrs Rosen to think that she was 'put upon', that there was anything unusual or pitiful in her lot. To be pitied was the deepest hurt anybody could know. And if Victoria once suspected Mrs Rosen's indignation, it would be all over. She would freeze her neighbour out, and that friendly voice, that quick pleasant chatter with the little foreign twist, would thenceforth be heard only at a distance, in the alley-way or across the fence. Victoria had a good heart, but she was terribly proud and could not bear the least criticism.

As soon as the grey light began to steal into the room, Mrs Harris would get up softly and wash at the basin on the oilcloth-covered box. She would wet her hair above her forehead, comb it with a little bone comb set in a tin rim, do it up in two smooth little horns over her ears, wipe the comb dry, and put it away in the pocket of her full-gathered calico skirt. She left nothing lying about. As soon as she was dressed, she made her bed, folding her nightgown and nightcap under the pillow, the sweater under the mattress. She smoothed the heavy quilts, and drew the red calico spread neatly over all. Her towel was hung on its special nail behind the curtain. Her soap she kept in a tin tobacco-box; the children's soap was in a crockery saucer. If her soap or towel got mixed up with the children's, Victoria was always sharp about it. The little rented house was much too small for the family, and Mrs Harris and her 'things' were almost required to be invisible. Two clean calico dresses hung in the curtained corner; another was on her back, and a fourth was in the wash. Behind the curtain there was always a good supply of aprons; Victoria bought them at church fairs, and it was a great satisfaction to Mrs Harris to put on a clean one whenever she liked. Upstairs, in Mandy's attic room over the kitchen, hung a black cashmere dress and a black bonnet with a long crêpe veil, for the rare occasions when Mr Templeton hired a double buggy and horses and drove his family to a picnic or to Decoration Day exercises. Mrs Harris rather dreaded these drives, for Victoria was usually cross afterwards.

When Mrs Harris went out into the kitchen to get breakfast, Mandy always had the fire started and the water boiling. They enjoyed a quiet half-hour before the little boys came running down the stairs, always in a good humour. In winter the boys had their breakfast in the kitchen, with Vickie. Mrs Harris made Mandy eat the cakes and fried ham the children left, so that she would not fast so long. Mr and Mrs Templeton breakfasted rather late, in the dining-room, and they always had fruit and thick cream, – a small pitcher of the very thickest was for Mrs Templeton. The children were never fussy about their food. As Grandmother often said feelingly to Mrs Rosen, they were as little trouble as children could possibly be. They sometimes tore their clothes, of course, or got sick. But even when Albert had an abscess in his ear and was in such pain, he would lie for hours in Grandmother's lounge with his cheek on a bag of hot salt, if only she or Vickie would read aloud to him.

'It's true, too, what de old lady says,' remarked Mrs Rosen to her husband one night at supper, 'dey are nice children. No one ever taught them anything, but they have good instincts, even dat Vickie. And think, if you please, of all the self-sacrificing mothers we know, – Fannie and Esther, to come near home; how they have planned for those children from infancy and given them every advantage. And now ingratitude and coldness is what dey meet with.'

Mr Rosen smiled his teasing smile. 'Evidently your sister and mine have the wrong method. The way to make your children unselfish is to be comfortably selfish yourself.'

'But dat woman takes no more responsibility for her

children than a cat takes for her kittens. Nor does poor young Mr Templeton, for dat matter. How can he expect to get so many children started in life, I ask you? It is not at all fair!'

Mr Rosen sometimes had to hear altogether too much about the Templetons, but he was patient, because it was a bitter sorrow to Mrs Rosen that she had no children. There was nothing else in the world she wanted so much.

III

Mrs Rosen in one of her blue working dresses, the indigo blue that became a dark skin and dusky red cheeks with a tone of salmon colour, was in her shining kitchen, washing her beautiful dishes – her neighbours often wondered why she used her best china and linen every day – when Vickie Templeton came in with a book under her arm.

'Good day, Mrs Rosen. Can I have the second volume?'

'Certainly. You know where the books are.' She spoke coolly, for it always annoyed her that Vickie never suggested wiping the dishes or helping with such household work as happened to be going on when she dropped in. She hated the girl's bringing-up so much that sometimes she almost hated the girl.

Vickie strolled carelessly through the dining-room into the parlour and opened the doors of one of the big bookcases. Mr Rosen had a large library, and a great many unusual books. There was a complete set of the Waverley Novels in German, for example; thick, dumpy little volumes bound in tooled leather, with very black type and dramatic engravings printed on wrinkled, yellowing pages. There were many French books, and some of the German classics done into English, such as Coleridge's translation of Schiller's *Wallenstein*.

Of course no other house in Skyline was in the least like Mrs Rosen's; it was the nearest thing to an art gallery and a museum that the Templetons had ever seen. All the rooms were carpeted alike (that was very unusual), with a soft velvet carpet, little blue and rose flowers scattered on a rose-grey ground. The deep chairs were upholstered in dark blue velvet. The walls were hung with engravings in pale gold frames: some of Raphael's 'Hours', a large soft engraving of a castle on the Rhine, and another of cypress trees about a Roman ruin, under a full moon. There were a number of water-colour sketches, made in Italy by Mr Rosen himself when he was a boy. A rich uncle had taken him abroad as his secretary. Mr Rosen was a reflective, unambitious man, who didn't mind keeping a clothing-store in a little Western town, so long as he had a great deal of time to read philosophy. He was the only unsuccessful member of a large, rich Jewish family.

Last August, when the heat was terrible in Skyline, and the crops were burned up on all the farms to the north, and the wind from the pink and yellow sand-hills to the south blew so hot that it singed the few green lawns in the town, Vickie had taken to dropping in upon Mrs Rosen at the very hottest part of the afternoon. Mrs Rosen knew, of course, that it was probably because the girl had no other cool and quiet place to go – her room at home under the roof would be hot enough! Now, Mrs Rosen liked to undress and take a nap from three to five, – if only to get out of her tight corsets, for she would have an hour-glass figure at any cost. She told Vickie firmly that she was welcome to come if she would read in the parlour with the blind up only a little way, and would be as still as a mouse. Vickie came, meekly enough, but she seldom read. She would take a sofa pillow and lie down on the soft carpet and look up at the pictures in the dusky room, and feel a happy, pleasant excitement from the heat and glare outside and the deep shadow and quiet within. Curiously enough, Mrs Rosen's house never made her dissatisfied with her own; she thought that very nice, too.

Mrs Rosen, leaving her kitchen in a state of such perfection as the Templetons were unable to sense or to admire, came into the parlour and found her visitor sitting cross-legged on the floor before one of the bookcases.

'Well, Vickie, and how did you get along with *Wilhelm Meister?*'

'I like it,' said Vickie.

Mrs Rosen shrugged. The Templetons always said that; quite as if a book or a cake were lucky to win their approbation.

'Well, *what* did you like?'

'I guess I liked all that about the theatre and Shakspere best.'

'It's rather celebrated,' remarked Mrs Rosen dryly. 'And are you studying every day? Do you think you will be able to win that scholarship?'

'I don't know. I'm going to try awful hard.'

Mrs Rosen wondered whether any Templeton knew how to try very hard. She reached for her work-basket and began to do cross-stitch. It made her nervous to sit with folded hands.

Vickie was looking at a German book in her lap, an illustrated edition of *Faust*. She had stopped at a very German picture of Gretchen entering the church, with Faustus gazing at her from behind a rose tree, Mephisto at his shoulder.

'I wish I could read this,' she said, frowning at the black Gothic text. 'It's splendid, isn't it?'

Mrs Rosen rolled her eyes upward and sighed. 'Oh, my dear, one of de world's masterpieces!'

That meant little to Vickie. She had not been taught to respect masterpieces, she had no scale of that sort in her mind. She cared about a book only because it took hold of her.

She kept turning over the pages. Between the first and second parts, in this edition, there was inserted the *Dies Irae* hymn in full. She stopped and puzzled over it for a long while.

'Here is something I can read,' she said, showing the page to Mrs Rosen.

Mrs Rosen looked up from her cross-stitch. 'There you have the advantage of me. I do not read Latin. You might translate it for me.'

Vickie began:

> 'Day of wrath, upon that day
> The world of ashes melts away,
> As David and the Sibyl say.

'But that don't give you the rhyme; every line ought to end in two syllables.'

'Never mind if it doesn't give the metre,' corrected Mrs Rosen kindly; 'go on, if you can.'

Vickie went on stumbling through the Latin verses, and Mrs Rosen sat watching her. You couldn't tell about Vickie. She wasn't pretty, yet Mrs Rosen found her attractive. She liked her sturdy build, and the steady vitality that glowed in her rosy skin and dark blue eyes, – even gave a springy quality to her curly reddish-brown hair, which she still wore in a single braid down her back. Mrs Rosen liked to have Vickie about because she was never listless or dreamy or apathetic. A half-smile nearly always played about her lips and eyes, and it was there because she was pleased with something, not because she wanted to be agreeable. Even a half-smile made her cheeks dimple. She had what her mother called 'a happy disposition.'

When she finished the verses, Mrs Rosen nodded approvingly. 'Thank you, Vickie. The very next time I go to Chicago, I will try to get an English translation of *Faust* for you.'

'But I want to read this one.' Vickie's open smile darkened. 'What I want is to pick up any of these books and just read them, like you and Mr Rosen do.'

The dusky red of Mrs Rosen's cheeks grew a trifle deeper. Vickie never paid compliments, absolutely never; but if she really admired anyone, something in her voice betrayed it so convincingly that one felt flattered. When she dropped a remark of this kind, she added another link to the chain of responsibility which Mrs Rosen unwillingly bore and tried to shake off – the irritating sense of being somehow responsible for Vickie, since, God knew, no one else felt responsible.

Once or twice, when she happened to meet pleasant young Mr Templeton alone, she had tried to talk to him seriously about his daughter's future. 'She has finished de school here, and she should be getting training of some sort; she is growing up,' she told him severely.

He laughed and said in his way that was so honest, and so disarmingly sweet and frank: 'Oh, don't remind me, Mrs Rosen! I just pretend to myself she isn't. I want to keep my little daughter as long as I can.' And there it ended.

Sometimes Vickie Templeton seemed so dense, so utterly unperceptive, that Mrs Rosen was ready to wash her hands of her. Then some queer streak of sensibility in the child would make her change her mind. Last winter, when Mrs Rosen came home from a visit to her sister in Chicago, she brought with her a new cloak of the sleeveless dolman type, black velvet, lined with grey and white squirrel skins, a grey skin next a white. Vickie, so indifferent to clothes, fell in love with that cloak. Her eyes followed it with delight whenever Mrs Rosen wore it. She found it picturesque, romantic. Mrs Rosen had been captivated by the same thing in the cloak, and had bought it with a shrug, knowing it would be quite out of place in Skyline; and Mr Rosen, when she first produced it from her trunk, had laughed and said: 'Where did you get that? – out of *Rigoletto*?' It looked like that – but how could Vickie know?

Vickie's whole family puzzled Mrs Rosen; their feelings were so much finer than their way of living. She bought milk from the Templetons because they kept a cow – which Mandy milked, – and every night one of the twins brought the milk to her in a tin pail. Whichever boy brought it, she always called him Albert – she thought Adelbert a silly, Southern name.

One night when she was fitting the lid on an empty pail, she said severely:

'Now, Albert, I have put some cookies for Grandma in this pail, wrapped in a napkin. And they are for Grandma, remember, not for your mother or Vickie.'

'Yes'm.'

When she turned to him to give him the pail, she saw two full crystal globes in the little boy's eyes, just ready to break. She watched him go softly down the path and dash those tears away with the back of his hand. She was sorry. She hadn't thought the little boys realized that their household was somehow a queer one.

Queer or not, Mrs Rosen liked to go there better than to most houses in the town. There was something easy, cordial, and carefree in the parlour that never smelled of being shut up, and the ugly furniture looked hospitable. One felt a pleasantness in the human relationships. These people didn't seem to know there were such things as struggle or exactness or competition in the world. They were always genuinely glad to see you, had time to see you, and were usually gay in mood – all but Grandmother, who had the kind of gravity that people who take thought of human destiny must have. But even she liked light-heartedness in others; she drudged, indeed, to keep it going.

There were houses that were better kept, certainly, but the housekeepers had no charm, no gentleness of manner, were like hard little machines, most of them; and some were grasping and narrow. The Templetons were not selfish or scheming. Anyone could take advantage of them, and many people did. Victoria might eat all the cookies her neighbour sent in, but she would give away anything she had. She was always ready to lend her dresses and hats and bits of jewellery for the school theatricals, and she never worked people for favours.

As for Mr Templeton (people usually called him 'young Mr Templeton'), he was too delicate to collect his just debts. His boyish, eager-to-please manner, his fair complexion and blue eyes and young face, made him seem very soft to some of the hard old money-grubbers in Main Street, and the fact that he always said 'Yes, sir,' and 'No, sir,' to men older than himself furnished a good deal of amusement to bystanders.

Two years ago, when this Templeton family came to Skyline and moved into the house next door, Mrs Rosen was inconsolable. The new neighbours had a lot of children, who would always be making a racket. They put a cow and a horse into the empty barn, which would mean dirt and flies. They strewed their back yard with packing-cases and did not pick them up.

She first met Mrs Templeton at an afternoon card party, in a house at the extreme north end of the town, fully half a mile away, and she had to admit that her new neighbour was an attractive woman, and that there was something warm and genuine about her. She wasn't in the least willowy or languishing, as Mrs Rosen had usually found Southern ladies to be. She was high-spirited and direct; a trifle imperious, but with a shade of diffidence, too, as if she were trying to adjust herself to a new group of people and to do the right thing.

While they were at the party, a blinding snowstorm came on, with a hard wind. Since they lived next door to each other, Mrs Rosen and Mrs Templeton struggled homeward together through the blizzard. Mrs Templeton seemed delighted with the rough weather; she laughed like a big country girl whenever she made a mis-step off the obliterated sidewalk and sank up to her knees in a snow-drift.

'Take care, Mrs Rosen,' she kept calling, 'keep to the right. Don't spoil your nice coat. My, ain't this real winter? We never had it like this back with us.'

When they reached the Templeton's gate, Victoria wouldn't hear of Mrs Rosen's going farther, 'No, indeed, Mrs Rosen, you come right in with me and get dry, and Ma'll make you a hot toddy while I take the baby.'

By this time Mrs Rosen had begun to like her neighbour, so she went in. To her surprise, the parlour was neat and comfortable – the children did not strew things about there, apparently. The hard-coal burner threw out a warm red glow. A faded, respectable Brussels carpet covered the floor, an old-fashioned wooden clock ticked on the walnut bookcase. There were a few easy chairs, and no hideous ornaments about. She rather liked the old oil-chromos on the wall: 'Hagar and Ishmael in the Wilderness,' and 'The Light of the World.' While Mrs Rosen dried her feet on the nickel

base of the stove, Mrs Templeton excused herself and withdrew to the next room, – her bedroom, – took off her silk dress
and corsets, and put on a white challis négligée. She reappeared with the baby, who was not crying, exactly, but
making eager, passionate, gasping entreaties, – faster and
faster, tenser and tenser, as he felt his dinner nearer and
nearer and yet not his.

Mrs Templeton sat down in a low rocker by the stove and
began to nurse him, holding him snugly but carelessly, still
talking to Mrs Rosen about the card party, and laughing about
their wade home through the snow. Hughie, the baby, fell to
work so fiercely that beads of sweat came out all over his
flushed forehead. Mrs Rosen could not help admiring him and
his mother. They were so comfortable and complete. When he
was changed to the other side, Hughie resented the interrup-
tion a little; but after a time he became soft and bland, as
smooth as oil, indeed; began looking about him as he drew in
his milk. He finally dropped the nipple from his lips altogether,
turned on his mother's arm, and looked inquiringly at Mrs
Rosen.

'What a beautiful baby!' she exclaimed from her heart. And
he was. A sort of golden baby. His hair was like sunshine, and
his long lashes were gold over such gay blue eyes. There
seemed to be a gold glow in his soft pink skin, and he had the
smile of a cherub.

'We think he's a pretty boy,' said Mrs Templeton. 'He's the
prettiest of my babies. Though the twins were mighty cunning
little fellows. I hated the idea of twins, but the minute I saw
them, I couldn't resist them.'

Just then old Mrs Harris came in, walking widely in her
full-gathered skirt and felt-soled shoes, bearing a tray with
two smoking goblets upon it.

'This is my mother, Mrs Harris, Mrs Rosen,' said Mrs
Templeton.

'I'm glad to know you, ma'am,' said Mrs Harris. 'Victoria, let
me take the baby, while you two ladies have your toddy.'

'Oh, don't take him away, Mrs Harris, please!' cried Mrs
Rosen.

The old lady smiled, 'I won't, I'll set right here. He never frets with his grandma.'

When Mrs Rosen had finished her excellent drink, she asked if she might hold the baby, and Mrs Harris placed him on her lap. He made a few rapid boxing motions with his two fists, then braced himself on his heels and the back of his head, and lifted himself up in an arc. When he dropped back, he looked up at Mrs Rosen with his most intimate smile. 'See what a smart boy I am!'

When Mrs Rosen walked home, feeling her way through the snow by following the fence, she knew she could never stay away from a house where there was a baby like that one.

IV

Vickie did her studying in a hammock hung between two tall cottonwood trees over in the Roadmaster's green yard. The Roadmaster had the finest yard in Skyline, on the edge of the town, just where the sandy plain and the sage-brush began. His family went back to Ohio every summer, and Bert and Del Templeton were paid to take care of his lawn, to turn the sprinkler on at the right hours and to cut the grass. They were really too little to run the heavy lawn-mower very well, but they were able to manage because they were twins. Each took one end of the handlebar, and they pushed together like a pair of fat Shetland ponies. They were very proud of being able to keep the lawn so nice, and worked hard on it. They cut Mrs Rosen's grass once a week, too, and did it so well that she wondered why in the world they never did anything about their own yard. They didn't have the city water, to be sure (it was expensive), but she thought they might pick up a few velocipedes and iron hoops, and dig up the messy 'flower-bed', that was even uglier than the naked gravel spots. She was particularly offended by a deep ragged ditch, a miniature arroyo, which ran across the back yard, serving no purpose and looking very dreary.

One morning she said craftily to the twins, when she was paying them for cutting her grass:

'And, boys, why don't you just shovel the sand-pile by your fence into dat ditch, and make your back yard smooth?'

'Oh, no, ma'am,' said Adelbert with feeling. 'We like to have the ditch to build bridges over!'

Ever since vacation began, the twins had been busy getting the Roadmaster's yard ready for the Methodist lawn party. When Mrs Holliday, the Roadmaster's wife, went away for the summer, she always left a key with the Ladies' Aid Society and invited them to give their ice-cream social at her place.

This year the date set for the party was June fifteenth. The day was a particularly fine one, and as Mr Holliday himself had been called to Cheyenne on railroad business, the twins felt personally responsible for everything. They got out to the Holliday place early in the morning, and stayed on guard all day. Before noon the drayman brought a wagon-load of card-tables and folding chairs, which the boys placed in chosen spots under the cottonwood trees. In the afternoon the Methodist ladies arrived and opened up the kitchen to receive the freezers of home-made ice-cream, and the cakes which the congregation donated. Indeed, all the good cake-bakers in town were expected to send a cake. Grandma Harris baked a white cake, thickly iced and covered with freshly grated coconut, and Vickie took it over in the afternoon.

Mr and Mrs Rosen, because they belonged to no church, contributed to the support of all, and usually went to the church suppers in winter and the socials in summer. On this warm June evening they set out early, in order to take a walk first. They strolled along the hard gravelled road that led out through the sage toward the sand-hills; tonight it led toward the moon, just rising over the sweep of dunes. The sky was almost as blue as at midday, and had that look of being very near and very soft which it has in desert countries. The moon, too, looked very near, soft and bland

and innocent. Mrs Rosen admitted that in the Adirondacks, for which she was always secretly homesick in summer, the moon had a much colder brilliance, seemed farther off and made of a harder metal. This moon gave the sage-brush plain and the drifted sand-hills the softness of velvet. All countries were beautiful to Mr Rosen. He carried a country of his own in his mind, and was able to unfold it like a tent in any wilderness.

When they at last turned back toward the town, they saw groups of people, women in white dresses, walking toward the dark spot where the paper lanterns made a yellow light underneath the cottonwoods. High above, the rustling tree-tops stirred free in the flood of moonlight.

The lighted yard was surrounded by a low board fence, painted the dark red Burlington colour, and as the Rosens drew near, they noticed four children standing close together in the shadow of some tall elder bushes just outside the fence. They were the poor Maude children; their mother was the washwoman, the Rosens' laundress and the Templetons'. People said that every one of those children had a different father. But good laundresses were few, and even the members of the Ladies' Aid were glad to get Mrs Maude's services at a dollar a day, though they didn't like their children to play with hers. Just as the Rosens approached, Mrs Templeton came out from the lighted square, leaned over the fence, and addressed the little Maudes.

'I expect you children forgot your dimes, now didn't you? Never mind, here's a dime for each of you, so come along and have your ice-cream.'

The Maudes put out small hands and said: 'Thank you,' but not one of them moved.

'Come along, Francie' (the oldest girl was named Frances). 'Climb right over the fence.' Mrs Templeton reached over and gave her a hand, and the little boys quickly scrambled after their sister. Mrs Templeton took them to a table which Vickie and the twins had just selected as being especially private – they liked to do things together.

'Here, Vickie, let the Maudes sit at your table and take care they get plenty of cake.'

The Rosens had followed close behind Mrs Templeton, and Mr Rosen now overtook her and said in his most courteous and friendly manner: 'Good evening, Mrs Templeton. Will you have ice-cream with us?' He always used the local idioms, though his voice and enunciation made them sound altogether different from Skyline speech.

'Indeed I will, Mr Rosen. Mr Templeton will be late. He went out to his farm yesterday, and I don't know just when to expect him.'

Vickie and the twins were disappointed at not having their table to themselves, when they had come early and found a nice one; but they knew it was right to look out for the dreary little Maudes, so they moved closer together and made room for them. The Maudes didn't cramp them long. When the three boys had eaten the last crumb of cake and licked their spoons, Francie got up and led them to a green slope by the fence, just outside the lighted circle. 'Now set down, and watch and see how folks do,' she told them. The boys looked to Francie for commands and support. She was really Amos Maude's child, born before he ran away to the Klondike, and it had been rubbed into them that this made a difference.

The Templeton children made their ice-cream linger out, and sat watching the crowd. They were glad to see their mother go to Mr Rosen's table, and noticed how nicely he placed a chair for her and insisted upon putting a scarf about her shoulders. Their mother was wearing her new dotted Swiss, with many ruffles, all edged with black ribbon, and wide ruffly sleeves. As the twins watched her over their spoons, they thought how much prettier their mother was than any of the other women, and how becoming her new dress was. The children got as much satisfaction as Mrs Harris out of Victoria's good looks.

Mr Rosen was well pleased with Mrs Templeton and her new dress, and with her kindness to the little Maudes. He thought her manner with them just right, – warm, spontaneous, without anything patronizing. He always admired her way with her own children, though Mrs Rosen thought it too casual. Being a good mother, he believed, was much more a matter of physical poise and richness than of sentimentalizing and reading doctor-books. Tonight he was more talkative than usual, and in his quiet way made Mrs Templeton feel his real friendliness and admiration. Unfortunately, he made other people feel it, too.

Mrs Jackson, a neighbour who didn't like the Templetons, had been keeping an eye on Mr Rosen's table. She was a stout square woman of imperturbable calm, effective in regulating the affairs of the community because she never lost her temper, and could say the most cutting things in calm, even kindly, tones. Her face was smooth and placid as a mask, rather good-humoured, and the fact that one eye had a cast and looked askance made it the more difficult to see through her intentions. When she had been lingering about the Rosens' table for some time, studying Mr Rosen's pleasant attentions to Mrs Templeton, she brought up a trayful of cake.

'You folks are about ready for another helping,' she remarked affably.

Mrs Rosen spoke. 'I want some of Grandma Harris's cake. It's a white coconut, Mrs Jackson.

'How about you, Mrs Templeton, would you like some of your own cake?'

'Indeed I would,' said Mrs Templeton heartily, 'Ma said she had good luck with it. I didn't see it. Vickie brought it over.'

Mrs Jackson deliberately separated the slices on her tray with two forks. 'Well,' she remarked with a chuckle that really sounded amiable, 'I don't know but I'd like my cakes, if I kept somebody in the kitchen to bake them for me.'

Mr Rosen for once spoke quickly. 'If I had a cook like Grandma Harris in my kitchen, I'd live in it!' he declared.

Mrs Jackson smiled. 'I don't know as we feel like that, Mrs Templeton? I tell Mr Jackson that my idea of coming up in the world would be to forget I had a cook-stove, like Mrs Templeton. But we can't all be lucky.'

Mr Rosen could not tell how much was malice and how much was stupidity. What he chiefly detected was self-satisfaction; the craftiness of the coarse-fibred country girl putting catch questions to the teacher. Yes, he decided, the woman was merely showing off, — she regarded it as an accomplishment to make people uncomfortable. Mrs Templeton didn't at once take it in. Her training was all to the end that you must give a guest everything you have, even if he happens to be your worst enemy, and that to cause anyone embarrassment is a frightful and humiliating blunder. She felt hurt without knowing just why, but all evening it kept growing clearer to her that this was another of those thrusts from the outside which she couldn't understand. The neighbours were sure to take sides against her, apparently, if they came often to see her mother.

Mr Rosen tried to distract Mrs Templeton, but he could feel the poison working. On the way home the children knew something had displeased or hurt their mother. When they went into the house, she told them to go upstairs at once, as she had a headache. She was severe and distant. When Mrs Harris suggested making her some peppermint tea, Victoria threw up her chin.

'I don't want anybody waiting on me. I just want to be let alone.' And she withdrew without saying good-night, or 'Are you all right, Ma?' as she usually did.

Left alone, Mrs Harris sighed and began to turn down her bed. She knew, as well as if she had been at the social, what kind of thing had happened. Some of those prying ladies of the Woman's Relief Corps, or the Woman's Christian Temperance Union, had been intimating to Victoria that her mother was 'put upon.' Nothing ever made Victoria cross but criticism. She was jealous of small attentions paid to Mrs Harris, because she felt they were paid 'behind her back' or 'over her head', in a way that implied reproach to her. Victoria had been a belle in their own town in Tennessee, but here she was not very popular, no matter how many pretty dresses she wore, and she couldn't bear it. She felt as if her mother and Mr Templeton must be somehow to blame; at least they ought to protect her from whatever was disagreeable – they always had!

V

Mrs Harris wakened at about four o'clock, as usual, before
the house was stirring, and lay thinking about their position
in this new town. She didn't know why, the neighbours
acted so; she was as much in the dark as Victoria. At home,
back in Tennessee, her place in the family was not exceptional, but perfectly regular. Mrs Harris had replied to Mrs
Rosen, when that lady asked why in the world she didn't
break Vickie in to help her in the kitchen: 'We are only
young once, and trouble comes soon enough.' Young girls,
in the South, were supposed to be carefree and foolish; the
fault Grandmother found in Vickie was that she wasn't
foolish enough. When the foolish girl married and began to
have children, everything else must give way to that. She
must be humoured and given the best of everything,
because having children was hard on a woman, and it was
the most important thing in the world. In Tennessee every
young married woman in good circumstances had an older
woman in the house, a mother or mother-in-law or an old
aunt, who managed the household economies and directed
the help.

That was the great difference; in Tennessee there had
been plenty of helpers. There was old Miss Sadie Crummer,
who came to the house to spin and sew and mend; old Mrs
Smith, who always arrived to help at butchering- and
preserving-time; Lizzie, the coloured girl, who did the
washing and who ran in every day to help Mandy. There
were plenty more, who came whenever one of Lizzie's
barefoot boys ran to fetch them. The hills were full of
solitary old women, or women but slightly attached to some
household, who were glad to come to Miz' Harris's for good
food and a warm bed, and the little present that either Mrs
Harris or Victoria slipped into their carpet-sack when they
went away.

To be sure, Mrs Harris, and the other women of her age
who managed their daughter's house, kept in the background; but it was their own background, and they ruled it

jealously. They left the front porch and the parlour to the young married couple and their young friends; the old women spent most of their lives in the kitchen and pantries and back dining-room. But there they ordered life to their own taste, entertained their friends, dispensed charity, and heard the troubles of the poor. Moreover, back there it was Grandmother's own house they lived in. Mr Templeton came of a superior family and had what Grandmother called 'blood,' but no property. He never so much as mended one of the steps to the front porch without consulting Mrs Harris. Even 'back home', in the aristocracy, there were old women who went on living like young ones, – gave parties and drove out in their carriage and 'went North' in the summer. But among the middle-class people and the country-folk, when a woman was a widow and had married daughters, she considered herself an old woman and wore full-gathered black dresses and a black bonnet and became a housekeeper. She accepted this estate unprotestingly, almost gratefully.

The Templetons' troubles began when Mr Templeton's aunt died and left him a few thousand dollars, and he got the idea of bettering himself. The twins were little then, and he told Mrs Harris his boys would have a better chance in Colorado – everybody was going West. He went alone first, and got a good position with a mining company in the mountains of southern Colorado. He had been book-keeper in the bank in his home town, had 'grown up in the bank', as they said. He was industrious and honourable, and the managers of the mining company liked him, even if they laughed at his polite, soft-spoken manners. He could have held his position indefinitely, and maybe got a promotion. But the altitude of that mountain town was too high for his family. All the children were sick there; Mrs Templeton was ill most of the time and nearly died when Ronald was born. Hillary Templeton lost his courage and came north to the flat, sunny, semi-arid country between Wray and Cheyenne, to work for an irrigation project. So far, things had not gone well with him. The pinch told on everyone, but most on Grandmother. Here, in Skyline, she had all her accustomed responsibilities, and no helper but Mandy. Mrs Harris was no longer living in a feudal society, where there were plenty of landless people glad to render service to the more fortunate, but in a snappy little Western democracy, where every man was as good as his neighbour and out to prove it.

Neither Mrs Harris nor Mrs Templeton understood just what was the matter; they were hurt and dazed, merely. Victoria knew that here she was censured and criticized, she who had always been so admired and envied! Grandmother knew that these meddlesome 'Northerners' said things that made Victoria suspicious and unlike herself; made her unwilling that Mrs Harris should receive visitors alone, or accept marks of attention that seemed offered in compassion for her state.

These women who belonged to clubs and Relief Corps lived differently, Mrs Harris knew, but she herself didn't like the way they lived. She believed that somebody ought to be in the parlour, and somebody in the kitchen. She wouldn't for the world have had Victoria go about every morning in a short gingham dress, with bare arms, and a dust-cap on her head to hide the curling-kids, as these brisk housekeepers did. To Mrs Harris that would have meant real poverty, coming down in the world so far that one could no longer keep up appearances. Her life was hard now, to be sure, since the family went on increasing and Mr Templeton's means went on decreasing; but she certainly valued respectability above personal comfort, and she could go on a good way yet if they always had a cool pleasant parlour, with Victoria properly dressed to receive visitors. To keep Victoria different from these 'ordinary' women meant everything to Mrs Harris. She realized that Mrs Rosen managed to be mistress of any situation, either in kitchen or parlour, but that was because she was 'foreign'. Grandmother perfectly understood that their neighbour had a superior cultivation which made everything she did an exercise of skill. She knew well enough that their own ways of cooking and cleaning were primitive beside Mrs Rosen's.

If only Mr Templeton's business affairs would look up, they could rent a larger house, and everything would be better. They might even get a German girl to come in and help, – but now there was no place to put her. Grandmother's own lot could improve only with the family fortunes – any comfort for herself, aside from that of the family, was inconceivable to her; and on the other hand she could have no real unhappiness, while the children were well, and good, and fond of her and their mother. That was why it was worth while to get up early in the morning and make her bed neat and draw the red spread smooth. The little boys loved to lie on her lounge and her pillows when they were tired. When they were sick, Ronald and Hughie wanted to be in her lap. They had no physical shrinking from her because she was old. And Victoria was never jealous of the children's wanting to be with her so much; that was a mercy!

Sometimes, in the morning, if her feet ached more than usual, Mrs Harris felt a little low. (Nobody did anything about broken arches in those days, and the common endurance test of old age was to keep going after every step cost something.) She would hang up her towel with a sigh and go into the kitchen, feeling that it was hard to make a start. But the moment she heard the children running down the uncarpeted back stairs, she forgot to be low. Indeed, she ceased to be an individual, an old woman with aching feet; she became part of a group, became a relationship. She was drunk up into their freshness when they burst in upon her, telling her about their dreams, explaining their troubles with buttons and shoe-laces and underwear shrunk too small. The tired, solitary old woman Grandmother had been at daybreak vanished; suddenly the morning seemed as important to her as it did to the children, and the mornings ahead stretched out sunshiny, important.

VI

The day after the Methodist social, Blue Boy didn't come for his morning milk; he always had it in a clean saucer on the covered back porch, under the long bench where the tin wash-tubs stood ready for Mrs Maude. After the children had finished breakfast, Mrs Harris sent Mandy out to look for the cat.

The girl came back in a minute, her eyes big.

'Law me, Miz' Harris, he's awful sick. He's a-layin' in the straw in the barn. He's swallered a bone, or having' a fit or somethin'.'

Grandmother threw an apron over her head and went out to see for herself. The children went with her. Blue Boy was retching and choking, and his yellow eyes were filled up with rhume.

'Oh, Gram'ma, what's the matter?' the boys cried.

'It's the distemper. How could he have got it?' Her voice was so harsh that Ronald began to cry. 'Take Ronald back to the house, Del. He might get bit. I wish I'd kept my word and never had a cat again!'

'Why, Gram'ma!' Albert looked at her. 'Won't Blue Boy get well?'

'Not from the distemper, he won't.'

'But Gram'ma, can't I run for the veter'nary?'

'You gether up an armful of hay. We'll take him into the coal-house, where I can watch him.'

Mrs Harris waited until the spasm was over, then picked up the limp cat and carried him to the coal-shed that opened off the back porch. Albert piled the hay in one corner – the coal was low, since it was summer – and they spread a piece of old carpet on the hay and made a bed for Blue Boy. 'Now you run along with Adelbert. There'll be a lot of work to do on Mr Holliday's yard, cleaning up after the sociable. Mandy an' me'll watch Blue Boy. I expect he'll sleep for a while.'

Albert went away regretfully, but the drayman and some of the Methodist ladies were in Mr Holliday's yard, packing chairs and tables and ice-cream freezers into the wagon, and the twins forgot the sick cat in their excitement. By noon they had picked up the last paper napkin, raked over the gravel walks where the salt from the freezers had left white patches, and hung the hammock in which Vickie did her studying back in its place. Mr Holliday paid the boys a dollar a week for keeping up the yard, and they gave the money to their mother – it didn't come amiss in a family where actual cash was so short. She let them keep half the sum Mrs Rosen paid for her milk every Saturday, and that was more spending money than most boys had. They often made a few extra quarters by cutting grass for other people, or by distributing handbills. Even the disagreeable Mrs Jackson next door had remarked over the fence to Mrs Harris: 'I do believe Bert and Del are going to be industrious. They must have got it from you, Grandma.'

The day came on very hot, and when the twins got back from the Roadmaster's yard, they both lay down on Grandmother's lounge and went to sleep. After dinner they had a rare opportunity; the Roadmaster himself appeared at the front door and invited them to go up to the next town with him on his railroad velocipede. That was great fun: the velocipede always whizzed along so fast on the bright rails, the gasoline engine puffing; and grasshoppers jumped up out of the sage-brush and hit you in the face like sling-shot bullets. Sometimes the wheels cut in two a lazy snake who was sunning himself on the track, and the twins always hoped it was a rattler and felt they had done a good work.

The boys got back from their trip with Mr Holliday late in the afternoon. The house was cool and quiet. Their mother had taken Ronald and Hughie down town with her, and Vickie was off somewhere, Grandmother was not in her room, and the kitchen was empty. The boys went out to the back porch to pump a drink. The coal-shed door was open, and inside, on a low stool, sat Mrs Harris beside her cat. Bert and Del didn't stop to get a drink; they felt ashamed that they had gone off for a gay ride and forgotten Blue Boy. They sat down on a big lump of coal beside Mrs Harris. They would never have known that this miserable rumpled animal was their proud tom. Presently he went off into a spasm and began to froth at the mouth.

'Oh, Gram'ma, can't you do anything?' cried Albert,

struggling with his tears. 'Blue Boy was such a good cat, – why has he got to suffer?'

'Everything that's alive has got to suffer,' said Mrs Harris. Albert put out his hand and caught her skirt, looking up at her beseechingly, as if to make her unsay that saying, which he only half understood. She patted his hand. She had forgot she was speaking to a little boy.

'Where's Vickie?' Adelbert asked aggrievedly. 'Why don't she do something? He's part her cat.'

Mrs Harris sighed. 'Vickie's got her head full of things lately; that makes people kind of heartless.'

The boys resolved they would never put anything into their heads, then!

Blue Boy's fit passed, and the three sat watching their pet that no longer knew them. The twins had not seen much suffering; Grandmother had seen a great deal. Back in Tennessee, in her own neighbourhood, she was accounted a famous nurse. When any of the poor mountain people were in great distress, they always sent for Miz' Harris. Many a time she had gone into a house where five or six children were all down with scarlet fever or diptheria, and done what she could. Many a child and many a woman she had laid out and got ready for the grave. In her primitive community the undertaker made the coffin, – he did nothing more. She had seen so much misery that she wondered herself why it hurt so to see her tom-cat die. She had taken her leave of him, and she got up from her stool. She didn't want the boys to be too much distressed.

'Now you boys must wash and put on clean shirts. Your mother will be home pretty son. We'll leave Blue Boy; he'll likely be easier in the morning.' She knew the cat would die at sundown.

After supper, when Bert looked into the coal-shed and found the cat dead, all the family were sad. Ronald cried miserably, and Hughie cried because Ronald did. Mrs Templeton herself went out and looked into the shed, and she was sorry, too. Though she didn't like cats, she had been fond of this one.

'Hillary,' she told her husband, 'when you go down town tonight, tell the Mexican to come and get that cat early in the morning, before the children are up.'

The Mexican had a cart and two mules, and he hauled away tin cans and refuse to a gully out in the sage-brush.

Mrs Harris gave Victoria an indignant glance when she heard this, and turned back to the kitchen. All evening she was gloomy and silent. She refused to read aloud, and the twins took Ronald and went mournfully out to play under the electric light. Later, when they had said good-night to their parents in the parlour and were on their way upstairs, Mrs Harris followed them into the kitchen, shut the door behind her, and said indignantly:

'Air you two boys going to let that Mexican take Blue Boy and throw him onto some trash-pile?'

The sleepy boys were frightened at the anger and bitterness on her tone. They stood still and looked up at her, while she went on:

'You git up early in the morning, and I'll put him in a sack, and one of you take a spade and go to that crooked old willer tree that grows just where the sand creek turns off the road, and you dig a little grave for Blue Boy, an' bury him right.'

They had seldom seen such resentment in their grand-mother. Albert's throat choked up, he rubbed the tears away with his fist.

'Yes'm, Gram'ma, we will, we will,' he gulped.

VII

Only Mrs Harris saw the boys go out next morning. She slipped a bread-and-butter sandwich into the hand of each, but she said nothing, and they said nothing.

The boys did not get home until their parents were ready to leave the table. Mrs Templeton made no fuss, but told them to sit down and eat their breakfast. When they had finished, she said commandingly:

'Now you march into my room.' That was where she heard explanations and administered punishment. When she whipped them, she did it thoroughly.

She followed them and shut the door.

'Now, what were you boys doing this morning?'

'We went off to bury Blue Boy.'

'Why didn't you tell me where you were going?'

They looked down at their toes, but said nothing. Their mother studied their mournful faces, and her overbearing expression softened.

'The next time you get up and go off anywhere, you come and tell me beforehand, do you understand?'

'Yes'm.'

She opened the door, motioned them out, and went with them into the parlour. 'I'm sorry about your cat, boys,' she said. 'That's why I don't like to have cats around; they're always getting sick and dying. Now run along and play. Maybe you'd like to have a circus in the back yard this afternoon? And we'll all come.'

The twins ran out in a joyful frame of mind. Their grandmother had been mistaken; their mother wasn't indifferent about Blue Boy, she was sorry. Now everything was all right, and they could make a circus ring.

They knew their grandmother got put out about strange things, anyhow. A few months ago it was because their mother hadn't asked one of the visiting preachers who came to the church conference to stay with them. There was no place for the preacher to sleep except on the folding lounge in the parlour, and no place for him to wash – he would have been very uncomfortable, and so would all the household. But Mrs Harris was terribly upset that there should be a conference in the town, and they not keeping a preacher! She was quite bitter about it.

The twins called in the neighbour boys, and they made a ring in the back yard, around their turning-bar. Their mother came to the show and paid admission, bringing Mrs Rosen and Grandma Harris. Mrs Rosen thought if all the children in the neighbourhood were to be howling and running in a

circle in the Templetons' back yard, she might as well be
there, too, for she would have no peace at home.

After the dog races and the Indian fight were over, Mrs
Templeton took Mrs Rosen into the house to revive her
with cake and lemonade. The parlour was cool and dusky.
Mrs Rosen was glad to get into it after sitting on a wooden
bench in the sun. Grandmother stayed in the parlour with
them, which was unusual. Mrs Rosen sat waving a palm-
leaf fan, – she felt the heat very much, because she wore
her stays so tight – while Victoria went to make the lemonade.

'De circuses are not so good, widout Vickie to manage
them, Grandma,' she said.

'No'm. The boys complain right smart about losing Vickie
from their plays. She's at her books all the time now. I don't
know what's got into the child.'

'If she wants to go to college, she must prepare herself,
Grandma. I am agreeably surprised in her. I didn't think
she'd stick to it.'

Mrs Templeton came in with a tray of tumblers, and the
glass pitcher all frosted over. Mrs Rosen wistfully admired
her neighbour's tall figure and good carriage; she was
wearing no corsets at all today under her flowered organdie
afternoon dress, Mrs Rosen had noticed, and yet she could
carry herself so smooth and straight, – after having had so
many children, too! Mrs Rosen was envious, but she gave
credit where credit was due.

When Mrs Templeton brought in the cake, Mrs Rosen
was still talking to Grandmother about Vickie's studying.
Mrs Templeton shrugged carelessly.

'There's such a thing as overdoing it, Mrs Rosen,' she
observed as she poured the lemonade. 'Vickie's very apt to
run to extremes.'

'But, my dear lady, she can hardly be too extreme in dis
matter. If she is to take a competitive examination with girls
from much better schools than ours she will have to do
better than the others, or fail; no two ways about it. We
must encourage her.'

Mrs Templeton bridled a little. 'I'm sure I don't interfere with her studying, Mrs Rosen. I don't see where she got this notion, but I let her alone.'

Mrs Rosen accepted a second piece of chocolate cake. 'And what do you think about it, Grandma?'

Mrs Harris smiled politely. 'None of our people, or Mr Templeton's either, ever went to college. I expect it is all on account of the young gentleman who was here last summer.'

Mrs Rosen laughed and lifted her eyebrows. 'Something very personal in Vickie's admiration for Professor Chalmers we think, Grandma? A very sudden interest in de sciences, I should say!'

Mrs Templeton shrugged. 'You're mistaken, Mrs Rosen. There ain't a particle of romance in Vickie.'

'But there are several kinds of romance, Mrs Templeton. She may not have your kind.'

'Yes'm, that's so,' said Mrs Harris in a low, grateful voice. She thought that a hard word Victoria had said of Vickie.

'I didn't see a thing in that Professor Chalmers, myself,' Victoria remarked. 'He was a gawky kind of fellow, and never had a thing to say in company. Did you think he amounted to much?'

'Oh, widout doubt Doctor Chalmers is a very scholarly man. A great many brilliant scholars are widout de social graces, you know.' When Mrs Rosen, from a much wider experience, corrected her neighbour, she did so somewhat playfully, as if insisting upon something Victoria capriciously chose to ignore.

At this point old Mrs Harris put her hands on the arms of the chair in preparation to rise. 'If you ladies will excuse me, I think I will go and lie down a little before supper.' She rose and went heavily out on her felt soles. She never really lay down in the afternoon, but she dozed in her own black rocker. Mrs Rosen and Victoria sat chatting about Professor Chalmers and his boys.

Last summer the young professor had come to Skyline with four of his students from the University of Michigan,

and had stayed three months, digging for fossils out in the
sandhills. Vickie had spent a great many mornings at their
camp. They lived at the town hotel, and drove out to their
camp every day in a light spring-wagon. Vickie used to wait
for them at the edge of the town, in front of the Roadmaster's house, and when the spring-wagon came rattling
along, the boys could call: 'There's our girl!' slow the
horses, and give her a hand up. They said she was their
mascot, and were very jolly with her. They had a splendid
summer, – found a great bed of fossil elephant bones,
where a whole herd must once have perished. Later on
they came upon the bones of a new kind of elephant,
scarcely larger than a pig. They were greatly excited about
their finds, and so was Vickie. That was why they liked her.
It was they who told her about a memorial scholarship at
Ann Arbor, which was open to any girl from Colorado.

VIII

In August Vickie went down to Denver to take her examinations. Mr Holliday, the Roadmaster, got her a pass, and
arranged that she should stay with the family of one of his
passenger conductors.

For three days she wrote examination papers along with
other contestants, in one of the Denver high schools, proc-
tored by a teacher. Her father had given her five dollars for
incidental expenses, and she came home with a box of
mineral specimens for the twins, a singing top for Ronald,
and a toy burro for Hughie.

Then began days of suspense that stretched into weeks.
Vickie went to the post-office every morning, opened her
father's combination box, and looked over the letters, long
before he got down town, – always hoping there might be a
letter from Ann Arbor. The night mail came in at six, and
after supper she hurried to the post-office and waited about
until the shutter at the general-delivery window was drawn
back, a signal that the mail had all been 'distributed'. While
the tedious process of distribution was going on, she usually

withdrew from the office, full of joking men and cigar smoke, and walked up and down under the big cottonwood trees that overhung the side street. When the crowd of men began to come out, then she knew the mail-bags were empty, and she went in to get whatever letters were in the Templeton box and take them home.

After two weeks went by, she grew downhearted. Her young professor, she knew, was in England for his vacation. There would be no one at the University of Michigan who was interested in her fate. Perhaps the fortunate contestant had already been notified of her success. She never asked herself, as she walked up and down under the cottonwoods on those summer nights, what she would do if she didn't get the scholarship. There was no alternative. If she didn't get it, then everything was over.

During the weeks when she lived only to go to the post-office, she managed to cut her finger and get ink into the cut. As a result, she had a badly infected hand and had to carry it in a sling. When she walked her nightly beat under the cottonwoods, it was a kind of comfort to feel that finger throb; it was companionship, made her case more complete.

The strange thing was that one morning a letter came, addressed to Miss Victoria Templeton; in a long envelope such as her father called 'legal size', with 'University of Michigan, in the upper left-hand corner. When Vickie took it from the box, such a wave of fright and weakness went through her that she could scarcely get out of the post-office. She hid the letter under her striped blazer and went a weak, uncertain trail down the sidewalk under the big trees. Without seeing anything or knowing what road she took, she got to the Roadmaster's green yard and her hammock, where she always felt not on the earth, yet of it.

Three hours later, when Mrs Rosen was just tasting one of those clear soups upon which the Templetons thought she wasted so much pains and good meat, Vickie walked in at the kitchen door and said in a low but somewhat unnatural voice:

'Mrs Rosen, I got the scholarship.'

Mrs Rosen looked up at her sharply, then pushed the soup back to a cooler part of the stove.

'What is dis you say, Vickie? You have heard from de University?'

'Yes'm. I got the letter this morning.' She produced it from under her blazer.

Mrs Rosen had been cutting noodles. She took Vickie's face in two hot, plump hands that were still floury, and looked at her intently. 'Is dat true, Vickie? No mistake? I am delighted – and surprised! Yes, surprised. Den you will *be* something, you won't just sit on de front porch.' She squeezed the girl's round, good-natured cheeks, as if she could mould them into something definite then and there. 'Now you must stay for lunch and tell us all about it. Go in and announce yourself to Mr Rosen.'

Mr Rosen had come home for lunch and was sitting, a book in his hand, in a corner of the darkened front parlour where a flood of yellow sun streamed in under the dark green blind. He smiled his friendly smile at Vickie and waved her to a seat, making her understand that he wanted to finish his paragraph. The dark engraving of the pointed cypresses and the Roman tomb was on the wall just behind him.

Mrs Rosen came into the back parlour, which was the dining-room, and began taking things out of the silver-drawer to lay a place for their visitor. She spoke to her husband rapidly in German.

He put down his book, came over, and took Vickie's hand.

'Is it true, Vickie? Did you really win the scholarship?'

'Yes, sir.'

He stood looking down at her through his kind, remote smile, – a smile in the eyes, that seemed to come up through layers and layers of something – gentle doubts, kindly reservations.

'Why do you want to go to college, Vickie?' he asked playfully.

'To learn,' she said with surprise.

'But why do you want to learn? What do you want to do with it?'

'I don't know. Nothing, I guess.'

'Then what do you want it for?'

'I don't know. I just want it.'

For some reason Vickie's voice broke there. She had been terribly strung up all morning, lying in the hamock with her eyes tight shut. She had not been home at all, she had wanted to take her letter to the Rosens first. And now one of the gentlest men she knew made her choke by something strange and presageful in his voice.

'Then if you want it without any purpose at all, you will not be disappointed.' Mr Rosen wished to distract her and help her to keep back the tears. 'Listen: a great man once said: "*Le but n'est rien; le chemin, c'est tout.*" That means: The end is nothing, the road is all. Let me write it down for you and give you your first French lesson.'

He went to the desk with its big silver inkwell, where he and his wife wrote so many letters in several languages, and inscribed the sentence on a sheet of purple paper, in his delicately shaded foreign script, signing under it a name: *J. Michelet*. He brought it back and shook it before Vickie's eyes. 'There, keep it to remember me by. Slip it into the envelope with your college credentials, – that is a good place for it.' From his deliberate smile and the twitch of one eyebrow, Vickie knew he meant her to take it along as an antidote, a corrective for whatever colleges might do to her. But she had always known that Mr Rosen was wiser than professors.

Mrs Rosen was frowning, she thought that sentence a bad precept to give any Templeton. Moreover, she always promptly called her husband back to earth when he soared a little; though it was exactly for this transcendental quality of mind that she reverenced him in her heart, and thought him so much finer than any of his successful brothers.

'Luncheon is served,' she said in the crisp tone that put people in their places. 'And Miss Vickie, you are to eat your tomatoes with an oil dressing, as we do. If you are going off into the world, it is quite time you learn to like things that are everywhere accepted.'

Vickie said: 'Yes'm' and slipped into the chair Mr Rosen had placed for her. Today she didn't care what she ate, though ordinarily she thought a French dressing tasted a good deal like castor oil.

IX

Vickie was to discover that nothing comes easily in this world. Next day she got a letter from one of the jolly students of Professor Chalmers's party, who was watching over her case in his chief's absence. He told her the scholarship meant admission to the freshman class without further examinations, and two hundred dollars toward her expenses; she would have to bring along about three hundred more to put her through the year.

She took this letter to her father's office. Seated in his revolving desk-chair, Mr Templeton read it over several times and looked embarrassed.

'I'm sorry, daughter,' he said at last, 'but really, just now, I couldn't spare that much. Not this year. I expect next year will be better for us.'

'But the scholarship is for this year, Father. It wouldn't count next year. I just have to go in September.'

'I really ain't got it, daughter.' He spoke, oh so kindly! He had lovely manners with his daughter and his wife. 'It's just all I can do to keep the store bills paid up. I'm away behind with Mr Rosen's bill. Couldn't you study here this winter and get along about as fast? It isn't that I wouldn't like to let you have the money if I had it. And with young children, I can't let my life insurance go.'

Vickie didn't say anything more. She took her letter and wandered down Main Street with it, leaving young Mr Templeton to a very bad half-hour.

At dinner Vickie was silent, but everyone could see she had been crying. Mr Templeton told *Uncle Remus* stories to keep up the family morale and make the giggly twins laugh. Mrs Templeton glanced covertly at her daughter from time to time. She was sometimes a little afraid of Vickie, who seemed to her to have a hard streak. If it were a love-affair that the girl was crying about, that would be so much more natural – and more hopeful!

At two o'clock Mrs Templeton went to the Afternoon Euchre Club, the twins were to have another ride with the Roadmaster on his velocipede, the little boys took their nap on their mother's bed. The house was empty and quiet. Vicky felt an aversion for the hammock under the cottonwoods where she had been betrayed into such bright hopes. She lay down on her grandmother's lounge in the cluttered play-room and turned her face to the wall.

When Mrs Harris came in for her rest and began to wash her face at the tin basin, Vickie got up. She wanted to be alone. Mrs Harris came over to her while she was still sitting on the edge of the lounge. 'What's the matter, Vickie child?' She put her hand on her grand-daughter's shoulder, but Vickie shrank away. Young misery is like that, sometimes.

'Nothing. Except that I can't go to college after all. Papa can't let me have the money.'

Mrs Harris settled herself on the faded cushions of her rocker. 'How much is it? Tell me about it, Vickie. Nobody's around.'

Vickie told her what the conditions were, briefly and dryly, as if she were talking to an enemy. Everyone was an enemy; all society was against her. She told her grandmother the facts and then went upstairs, refusing to be comforted.

Mrs Harris saw her disappear through the kitchen door, and then sat looking at the door, her face grave, her eyes stern and sad. A poor factory-made piece of joiner's work seldom has to bear a look of such intense, accusing sorrow; as if that flimsy pretence of 'grained' yellow pine were the door shut against all young aspiration.

X

Mrs Harris had decided to speak to Mr Templeton, but opportunities for seeing him alone were not frequent. She watched out of the kitchen window, and when she next saw him go into the barn to fork down hay for his horse, she threw an apron over her head and followed him. She waylaid him as he came down from the hayloft.

'Hillary, I want to see you about Vickie. I was wondering if you could lay hand on any of the money you got from the sale of my house back home.'

Mr Templeton was nervous. He began brushing his trousers with a little whisk-broom he kept there, hanging on a nail.

'Why, no'm, Mrs Harris. I couldn't just conveniently call in any of it right now. You know we had to use part of it to get moved up here from the mines.'

'I know. But I thought if there was any left you could get at, we could let Vickie have it. A body'd like to help the child.'

'I'd like to, powerful well, Mrs Harris. I would, indeedy. But I'm afraid I can't manage it right now. The fellers I've loaned to can't pay up this year. Maybe next year – ' He was like a little boy trying to escape a scolding, though he had never had a nagging word from Mrs Harris.

She looked downcast, but said nothing.

'It's all right, Mrs Harris,' he took on his brisk business tone and hung up the brush. 'The money's perfectly safe. It's well invested.'

Invested; that was a word men always held over women, Mrs Harris thought, and it always meant they could have none of their own money. She sighed deeply.

'Well, if that's the way it is . . .' She turned away and went back to the house on her flat heelless slippers, just in time; Victoria was at that moment coming out to the kitchen with Hughie.

'Ma,' she said, 'can the little boy play out here, while I go down town?'

XI

For the next few days Mrs Harris was very sombre, and she was not well. Several times in the kitchen she was seized with what she called giddy spells, and Mandy had to help her to a chair and give her a little brandy.

'Don't you say nothin', Mandy,' she warned the girl. But Mandy knew enough for that.

Mrs Harris scarcely noticed how her strength was failing, because she had so much on her mind. She was very proud, and she wanted to do something that was hard for her to do. The difficulty was to catch Mrs Rosen alone.

On the afternoon when Victoria went to her weekly euchre, the old lady beckoned Mandy and told her to run across the alley and fetch Mrs Rosen for a minute.

Mrs Rosen was packing her trunk, but she came at once. Grandmother awaited her in her chair in the play-room.

'I take it very kindly of you to come, Mrs Rosen. I'm afraid it's warm in here. Won't you have a fan?' She extended the palm leaf she was holding.

'Keep it yourself, Grandma. You are not looking very well. Do you feel badly, Grandma Harris?' She took the old lady's hand and looked at her anxiously,

'Oh no, ma'am! I'm as well as usual. The heat wears on me a little, maybe. Have you seen Vickie lately, Mrs Rosen?'

'Vickie? No, She hasn't run in for several days. These young people are full of their own affairs, you know.'

'I expect she's backward about seeing you, now that she's so discouraged.'

'Discouraged? Why, didn't the child get her scholarship after all?'

'Yes'm, she did. But they write her she has to bring more money to help her out; three hundred dollars. Mr Templeton can't raise it just now. We had so much sickness in that mountain town before we moved up here, he got behind. Pore Vickie's downhearted.'

'Oh, that is too bad! I expect you've been fretting over it, and that is why you don't look like yourself. Now what can we do about it?'

Mrs Harris sighed and shook her head. ''Vickie's trying to muster courage to go around to her father's friends and borrow from one and another. But we ain't been here long, – it ain't like we had old friends here. I hate to have the child do it.'

Mrs Rosen looked perplexed. 'I'm sure Mr Rosen would help her. He takes a great interest in Vickie.'

'I thought maybe he could see his way to. That's why I sent Mandy to fetch you.'

'That was right, Grandma. Now let me think.' Mrs Rosen put up her plump red-brown hand and leaned her chin upon it. 'Day after tomorrow I am going to run on to Chicago for my niece's wedding.' She saw her old friend's face fall. 'Oh, I shan't be gone long; ten days, perhaps. I will speak to Mr Rosen tonight, and if Vickie goes to him after I am off his hands, I'm sure he will help her.'

Mrs Harris looked up at her with solemn gratitude. 'Vickie ain't the kind of girl would forget anything like that, Mrs Rosen. Nor I wouldn't forget it.'

Mrs Rosen patted her arm. 'Grandma Harris,' she exclaimed, ' I will just ask Mr Rosen to do it for you! You know I care more about the old folks than the young. If I take this worry off your mind, I shall go away to the wedding with a light heart. Now dismiss it. I am sure Mr Rosen can arrange this himself for you, and Vickie won't have to go about to these people here, and our gossipy neighbours will never be the wiser.' Mrs Rosen poured this out in her quick, authoritative tone, converting her *th*'s into *d*'s, as she did when she was excited.

Mrs Harris's red-brown eyes slowly filled with tears, – Mrs Rosen had never seen that happen before. But she simply said, with quiet dignity: 'Thank you, ma'am. I wouldn't have turned to nobody else.'

'That means I am an old friend already, doesn't it, Grandma? And that's what I want to be. I am very jealous where Grandma Harris is concerned!' She lightly kissed the back of the purple-veined hand she had been holding, and ran home to her packing. Grandma sat looking down at her hand. How easy it was for these foreigners to say what they felt!

XII

Mrs Harris knew she was failing. She was glad to be able to conceal it from Mrs Rosen when that kind neighbour dashed in to kiss her good-bye on the morning of her departure for Chicago. Mrs Templeton was, of course, present, and secrets could not be discussed. Mrs Rosen, in her stiff little brown travelling-hat, her hands tightly gloved in brown kid, could only wink and nod to Grandmother to tell her all was well. Then she went out and climbed into the 'hack' bound for the depot, which had stopped for a moment at the Templetons' gate.

Mrs Harris was thankful that her excitable friend hadn't noticed anything unusual about her looks, and above all, that she had made no comment. She got through the day, and that evening, thank goodness, Mr Templeton took his wife to hear a company of strolling players sing *The Chimes of Normandy* at the Opera House. He loved music, and just now he w~s very eager to distract and amuse Victoria. Grandma sent the twins out to play and went to bed early.

Next morning, when she joined Mandy in the kitchen, Mandy noticed something wrong.

'You set right down, Miz' Harris, an' let me git you some whisky. Deed, ma'am, you look awful porely. You ought to tell Miss Victoria an' let her send for the doctor.'

'No, Mandy, I don't want no doctor. I've seen more sickness than ever he has. Doctors can't do no more than linger you out, an' I've always prayed I wouldn't last to be a burden. You git me some whisky in hot water, and pour it on a piece of toast. I feel real empty.'

That afternoon when Mrs Harris was taking her rest, for once, she lay down upon her lounge. Vickie came in, tense and excited, and stopped for a moment.

'It's all right, Grandma. Mr Rosen is going to lend me the money. I won't have to go to anybody else. He won't ask Father to endorse my note, either. He'll just take my name.' Vickie rather shouted this news at Mrs Harris, as if the old lady were deaf, or slow of understanding. She didn't thank her; she didn't know her grandmother was in any way responsible for Mr Rosen's offer, though at the close of their interview he had said: 'We won't speak of our arrangement to anyone but your father. And I want you to mention it to the old lady Harris. I know she has been worrying about you.'

Having brusquely announced her news, Vickie hurried away. There was so much to do about getting ready, she didn't know where to begin. She had no trunk and no clothes. Her winter coat, bought two years ago, was so outgrown that she couldn't get into it. All her shoes were run over at the heel and must go to the cobbler. And she had only two weeks in which to do everything! She dashed off.

Mrs Harris sighed and closed her eyes happily. She thought with modest pride that with people like the Rosens she had always 'got along nicely.' It was only with the ill-bred and unclassified, like this Mrs Jackson next door, that she had disagreeable experiences. Such folks, she told herself, had come out of nothing and knew no better. She was afraid this inquisitive woman might find her ailing and come prying round with unwelcome suggestions.

Mrs Jackson did, indeed, call that very afternoon, with a miserable contribution of veal-loaf as an excuse (all the Templetons hated veal), but Mandy had been forewarned, and she was resourceful. She met Mrs Jackson at the kitchen door and blocked the way.

'Sh-h-h ma'am, Miz' Harris is asleep, havin' her nap. No'm, she ain't porely, she's as usual. But Hughie had the colic last night when Miss Victoria was at the show, an' kep' Miz' Harris awake.'

Mrs Jackson was loath to turn back. She had really come to find out why Mrs Rosen drove away in the depot hack yesterday morning. Except at church socials, Mrs Jackson did not meet people in Mrs Rosen's set.

The next day, when Mrs Harris got up and sat on the edge of her bed, her head began to swim, and she lay down again. Mandy peeped into the play-room as soon as she came downstairs, and found the old lady still in bed. She leaned over her and whispered:

'Ain't you feelin' well, Miz' Harris?'

'No, Mandy, I'm right porely,' Mrs Harris admitted.

'You stay where you air, ma'am. I'll git the breakfast fur the chillun, an' take the other breakfast in fur Miss Victoria an' Mr Templeton.' She hurried back to the kitchen, and Mrs Harris went to sleep.

Immediately after breakfast Vickie dashed off about her own concerns, and the twins went to cut grass while the dew was still on it. When Mandy was taking the other breakfast into the dining-room, Mrs Templeton came through the play-room.

'What's the matter, Ma? Are you sick?' she asked in an accusing tone.'

'No, Victoria, I ain't sick. I had a little giddy spell, and I thought I'd lay still.'

'You ought to be more careful what you eat, Ma. If you're going to have another bilious spell, when everything is so upset anyhow, I don't know what I'll do!' Victoria's voice broke. She hurried back into her bedroom, feeling bitterly that there was no place in that house to cry in, no spot where one could be alone, even with misery; that the house and the people in it were choking her to death.

Mrs Harris sighed and closed her eyes. Things did seem to be upset, though she didn't know just why. Mandy, however, had her suspicions. While she waited on Mr and Mrs Templeton at breakfast, narrowly observing their manner toward each other and Victoria's swollen eyes and desperate expression, her suspicions grew stronger.

Instead of going to his office, Mr Templeton went to the barn and ran out the buggy. Soon he brought out Cleveland, the black horse, with his harness on. Mandy watched from the back window. After he had hitched the horse to the buggy, he came into the kitchen to wash his hands. While he dried them on the roller towel, he said in his most businesslike tone:

'I likely won't be back tonight, Mandy. I have to go out to my farm, and I'll hardly get through my business there in time to come home.'

Then Mandy was sure. She had been through these times before and at such a crisis poor Mr Templeton was always called away on important business. When he had driven out through the alley and up the street past Mrs Rosen's, Mandy left the dishes and went in to Mrs Harris. She bent over and whispered low:

'Miz' Harris, I'spect Miss Victoria's done found out she's goin' to have another baby! It looks that way. She's gone back to bed.'

Mrs Harris lifted a warning finger. 'Sh-h-h!'

'Oh yes'm, I won't say nothin'. I never do.'

Mrs Harris tried to face this possibility, but her mind didn't seem strong enough – she dropped off into another doze.

All that morning Mrs Templeton lay on her bed alone, the room darkened and a handkerchief soaked in camphor tied round her forehead. The twins had taken Ronald off to watch them cut grass, and Hughie played in the kitchen under Mandy's eye.

Now and then Victoria sat upright on the edge of the bed, beat her hands together softly and looked desperately at the ceiling, then about at those frail, confining walls. If only she could meet the situation with violence, fight it, conquer it! But there was nothing for it but stupid animal patience. She would have to go through all that again, and nobody, not even Hillary, wanted another baby, – poor as they were, and in this overcrowded house. Anyhow, she told herself, she was ashamed to have another baby, when she had a daughter old enough to go to college! She was sick of it all; sick of dragging this chain of life that never let her rest and periodically knotted and overpowered her; made her ill and hideous for months, and then dropped another baby into her arms. She had had babies enough; and there ought to be an end to such apprehensions some time before you were old and ugly.

She wanted to run away, back to Tennessee, and lead a free, gay life, as she had when she was first married. She could do a great deal more with freedom than ever Vickie could. She was still young, and she was still handsome; why must she be for ever shut up in a little cluttered house with children and fresh babies and an old woman and a stupid bound girl and a husband who wasn't very successful? Life hadn't brought her what she expected when she married Hillary Templeton; life hadn't used her right. She had tried to keep up appearances, to dress well with very little to do it on, to keep young for her husband and children. She had tried, she had tried! Mrs Templeton buried her face in the pillow and smothered the sobs that shook the bed.

Hillary Templeton, on his drive out through the sage-brush, up into the farming country that was irrigated from the North Platte, did not feel altogether cheerful, though he whistled and sang to himself on the way. He was sorry Victoria would have to go through another time. It was awkward just now, too, when he was so short of money. But he was naturally a cheerful man, modest in his demands upon fortune, and easily diverted from unpleasant thoughts. Before Cleveland had travelled half the eighteen miles to the farm, his master was already looking forward to a visit with his tenants, an old German couple who were fond of him because he never pushed them in a hard year — so far, all the years had been hard — and he sometimes brought them bananas and such delicacies from town.

Mrs Heyse would open her best preserves for him, he knew, and kill a chicken, and tonight he would have a clean bed in her spare room. She always put a vase of flowers in his room when he stayed overnight with them, and that pleased him very much. He felt like a youth out there, and forgot all the bills he had somehow to meet, and the loans he had made and couldn't collect. The Heyses kept bees and raised turkeys, and had honeysuckle vines running over the front porch. He loved all those things. Mr Templeton touched Cleveland with the whip, and as they sped along into the grass country, sang softly:

> 'Old Jesse was a gem'man,
> Way down in Tennessee.'

XIII

Mandy had to manage the house herself that day, and she was not at all sorry. There wasn't a great deal of variety in her life, and she felt very important, taking Mrs Harris's place, giving the children their dinner, and carrying a plate of milk toast to Mrs Templeton. She was worried about Mrs Harris, however, and remarked to the children at noon that she thought somebody ought to 'set' with their grandma. Vicky wasn't home for dinner. She had her father's office to herself for the day and was making the most of it, writing a long letter to Professor Chalmers. Mr Rosen had invited her to have dinner with him at the hotel (he boarded there when his wife was away), and that was a great honour.

When Mandy said someone ought to be with the old lady, Bert and Del offered to take turns. Adelbert went off to rake up the grass they had been cutting all morning, and Albert sat down in the play-room. It seemed to him his grandmother looked pretty sick. He watched her while Mandy gave her toast-water with whisky in it, and thought he would like to make the room look a little nicer. While Mrs Harris lay with her eyes closed, he hung up the caps and coats lying about, and moved away the big rocking-chair that stood by the head of Grandma's bed. There ought to be a table there, he believed, but the small tables in the house all had something on them. Upstairs in the room where he and Adelbert and Ronald slept, there was a nice clean wooden cracker-box, on which they sat in the morning to put on their shoes and stockings. He brought this down and stood it on end at the head of Grandma's lounge, and put a clean napkin over the top of it.

She opened her eyes and smiled at him. 'Could you git me a tin of fresh water, honey?'

He went to the back porch and pumped till the water ran cold. He gave it to her in a tin cup as she had asked, but he didn't think that was the right way. After she dropped back on the pillow, he fetched a glass tumbler from the cupboard, filled it, and set it on the table he had just manufactured. When Grandmother drew a red cotton handkerchief from under her pillow and wiped the moisture from her face, he ran upstairs again and got one of his Sunday-school handkerchiefs, linen ones, that Mrs Rosen had given him and Del for Christmas. Having put this in Grandmother's hand and taken away the crumpled red one, he could think of nothing else to do — except to darken the room a little. The windows had no blinds, but flimsy cretonne curtains tied back, — not really tied, but caught back over nails driven into the sill. He loosened them and let them hang down over the bright afternoon sunlight. Then he sat down on the low sawed-off chair and gazed about, thinking that now it looked quite like a sick-room.

It was hard for a little boy to keep still. 'Would you like me to read *Joe's Luck* to you, Gram'ma?' he said presently.

'You might, Bertie.'

He got the 'boy's book' she had been reading aloud to them, and began where she had left off. Mrs Harris liked to hear his voice, and she liked to look at him when she opened her eyes from time to time. She did not follow the story. In her mind she was repeating a passage from the second part of *Pilgrim's Progress*, which she had read aloud to the children so many times; the passage where Christiana and her band come to the arbour on the Hill of Difficulty: '*Then said Mercy, how sweet is rest to them that labour.*'

At about four o'clock Adelbert came home, hot and sweaty from raking. He said he had got in the grass and taken it to their cow, and if Bert was reading, he guessed he'd like to listen. He dragged the wooden rocking-chair up close to Grandma's bed and curled up in it.

Grandmother was perfectly happy. She and the twins were about the same age; they had in common all the realest and truest things. The years between them and her, it seemed to Mrs Harris, were full of trouble and unimportant. The twins and Ronald and Hughie were important. She opened her eyes.

'Where is Hughie?' she asked.

'I guess he's asleep. Mother took him into her bed.'

'And Roland?'

'He's upstairs with Mandy. There ain't nobody in the kitchen now.'

'Then you might git me a fresh drink, Del.'

'Yes'm, Gram'ma.' He tiptoed out to the pump in his brown canvas sneakers.

When Vickie came home at five o'clock, she went to her mother's room, but the door was locked – a thing she couldn't remember ever happening before. She went into the play-room – old Mrs Harris was asleep, with one of the twins on guard, and he held up a warning finger. She went into the kitchen. Mandy was making biscuits, and Ronald was helping her to cut them out.

'What's the matter, Mandy? Where is everybody?'

'You know your papa's away, Miss Vickie; an' your mama's got a headache, an' Miz' Harris has had a bad spell. Maybe I'll just fix supper for you an' the boys in the kitchen, so you won't all have to be runnin' through her room.

'Oh, very well,' said Vickie bitterly, and she went upstairs. Wasn't it just like them all to go and get sick, when she had now only two weeks to get ready for school, and no trunk and no clothes or anything? Nobody but Mr Rosen seemed to take the least interest, 'when my whole life hangs by a thread,' she told herself fiercely. What were families for, anyway?

After supper Vickie went to her father's office to read; she told Mandy to leave the kitchen door open, and when she got home she would go to bed without disturbing anybody. The twins ran out to play under the electric light with the neighbour boys for a little while, then slipped softly up the back stairs to their room. Mandy came to Mrs Harris after the house was still.

'Kin I rub your legs fur you, Miz' Harris?'

'Thank you, Mandy. And you might get me a clean nightcap out of the press.'

Mandy returned with it.

'Lawsie me! But your legs is cold, ma'am!'

'I expect it's about time, Mandy,' murmured the old lady. Mandy knelt on the floor and set to work with a will. It brought the sweat out on her, and at last she sat up and wiped her face with the back of her hand.

'I can't seem to get no heat into em, Miz' Harris. I got a hot flat-iron on the stove; I'll wrap it in a piece of old blanket and put it to your feet. Why didn't you have the boys tell me you was cold, pore soul?'

Mrs Harris did not answer. She thought it was probably a cold that neither Mandy nor the flat-iron could do much with. She hadn't nursed so many people back in Tennessee without coming to know certain signs.

After Mandy was gone, she fell to thinking of her blessings. Every night for years, when she said her prayers, she had prayed that she might never have a long sickness or be a burden. She dreaded the heart-ache and humiliation of being helpless on the hands of people who would be impatient under such a care. And now she felt certain that she was going to die tonight, without troubling anybody.

She was glad Mrs Rosen was in Chicago. Had she been at home, she would certainly have come in, would have seen that her old neighbour was very sick, and bustled about. Her quick eye would have found all Grandmother's little secrets: how hard her bed was, that she had no proper place to wash, and kept her comb in her pocket; that her nightgowns were patched and darned. Mrs Rosen would have been indignant, and that would have made Victoria cross. She didn't have to see Mrs Rosen again to know that Mrs Rosen thought highly of her and admired her – yes,

admired her. Those funny little pats and arch pleasantries
had meant a great deal to Mrs Harris.

It was a blessing that Mr Templeton was away, too.
Appearances had to be kept up when there was a man in
the house; and he might have taken it into his head to send
for the doctor, and stir everybody up. Now everything
would be so peaceful. *'The Lord is my shepherd,'* she whispered gratefully. 'Yes, Lord, I always spoiled Victoria. She
was so much the prettiest. But nobody won't ever be the
worse for it: Mr Templeton will always humour her and the
children love her more than most. They'll always be good to
her; she has that way with her.'

Grandma fell to remembering the old place at home:
what a dashing, high-spirited girl Victoria was, and how
proud she had always been of her; how she used to hear
her laughing and teasing out in the lilac arbour when
Hillary Templeton was courting her. Toward morning all
these pleasant reflections faded out. Mrs Harris felt that she
and her bed were softly sinking, through the darkness to a
deeper darkness.

Old Mrs Harris did not really die that night, but she
believed she did. Mandy found her unconscious in the
morning. Then there was a great stir and bustle; Victoria,
and even Vickie, were startled out of their intense self-
absorption. Mrs Harris was hastily carried out of the play-
room and laid in Victoria's bed, put into one of Victoria's
best nightgowns. Mr Templeton was sent for, and the
doctor was sent for. The inquisitive Mrs Jackson from next
door got into the house at last, – installed herself as nurse,
and no one had the courage to say her nay. But Grandmother was out of it all, never knew that she was the object
of so much attention and excitement. She died a little while
after Mr Templeton got home.

Thus Mrs Harris slipped out of the Templetons' story; but
Victoria and Vickie had still to go on, to follow the long road
that leads through things unguessed at and unforeseeable.
When they are old, they will come closer and closer to
Grandma Harris. They will think a great deal about her, and

remember things they never noticed; and their lot will be more or less like hers. They will regret that they heeded her so little; but they, too, will look into the eager, unseeing eyes of young people and feel themselves alone. They will say to themselves: 'I was heartless, because I was young and strong and wanted things so much. But now I know.'

First published in *Ladies' Home Journal*, September–November 1932.

THE OLD BEAUTY

I

ONE brilliant September morning in 1922 a slender, fair-skinned man with white moustaches, waxed and turned up at the ends, stepped hurriedly out of the Hôtel Splendide at Aix-les-Bains and stood uncertainly at the edge of the driveway. He stood there for some moments, holding, or rather clutching, his gloves in one hand, a light cane in the other. The pavement was wet, glassy with water. The boys were still sprinkling the walk farther down the hill, and the fuchsias and dahlias in the beds sparkled with water drops. The clear air had the freshness of early morning and the smell of autumn foliage.

Two closed litters, carried by porters, came out of a side door and went joggling down the hill toward the baths. The gentleman standing on the kerb followed these eagerly with his eyes, as if about to dash after them; indeed, his mind seemed to accompany them to the turn in the walk where they disappeared, then to come back to him where he stood and at once to dart off in still another direction.

The gentleman was Mr Henry Seabury, aged fifty-five, American-born, educated in England, and lately returned from a long business career in China. His evident nervousness was due to a shock: an old acquaintance, who had been one of the brilliant figures in the world of the 1890's, had died a few hours ago in this hotel.

As he stood there he was thinking that he ought to send telegrams . . . but to whom? The lady had no immediate family, and the distinguished men of her time who had cherished the slightest attention from her were all dead. No, there was one (perhaps the most variously gifted of that group) who was still living: living in seclusion down on the Riviera, in a great white mansion set in miles of park and garden. A cloud had come over this man in the midst of a triumphant public life. His opponents had ruined his career by a whispering campaign. They had set going a rumour which would have killed any public man in England at that time. Mr Seabury began composing his telegram to Lord H——. Lord H—— would recognize that this death was more than the death of an individual. To him her name would recall a society whose manners, dress, conventions, loyalties, codes of honour, were different from anything existing in the world today.

And there were certainly old acquaintances like himself, men not of her intimate circle, scattered about over the world; in the States, in China, India. But how to reach them?

Three young men came up the hill to resolve his perplexity; three newspaper corespondents, English, French, American. The American spoke to his companions. 'There's the man I've seen about with her so much. He's the one we want.'

The three approached Mr Seabury, and the American addressed him. 'Mr Seabury, I believe? Excuse my stopping you, but we have just learned through the British Consulate that the former Lady Longstreet died in this hotel last night. We are newspaper men, and must send dispatches to our papers.' He paused to introduce his companions by their names and the names of their journals. 'We thought you might be good enough to tell us something about Lady Longstreet, Madame de Couçy, as she was known here.'

'Nothing but what all the world knows.' This intrusion had steadied Mr Seabury, brought his scattered faculties to a focus.

'But we must jog the world's memory a little. A great many things have happened since Lady Longstreet was known everywhere.'

'Certainly. You have only to cable your papers that Madame de Couçy, formerly Lady Longstreet, died here last night. They have in their files more that I could tell you if I stood here all morning.'

'But the circumstances of her death?'

'You can get that from the management. Her life was interesting, but she died like anyone else – just as you will, some day.'

'Her old friends, everywhere, would of course like to learn something about her life here this summer. No one knew her except as Madame de Couçy, so no one observed her very closely. You were with her a great deal, and the simple story of her life here would be –'

'I understand, but it is quite impossible. Good morning, gentlemen.' Mr Seabury went to his room to write his telegram to Lord H—.

II

Two months ago Henry Seabury had come here almost directly from China. His hurried trip across America and his few weeks in London scarcely counted. He was hunting for something, some spot that was still more or less as it used to be. Here, at Aix-les-Bains, he found the place unchanged, – and in the hotels many people very like those who used to come there.

The first night after he had settled himself at the Splendide he became interested in two old English ladies who dined at a table not far from his own. They had been coming here for many years, he felt sure. They had the old manner. They were at ease and reserved. Their dress was conservative. They were neither painted nor plucked, their nails were neither red nor green. One was plump, distinctly plump, indeed, but as she entered the dining-room he had noticed that she was quick in her movements and light on her feet. She was radiantly cheerful and talkative. But it was the other lady who interested him. She had an air of distinction, that unmistakable thing, which told him she had been a personage. She was tall, had a fine figure and carriage, but either she was much older than her friend, or life had used her more harshly. Something about her eyes and brow teased his memory. Had he once known her, or did she merely recall a type of woman he used to know? No, he felt that he must have met her, at least, long ago, when she was not a stern, gaunt-cheeked old woman with a yellowing complexion. The hotel management informed him that the lady was Madame de Couçy. He had never known anyone of that name.

The next afternoon when he was sitting under the plane trees in the *Place*, he saw the two ladies coming down the hill; the tall one moving with a peculiar drifting ease, looking into the distance as if the unlevel walk beneath her would natur-ally accommodate itself to her footing. She kept a white fur well up about her cheeks, though the day was hot. The short one tripped along beside her. They crossed the Square, sat down under the trees, and had tea brought out from the confectioner's. Then the muffled lady let her fur fall back a little and glanced about her. He was careful not to stare, but once when he suddenly lifted his eyes, she was looking directly at him. He thought he saw a spark of curiosity, perhaps recognition.

The two ladies had tea in the *Place* every afternoon unless it rained; when they did not come Seabury felt disappointed. Sometimes the taller one would pause before she sat down and suggest going farther, to the Casino. Once he was near enough to hear the rosy one exclaiming: 'Oh, no! It's much nicer here, really. You are always dissatisfied when we go to the Casino. There are more of the kind you hate there.'

The older one with a shrug and a mournful smile sat down resignedly in front of the pastry shop. When she had finished her tea she drew her wrap up about her chin as if about to leave, but her companion began to coax: 'Let us wait for the newspaper woman. It's almost time for her, and I do like to get the home papers.'

The other reminded her that there would be plenty of papers at the hotel.

'Yes, yes, I know. But I like to get them from her. I'm sure she's glad of our pennies.'

When they left their table they usually walked about the Square for a time, keeping to the less frequented end toward the Park. They bought roses at the flower booths, and cyclamen from an old country woman who tramped about with a basketful of them. Then they went slowly up the hill toward the hotel.

III

Seabury's first enlightenment about these solitary women came from a most unlikely source.

Going up to the summit of Mont Revard in the little railway train one morning, he made the acquaintance of an English family (father, mother, and two grown daughters) whom he liked very much. He spent the day on the mountain in their company, and after that he saw a great deal of them. They were from Devonshire, home-staying people, not tourists. (The daughters had never been on the Continent before.) They had come over to visit the son's grave in one of the war cemeteries in the north of France. The father brought them down to Aix to cheer them up a little. (He and his wife had come there on their honeymoon, long ago.) As the Thompsons were stopping at a cramped, rather mean little hotel down in the town, they spent most of the day out of doors. Usually the mother and one of the daughters sat the whole morning in the *Place*, while the other girl went off tramping with the father. The mother knitted, and the girl read aloud to her. Whichever daughter it happened to be kept watchful eye on Mrs Thompson. If her face grew too pensive, the girl would close the book and say:

'Now, Mother, do let us have some chocolate and croissants. The breakfast at that hotel is horrid, and I'm famished.'

Mr Seabury often joined them in the morning. He found it very pleasant to be near that kind of family feeling. They felt his friendliness, the mother especially, and were pleased to have him join them at their chocolate, or to go with him to afternoon concerts at the Grand-Cercle.

One afternoon when the mother and both daughters were

having tea with him near the Roman Arch, the two English ladies from his hotel crossed the Square and sat down at a table not far away. He noticed that Mrs Thompson glanced often in their direction. Seabury kept his guests a long while at tea, – the afternoon was hot, and he knew their hotel was stuffy. He was telling the girls something about China, when the two unknown English ladies left their table and got into a taxi. Mrs Thompson turned to Seabury and said in a low, agitated voice:

'Do you know, I believe the tall one of those two was Lady Longstreet.'

Mr Seabury started. 'Oh, no! Could it be possible?'

'I am afraid it is. Yes, she is greatly changed. It's very sad. Six years ago she stayed at a country place near us, in Devonshire, and I used often to see her out on her horse. She still rode then. I don't think I can be mistaken.'

In a flash everything came back to Seabury. 'You're right, I'm sure of it, Mrs Thompson. The lady lives at my hotel, and I've been puzzling about her. I knew Lady Longstreet slightly many years ago. Now that you tell me, I can see it. But . . . as you say, she is greatly changed. At the hotel she is known as Madame de Couçy.'

'Yes, she married during the war; a Frenchman. But it must have been after she had lost her beauty. I had never heard of the marriage until he was killed, – in '17, I think. Then some of the English papers mentioned that he was the husband of Gabrielle Longstreet. It's very sad when those beautiful ones have to grow old, isn't it? We never have too many of them, at best.'

The younger daughter threw her arms about Mrs Thompson. 'Oh, Mother, I wish you hadn't told us! I'm afraid Mr Seabury does, too. It's such a shock.'

He protested. 'Yes, it is a shock, certainly. But I'm grateful to Mrs Thompson. I must be very stupid not to have seen it, I'm glad to know. The two ladies seem very much alone, and the older one looks ill. I might be of some service, if she remembers me. It's all very strange: but one might be useful, perhaps, Mrs Thompson?'

'That's the way to look at it, Mr Seabury.' Mrs Thompson spoke gently, 'I think she does remember you. When you were talking to Dorothy, turned away from them, she glanced at you often. The lady with her is a friend, don't you think, not a paid companion?'

He said he was sure of it, and she gave him a warm, grateful glance as if he and she could understand how much that meant, then turned to her daughters: 'Why, there is Father, come to look for us!' She made a little signal to the stout, flushed man who was tramping across the Square in climbing boots.

IV

Mr Seabury did not go back to his hotel for dinner. He dined at a little place with tables in the garden and returned late to the Splendide. He felt rather knocked up by what Mrs Thompson had told him, – felt that in this world people have to pay an extortionate price for any exceptional gift whatever. Once in his own room, he lay for a long while in a chaise longue before an open window, watching the stars and the fireflies, recalling the whole romantic story, – all he had ever known of Lady Longstreet. And in this hotel, full of people, she was unknown – she!

Gabrielle Longstreet was a name known all over the globe, – even in China, when he went there twenty-seven years ago. Yet she was not an actress or an adventuress. She had come into the European world in a perfectly regular, if somewhat unusual, way.

Sir Wilfred Longstreet, a lover of yachting and adventure on the high seas, had been driven into Martinique by a tropical hurricane. Strolling about the harbour town, he saw a young girl coming out of a church with her mother; the girl was nineteen, the mother perhaps forty. They were the two most beautiful women he had ever seen. The hurricane passed and was forgotten, but Sir Wilfred Longstreet's yacht still lay in the harbour of Fort de France. He sought out the girl's father, an English colonial from Barbados, who was easily convinced. The mother not so easily: she was a person of character as well as severe beauty. Longstreet had sworn that he would never take his yacht out to sea unless she carried Gabrielle aboard her. The *Sea Nymph* might lie and rot there.

In time the mother was reassured by letters and documents from England. She wished to do well for her daughter, and what very brilliant opportunities were there in Martinique? As for the girl, she wanted to see the world; she had never been off the island. Longstreet made a settlement upon Madame the mother, and submitted to the two services, civil and religious. He took his bride directly back to England. He had not advised his friends of his marriage; he was a young man who kept his affairs to himself.

He kept his wife in the country for some months. When he opened his town house and took her to London, things went as he could not possibly have foreseen. In six weeks she was the fashion of the town; the object of admiration among his friends, and his father's friends. Gabrielle was not socially ambitious, made no effort to please. She was not witty or especially clever, – had no accomplishments beyond speaking French as naturally as English. She was beautiful, that was all. And she was fresh. She came into that society of old London like a quiet country dawn.

She showed no great zest for this life so different from anything she had ever known; a quiet wonderment rather, faintly tinged wth pleasure. There was no glitter about her, no sparkle. She never dressed in the mode: refused to wear crinoline in a world that billowed and swelled with it. Into drawing-rooms full of ladies enriched by marvels of hairdressing (switches, ringlets, puffs, pompadours, waves starred with gems), she came with her brown hair parted in the middle and coiled in a small knot at the back of her head. Hairdressers protested, as one client after another adopted the 'mode Gabrielle'. (The knot at the nape of the neck! Charwomen had always worn it; it was as old as mops and pails.)

The English liked high colour, but Lady Longstreet had no

red roses in her cheeks. Her skin had the soft glow of orient pearls, – the jewel to which she was most often compared. She was not spirited, she was not witty, but no one ever heard her say a stupid thing. She was often called cold. She seemed unawakened, as if she were still an island girl with reserved island good manners. No woman had been so much discussed and argued about for a long stretch of years. It was to the older men that she was (unconsciously, as it seemed) more gracious. She like them to tell her about events and personages already in the past; things she had come too late to see.

Longstreet, her husband, was none too pleased by the flutter she caused. It was no great credit to him to have discovered a rare creature; since everyone else discovered her the moment they had a glimpse of her. Men much his superiors in rank and importance looked over his head at his wife, passed him with a nod on their way to her. He began to feel annoyance, and waited for this flurry to pass over. But pass it did not. With her second and third seasons in town her circle grew. Statesmen and officers twenty years Longstreet's senior seemed to find in Gabrielle an escape from long boredom. He was jealous without having the common pretexts for jealousy. He began to spend more and more time on his yacht in distant waters. He left his wife in his town house with his spinster cousin as chaperone. Gabrielle's mother came on from Martinique for a season, and was almost as much admired as her daughter. Sir Wilfred found that the Martiniquaises had considerably overshadowed him. He was no longer the interesting 'original' he had once been. His unexpected appearances and disappearances were mere incidents in the house and the life which his wife and his cousin had so well organized. He bore this for six years and then, unexpectedly, demanded divorce. He established the statutory grounds, she petitioning for the decree. He made her a generous settlement.

This brought about a great change in Gabrielle Longsreet's life. She remained in London and bought a small house near St James's Park. Longstreet's old cousin, to his great annoyance, stayed on with Gabrielle, – the only one of his family who had not treated her like a poor relation. The loyalty of this spinster, a woman of spirit, Scotch on the father's side, did a good deal to ease Gabrielle's fall in the world. For fall it was, of course. She had her circle, but it was smaller and more intimate. Fewer women invited her now, fewer of the women she used to know. She did not go afield for those who affected art and advanced ideas; they would gladly have championed her cause. She replied to their overtures that she no longer went into society. Her men friends never flinched in their loyalty. Those unembarrassed by wives, the bachelors and widowers, were more assiduous than ever. At that dinner table where Gabrielle and 'the Honourable MacPhairson,' as the old cousin was called, were sometimes the only women, one met promising young men, not yet settled in their careers, and much older men, so solidly and successfully settled that their presence in a company established its propriety.

Nobody could ever say exactly why Gabrielle's house was so attractive. The men who had the entrée there were not skilful at defining such a thing as 'charm' in words: that was not at all their line. And they would have been reluctant to admit that a negligible thing like temperature had anything to do with the pleasant relaxation they enjoyed there. The chill of London houses had been one of the cruellest trials the young Martiniquaise had to bear. When she took a house of her own, she (secretly, as if it were a disgraceful thing to do) had a hot-air furnace put in her cellar, and she kept coal fires burning in the grates at either end of the drawing-room. In colour, however, the rooms were not warm, but rather cool and spring-like. Always flowers, and not too many. There was something more flower-like than the flowers, – something in Gabrielle herself (now more herself than ever she had been as Lady Longstreet); the soft pleasure that came into her face when she put out her hand to greet a hero of perhaps seventy years, the look of admiration in her calm grey eyes. A century earlier her French grandmothers may have greeted the dignitaries of the Church with such a look,

— deep feeling, without eagerness of any kind. To a badgered Minister, who came in out of committee meetings and dirty weather, the warm house, the charming companionship which had no request lurking behind it, must have been grateful. The lingering touch of a white hand on his black sleeve can do a great deal for an elderly man who has left a busy and fruitless day behind him and who is worn down by the unreasonable demands of his own party. Nothing said in that room got out into the world. Gabrielle never repeated one man to another, — and as for the Honourable MacPhairson, she never gave anything away, not even a good story!

In time there came about a succession of Great Protectors, and Gabrielle Longstreet was more talked about than in the days of her sensational debut. Whether any of them were ever her lovers, no one could say. They were all men much older than she and only one of them was known for light behaviour with women. Young men were sometimes asked to her house, but they were made to feel it was by special kindness. Henry Seabury himself had been taken there by young Hardwick, when he was still an undergraduate. Seabury had not known her well, however, until she leased a house in New York and spent two winters there. A jealous woman, and a very clever one, had made things unpleasant for her in London and Gabrielle had quitted England for a time.

Sitting alone that night, recalling all he had heard of Lady Longstreet, Seabury tried to remember her face just as it was in the days when he used to know her; the beautiful contour of the cheeks, the low, straight brow, the lovely line from the chin to the base of the throat. Perhaps it was her eyes he remembered best; no glint in them, no sparkle, no drive. When she was moved by admiration, they did not glow, but became more soft, more grave; a kind of twilight shadow deepened in them. That look, with her calm white shoulders, her unconsciousness of her body and whatever clothed it, gave her the air of having come from afar off.

And now it was all gone. There was something tense, a

little defiant in the shoulders now. The hands that used to
lie on her dress forgotten, as a bunch of white violets might
lie there . . . Well, it was all gone.

Plain women, he reflected, when they grow old are –
simply plain women. Often they improve. But a beautiful
woman may become a ruin. The more delicate her beauty,
the more it owes to some exquisite harmony in modelling
and line, the more completely it is destroyed. Gabrielle
Longstreet's face was now unrecognizable. She gave it no
assistance, certainly. She was the only woman in the dining
room who used no make-up. She met the winter barefaced.
Cheap counterfeits meant nothing to a woman who had
had the real thing for so long. She must have been close
upon forty when he knew her in New York, – and where
was there such a creature in the world today? Certainly in
his hurried trip across America and England he had not
been gladdened by the sight of one. He had seen only
cinema stars, and women curled and plucked and painted
to look like them. Perhaps the few very beautiful women he
remembered in the past had been illusions, had benefited
by a romantic tradition which played upon them like a
kindly light . . . and by an attitude in men which no longer
existed.

v

When Mr Seabury awoke the next day it was clear to him
that any approach to Madame de Couçy must be made
through the amiable-seeming friend, Madame Allison as she
was called at the hotel, who always accompanied her. He
had noticed that this lady usually went down into the town
alone in the morning. After breakfasting he walked down
the hill and loitered about the little streets. Presently he saw
Madame Allison come out of the English bank,with several
small parcels tucked under her arm. He stepped beside her.

'Pardon me, Madame, but I am stopping at your hotel,
and I have noticed that you are a friend of Madame de
Couçy, whom I think I used to know as Gabrielle

Longstreet. It was many years ago, and naturally she does not recognize me. Would it displease her if I sent up my name, do you think?'

Mrs Allison answered brightly. 'Oh, she did recognize you, if you are Mr Seabury. Shall we sit down in the shade for a moment? I find it very warm here, even for August.'

When they were seated under the plane trees she turned to him with a friendly smile and frank curiosity. 'She is here for a complete rest and isn't seeing people, but I think she would be glad to see an old friend. She remembers you very well. At first she was not sure about your name, but I asked the porter. She recalled it at once and said she met you with Hardwick, General Hardwick, who was killed in the war. Yes, I'm sure she would be glad to see an old friend.'

He explained that he was scarcely an old friend, merely one of many admirers; but he used to go to her house when she lived in New York.

'She said you did. She thought you did not recognize her. But we have all changed, haven't we?'

'And have you and I met before, Madame Allison?'

'Oh, drop the Madame, please! We both speak English, and I am Mrs Allison. No, we never met. You may have seen me, if you went to the Alhambra. I was Cherry Beamish in those days.'

'Then I last saw you in an Eton jacket, with your hair cropped. I never had the pleasure of seeing you out of your character parts, which accounts for my not recognizing –'

She cut him short with a jolly laugh. 'Oh, thirty years and two stone would account, would account perfectly! I always did boy parts, you remember. They wouldn't have me in skirts. So I had to keep my weight down. Such a comfort not to fuss about it now. One has a right to a little of one's life, don't you think?'

He agreed. 'But I saw you in America also. You had great success there.'

She nodded. 'Yes, three seasons, grand engagements. I laid by a pretty penny. I was married over there, and divorced over there, quite in the American style! He was a Scotch boy, stranded in Philadelphia. We parted with no hard feelings, but he was too expensive to keep.' Seeing the hotel bus, Mrs Allison hailed it. 'I *shall* be glad if Gabrielle feels up to seeing you. She is frightfully dull here and not very well.'

VI

The following evening, as Seabury went into the dining-room and bowed to Mrs Allison, she beckoned him to Madame de Couçy's table. That lady put out her jewelled hand and spoke abruptly.

'Chetty tells me we are old acquaintances, Mr Seabury. Will you come up to us for coffee after dinner? This is the number of our apartment.' As she gave him her card he saw that her hand trembled slightly. Her voice was much deeper than it used to be, and cold. It had always been cool, but soft, like a cool fragrance, – like her eyes and her white arms.

When he rang at Madame de Couçy's suite an hour later, her maid admitted him. The two ladies were seated before an open window, the coffee table near them and the percolator bubbling. Mrs Allison was the first to greet him. In a moment she retired, leaving him alone with Madame de Couçy.

'It is very pleasant to meet you again, after so many years, Seabury. How did you happen to come?'

Because he had liked the place long ago, he told her.

'And I, for the same reason. I live in Paris now. Mrs Allison tells me you have been out in China all this while. And how are things there?'

'Not so good, Lady Longstreet, may I still call you? China is rather falling to pieces.'

'Just as here, eh? No, call me as I am known in this hotel, please. When we are alone, you may use my first name; that has survived time and change. As to change, we have got used to it. But you, coming back upon it, this Europe, suddenly . . . it must give you rather a shock.'

It was she herself who had given him the greatest shock

of all, and in one quick, penetrating glance she seemed to read the fact. She shrugged: there was nothing to be done about it. 'Chetty, where are you?' she called.

Mrs Allison came quickly from another room and poured the coffee. Her presence warmed the atmosphere considerably. She seemed unperturbed by the grimness of her friend's manner; and she herself was a most comfortable little person. Even her too evident plumpness was comfortable, since she didn't seem to mind it. She didn't like living in Paris very well, she said; something rather stiff and chilly about it. But she often ran away and went home to see her nieces and nephews, and they were a jolly lot. And now that an old friend of Gabrielle's had obligingly turned up, they would have someone to talk to, and that would be a blessing.

Madame de Couçy gave a low, mirthless laugh. 'She seems to take a good deal for granted, doesn't she?'

'Not where I am concerned, if you mean that. I should be deeply grateful for someone to talk to. Between the three of us we may find a great deal.'

'Be sure we shall,' said Mrs Allison. 'We have the past, and the present – which is really very interesting, if only you will let yourself think so. Some of the people here are very novel and amusing, and others are quite like people we used to know. Don't you find it so, Mr Seabury?'

He agreed with her and turned to Madame de Couçy. 'May I smoke?'

'What a question to ask in these days! Yes, you and Chetty may smoke. I will take a liqueur.'

Mrs Allison rose. 'Gabrielle has a cognac so old and precious that we keep it locked in a cabinet behind the piano.' In opening the cabinet she overturned a framed photograph which fell to the floor. 'There goes the General again! No, he didn't break, dear. We carry so many photographs about with us, Mr Seabury.'

Madame de Couçy turned to Seabury. 'Do you recognize some of my old friends? There are some of yours too, perhaps. I think I was never sentimental when I was young, but now I travel with my photographs. My friends mean more to me now than when they were alive. I was too ignorant then to realize what remarkable men they were. I supposed the world was always full of great men.'

She left the chair and walked with him about the salon and the long entrance hall, stopping before one and another; uniforms, military and naval, caps and gowns; photographs, drawings, engravings. As she spoke of them the character of her voice changed altogether, – became, indeed, the voice Seabury remembered. The hard, dry tone was a form of disguise, he conjectured; a protection behind which she addressed people from whom she expected neither recognition nor consideration.

'What an astonishing lot they are, seeing them together like this,' he exclaimed with feeling. 'How can a world manage to get on without them?'

'It hasn't managed very well, has it? You may remember that I was a rather ungrateful young woman. I took what came. A great man's time, his consideration, his affection, were mine in the natural course of things, I supposed. But it's not so now. I bow down to them in admiration . . . gratitude. They are dearer to me than when they were my living friends, – because I understand them better.'

Seabury remarked that the men whose pictures looked down at them were too wise to expect youth and deep discernment in the same person.

'I'm not speaking of discernment; that I had, in a way. I mean ignorance. I simply didn't know all that lay behind them. I am better informed now. I read everything they wrote, and everything that has been written about them. That is my chief pleasure.'

Seabury smiled indulgently and shook his head. 'It wasn't for what you knew about them that they loved you.'

She put her hand quickly on his arm. 'Ah, you said that before you had time to think! You believe, then, that I did mean something to them?' For the first time she fixed on him the low, level wondering look that he remembered of old: the woman he used to know seemed breathing beside him. When she turned away from him suddenly, he knew it was to hide the tears in her eyes. He had seen her cry once, a long time ago. He had not forgotten.

He took up a photograph and talked, to bridge over a silence in which she could not trust her voice. 'What a fine likeness of X—! He was my hero, among the whole group. Perhaps his contradictions fascinated me. I could never see how one side of him managed to live with the other. Yet I know that both sides were perfectly genuine. He was a mystery. And his end was mysterious. No one will ever know where or how. A secret departure on a critical mission, and never an arrival anywhere. It was like him.'

Madame de Couçy turned, with a glow in her eyes such as he had never seen there in her youth. 'The evening his disappearance was announced . . . Shall I ever forget it! I was in London. The newsboys were crying in the street. I did not go to bed that night. I sat up in the drawing-room until daylight; hoping, saying the old prayers I used to say with my mother. It was all one could do. . . . Young Harney was with him, you remember. I have always been glad of that. Whatever fate was in store for his chief, Harney would have chosen to share it.'

Seabury stayed much longer with Madame de Couçy than he had intended. The ice once broken, he felt he might never find her so much herself again. They sat talking about people who were no longer in this world. She knew much more about them than he. Knew so much that her talk brought back not only the men, but their period; its security, the solid exterior, the exotic contradictions behind the screen; the deep, claret-coloured closing years of Victoria's reign. Nobody ever recognizes a period until it has gone by, he reflected: until it lies behind one it is merely everyday life.

VII

The next evening the Thompsons, all four of them, were to dine with Mr Seabury at the Maison des Fleurs. Their holiday was over, and they would be leaving on the following afternoon. They would stop once more at that spot in the north, to place fresh wreaths, before they took the Channel boat.

When Seabury and his guests were seated and the dinner had been ordered, he was aware that the mother was looking at him rather wistfully. He felt he owed her some confidence, since it was she, really, who had enlightened him. He told her that he had called upon Gabrielle Longstreet last evening.

'And how is she, dear Mr Seabury? Is she less — less forbidding than when we see her in the Square?'

'She was on her guard at first, but that soon passed. I stayed later than I should have done, but I had a delightful evening. I gather that she is a little antagonistic to the present order, — indifferent, at least. But when she talks about her old friends she is quite herself.'

Mrs Thompson listened eagerly. She hesitated and then asked: 'Does she find life pleasant at all, do you think?'

Seabury told her how the lady was surrounded by the photographs and memoirs of her old friends; how she never travelled without them. It had struck him that she was living her life over again, — more understandingly than she lived it the first time.

Mrs Thompson breathed a little sigh. 'Then I know that all is well with her. You have done so much to make our stay here pleasant, Mr Seabury, but your telling us this is the best of all. Even Father will be interested to know that.'

The stout man, who wore an ancient tail coat made for him when he was much thinner, came out indignantly. 'Even Father! I like that! One of the great beauties of our time, and very popular before the divorce.'

His daughter laughed and patted his sleeve. Seabury went on to tell Mrs Thompson that she had been quite right in surmising the companion to be a friend, not a paid attendant. 'And a very charming person, too. She was one of your cleverest music-hall stars. Cherry Beamish.'

Here Father dropped his spoon into his soup. 'What's that? Cherry Beamish? But we haven't had such another since! Remember her in that coster song, Mother? It went round the world, that did. We were all crazy about her, the boys called her Cherish Beamy. No monkeyshines for her, never got herself mixed up in anything shady.'

'Such a womanly woman in private life,' Mrs Thompson murmured. 'My Dorothy went to school with two of her nieces. An excellent school, and quite dear. Their Aunt Chetty does everything for them. And now she is with Lady Longstreet! One wouldn't have supposed they'd ever meet, those two. But then things *are* strange now?'

There was no lull in conversation at that dinner. After the father had enjoyed several glasses of champagne he delighted his daughters with an account of how Cherry Beamish used to do the tipsy schoolboy coming in at four in the morning and meeting his tutor in the garden.

VIII

Mr Seabury sat waiting before the hotel in a comfortable car which he now hired by the week. Gabrielle and Chetty drove out with him every day. This afternoon they were to go to Annecy by the wild road along the Echelles. Presently Mrs Allison came down alone. Gabrielle was staying in bed, she said. Last night Seabury had dined with them in their apartment, and Gabrielle had talked too much, she was afraid. 'She didn't sleep afterward, but I think she will make it up today if she is quite alone.'

Seabury handed her into the car. In a few minutes they were running past the lake of Bourget.

'This gives me an opportunity, Mrs Allison, to ask you how it came about that you've become Lady Longstreet's protector. It's a beautiful friendship.'

She laughed. 'And an amazing one? But I think you must call me Chetty, as she does, if we are to be confidential. Yes, I suppose it must seem to you the queerest partnership that war and desolation have made. But you see, she was so strangely left. When I first began to look after her a little, two years ago, she was ill in an hotel in Paris (we have taken a flat since), and there was no one, positively no one but the hotel people, the French doctor, and an English nurse who had chanced to be within call. It was the nurse, really, who gave me my cue. I had sent flowers, with no name, of course. (What would a bygone music-hall name mean to Gabrielle Longstreet?) And I called often to inquire. One morning I met Nurse Ames just as she was going out into the Champs-Élysées for her exercise, and she asked me to accompany her. She was an experienced woman, not young. She remembered when Gabrielle Longstreet's name and photographs were known all over the Continent, and when people at home were keen enough upon meeting her. And here she was, dangerously ill in a foreign hotel, and there was no one, simply no one. To be sure, she was registered under the name of her second husband.'

Seabury interrupted. 'And who was he, this de Couçy? I have heard nothing about him.'

'I know very little myself, I never met him. They had been friends a long while, I believe. He was killed in action – less than a year after they were married. His name was a disguise for her, even then. She came from Martinique, you remember, and she had no relatives in England. Longstreet's people had never liked her. So, you see, she was quite alone.'

Seabury took her plump little hand. 'And that was where you came in, Chetty?'

She gave his fingers a squeeze. 'Thank you! That's nice. It was Nurse Ames who did it. The war made a lot of wise nurses. After Gabrielle was well enough to see people, there was no one for her to see! The same thing that had happened to her friends in England had happened over here. The old men had paid the debt of nature, and the young ones were killed or disabled or had lost touch with her. She once had many friends in Paris. Nurse Ames told me that an old French officer, blinded in the war, sometimes came to see her, guided by his little granddaughter. She said her patient had expressed curiosity about the English woman who had sent so many flowers. I wrote a note asking whether I could be of any service, and signed my professional name. She might recognize it, she might not.

We had been on a committee together during the war. She told the nurse to admit me, and that's how it began.'

Seabury took her hand again. 'Now I want you to be frank with me. Had she then, or has she now, money worries at all?'

Cherry Beamish chuckled. 'Not she, you may believe! But I have had a few for her. On the whole, she's behaved very well. She sold her place in Devonshire to advantage, before the war. Her capital is in British bonds. She seems to you harassed?'

'Sometimes.'

Mrs Allison looked grave and was silent for a little.'Yes,' with a sigh, 'she gets very low at times. She suffers from strange regrets. She broods on the things she might have done for her friends and didn't, — thinks she was cold to them. Was she, in those days, so indifferent as she makes herself believe?'

Seabury reflected. 'Not exactly indifferent. She wouldn't have been so attractive if she'd been that. She didn't take things very hard, perhaps. She used to strike me as . . . well, we might call it unawakened.'

'But wasn't she the most beautiful creature then! I used to see her at the races, and at charity bazaars, in my early professional days. After the war broke out and everybody was all mixed up, I was put on an entertainment committee with her. She wasn't quite the Lady Longstreet of my youth, but she still had that grand style. It was the illness in Paris that broke her. She's changed very fast ever since. You see she thought, once the war was over, the world would be just as it used to be. Of course it isn't.'

By this time the car had reached Annecy, and they stopped for tea. The shore of the lake was crowded with young people taking their last dip for the day; sunbrowned backs and shoulders, naked arms and legs. As Mrs Allison was having her tea on the terrace, she watched the bathers. Presently she twinkled a sly smile at her host. 'Do you know, I'm rather glad we didn't bring Gabrielle! It puts her out terribly to see young people bathing naked. She makes comments that are indecent, really! If only she had a swarm of young nieces and nephews, as I have, she'd see things quite differently, and she'd be much happier. Legs were never wicked to us stage people, and now all the young things know they are not wicked.'

IX

When Madame de Couçy went out with Seabury alone, he missed the companionship of Cherry Beamish. With Cherry the old beauty always softened a little; seemed amused by the other's interest in whatever the day produced: the countryside, the weather, the number of cakes she permitted herself for tea. The imagination which made this strange friendship possible was certainly on the side of Cherry Beamish. For her, he could see, there was something in it; to be the anchor, the refuge, indeed, of one so out of her natural orbit, – selected by her long ago as an object of special admiration.

One afternoon when he called, the maid, answering his ring, said that Madame would not go out this afternoon, but hoped he would stay and have tea with her in her salon. He told the lift boy to dismiss the car and went in to Madame de Couçy. She received him with unusual warmth.

'Chetty is out for the afternoon, with some friends from home. Oh, she still has a great many! She is much younger than I, in every sense. Today I particularly wanted to see you alone. It's curious how the world runs away from one, slips by without one's realizing it.'

He reminded her that the circumstances had been unusual. 'We have lived through a storm to which the French Revolution, which used to be our standard of horrors, was merely a breeze. A rather gentlemanly affair, as one looks back on it . . . As for me, I am grateful to be alive, sitting here with you in a comfortable hotel (I might be in a prison full of rats), in a France still undestroyed.'

The old lady looked into his eyes with the calm, level gaze so rare with her now. 'Are you grateful? I am not. I think one should go out with one's time. I particularly wished to see you alone this afternoon. I want to thank you for your tact and gentleness with me one hideous evening long ago; in my house in New York. You were a darling boy to me that night. If you hadn't come along, I don't know how I would have got over it – out of it, even. One can't call the servants.'

'But Gabrielle, why recall a disagreeable incident when you have so many agreeable ones to remember?'

She seemed not to hear him, but went on, speaking deliberately, as if she were reflecting aloud. 'It was strange, your coming in just when you did: that night it seemed to me like a miracle. Afterward, I remembered you had been expected at eight. But I had forgotten all that, forgotten everything. Never before or since have I been so frightened. It was something worse than fear.'

There was a knock at the door. Madame de Couçy called: '*Entrez!*' without turning round. While the tea was brought she sat looking out of the window, frowning. When the waiter had gone she turned abruptly to Seabury:

'After that night I never saw you again until you walked into the dining-room of this hotel a few weeks ago. I had gone into the country somewhere, hiding with friends, and when I came back to New York, you were already on your way to China. I never had a chance to explain.'

'There was certainly no need for that.'

'Not for you, perhaps. But for me. You may have thought such scenes were frequent in my life. Hear me out, please,' as he protested. 'That man had come to my house at seven o'clock that evening and sent up a message begging me to see him about some business matters. (I had been stupid enough to let him make investments for me.) I finished dressing and hurried down to the drawing-room.' Here she stopped and slowly drank a cup of tea. 'Do you know, after you came in I did not see you at all, not for some time, I think. I was mired down in something ... *the power of the dog*, the English Prayer Book calls it. But the moment I heard your voice, I knew that I was safe ... I felt the leech drop off. I have never forgot the sound of your voice that night; so calm, with all a ·

man's strength behind it, – and you were only a boy. You merely asked if you had come too early. I felt the leech drop off. After that I remember nothing. I didn't see you, with my eyes, until you gave me your handkerchief. You stayed with me and looked after me all evening.

'You see, I had let the beast come to my house, oh, a number of times! I had asked his advice and allowed him to make investments for me. I had done the same thing at home with men who knew about such matters; they were men like yourself and Hardwick. In a strange country one goes astray in one's reckonings. I had met that man again and again at the houses of my friends, – your friends! Of course his personality was repulsive to me. One knew at once that under his smoothness he was a vulgar person. I supposed that was not unusual in great bankers in the States.'

'You simply chose the wrong banker, Gabrielle. The man's accent must have told you that he belonged to a country you did not admire.'

'But I tell you I met him at the houses of decent people.'

Seabury shook his head, 'Yes, I am afraid you must blame us for that. Americans, even those whom you call the decent ones, do ask people to their houses who shouldn't be there. They are often asked *because* they are outrageous, – and therefore considered amusing. Besides, that fellow had a very clever way of pushing himself. If a man is generous in his contributions to good causes, and is useful on committees and commissions, he is asked to the houses of the people who have these good causes at heart.'

'And perhaps I, too, was asked because I was considered notorious? A divorcée, known to have more friends among men than among women at home? I think I see what you mean. There are not many shades in your society. I left the States soon after you sailed for China. I gave up my New York house at a loss to be rid of it. The instant I recognized you in the dining-room downstairs, that miserable evening came back to me. In so far as our acquaintance was concerned, all that had happened only the night before.'

'Then I am reaping a reward I didn't deserve, some thirty

years afterward! If I had not happened to call that evening
when you were so – so unpleasantly surprised, you would
never have remembered me at all! We shouldn't be sitting
together at this moment. Now may I ring for some fresh tea,
dear? Let us be comfortable. This afternoon has brought us
closer together. And this little spot in Savoie is a nice place to
renew old friendships, don't you think?'

X

Some hours later, when Mr Seabury was dressing for dinner,
he was thinking of that strange evening in Gabrielle Longstreet's house on Fifty-third Street, New York.

He was then twenty-four years old. She had been very
gracious to him all the winter.

On that particular evening he was to take her to dine at
Delmonico's. Her cook and butler were excused to attend a
wedding. The maid who answered his ring asked him to go
up to the drawing-room on the second floor, where Madame
was awaiting him. She followed him as far as the turn of the
stairway, then, hearing another ring at the door, she excused
herself.

He went on alone. As he approached the wide doorway
leading into the drawing-room, he was conscious of something unusual; a sound, or perhaps an unnatural stillness.
From the doorway he beheld something quite terrible. At the
far end of the room Gabrielle Longstreet was seated on a little
French sofa – not seated, but silently struggling. Behind the
sofa stood a stout, dark man leaning over her. His left arm,
about her waist, pinioned her against the flowered silk
upholstery. His right hand was thrust deep into the low-cut
bodice of her dinner gown. In her struggle she had turned a
little on her side; her right arm was in the grip of his left
hand, and she was trying to free the other, which was held
down by the pressure of his elbow. Neither of those two
made a sound. Her face was averted, half hidden against the
blue silk back of the sofa. Young Seabury stood still just long
enough to see what the situation really was. Then he stepped

across the threshold and said with such coolness as he could command: 'Am I too early, Madame Longstreet?'

The man behind her started from his crouching position, darted away from the sofa, and disappeared down the stairway. To reach the stairs he passed Seabury, without lifting his eyes, but his face was glistening wet.

The lady lay without stirring, her face now completely hidden. She looked so crushed and helpless, he thought she must be hurt physically. He spoke to her softly: 'Madame Longstreet, shall I call – '

'Oh, don't°call! Don't call anyone.' She began shuddering violently, her face still turned away. 'Some brandy, please. Downstairs, in the dining-room.'

He ran down the stairs, had to tell the solicitous maid that Madame wished to be alone for the present. When he came back Gabrielle had caught up the shoulder straps of her gown. Her right arm bore red finger marks. She was shivering and sobbing. He slipped his handkerchief into her hand, and she held it over her mouth. She took a little brandy. Then another fit of weeping came on. He begged her to come nearer to the fire. She put her hand on his arm, but seemed unable to rise. He lifted her from that seat of humiliation and took her, wavering between his supporting hands, to a low chair beside the coal grate. She sank into it and he put a cushion under her feet. He persuaded her to drink the rest of the brandy. She stopped crying and leaned back, her eyes closed, her hands lying nerveless on the arms of the chair. Seabury thought he had never seen her when she was more beautiful . . . probably that was because she was helpless and he was young.

'Perhaps you would like me to go now?' he asked her.

She opened her eyes. 'Oh, no! Don't leave me, please. I am so much safer with you here.' She put her hand, still cold, on his for a moment, then closed her eyes and went back into that languor of exhaustion. Perhaps half an hour went by. She did not stir, but he knew she was not asleep: an occasional trembling of the eyelids, tears stealing out from under her black lashes and glistening unregarded on her cheeks; like pearls he thought they were, transparent shimmers on velvet cheeks gone very white.

When suddenly she sat up, she spoke in her natural voice.

'But, my dear boy, you have gone dinnerless all this while! Won't you stay with me and have just a bit of something up here? Do ring for Hopkins, please.'

The young man caught at the suggestion. If once he could get her mind on the duties of caring for a guest, that might lead to something. He must try to be very hungry.

The kitchen maid was in and, under Hopkins's direction, got together a creditable supper and brought it up to the drawing room. Gabrielle took nothing but the hot soup and a little sherry. Young Seabury, once he tasted food, found he had no difficulty in doing away with cold pheasant and salad.

Gabrielle had quite recovered her self-control. She talked very little, but that was not unusual with her. He told her about Hardwick's approaching marriage. For him, the evening went by very pleasantly. He felt with her a closer intimacy than ever before.

When at midnight he rose to take his leave, she detained him beside her chair, holding his hand. 'At some other time I shall explain what you saw here tonight. How could such a thing happen in one's own house, in an English-speaking city . . .?'

'But that was not an English-speaking man who went out from here. He is an immigrant who has made a lot of money. He does not belong.'

'Yes, that is true. I wish you weren't going out to China. Not for long, I hope. It's a bad thing to be away from one's own people.' Her voice broke, and tears came again. He kissed her hand softly, devotedly, and went downstairs.

He had not seen her again until his arrival at this hotel some weeks ago, when he did not recognize her.

XI

One evening when Mrs Allison and Madame de Couçy had been dining with Seabury at the Maison des Fleurs, they went into the tea room to have their coffee and watch the dancing. It was now September, and almost everyone would be leaving next week. The floor was full of young people, English, American, French, moving monotonously to monotonous rhythms, – some of them scarcely moving at all. Gabrielle watched them through her lorgnette, with a look of resigned boredom.

Mrs Allison frowned at her playfully. 'Of course it's all very different,' she observed, 'but then so is everything.' She turned to Seabury: 'You know we used to have to put so much drive into a dance act, or it didn't go at all. Lottie Collins was the only lazy dancer who could get anything over. But the truth was, the dear thing couldn't dance at all; got on by swinging her foot! There must be something in all this new manner, if only one could get it. That couple down by the bar now, the girl with the *very* low back: they are doing it beautifully; she dips and rises like a bird in the air . . . a tired bird, though. That's the disconcerting thing. It all seems so tired.'

Seabury agreed with her cheerfully that it was charming, though tired. He felt a gathering chill in the lady on his right. Presently she said impatiently: 'Haven't you had enough of this, Chetty?'

Mrs Allison sighed. 'You never see anything in it, do you, dear?'

'I see wriggling. They look to me like lizards dancing – or reptiles coupling.'

'Oh, no, dear! No! They are such sweet young things. But they are dancing in a dream. I want to go and wake them up. Dancing ought to be open and free, with the lungs full; not mysterious and breathless. I wish I could see a *spirited* waltz again.'

Gabrielle shrugged and gave a dry laugh. 'I wish I could dance one! I think I should try, if by any chance I should ever hear a waltz played again.'

Seabury rose from his chair. 'May I take you up on that? Will you?'

She seemed amused and incredulous, but nodded.

'Excuse me for a moment.' He strolled toward the orchestra.

When the tango was over he spoke to the conductor, handing him something from his vest pocket. The conductor smiled and bowed, then spoke to his men, who smiled in turn. The saxophone put down his instrument and grinned. The strings sat up in their chairs, pulled themselves up, as it were, tuned for a moment, and sat at attention. At the lift of the leader's hand they began the 'Blue Danube.'

Gabrielle took Mr Seabury's arm. They passed a dozen couples who were making a sleepy effort and swung into the open square where the line of tables stopped. Seabury had never danced with Gabrielle Longstreet, and he was astonished. She had attack and style, the grand style, slightly military, quite right for her tall, straight figure. He held her hand very high, accordingly. The conductor caught the idea; smartened the tempo slightly, made the accents sharper. One by one the young couples dropped out and sat down to smoke. The two old waltzers were left alone on the floor. There was a stir of curiosity about the room; who were those two, and why were they doing it? Cherry Beamish heard remarks from the adjoining tables.

'She's rather stunning, the old dear!'

'Aren't they funny?'

'It's so quaint and theatrical. Quite effective in its way.'

Seabury had not danced for some time. He thought the musicians drew the middle part out interminably; rather suspected they were playing a joke on him. But his partner lost none of her brilliance and verve. He tried to live up to her. He was grateful when those fiddlers snapped out the last phrase. As he took Gabrielle to her seat, a little breeze of applause broke out from the girls about the room.

'Dear young things!' murmured Chetty, who was flushed with pleasure and excitement. A group of older men who had come in from the dining-room were applauding.

'Let us go, Seabury. I am afraid we have been making rather an exhibition,' murmured Madame de Couçy. As they got into the car awaiting them outside, she laughed good-humouredly. 'Do you know, Chetty, I quite enjoyed it!'

XII

The next morning Mrs Allison telephoned Seabury that Gabrielle had slept well after an amusing evening: felt so fit that she thought they might seize upon this glorious morning for a drive to the Grande-Chartreuse. The drive, by the route they preferred, was a long one, and hitherto she had not felt quite equal to it. Accordingly, the three left the hotel at eleven o'clock with Seabury's trusty young Savoyard driver, and were soon in the mountains.

It was one of those high-heavenly days that often come among the mountains of Savoie in autumn. In the valleys the hillsides were pink with autumn crocuses thrusting up out of the short sunburned grass. The beech trees still held their satiny green. As the road wound higher and higher toward the heights, Seabury and his companions grew more and more silent. The lightness and purity of the air gave one a sense of detachment from everything one had left behind 'down there, back yonder.' Mere breathing was a delicate physical pleasure. One had the feeling that life would go on thus forever in high places, among naked peaks cut sharp against a stainless sky.

Ever afterward Seabury remembered that drive as strangely impersonal. He and the two ladies were each lost in a companionship much closer than any they could share with one another. The clean-cut mountain boy who drove them seemed lost in thoughts of his own. His eyes were on the road: he never spoke. Once, when the gold tones of an alpine horn floated down from some hidden pasture far overhead, he stopped the car of his own accord and shut off the engine. He threw a smiling glance back at Seabury and then sat still, while the simple, melancholy song floated down through the blue air. When it ceased, he waited a little, looking up. As the horn did not sing again, he drove on without comment.

At last, beyond a sharp turn in the road, the monastery came into view; acres of slate roof, of many heights and pitches, turrets and steep slopes. The terrifying white mountain crags overhung it from behind, and the green beech wood lay all about its walls. The sunlight blazing down upon that mothering roof showed ruined patches: the Government could not afford to keep such a wilderness of leading in repair.

The monastery, superb and solitary among the lonely mountains, was after all a destination: brought Seabury's party down into man's world again, though it was the world of the past. They began to chatter foolishly, after hours of silent reflection. Mrs Allison wished to see the kitchen of the Carthusians, and the chapel, but she thought Gabrielle should stay in the car. Madame de Couçy insisted that she was not tired: she would walk about the stone courtyard while the other two went into the monastery.

Except for a one-armed guard in uniform, the great court was empty. Herbs and little creeping plants grew between the cobblestones. The three walked toward the great open well and leaned against the stone wall that encircled it, looking down into its wide mouth. The hewn blocks of the coping were moss-grown, and there was water at the bottom. Madame de Couçy slipped a little mirror from her handbag and threw a sunbeam down into the stone-lined well. That yellow ray seemed to waken the black water at the bottom: little ripples stirred over the surface. She said nothing, but she smiled as she threw the gold plaque over the water and the wet moss of the lower coping. Chetty and Seabury left her there. When he glanced back, just before they disappeared into the labyrinth of buildings she was still looking down into the well and playing with her little reflector, a faintly contemptuous smile on her lips.

After nearly two hours at the monastery the party started homeward. Seabury told the driver to regulate his speed so that they would see the last light on the mountains before they reached the hotel.

The return trip was ill-starred: they narrowly escaped a serious accident. As they rounded one of those sharp curves, with a steep wall on their right and an open gulf on the left, the chauffeur was confronted by a small car with two women, crossing the road just in front of him. To avoid throwing them over the precipice he ran sharply to the right, grazing the rock wall until he could bring his car to a stop. His passengers were thrown violently forward over the driver's seat. The light car had been on the wrong side of the road. and had attempted to cross on hearing the Savoyard's horn. His nerve and quickness had brought every one off alive, at least.

Immediately the two women from the other car sprang out and ran up to Seabury with shrill protestations; they were very careful drivers, had run this car twelve thousand miles and never had an accident, etc. They were Americans; bobbed, hatless, clad in dirty white knickers and sweaters. They addressed each other as 'Marge' and 'Jim'. Seabury's forehead was bleeding: they repeatedly offered to plaster it up for him.

The Savoyard was in the road, working with his mudguard and his front wheel. Madame de Couçy was lying back in her seat, pale, her eyes closed, something very wrong with her breathing. Mrs Allison was fanning her with Seabury's hat. The two girls who had caused all the trouble had lit cigarettes and were swaggering about with their hands in their trousers pockets, giving advice to the driver about his wheel. The Savoyard never lifted his eyes. He had not spoken since he ran his car into the wall. The sharp voices, knowingly ordering him to '*regardez, attendez*,' did not pierce his silence or his contempt. Seabury paid no attention to them because he was alarmed about Madame de Couçy, who looked desperately ill. She ought to lie down, he felt sure, but there was no place to put her – the road was cut along the face of a cliff for a long way back. Chetty had aromatic ammonia in her handbag; she persuaded Gabrielle to take it from the bottle, as they had no cup. While Seabury was leaning over her she opened her eyes and said distinctly:

'I think I am not hurt . . . faintness, a little palpitation. If you could get those creatures away . . .'

He sprang off the running-board and drew the two intruders aside. He addressed them; first politely, then forcibly.

Their reply was impertinent, but they got into their dirty little car and went. The Savoyard was left in peace; the situation was simplified. Three elderly people had been badly shaken up and bruised, but the brief submersion in frightfulness was over. At last the driver said he could get his car home safely.

During the rest of the drive Madame de Couçy seemed quite restored. Her colour was not good, but her self-control was admirable.

'You must let me give that boy something on my own account, Seabury. Oh, I know you will be generous with him! But I feel a personal interest. He took a risk, and he took the right one. He couldn't run the chance of knocking two women over a precipice. They happened to be worth nobody's consideration, but that doesn't alter the code.'

'Such an afternoon to put you through!' Seabury groaned.

'It was natural, wasn't it, after such a morning. After one has been *exaltée*, there usually comes a shock. Oh, I don't mean the bruises we got! I mean the white breeches.' Gabrielle laughed, her good laugh, with no malice in it. She put her hand on his shoulder. 'How ever did you manage to dispose of them so quickly?'

When the car stopped before the hotel, Madame de Couçy put a tiny card case into the driver's hand with a smile and a word. But when she tried to rise from the seat, she sank back. Seabury and the Savoyard lifted her out, carried her into the hotel and up the lift, into her own chamber. As they placed her on the bed, Seabury said he would call a doctor. Madame de Couçy opened her eyes and spoke firmly:

'That is not necessary. Chetty knows what to do for me, I shall be myself tomorrow. Thank you both, thank you.'

Outside the chamber door Seabury asked Mrs Allison whether he should telephone for Doctor Françon.

'I think not. A new person would only disturb her. I have all the remedies her own doctor gave me for these attacks. Quiet is the most important thing, really.'

The next morning Seabury was awakened very early, something before six o'clock, by the buzz of his telephone. Mrs

Allison spoke, asking in a low voice if he would come to their apartment as soon as possible. He dressed rapidly. The lift was not yet running, so he went up two flights of stairs and rang at their door. Cherry Beamish, in her dressing-gown, admitted him. From her face he knew, at once, – though her smile was almost radiant as she took his hand.

'Yes, it is over for her, poor dear,' she said softly, 'It must have happened in her sleep. I was with her until after midnight. When I went in again, a little after five, I found her just as I want you to see her now; before the maid comes, before anyone has been informed.'

She led him on tiptoe into Gabrielle's chamber. The first shafts of the morning sunlight slanted through the Venetian blinds. A blue dressing-gown hung on a tall chair beside the bed, blue slippers beneath it. Gabrielle lay on her back, her eyes closed. The face that had outfaced so many changes in fortune had no longer need to muffle itself in furs, to shrink away from curious eyes, or harden itself into scorn. It lay on the pillow regal, calm, victorious, – like an open confession.

Seabury stood for a moment looking down at her. Then he went to the window and peered out through the open slats at the sun, come at last over the mountains into a sky that had long been blue: the same mountains they were driving among yesterday.

Presently Cherry Beamish spoke to him. She pointed to the hand that lay on the turned-back sheet. 'See how changed her hands are; like those of a young woman. She forgot to take off her rings last night, or she was too tired. Yes, dear, you needed a long rest. And now you are with your own kind.'

'I feel that, too, Chetty. She is with them. All is well. Thank you for letting me come.' He stooped for a moment over the hand that had been gracious to his youth. They went out into the salon, carefully closing the door behind them.

'Now, my dear, stay here, with her. I will go to the management, and I will arrange all that must be done.'

Some hours later, after he had gone through the

formalities required by French law, Seabury encountered the three journalists in front of the hotel.

Next morning the great man from the Riviera to whom Seabury had telegraphed came in person, his car laden with flowers from his conservatories. He stood on the platform at the railway station, his white head uncovered, all the while that the box containing Gabrielle Longstreet's coffin was being carried across and put on the express. Then he shook Seabury's hand in farewell, and bent gallantly over Chetty's. Seabury and Chetty were going to Paris on that same express.

After her illness two years ago Gabrielle de Couçy had bought a lot *à perpétuité* in Père-Lachaise. That was rather a fashion then: Adelina Patti, Sarah Bernhardt, and other ladies who had once held a place in the world made the same choice.

1936

BEFORE BREAKFAST

HENRY Grenfell, of Grenfell & Saunders, got resentfully out of bed after a bad night. The first sleepless night he had ever spent in his own cabin, on his own island, where nobody knew that he was senior partner of Grenfell & Saunders, and where the business correspondence was never forwarded to him. He slipped on a blanket dressing-gown over his pyjamas (island mornings in the North Atlantic are chill before dawn), went to the front windows of his bed-room, and ran up the heavy blue shades which shut out the shameless blaze of the sunrise if one wanted to sleep late – and he usually did on the first morning after arriving. (The trip up from Boston was long and hard, by trains made up of the cast-off coaches of liquidated railroads, and then by the two worst boats in the world.) The cabin modestly squatted on a tiny clearing between a tall spruce wood and the sea, – sat about fifty yards back from the edge of the red sandstone cliff which dropped some two hundred feet to a narrow beach – so narrow that it was covered at high tide. The cliffs rose sheer on this side of the island, were undercut in places, and faced the east.

The east was already lightening; a deep red streak burnt over the sky-line water, and the water itself was thick and dark, indigo blue – occasionally a silver streak, where the tide was going out very quietly. While Grenfell stood at his window, a big snowshoe hare ran downhill from the spruce wood, bounded into the grass plot at the front door, and began nervously nibbling the clover. He was puzzled and furtive; his jaws quivered, and his protruding eyes kept watch behind him as well as before. Grenfell was sure it was the hare that used to come every morning two summers ago and had become quite friendly. But now he seemed ill at ease; presently he started, sat still for an instant, then scampered up the grassy hillside and disappeared into the dark spruce wood. Silly thing! Still, it was a kind of greeting.

Grenfell left the window and went to his walnut wash-stand (no plumbing) and mechanically prepared to take a shower in the shed room behind his sleeping-chamber. He began his morning routine, still thinking about the hare.

First came the eye-drops. Tilting his head back, thus staring into the eastern horizon, he raised the glass dropper, but he didn't press the bulb. He saw something up there. While he was watching the rabbit the sky had changed. Above the red streak on the water line the sky had lightened to faint blue, and across the horizon a drift of fleecy rose cloud was floating. And through it a white-bright, gold-bright planet was shining. The morning star, of course. At this hour, and so near the sun, it would be Venus.

Behind her rose-coloured veils, quite alone in the sky already blue, she seemed to wait. She had come in on her beat, taken her place in the figure. Serene, impersonal splendour. Merciless perfection, ageless sovereignty. The poor hare and his clover, poor Grenfell and his eye-drops!

He braced himself against his washstand and still stared up at her. Something roused his temper so hot that he began to mutter aloud.

'And what's a hundred and thirty-six million years to you, Madam? That Professor needn't blow. You were winking and blinking up there maybe a hundred and thirty-six million times before that date they are so proud of. The rocks can't tell any tales on you. You were doing your stunt up there long before there was anything down here but – God knows what! Let's leave that to the professors, Madam, you and me!'

This childish bitterness toward 'millions' and professors

was the result of several things. Two of Grenfell's sons were 'professors'; Harrison a distinguished physicist at thirty. This morning, however, Harrison had not popped up in his father's mind. Grenfell was still thinking of a pleasant and courtly scientist whom he had met on the boat yesterday – a delightful man who had, temporarily at least, wrecked Grenfell's life with civilities and information.

It was natural, indeed inevitable, that two clean, close-shaven gentlemen in tailored woods clothes, passengers on the worst tub owned by the Canadian Steamships Company and both bound for a little island off the Nova Scotia coast, should get into conversation. It was all the more natural since the scientist was accompanied by a lovely girl – his daughter.

It was a pleasure to look at her, just as it is a pleasure to look at any comely creature who shows breeding, delicate preferences. She had lovely eyes, lovely skin, lovely manners. She listened closely when Grenfell and her father talked, but she didn't bark up with her opinions. When he asked her about their life on the island last summer, he liked everything she said about the place and the people. She answered him lightly, as if her impressions could matter only to herself, but, having an opinion, it was only good manners to admit it. 'Sweet, but decided,' was his rough estimate.

Since they were both going to an island which wasn't even on the map, supposed to be known only to the motor launches that called after a catch of herring, it was natural that the two gentlemen should talk about that bit of wooded rock in the sea. Grenfell always liked to talk about it to the right person. At first he thought Profesor Fairweather was a right person. He had felt alarm when Fairweather mentioned that last summer he had put up a portable house on the shore about two miles from Grenfell's cabin. But he added that it would soon vanish as quietly as it had come. His geological work would be over this autumn, and his portable house would be taken to pieces and shipped to an island in the South Pacific. Having thus reassured him, Fairweather carelessly, in quite the tone of weather-comment small talk, proceeded to wreck one of Grenfell's happiest illusions; the escape-avenue he kept in the back of his mind when he was at his desk at Grenfell & Saunders, Bonds. The Professor certainly meant no harm. He was a man of the world, urbane, not self-important. He merely remarked that the island was interesting geologically because the two ends of the island belonged to different periods, yet the ice seemed to have brought them both down together.

'And about how old would our end be, Professor?' Grenfell meant simply to express polite interest, but he gave himself away, parted with his only defence – indifference.

'We call it a hundred and thirty-six million years,' was the answer he got.

'Really? That's getting it down pretty fine, isn't it? I'm just a blank where science is concerned. I went to work when I was thirteen – didn't have any education. Of course some business men read up on science. But I have to struggle with reports and figures a good deal. When I do read I like something human – the old fellows: Scott and Dickens and Fielding. I get a great kick out of them.'

The Professor was a perfect gentleman, but he couldn't resist the appeal of ignorance. He had sensed in half an hour that this man loved the island. (His daughter had sensed it a year ago, as soon as she arrived there with her father. Something about his cabin, the little patch of lawn in front, and the hedge of wild roses that fenced it in, told her that.) In their talk Professor Fairweather had come to realize that this man had quite an unusual feeling for the island, therefore he would certainly like to know more about it – all he could tell him!

The sun leaped out of the sea – the planet vanished. Grenfell rejected his eye-drops. Why patch up? What was the use . . . of anything? Why tear a man loose from his little rock and shoot him out into the eternities? All that stuff was inhuman. A man had his little hour, with heat and cold and a time-sense suited to his endurance. If you took that away from him you left him spineless, accidental, unrelated to anything. He himself was, he realized, sitting in his bathrobe by his washstand, limp! No wonder: what a night! What a dreadful night! The speeds which machinists had worked up in the last fifty years were mere baby-talk to what can go through a man's head between dusk and daybreak. In the last ten hours poor Grenfell had travelled over seas and continents, gone through boyhood and youth, founded a business, made a great deal of money, and brought up an expensive family. (There were three sons, to whom he had given every advantage and who had turned out well, two of them brilliantly.) And all this meant nothing to him except negatively — 'to avoid worse rape,' he quoted Milton to himself.

Last night had been one of those nights of revelation, revaluation, when everything seems to come clear . . . only to fade out again in the morning. In a low cabin on a high red cliff overhanging the sea, everything that was shut up in him, under lock and bolt and pressure, simply broke jail, spread out into the spaciousness of the night, undraped, unashamed.

When his father died, Henry had got a job as messenger boy with the Western Union. He always remembered those years with a certain pride. His mother took in sewing. There were two little girls, younger than he. When he looked back on that time, there was nothing in it to be ashamed of. Those are the years, he often told the reformers, that make character, make proficiency. A business man should have early training, like a pianist, *at the instrument*. The sense of responsibility makes a little boy a citizen: for him there is no 'dangerous age.' From his first winter with the telegraph company he knew he could get on if he tried hard, since most lads emphatically did not try hard. He read law at night, and when he was twenty was confidential clerk with one of the most conservative legal firms in Colorado.

Everything went well until he took his first long vacation — bicycling in the mountains above Colorado Springs. One morning he was pedalling hard uphill when another bicycle came round a curve and collided with him; a girl coasting. Both riders were thrown. She got her foot caught in her wheel; sprain and lacerations. Henry ran two miles down to her hotel and her family. New York people; the father's name was a legend in Henry's credulous Western world. And they liked him, Henry, these cultivated, clever, experienced people! The mother was the ruling power – remarkable woman. What she planned, she put through – relentless determination. He ought to know, for he married that only daughter one year after she coasted into him. A warning unheeded, that first meeting. It was his own intoxicated vanity that sealed his fate. He had never been 'made much over' before.

It had worked out as well as most marriages, he supposed. Better than many. The intelligent girl had been no discredit to him, certainly. She had given him two remarkable sons, any man would be proud of them . . . .

Here Grenfell had flopped over in bed and suddenly sat up, muttering aloud. 'But God, they're as cold as ice! I can't see through it. They've never lived at all, those two fellows. They've never run after the ball – they're so damned clever they don't *have* to. They just reach out and *take* the ball. Yes, fine hands, like their grandmother's; long . . . white . . . beautiful nails. The way Harrison picked up that book! I'm glad my paws are red and stubby.'

For a moment he recalled sharply a little scene. Three days ago he was packing for his escape to this island. Harrison, the eldest son, the physicist, after knocking, had entered to his father's 'Come in!' He came to ask who should take care of his personal mail (that which came to the house) if Miss O'Doyle should go on her vacation before he returned. He put the question rather grimly. The family seemed to resent the fact that, though he worked like a steam shovel while he was in town, when he went on a vacation he never told them how long he would be away or where he was going.

'Oh, I meant to tell you, Harrison, before I leave. But it was nice of you to think of it. Miss O'Doyle has decided to put off her vacation until the middle of October, and then she'll take a long one.' He was sure he spoke amiably as he stood looking at his son. He was always proud of Harrisons's fine presence, his poise and easy reserve. The little travelling bag (made to his order) which on a journey he always carried himself, never trusted to a porter, lay open on his writing table. On top of his pyjamas and razor case lay two little books bound in red leather. Harrison picked up one and glanced at the lettering on the back. *King Henry IV, Part I.*

'Light reading?' he remarked. Grenfell was stung by such impertinence. He resented any intrusion on his private, personal, non-family life.

'Light or heavy,' he remarked dryly, 'they're good company. And they're mighty human.'

'They have that reputation,' his son admitted.

A spark flashed into Grenfell's eye. Was the fellow sarcastic, or merely patronizing?

'Reputation, hell!' he broke out. 'I don't carry books around with my toothbrushes and razors on account of their reputation.'

'No, I wouldn't accuse you of that.' The young man spoke quietly, not warmly, but as if he meant it. He hesitated and left the room.

Sitting up in his bed in the small hours of the morning, Grenfell wondered if he hadn't flared up too soon. Maybe the fellow hadn't meant to be sarcastic. All the same he had no business to touch anything in his father's bag. That bag was like his coat pocket. Grenfell never bothered his family with his personal diversions, and he never intruded upon theirs. Harrison and his mother were a team – a close corporation! Grenfell respected it absolutely. No questions, no explanations demanded by him. The bills came in; Miss O'Doyle wrote the checks and he signed them. He hadn't the curiosity, the vulgarity to look at them.

Of course, he admitted, there were times when he got back at the corporation just a little. That usually occurred when his dyspepsia had kept him on very light food all day and, the dinner at home happening to be 'rich,' he confined himself to graham crackers and milk. He remembered such a little dinner scene last month. Harrison and his mother came downstairs dressed to go out for the evening. Soon, after the soup was served, Harrison wondered whether Koussevitzky would take the slow movement in the Brahms Second as he did last winter. His mother said she still remembered Muck's reading, and preferred it.

The theoretical head of the house spoke up. 'I take it that this is Symphony night, and that my family are going. You have ordered the car? Well, I am going to hear John McCormack sing *Kathleen Mavourneen*.'

His wife rescued him as she often did (in an innocent, well-bred way) by refusing to recognize his rudeness. 'Dear me! I haven't heard McCormack since he first came out in Italy years and years ago. His success was sensational. He was singing Mozart then.'

Yes, when he was irritable and the domestic line-up got the better of him, Margaret, by being faultlessly polite, often saved the situation.

When he thought everything over, here in this great quiet, in this great darkness, he admitted that his shipwreck had not been on the family rock. The bitter truth was that his worst enemy was closer even than the wife of his bosom – was his bosom itself!

Grenfell had what he called a hair-trigger stomach. When he was in his New York office he worked like a whirlwind; and to do it he had to live on a diet that would have tried the leanest anchorite. The doctors said he did everything too hard. He knew that – he always had done things hard, from the day he first went to work for the Western Union. Mother and two little sisters, no schooling – the only capital he had was the ginger to care hard and work hard. Apparently it was not the brain that desired and achieved. At least, the expense account came out of a very other part of one. Perhaps he was a throw-back to the Year One, when in the stomach was the only constant, never sleeping, never quite satisfied desire.

The humiliation of being 'delicate' was worse than the

actual hardship. He had found the one way in which he could make it up to himself, could feel like a whole man, not like a miserable dyspeptic. That way was by living rough, not by living soft. There wasn't a big-game country in North America where he hadn't hunted; mountain sheep in the wild Rockies, moose in darkest Canada, caribou in New-foundland. Long before he could really afford it, he took four months out of every year to go shooting. His greatest triumph was a white bear in Labrador. His guide and packmen and canoe men never guessed that he was a frail man. Out there, up there, he wasn't! Out there he was just a 'city man' who paid well; eccentric, but a fairly good shot. That was what he had got out of hard work and very good luck. He had got ahead wonderfully . . . but, somehow, ahead on the wrong road.

At this point in his audit Grenfell had felt his knees getting cold, so he got out of bed, opened a clothes closet, and found his eiderdown bath-robe hanging on the hook where he had left it two summers ago. That was a satisfaction. (He liked to be orderly, and it made this cabin seem more his own to find things, year after year, just as he had left them.) Feeling comfortably warm, he ran up the dark window blinds which last night he had pulled down to shut out the disturbing sight of the stars. He bethought him of his eye-drops, tilted back his head, and there was that planet, serene, terrible and splendid, looking in at him . . . immortal beauty . . . yes, but only when somebody *saw* it, he fiercely answered back!

He thought about it until he head went round. He would get out of this room and get out quick. He began to dress — wool stockings, moccasins, flannel shirt, leather coat. He would get out and find his island. After all, it still existed. The Professor hadn't put it in his pocket, he guessed! He scrawled a line for William, his man Friday: 'BREAKFAST WHEN I RETURN,' and stuck it on a hook in his dining-car kitchen. William was 'boarded out' in a fisherman's family. (Grenfell wouldn't stand anyone in the cabin with him. He wanted all this glorious loneliness for himself. He had paid dearly for it.)

He hurried out of the kitchen door and up the grassy hillside to the spruce wood. The spruces stood tall and still as ever in the morning air; the same dazzling spears of sunlight shot through their darkness. The path underneath had the dampness, the magical softness which his feet remembered. On either side of the trail yellow toadstools and white mushrooms lifted the heavy thatch of brown spruce needles and made little damp tents. Everything was still in the wood. There was not a breath of wind; deep shadow and new-born light, yellow as gold, a little unsteady like other new-born things. It was blinking, too, as if its own reflection on the dewdrops was too bright. Or maybe the light had been asleep down under the sea and was just waking up.

'Hello, Grandfather!' Grenfell cried as he turned a curve in the path. The grandfather was a giant spruce tree that had been struck by lightning (must have been about a hundred years ago, the islanders said). It still lay on a slant along a steep hillside, its shallow roots in the air, all its great branches bleached greyish white, like an animal skeleton long exposed to the weather. Grenfell put out his hand to twitch off a twig as he passed, but it snapped back at him like a metal spring. He stopped in astonishment, his hand smarted, actually.

'Well, Grandfather! Lasting pretty well, I should say. Compliments! You get good drainage on this hillside, don't you?'

Ten minutes more on the winding uphill path brought him to the edge of the spruce wood and out on a bald headland that topped a cliff two hundred feet above the sea. He sat down on a rock and grinned. Like Christian of old, he thought, he had left his burden at the bottom of the hill. Now why had he let Doctor Fairweather's perfectly unessential information give him a miserable night? He had always known this island existed long before he discovered it, and that it must once have been a naked rock. The soil-surface was very thin. Almost anywhere on the open downs you could cut with a spade through the dry turf and roll it back from the rock as you roll a rug back from the floor. One knew that the rock itself, since it rested on the bottom of the ocean, must be very ancient.

THE SHORT STORIES OF WILLA CATHER

But that fact had nothing to do with the green surface where men lived and trees lived and blue flags and butter-cups and daisies and meadowsweet and steeplebush and goldenrod crowded one another in all the clearings. Grenfell shook himself and hurried along up the cliff trail. He crossed the first brook on stepping-stones. Must have been recent rain, for the water was rushing down the deep-cut channel with sound and fury till it leaped hundreds of feet over the face of the cliff and fell into the sea: a white waterfall that never rested.

The trail led on through a long jungle of black alder . . . then through a lazy, rooty, brown swamp . . . and then out on another breezy, grassy headland which jutted far out into the air in a horseshoe curve. There one could stand beside a bushy rowan tree and see four waterfalls, white as silver, pouring down the perpendicular cliff walls.

Nothing had changed. Everything was the same, and he, Henry Grenfell, was the same: the relationship was unchanged. Not even a tree blown down; the stunted beeches (precious because so few) were still holding out against a climate unkind to them. The old white birches that grew on the edge of the cliff had been so long beaten and tormented by east wind and north wind that they grew more down than up, and hugged the earth that was kinder than the stormy air. Their growth was all one-sided; away from the sea, and their land-side branches actually lay along the ground and crept up the hillside through the underbrush, persistent, nearly naked, like great creeping vines, and at last, when they got into the sunshine, burst into tender leafage.

This knob of grassy headland with the bushy rowan tree had been his vague objective when he left the cabin. From this elbow he could look back on the cliff wall, both north and south, and see the four silver waterfalls in the morning light. A splendid sight, Grenfell was thinking, and all his own. Not even a gull — they had gone screaming down the coast toward the herring weirs when he first left his cabin. Not a living creature — but wait a minute: there was something moving down there, on the shingle by the water's edge. A human figure, in a long white bathrobe – and a rubber cap! Then it must be a woman? Queer. No island woman would go bathing at this hour, not even in the warm inland ponds. Yes, it was a woman! A girl, and he knew *what* girl! In the miseries of the night he had forgotten her. The geologist's daughter.

How had she got down there without breaking her neck? She picked her way along the rough shingle; presently stopped and seemed to be meditating, seemed to be looking out at an old sliver of rock that was almost submerged at high tide. She opened her robe, a grey thing lined with white. Her bathing-suit was pink. If a clam stood upright and graciously opened its shell, it would look like that. After a moment she drew her shell together again – felt the chill of the morning air, probably. People are really themselves only when they believe they are absolutely alone and unobserved, he was thinking. With a quick motion she shed her robe, kicked off her sandals, and took to the water.

At the same moment Grenfell kicked off his moccasins. 'Crazy kid! What does she think she's doing? This is the North Atlantic, girl, you can't treat it like that!' As he muttered, he was getting off his fox-lined jacket and loosening his braces. Just how he would get down to the shingle he didn't know, but he guessed he'd have to. He was getting ready while, so far, she was doing nicely. Nothing is more embarrassing than to rescue people who don't want to be rescued. The tide was out, slack – she evidently knew its schedule.

She reached the rock, put up her arms and rested for a moment, then began to weave her way back. The distance wasn't much, but Lord! the cold, – in the early morning! When he saw her come out dripping and get into her shell, he began to shuffle on his fur jacket and his moccasins. He kept on scolding. 'Silly creature! Why couldn't she wait till afternoon, when the death-chill is off the water?'

He scolded her ghost all the way home, but he thought he knew just how she felt. Probably she used to take her swim at that hour last summer, and she had forgot how cold the

water was. When she first opened her long coat the nip of
the air had startled her a little. There was no one watching
her, she didn't have to keep face – except to herself. That she
had to do and no fuss about it. She hadn't dodged. She had
gone out, and she had come back. She would have a happy
day. He knew just how she felt. She surely did look like a
little pink clam in her white shell!

He was walking fast down the winding trails. Everything
since he left the cabin had been reassuring, delightful –
everything was the same, and so was he! The air, or the smell
of fir trees – something had sharpened his appetite. He was
hungry. As he passed the grandfather tree he waved his
hand, but didn't stop. Plucky youth is more bracing than
enduring age. He crossed the sharp line from the deep shade
to the sunny hillside behind his cabin and saw the wood
smoke rising from the chimney. The door of the dining-car
kitchen stood open, and the smell of coffee drowned the
spruce smell and sea smell. William hadn't waited; he was
wisely breakfasting.

As he came down the hill Grenfell was chuckling to
himself: 'Anyhow, when that first amphibious frog-toad
found his water-hole dried up behind him, and jumped out
to hop along till he could find another – well, he started on a
long hop.'

1944

THE BEST YEARS

ON a bright September morning in the year 1899 Miss Evangeline Knightly was driving through the beautiful Nebraska land which lies between the Platte River and the Kansas line. She drove slowly, for she loved the country, and she held the reins loosely in her gloved hand. She drove about a great deal and always wore leather gauntlets. Her hands were small, well shaped and very white, but they freckled in hot sunlight.

Miss Knightly was a charming person to meet – and an unusual type in a new country: oval face, small head delicately set (the oval chin tilting inward instead of the square chin thrust out), hazel eyes, a little blue, a little green, tiny dots of brown . . . . Somehow these splashes of colour made light – and warmth. When she laughed, her eyes positively glowed with humour, and in each oval cheek a roguish dimple came magically to the surface. Her laugh was delightful because it was intelligent, discriminating, not the physical spasm which seizes children when they are tickled, and growing boys and girls when they are embarrassed. When Miss Knightly laughed, it was apt to be because of some happy coincidence or droll mistake. The farmers along the road always felt flattered if they could make Miss Knightly laugh. Her voice had as many colours as her eyes – nearly always on the bright side, though it had a beautiful gravity for people who were in trouble.

It is only fair to say that in the community where she lived

Miss Knightly was considered an intelligent young woman, but plain – distinctly plain. The standard of female beauty seems to be the same in all newly settled countries: Australia, New Zealand, the farming country along the Platte. It is, and was, the glowing, smiling calendar girl sent out to advertise agricultural implements. Colour was everything, modelling was nothing. A nose was a nose – any shape would do; a forehead was the place where the hair stopped, chin utterly negligible unless it happened to be more than two inches long.

Miss Knightly's old mare, Molly, took her time along the dusty, sunflower-bordered roads that morning, occasionally pausing long enough to snatch off a juicy, leafy sunflower top in her yellow teeth. This she munched as she ambled along. Although Molly had almost the slowest trot in the world, she really preferred walking. Sometimes she fell into a doze and stumbled. Miss Knightly also, when she was abroad on these long drives, preferred the leisurely pace. She loved the beautiful autumn country; loved to look at it, to breathe it. She was not a 'dreamy' person, but she was thoughtful and very observing. She relished the morning; the great blue of the sky, smiling, cloudless, – and the land that lay level as far as the eye could see. The horizon was like a perfect circle, a great embrace, and within it lay the cornfields, still green, and the yellow wheat stubble, miles and miles of it, and the pasture lands where the white-faced cattle led lives of utter content. All their movements were deliberate and dignified. They grazed through all the morning; approached their metal water tank and drank. If the windmill had run too long and the tank had overflowed, the cattle trampled the over-flow into deep mud and cooled their feet. Then they drifted off to graze again. Grazing was not merely eating, it was also a pastime, a form of reflection, perhaps meditation.

Miss Knightly was thinking, as Molly jogged along, that the barbed-wire fences, though ugly in themselves, had their advantages. They did not cut the country up into patterns as did the rail fences and stone walls of her native New England. They were, broadly regarded, invisible – did not impose themselves upon the eye. She seemed to be driving through a fineless land. On her left the Hereford cattle apparently wandered at will: the tall sunflowers hid the wire that kept them off the road. Far away, on the horizon line, a troop of colts were galloping, all in the same direction – purely for exercise, one would say. Between her and the horizon the white wheels of windmills told her where the farmhouses sat.

Miss Knightly was abroad this morning with a special purpose – to visit country schools. She was the County Superintendent of Public Instruction. A grim title, that, to put upon a charming young woman .... Fortunately it was seldom used except on reports which she signed, and there it was usually printed. She was not even called 'the Super-intendent.' A country school-teacher said to her pupils: 'I think Miss Knightly will come to see us this week. She was at Walnut Creek yesterday.'

After she had driven westward through the pasture lands for an hour or so, Miss Knightly turned her mare north and very soon came into a rich farming district, where the fields were too valuable to be used for much grazing. Big red barns, rows of yellow straw stacks, green orchards, trim white farmhouses, fenced gardens.

Looking at her watch, Miss Knightly found that it was already after eleven o'clock. She touched Molly delicately with the whip and roused her to a jog trot. Presently they stopped before a little one-storey schoolhouse. All the windows were open. At the hitch-bar in the yard five horses were tethered – their saddles and bridles piled in an empty buckboard. There was a yard, but no fence – though on one side of the play-ground was a woven-wire fence covered with the vines of sturdy rambler roses – very pretty in the spring. It enclosed a cemetery – very few graves, very much sun and waving yellow grass, open to the singing from the schoolroom and the shouts of the boys playing ball at noon. The cemetery never depressed the children, and surely the school cast no gloom over the cemetery.

When Miss Knightly stopped before the door, a boy ran

out to hand her from the the buggy and to take care of Molly. The little teacher stood on the doorstep, her face lost, as it were, in a wide smile of tremulous gladness.

Miss Knightly took her hand, held it for a moment and looked down into the child's face – she was scarcely more – and said in the very gentlest shade of her many-shaded voice, 'Everything going well, Lesley?'

The teacher replied in happy little gasps, 'Oh yes, Miss Knightly! It's all so much easier than it was last year. I have some such lovely children – and they're all *good*!'

Miss Knightly took her arm, and they went into the school-room. The pupils grinned a welcome to the visitor. The teacher asked the conventional question: What recitation would she like to hear?

Whatever came next in the usual order, Miss Knightly said.

The class in geography came next. The children were 'bounding' the States. When the North Atlantic States had been disposed of with more or less accuracy, the little teacher said they would now jump to the Middle West, to bring the lesson nearer home.

'Suppose we begin with Illinois. That is your State, Edward, so I will call on you.'

A pale boy rose and came front of the class; a little fellow aged ten, maybe, who was plainly a newcomer – wore knee pants and stockings, instead of long trousers or blue overalls like the other boys. His hands were clenched at his sides, and he was evidently much frightened. Looking appealingly at the little teacher, he began in a high treble: 'The State of Illinois is bounded on the north by Lake Michigan, on the east by Lake Michigan . . .' He felt he had gone astray, and language utterly failed. A quick shudder ran over him from head to foot, and an accident happened. His dark blue stockings grew darker still, and his knickerbockers very dark. He stood there as if nailed to the floor. The teacher went up to him and took his hand and led him to his desk.

'You're too tired, Edward,' she said. 'We're all tired, and it's almost noon. So you can all run out and play, while I talk to Miss Knightly and tell her how naughty you all are.'

The children laughed (all but poor Edward), laughed heartily, as if they were suddenly relieved from some strain. Still laughing and punching each other they ran out into the sunshine.

Miss Knightly and the teacher (her name, by the way, was Lesley Ferguesson) sat down on a bench in the corner.

'I'm so sorry that happened, Miss Knightly. I oughtn't to have called on him. He's so new here, and he's a nervous little boy. I thought he'd like to speak up for his State. He seems homesick.'

'My dear, I'm glad you did call on him, and I'm glad the poor little fellow had an accident, – if he doesn't get too much misery out of it. The way those children behaved astonished me. Not a wink, or grin, or even a look. Not a wink from the Haymaker boy. I watched him. His mother has no such delicacy. They have just the best kind of good manners. How do you do it, Lesley?'

Lesley gave a happy giggle and flushed as red as a poppy. 'Oh, I don't do anything! You see they really *are* nice children. I remember last year I did have a little trouble – till they got used to me.'

'But they all passed their finals, and one girl, who was older than her teacher, got a school.'

'Hush, hush, ma'am! I'm afraid for the walls to hear it! Nobody knows our secret but my mother.'

'I'm very well satisfied with the results of our crime, Lesley.'

The girl blushed again. She loved to hear Miss Knightly speak her name, because she always sounded the s like a z, which made it seem gentle and more intimate. Nearly everyone else, even her mother, hissed the s as if it were spelled 'Lessley.' It was embarrassing to have such a queer name, but she respected it because her father had chosen it for her.

'Where are you going to stay all night, Miss Knightly?' she asked rather timidly.

'I think Mrs Ericson expects me to stay with her.'

'Mrs Hunt, where I stay, would be awful glad to have you,

but I know you'll be more comfortable at Mrs Ericson's. She's a lovely housekeeper.' Lesley resigned the faint hope that Miss Knightly would stay where she herself boarded, and broke out eagerly:

'Oh, Miss Knightly, have you seen any of our boys lately? Mother's too busy to write to me often.'

'Hector looked in at my office last week. He came to the Court House with a telegram for the sheriff. He seemed well and happy.'

'Did he? But Miss Knightly, I wish he hadn't taken that messenger job. I hate so for him to quit school.'

'Now, I wouldn't worry about that, my dear. School isn't everything. He'll be getting good experience every day at the depot.'

'Do you think so? I haven't seen him since he went to work.'

'Why, how long has it been since you were home?'

'It's over a month now. Not since my school started. Father has been working all our horses on the farm. Maybe you can share my lunch with me?'

'I brought a lunch for the two of us, my dear. Call your favourite boy to go to my buggy and get my basket for us. After lunch I would like to hear the advanced arithmetic class.'

While the pupils were doing their sums at the blackboard, Miss Knightly herself was doing a little figuring. This was Thursday. Tomorrow she would visit two schools, and she had planned to spend Friday night with a pleasant family on Farmers' Creek. But she could change her schedule and give this homesick child a visit with her family in the county seat. It would inconvenience her very little.

When the class in advanced arithmetic was dismissed, Miss Knightly made a joking little talk to the children and told them about a very bright little girl in Scotland who knew nearly a whole play of Shakespeare's by heart, but who wrote in her diary: 'Nine times nine is the Devil'; which proved, she said, that there are two kinds of memory, and

God is very good to anyone to whom he gives both kinds.
Then she asked if the pupils might have a special recess of
half an hour, as a present from her. They gave her a cheer
and out they trooped, the boys to the ball ground, and the
girls to the cemetery, to sit neatly on the headstones and
discuss Miss Knightly.

During their recess the Superintendent disclosed her plan.
'I've been wondering, Lesley, whether you wouldn't like to
go back to town with me after school tomorrow. We could
get into MacAlpin by seven o'clock, and you could have all of
Saturday and Sunday at home. Then we would make an
early start Monday morning, and I would drop you here at
the schoolhouse at nine o'clock.'

The little teacher caught her breath – she became quite
pale for a moment.

'Oh Miss Knightly, could you? Could you?'

'Of course I can. I'll stop for you here at four o'clock
tomorrow afternoon.'

II

The dark secret between Lesley and Miss Knightly was that
only this September had the girl reached the legal age for
teachers, yet she had been teaching all last year when she
was still under age!

Last summer, when the applicants for teachers' certificates
took written examinations in the County Superintendent's
offices at the Court House in MacAlpin, Lesley Ferguesson
had appeared with some twenty-six girls and nine boys. She
wrote all morning and all afternoon for two days. Miss
Knightly found her paper one of the best in the lot. A week
later, when all the papers were filed, Miss Knightly told
Lesley she could certainly give her a school. The morning
after she had thus notified Lesley, she found the girl herself
waiting on the sidewalk in front of the house where Miss
Knightly boarded.

'Could I walk over to the Court House with you, Miss
Knightly? I ought to tell you something,' she blurted out at

once. 'On that paper I didn't put down my real age. I put down sixteen, and I won't be fifteen until this September.'

'But I checked you with the high-school records, Lesley.'

'I know. I put it down wrong there, too. I didn't want to be the class baby, and I hoped I could get a school soon, to help out at home.'

The County Superintendent thought she would long remember that walk to the Court House. She could see that the child had spent a bad night; and she had walked up from her home down by the depot, quite a mile away, probably without breakfast.

'If your age is wrong on both records, why do you tell me about it now?'

'Oh, Miss Knightly I got to thinking about it last night, how if you did give me a school it might all come out, and mean people would say you knew about it and broke the law.'

Miss Knightly was thoughtless enough to chuckle. 'But, my dear, don't you see that if I didn't know about it until this moment, I am completely innocent?'

The child who was walking beside her stopped short and burst into sobs. Miss Knightly put her arm around those thin, eager, forward-reaching shoulders.

'Don't cry, dear. I was only joking. There's nothing very dreadful about it. You didn't give your age under oath, you know.' The sobs didn't stop. 'Listen, let me tell you something. That big Hatch boy put his age down as nineteen, and I know he was teaching down in Nemaha County four years ago. I can't always be sure about the age applicants put down. I have to use my judgement.'

The girl lifted her pale, trouble face and murmured, 'Judgment?'

'Yes. Some girls are older at thirteen than others are at eighteen. Your paper was one of the best handed in this year, and I am going to give you a school. Not a big one, but a nice one, in a nice part of the country. Now let's go into Ernie's coffee shop and have some more breakfast. You have a long walk home.'

Of course, fourteen was rather young for a teacher in an ungraded school, where she was likely to have pupils of sixteen and eighteen in her classes. But Miss Knightly's 'judgment' was justified by the fact that in June the school directors of the Wild Rose district asked to have 'Miss Ferguesson' back for the following year.

III

At four o'clock on Friday afternoon Miss Knightly stopped at the Wild Rose schoolhouse to find the teacher waiting by the roadside and the pupils already scattering across the fields, their tin lunch pails flashing back the sun. Lesley was standing almost in the road itself, her grey 'telescope' bag at her feet. The moment old Molly stopped, she stowed her bag in the back of the buggy and climbed in beside Miss Knightly. Her smile was so eager and happy that her friend chuckled softly. 'You still get a little homesick, don't you, Lesley?'

She didn't deny it. She gave a guilty laugh and murmured, 'I do miss the boys.'

The afternoon sun was behind them, throwing over the pastures and the harvested, resting fields that wonderful light, so yellow that it is actually orange. The three hours and the fourteen miles seemed not overlong. As the buggy neared the town of MacAlpin, Miss Knightly thought she could feel Lesley's heart beat. The girl had been silent a long while when she exclaimed:

'Look, there's the standpipe!'

The object of this emotion was a red sheet-iron tube which thrust its naked ugliness some eighty feet into the air and held the water supply for the town of MacAlpin. As it stood on a hill, it was the first thing one saw on approaching the town from the west. Old Molly, too, seemed to have spied this heartening landmark, for she quickened her trot without encouragement from the whip. From that point on, Lesley said not a word. There were two more low hills (very low), and then Miss Knightly turned off the main road and drove by a short cut through the baseball ground, to the south appendix of the town proper, the 'depot settlement' where the Ferguessons lived.

Their house stood on a steep hillside – a storey-and-a-half frame house with a basement on the downhill side, faced with brick up to the first-floor level. When the buggy stopped before the yard gate, two little boys came running out of the front door. Miss Knightly's passenger vanished from her side – she didn't know just when Lesley alighted. Her attention was distracted by the appeareance of the mother, with a third boy, still in kilts, trotting behind her.

Mrs Ferguesson was not a person who could be overlooked. All the merchants in MacAlpin admitted that she was a fine figure of a woman. As she came down the little yard and out of the gate, the evening breeze ruffled her wavy auburn hair. Her quick step and alert, upright carriage gave one the impression that she got things done. Coming up to the buggy, she took Miss Knightly's hand.

'Why, it's Miss Knightly! And she's brought our girl along to visit us. That was mighty clever of you, Miss, and these boys will surely be a happy family. They do miss their sister.' She spoke clearly, distinctly, but with a slight Missouri turn of speech.

By this time Lesley and her brothers had become telepathically one. Miss Knightly couldn't tell what the boys said to her, or whether they said anything, but they had her old canvas bag out of the buggy and up on the porch in no time at all. Lesley ran toward the front door, hurried back to thank Miss Knightly, and then disappeared, holding fast to the little chap in skirts. She had forgotten to ask at what time Miss Knightly would call for her on Monday, but her mother attended to that. When Mrs Ferguesson followed the children through the hall and the little back parlour into the dining-room, Lesley turned to her and asked breathlessly, almost sharply:

'Where's Hector?'

'He's often late on Friday night, dear. He telephoned me from the depot and said not to wait supper for him – he'd get a sandwich at the lunch counter. Now how *are* you, my girl?'

Mrs Ferguesson put her hands on Lesley's shoulders and looked into her glowing eyes.

'Just fine, Mother. I like my school so much! And the scholars are nicer even than they were last year. I just love some of them.'

At this the little boy in kilts (the fashion of the times, though he was four years old) caught his sister's skirt in his two hands and jerked it to get her attention. 'No, no!' he said mournfully, 'you don't love anybody but us!'

His mother laughed, and Lesley stooped and gave him the tight hug he wanted.

The family supper was over. Mrs Ferguesson put on her apron. 'Sit right down, Lesley, and talk to the children. No, I won't let you help me. You'll help me most by keeping them out of my way. I'll scramble you an egg and fry you some ham, so sit right down in your own place. I have some stewed plums for your dessert, and a beautiful angel cake I bought at the Methodist bake sale. Your father's gone to some political meeting, so we had supper early. You'll be a nice surprise for him when he gets home. He hadn't been gone half an hour when Miss Knightly drove up. Sit still, dear, it only bothers me if anybody tries to help me. I'll let you wash the dishes afterward, like we always do.'

Lesley sat down at the half-cleared table; an oval-shaped table which could be extended by the insertion of 'leaves' when Mrs Ferguesson had company. The room was already dusky (twilights are short in a flat country), and one of the boys switched on the light which hung by a cord high above the table. A shallow china shade over the bulb threw a glaring white light down on the sister and the boys who stood about her chair. Lesley wrinkled up her brow, but it didn't occur to her that the light was too strong. She gave herself up to the feeling of being at home. It went all through her, that feeling, like getting into a warm bath when one is tired. She was safe from everything, was where she wanted to be, where she ought to be. A plant that has been washed out by a rain storm feels like that, when a kind gardener puts it gently back into its own earth with its own group.

The two older boys, Homer and Vincent, kept interrupting each other, trying to tell her things, but she didn't really listen to what they said. The little fellow stood close beside her chair, holding on to her skirt, fingering the glass buttons on her jacket. He was named Bryan, for his father's hero, but he didn't fit the name very well. He was a rather wistful and timid child.

Mrs Ferguesson brought the ham and eggs and the warmed-up coffee. Then she sat down opposite her daughter to watch her enjoy her supper. 'Now don't talk to her, boys. Let her eat in peace.'

Vincent spoke up. 'Can't I just tell her what happened to my lame pigeon?'

Mrs Ferguesson merely shook her head. She had control in that household, sure enough!

Before Lesley had quite finished her supper she heard the front door open and shut. The boys started up, but the mother raised a warning finger. They understood; a surprise. They were still as mice, and listened: A pause in the hall . . . he was hanging up his cap. Then he came in – the flower of the family.

For a moment he stood speechless in the doorway, the 'incandescent' glaring full on his curly yellow hair and his amazed blue eyes. He was surprised indeed!

'Lesley!' he breathed, as if he were talking in his sleep.

She couldn't sit still. Without knowing that she got up and took a step, she had her arms around her brother. 'It's me, Hector! Ain't I lucky? Miss Knightly brought me in.'

'What time did you get here? You might have telephoned me, Mother.'

'Dear, she ain't been here much more than half an hour.'

'And Miss Knightly brought you in with old Molly, did she?' Oh, the lovely voice he had, that Hector! – warm, deliberate . . . it made the most commonplace remark full of meaning. He had to say merely that – and it told his appreciation of Miss Knightly's kindness, even a playful gratitude to Molly, her clumsy, fat, road-pounding old mare. He was tall for his age, was Hector, and he had the fair

pink-cheeked complexion which Lesley should have had and
didn't.

Mrs Ferguesson rose. 'Now let's all go into the parlour and
talk. We'll come back and clear up afterward.' With this she
opened the folding doors, and they followed her and found
comfortable chairs – there was even a home-made hassock
for Bryan. There were real books in the sectional bookcases
(old Ferg's fault),and there was a real Brussels carpet in soft
colours on the floor. That was Lesley's fault. Most of her
savings from her first year's teaching had gone into that
carpet. She had chosen it herself from the samples which
Marshall Field's travelling man brought to MacAlpin. There
were comfortable old-fashioned pictures on the walls –
'Venice by Moonlight' and such. Lesley and Hector thought it
a beautiful room.

Of course the room was pleasant because of the feeling the
children had for one another, and because in Mrs Ferguesson
there was authority and organization. Here the family sat
and talked until Father came home. He was always treated a
little like company. His wife and his children had a deep
respect for him and for experimental farming, and profound
veneration for William Jennings Bryan. Even little Bryan
knew he was named for a great man, and must some day
stop being afraid of the dark.

James Grahame Ferguesson was a farmer. He spent most of
his time on what he called an 'experimental farm.' (The
neighbours had other names for it – some of them amusing.)
He was a loosely built man; had drooping shoulders carried
with a forward thrust. He was a ready speaker, and usually
made the Fourth of July speech in MacAlpin – spoke from a
platform in the Court House grove, and even the farmers
who joked about Ferguesson came to hear him. Alf Delaney
declared: 'I like to see anything done well – even talking. If
old Ferg could shuck corn as fast as he can rustle the
dictionary, I'd hire him, even if he is a Pop.'

Old Ferg was not at all old – just turned forty – but he was
fussy about the spelling of his name. He wrote it James

Ferguesson. The merchants, even the local newspaper, simply would not spell it that way. They left letters out, or they put letters in. He complained about this repeatedly,and the result was that he was simply called 'Ferg' to his face, and 'old Ferg' to his back. His neighbours, both in town and in the country where he farmed, liked him because he gave them so much to talk about. He couldn't keep a hired man long at any wages. His habits were too unconventional. He rose early, saw to the chores like any other man, and went into the field for the morning. His lunch was a cold spread from his wife's kitchen, reinforced by hot tea. (The hired man was expected to bring his own lunch − outrageous!) After lunch Mr Ferguesson took off his boots and lay down on the blue gingham sheets of a wide bed, and remained there until what he called 'the cool of the afternoon.' When that refreshing season arrived, he fed and watered his work horses, put the young gelding to his buckboard, and drove four miles to MacAlpin for his wife's hot supper. Mrs Ferguesson, though not at all a meek woman or a stupid one, unquestioningly believed him when he told her that he did his best thinking in the afternoon. He hinted to her that he was working out in his head something that would benefit the farmers of the county more than all the corn and wheat they could raise even in a good year.

Sometimes Ferguesson did things she regretted − not because they were wrong, but because other people had mean tongues. When a fashion came in for giving names to farms which had hitherto been designated by figures (range, section, quarter, etc.), and his neighbours came out with 'Lone Tree Farm,' 'Cold Spring Farm,' etc., Ferguesson tacked on a cottonwood tree by his gate a neatly painted board inscribed: WIDE AWAKE FARM.

His neighbours, who could never get used to his afternoon siesta, were not long in converting this prophetic christening into 'Hush-a-bye Farm.' Mrs Ferguesson overheard some of this joking on a Saturday night (she was marketing late after a lodge meeting on top of a busy day), and she didn't like it. On Sunday morning when he was dressing for church, she

asked her husband why he ever gave the farm such a foolish
name. He explained to her that the important crop on that
farm was an idea. His farm was like an observatory where
one watched the signs of the times and saw the great change
that was coming for the benefit of all mankind. He even
quoted Tennyson about looking into the future 'far as
human eye could see.' It had been a long time since he had
quoted any poetry to her. She sighed and dropped the
matter.

On the whole, Ferg did himself a good turn when he put
up that piece of nomenclature. People drove out of their way
for miles to see it. They felt more kindly toward old Ferg
because he wrote himself down such an ass. In a hard-
working farming community a good joke is worth something. Ferguesson himself felt a gradual warming toward him
among his neighbours. He ascribed it to the power of his
oratory. It was really because he had made himself so absurd,
but this he never guessed. Idealists are seldom afraid of
ridicule – if they recognize it.

The Ferguesson children believed that their father was
misunderstood by people of inferior intelligence, and that
conviction gave them a 'cause' which bound them together.
They must do better than other children; better in school,
and better on the playground. They must turn in a quarter of
a dollar to help their mother out whenever they could.
Experimental farming wasn't immediately remunerative.

Fortunately there was never any rent to pay. They owned
their house down by the depot. When Mrs Ferguesson's
father died down in Missouri, she bought that place with
what he left her. She knew that was the safe thing to do, her
husband being a thinker. Her children were bound to her,
and to that house, by the deepest, the most solemn loyalty.
They never spoke of that covenant to each other, never even
formulated it in their minds – never. It was a consciousness
they shared, and it gave them a family complexion.

On this Saturday of Lesley's surprise visit home, Father
was with the family for breakfast. That was always a pleasant
way to begin the day – especially on Saturday, when no one

was in a hurry. He had grave good manners towards his wife and his children. He talked to them as if they were grown-up, reasonable beings – talked a trifle as if from a rostrum, perhaps, – and he never indulged in small-town gossip. He was much more likely to tell them what he had read in the *Omaha World-Herald* yesterday; news of the State capital and the national capital. Sometimes he told them what a grasping, selfish country England was. Very often he explained to them how the gold standard had kept the poor man down. The family seldom bothered him about petty matters – such as that Homer needed new shoes, or that the iceman's bill for the whole summer had come in for the third time. Mother would take care of that.

On this particular Saturday morning Ferguesson gave especial attention to Lesley. He asked her about her school, and had her name her pupils. 'I think you are fortunate to have the Wild Rose school, Lesley,' he said as he rose from the table. 'The farmers up there are open-minded and prosperous. I have sometimes wished that I had settled up there, though there are certain advantages in living at the county seat. The educational opportunities are better. Your friendship with Miss Knightly has been a broadening influence.'

He went out to hitch up the buckboard to drive to the farm, while his wife put up the lunch he was to take along with him, and Lesley went upstairs to make the beds.

'Upstairs' was a story in itself, a secret romance. No caller or neighbour had ever been allowed to go up there. All the children loved it – it was their very own world where there were no older people poking about to spoil things. And it was unique – not at all like other people's upstairs chambers. In her stuffy little bedroom out in the country Lesley had more than once cried for it.

Lesley and the boys liked space, not tight cubbyholes. Their upstairs was a long attic which ran the whole length of the house, from the front door downstairs to the kitchen at the back. Its great charm was that it was unlined. No plaster, no beaver-board lining; just the roof shingles, supported by long, unplaned, splintery rafters that sloped from the sharp roof-peak down to the floor of the attic. Bracing these long roof rafters were cross rafters on which one could hang things – a little personal washing, a curtain for tableaux, a rope swing for Bryan.

In this spacious, undivided loft were two brick chimneys, going up in neat little stair-steps from the plank floor to the shingle roof – and out of it to the stars! The chimneys were of red, unglazed brick, with lines of white mortar to hold them together.

Last year, after Lesley first got her school, Mrs Ferguesson exerted her authority and partitioned off a little room over the kitchen end of the 'upstairs' for her daughter. Before that, all the children slept in this delightful attic. The three older boys occupied two wide beds, their sister her little single bed. Bryan, subject to croup, still slumbered downstairs near his mother, but he looked forward to his ascension as to a state of pure beatitude.

There was certainly room enough up there for widely scattered quarters, but the three beds stood in a row, as in a hospital ward. The children liked to be close enough together to share experiences.

Experiences were many. Perhaps the most exciting was when the driving, sleety snowstorms came on winter nights. The roof shingles were old and had curled under hot summer suns. In a driving snowstorm the frozen flakes sifted in through all those little cracks, sprinkled the beds and the children, melted on their faces, in their hair! That was delightful. The rest of you was snug and warm under blankets and comforters, with a hot brick at one's feet. The wind howled outside; sometimes the white light from the snow and the half-strangled moon came in through the single end window. Each child had his own dream-adventure. They did not exchange confidences; every 'fellow' had a right to his own. They never told their love.

If they turned in early, they had a good while to enjoy the outside weather; they never went to sleep until after ten o'clock, for then came the sweetest morsel of the night. At that hour Number Seventeen, the westbound passenger, whistled in. The station and the engine house were perhaps an eighth of a mile down the hill, and from far away across the meadows the children could hear that whistle. Then came the heavy pants of the locomotive in the frosty air. Then a hissing – then silence: she was taking water.

On Saturdays the children were allowed to go down to the depot to see Seventeen come in. It was a fine sight on winter nights. Sometimes the great locomotive used to sweep in armoured in ice and snow, breathing fire like a dragon, its great red eye shooting a blinding beam along the white roadbed and shining wet rails. When it stopped, it panted like a great beast. After it was watered by the big hose from the overhead tank, it seemed to draw long deep breaths, ready to charge afresh over the great Western land.

Yes, they were grand old warriors, those towering locomotives of other days. They seemed to mean power, conquest, triumph – Jim Hill's dream. They set children's hearts beating from Chicago to Los Angeles. They were the awakeners of many a dream.

As she made the boys' beds that Saturday morning and put on clean sheets, Lesley was thinking she would give a great deal to sleep out here as she used to. But when she got her school last year, her mother had said she must have a room of her own. So a carpenter brought sheathing and 'lined' the end of the long loft – the end over the kitchen; and Mrs Ferguesson bought a little yellow washstand and a bowl and pitcher, and said with satisfaction: 'Now you see, Lesley, if you were sick, we would have some place to take the doctor.' To be sure, the doctor would have to be admitted through the kitchen, and then come up a dark winding stairway with two turns. (Mr Ferguesson termed it 'the turnpike.' His old Scotch grandmother, he said, had always thus called a winding stairway.) And Lesley's room, when you got there, was very like a snug wooden box. It was possible, of course, to leave her door open into the long loft, where the wood was brown and the chimneys red and the weather always so close to one. Out there things were still wild and rough – it wasn't a bedroom or a chamber – it was a hall, in the old baronial sense, reminded her of the lines in their *Grimm's Fairy Tales* book:

> Return, return, thou youthful bride,
> This is a robbers' hall inside.

IV

When her daughter had put the attic to rights, Mrs Ferguesson went uptown to do her Saturday marketing. Lesley slipped out through the kitchen door and sat down on the back porch. The front porch was kept neat and fit to receive callers, but the back porch was given over to the boys. It was a messy-looking place, to be sure. From the wooden ceiling hung two trapezes. At one corner four boxing gloves were piled in a broken chair. In the trampled, grassless back yard, two-by-fours, planted upright, supported a length of lead pipe on which Homer practised bar exercises. Lesley sat down on the porch floor, her feet on the ground, and sank into idleness and safety and perfect love.

The boys were much the dearest things in the world to her. To love them so much was just . . . happiness. To think about them was the most perfect form of happiness. Had they been actually present, swinging on the two trapezes, turning on the bar, she would have been too much excited, too actively happy to be perfectly happy. But sitting in the warm sun, with her feet on the good ground, even her mother away, she almost ceased to exist. The feeling of being at home was complete, absolute: it made her sleepy. And that feeling was not so much the sense of being protected by her father and mother as of being with, and being one with, her brothers. It was the clan feeling, which meant life or death for the blood, not for the individual. For some reason, or for no reason, back in the beginning, creatures wanted the blood to continue.

After the noonday dinner Mrs Ferguesson thoughtfully confided to her daughter while they were washing the dishes:

'Lesley, I'm divided in my mind. I would so appreciate a
quiet afternoon with you, but I've a sort of engagement with
the P.E.O. A lady from Canada is to be there to talk to us, and
I've promised to introduce her. And just when I want to have
a quiet time with you.'

Lesley gave a sigh of relief and thought how fortunate it is
that circumstances do sometimes make up our mind for us.
In that battered canvas bag upstairs there was a roll of
arithmetic papers and 'essays' which hung over her like a
threat. Now she would have a still hour in their beautiful
parlour to correct them; the shades drawn down, just
enough light to read by, her father's unabridged at hand, and
the boys playing bat and pitch in the back yard.

Lesley and her brothers were proud of their mother's good
looks, and that she never allowed herself to become a
household drudge, as so many of her neighbours did. She
'managed,' and the boys helped her to manage. For one
thing, there were never any dreary tubs full of washing
standing about, and there was no ironing day to make a hole
in the week. They sent all the washing, even the sheets, to
the town steam laundry. Hector, with his weekly wages as
messenger boy, and Homer and Vincent with their stable
jobs, paid for it. That simple expedient did away with the
worst blight of the working man's home.

Mrs Ferguesson was 'public-spirited,' and she was the friend
of all good causes. The business men of the town agreed that she
had a great deal of influence, and that her name added strength
to any committee. She was generally spoken of as a very *practical* woman, with an emphasis which implied several things.
She was a 'joiner,' too! She was a Royal Neighbor, and a Neighborly Neighbor, and a P.E.O., and an Eastern Star. She had even
joined the Methodist Win-a-Couple, though she warned them
that she could not attend their meetings, as she liked to spend
some of her evenings at home.

Promptly at six thirty Monday morning Miss Knightly's old

mare stopped in front of the Ferguesson's house. The four boys were all on the front porch. James himself carried Lesley's bag down and put it into the buggy. He thanked the Superintendent very courteously for her kindness and kissed his daughter good-bye.

It had been at no trifling sacrifice that Miss Knightly was able to call for Lesley at six thirty. Customarily she started on her long drives at nine o'clock. This morning she had to give an extra half-dollar to the man who came to curry and harness her mare. She herself got no proper breakfast, but a cold sandwich and a cup of coffee at the station lunch counter – the only eating-place open at six o'clock. Most serious of all, she must push Molly a little on the road, to land her passenger at the Wild Rose schoolhouse at nine o'cock. Such small inconveniences do not sum up to an imposing total, but we assume them only for persons we really care for.

V

It was Christmas Eve. The town was busy with Christmas 'exercises,' and all the churches were lit up. Hector Ferguesson was going slowly up the hill which separated the depot settlement from the town proper. He walked at no messenger-boy pace tonight, crunching under his feet the snow which had fallen three days ago, melted, and then frozen hard. His hands were in the pockets of his new overcoat, which was so long that it almost touched the ground when he toiled up the steepest part of the hill. It was very heavy and not very warm. In those days there was a theory that in topcoats very little wool was necessary if they were woven tight enough and hard enough to 'keep out the cold.' A barricade was the idea. Hector carried the weight and clumsiness bravely, proudly. His new overcoat was a Christmas present from his sister. She had gone to the big town in the next county to shop for it, and bought it with her own money. He was thinking how kind Lesley was, and how hard she had worked for that money, and how much she had to put up with in the rough farmhouse where she boarded, out in the country. It was usually a poor housekeeper who was willing to keep a teacher, since they paid so little. Probably the amount Lesley spent for that coat would have kept her at a comfortable house all winter. When he grew up, and made lots of money (a brakeman – maybe an engineer), he would certainly be good to his sister.

Hector was a strange boy; a blend of the soft and the hard. In action he was practical, executive, like his mother. But in his mind, in his thoughts and plans, he was extravagant, often absurd. His mother suspected that he was 'dreamy.' Tonight, as he trailed up the frozen wooden sidewalk toward the town, he kept looking up the stars, which were unusually bright, as they always seem over a stretch of snow. He was wondering if there were angels up there, watching the world on Christmas Eve. They came before, on the first Christmas Eve, he knew. Perhaps they kept the Anniversary. He thought about a beautiful coloured picture tacked up in Lesley's bedroom; two angels with white robes and long white wings, flying toward a low hill in the early dawn before sunrise, and on that distant hill, against the soft daybreak light, were three tiny crosses. He never doubted angels looked like that. He was credulous and truthful by nature. There was that look in his blue eyes. He would get it knocked out of him, his mother knew. But she believed he would always keep some of it – enough to make him open-handed and open-hearted.

Tonight Hector had his leather satchel full of Christmas telegrams. After he had delivered them all, he would buy his presents for his mother and the children. The stores sold off their special Christmas things at a discount after eleven o'clock on Christmas Eve.

VI

Miss Knightly was in Lincoln, attending a convention of Superintendents of Public Instruction, when the long-to-be-remembered blizzard swept down over the prairie State.

Travel and telephone service were discontinued. A Chicago passenger train was stalled for three days in a deep cut west of W–. There she lay, and the dining-car had much ado to feed the passengers.

Miss Knightly was snowbound in Lincoln. She tarried there after the convention was dismissed and her fellow superintendents had gone home to their respective counties. She was caught by the storm because she had stayed over to see Julia Marlowe (then young and so fair!) in *The Love Chase*. She was not inconsolable to be delayed for some days. Why worry? She was staying at a small but very pleasant hotel, where the food was good and the beds were comfortable. She was New England born and bred, too conscientious to stay over in the city from mere self-indulgence, but quite willing to be lost to MacAlpin and X– County by the intervention of fate. She stayed, in fact, a week, greatly enjoying such luxuries as plenty of running water, hot baths, and steam heat. At that date MacAlpin houses, and even her office in the Court House, were heated by hard-coal stoves.

At last she was jogging home on a passenger train which left Lincoln at a convenient hour (it was two hours late, travel was still disorganized), when she was pleased to see Mr Redman in conductor's uniform come into the car. Two of his boys had been her pupils when she taught in high school, before she was elected to a county office. Mr Redman also seemed pleased, and after he had been through the train to punch tickets, he came back and sat down in the green plush seat opposite Miss Knightly and began to 'tease.'

'I hear there was a story going up at the Court House that you'd eloped. I was hoping you hadn't made a mistake.'

'No. I thought it over and avoided the mistake. But what about you, Mr Redman? You belong on the run west out of MacAlpin, don't you?'

'I don't know where I belong, Ma'm, and nobody else does. This is Jack Kelly's run, but he got his leg broke trying to help the train crew shovel the sleeping-car loose in that deep cut out of W–. The passengers were just freezing. This blizzard has upset everything. There's got to be better organization from higher up. This has taught us we just can't handle an emergency. Hard on stock, hard on people. A little neighbour of ours – why, you must know her, she was one of your teachers – Jim Ferguesson's little girl. She got pneumonia out there in the country and died out there.'

Miss Knightly went so white that Redman without a word hurried to the end of the car and brought back a glass of water. He kept muttering that he was sorry . . . that he 'always put his foot in it.'

She did not disappoint him. She came back quickly. 'That's all right, Mr Redman. I'd rather hear it before I get home. Did she get lost in the storm? I don't understand.'

Mr Redman sat down and did the best he could to repair damages.

'No, Ma'm, little Lesley acted very sensible, didn't lose her head. You see, the storm struck us about three o'clock in the afternoon. The whole day it had been mild and soft, like spring. Then it came down instanter, like a thousand tons of snow dumped out of the sky. My wife was out in the back yard taking in some clothes she'd hung to dry. She hadn't even a shawl over her head. The suddenness of it confused her so (she couldn't see three feet before her), she wandered around in our back yard, couldn't find her way back to the house. Pretty soon our old dog – he's part shepherd – came yappin' and whinin'. She dropped the clothes and held onto his hair, and he got her to the back porch. That's how bad it was in MacAlpin.'

'And Lesley?' Miss Knightly murmured.

'Yes, Ma'm! I'm coming to that. Her scholars tell about how the schoolroom got a little dark, and they all looked out, and there was no graveyard, and no horses that some of them had rode to school on. The boys jumped up to run out and see after the horses, but Lesley stood with her back against the door and wouldn't let 'em go out. Told 'em it would be over in a few minutes. Well, you see it wasn't. Over four feet of snow fell in less'n an hour. About six o'clock some of the fathers of the children that lived aways off started out on horseback, but the horses waded belly-deep, and a wind come up and it turned cold.

'Ford Robertson is the nearest neighbour, you know, – scarcely more than across the road – eighth of a mile, maybe. As soon as he come in from his corral – the Herefords had all bunched up together, over a hundred of 'em, under the lee of a big haystack, and he knew they wouldn't freeze. As soon as he got in, the missus made him go over to the schoolhouse an' take a rope along an' herd 'em all over to her house, teacher an' all, with the boys leading their horses. That night Mrs Robertson cooked nearly everything in the house for their supper, and she sent Ford upstairs to help Lesley make shakedown beds on the floor. Mrs Robertson remembers when the big supper was ready and the children ate like wolves, Lesley didn't eat much – said she had a little headache. Next morning she was pretty sick. That day all the fathers came on horseback for the children. Robertson got one of them to go for old Doctor Small, and he came down on his horse. Doctor said it was pneumonia, and there wasn't much he could do. She didn't seem to have strength to rally. She was out of her head when he got there. She was mostly unconscious for three days, and just slipped out. The funeral is tomorrow. The roads are open now. They were to bring her home today.'

The train stopped at a station, and Mr Redman went to attend to his duties. When he next came through the car Miss Knightly spoke to him. She had recovered herself. Her voice was steady, though very low and very soft when she asked him:

'Were any of her family out there with her when she was ill?'

'Why, yes, Mrs Ferguesson was out there. That boy Hector got his mother through, before the roads were open. He'd stop at a farmhouse and explain the situation and borrow a team and get the farmer or one of his hands to give them a lift to the next farm, and there they'd get a lift a little further. Everybody knew about the school and the teacher by that time, and wanted to help, no matter how bad the roads were.

You see, Miss Knightly, everything would have gone better if it hadn't come on so freezing cold, and if the snow hadn't been so darn soft when it first fell. That family are terrible broke up. We all are, down at the depot. She didn't recognize them when they got there, I heard.'

VII

Twenty years after that historic blizzard Evangeline Knightly – now Mrs Ralph Thorndike – alighted from the fast east-bound passenger at the MacAlpin station. No one at the station knew who she was except the station master, and he was not quite sure. She looked older, but she also looked more prosperous, more worldly. When she approached him at his office door and asked, 'Isn't this Mr Beardsley?' he recognized her voice and speech.

'That's who. And it's my guess this is, or used to be, Miss Knightly. I've been here almost forever. No ambition. But you left us a long time ago. You're looking fine, Ma'm, if I may say so.'

She thanked him and asked him to recommend a hotel where she could stay for a day or two.

He scratched his head. 'Well, the Plummer House ain't no Waldorf-Astoria, but the travelling men give a good report of it. The Bishop always stays there when he comes to town. You like me to telephone for an otto [automobile] to take you up? Lord, when you left here there wasn't an otto in the town!'

Mrs Thorndike smiled. 'Not many in the world, I think. And can you tell me, Mr Beardsley, where the Ferguessons live?'

'The depot Ferguessons? Oh, they live uptown now. Ferg built right west of the Court House, right next to where the Donaldsons used to live. You'll find lots of changes. Some's come up, and some's come down. We used to laugh at Ferg and tell him politics didn't bring in the bacon. But he's got it on us now. The Democrats are sure grand job-givers. Throw 'em round for value received. I still vote the Republican ticket. Too old to change. Anyhow, all those new jobs don't affect the railroads much. They can't put a college professor on to run trains. Now I'll telephone for an otto for you.'

Miss Knightly, after going to Denver, had married a very successful young architect, from New England, like herself, and now she was on her way back to Brunswick, Maine, to revisit the scenes of her childhood. Although she had never been in MacAlpin since she left it fifteen years ago, she faithfully read the MacAlpin *Messenger* and knew the important changes in the town.

After she had settled her room at the hotel, and unpacked her toilet articles, she took a cardboard box she had brought with her in the sleeping-car, and went out on a personal errand. She came back to the hotel late for lunch – had a tray sent up to her room, and at four o'clock went to the office in the Court House which used to be her office. This was the autumn of the year, and she had a great desire to drive out among the country schools and see how much fifteen years had changed the land, the pupils, the teachers.

When she introduced herself to the present incumbent, she was cordially received. The young Superintendent seemed a wide-awake, breezy girl, with bobbed blond hair and crimson lips. Her name was Wanda Bliss.

Mrs Thorndike explained that her stay would not be long enough to let her visit all the country schools, but she would like Miss Bliss's advice as to which were the most interesting.

'Oh, I can run you around to nearly all of them in a day, in my car!'

Mrs Thorndike thanked her warmly. She liked young people who were not in the least afraid of life or luck or responsibility. In her own youth there were very few like that. The teachers, and many of the pupils out in the country schools, were eager – but anxious. She laughed and told Miss Bliss that she meant to hire a buggy, if there was such a thing left in MacAlpin, and drive out into the country alone.

'I get you. You want to put on an old-home act. You might phone around to any farmers you used to know. Some of them still keep horses for haying.'

Mrs Thorndike got a list of the country teachers and the districts in which they taught. A few of them had been pupils in the schools she used to visit. Those she was determined to see.

The following morning she made the call she had stopped off at MacAlpin to make. She rang the doorbell at the house pointed out to her, and through the open window heard a voice call: 'Come in, come in, please. I can't answer the bell.'

Mrs Thorndike opened the door into a shining oak hall with a shining oak stairway.

'Come right through, please. I'm in the back parlour. I sprained my ankle and can't walk yet.'

The visitor followed the voice and found Mrs Ferguesson sitting in a spring rocker, her bandaged right foot resting on a low stool.

'Come in, Ma'm. I have a bad sprain, and the little girl who does for me is downtown marketing. Maybe you came to see Mr Ferguesson, but his office is —' here she broke off and looked up sharply — intently — at her guest. When the guest smiled, she broke out: 'Miss Knightly! *Are* you Miss Knightly? Can it be?'

'They call me Mrs Thorndike now, but I'm Evangeline Knightly just the same.' She put out her hand, and Mrs Ferguesson seized it with both her own.

'It's too good to be true!' she gasped with tears in her voice, 'just too good to be true. The things we dream about that way don't happen.' She held fast to Mrs Thorndike's hand as if she were afraid she might vanish. 'When did you come to town, and why didn't they let me know!'

'I came only yesterday, Mrs Ferguesson, and I wanted to slip in on you just like this, with no one else around.'

'Mr Ferguesson must have known. But his mind is always off on some trail, and he never brings me any news when I'm laid up like this. Dear me! It's a long time.' She pressed the visitor's hand again before she released it. 'Get yourself a comfortable chair, dear, and sit down by me. I do hate to be helpless like this. It wouldn't have happened but for those slippery front stairs. Mr Ferguesson just wouldn't put a carpet on them, because he says folks don't carpet hardwood stairs, and I tried to answer the doorbell in a hurry, and this is what come of it. I'm not naturally a clumsy woman on my feet.'

Mrs Thorndike noticed an aggrieved tone in her talk which had never been there in the old days when she had so much to be aggrieved about. She brought a chair and sat down close to Mrs Ferguesson, facing her. The good woman had not changed much, she thought. There was a little grey in her crinkly auburn hair, and there were lines about her mouth which used not to be there, but her eyes had all the old fire.

'How comfortably you are fixed here, Mrs Ferguesson! I'm so glad to find you like this.'

'Yes, we're comfortable – now that they're all gone! It's mostly his taste. He took great interest.' She spoke rather absently, and kept looking out through the polished hall toward the front door, as if she were expecting someone. It seemed a shame that anyone naturally so energetic should be enduring this foolish antiquated method of treating a sprain. The chief change in her, Mrs Thorndike thought, was that she had grown softer. She reached for the visitor's hand again and held it fast. Tears came to her eyes.

Mrs Thorndike ventured that she had found the town much changed for the better.

Yes, Mrs Ferguesson supposed it was.

Then Mrs Thorndike began in earnest. 'How wonderful it is that all your sons have turned out so well! I take the MacAlpin paper chiefly to keep track of the Ferguesson boys. You and Mr Ferguesson must be very proud.'

'Yes'm, we are. We are thankful.'

'Even the Denver papers have long articles about Hector and Homer and their great sheep ranches in Wyoming. And Vincent has become such a celebrated chemist, and is helping to destroy all the irreducible elements that I learned when I went to school. And Bryan is with Marshall Field!'

Mrs Ferguesson nodded and pressed her hand, but she still

kept looking down the hall toward the front door. Suddenly
she turned with all herself to Mrs Thorndike and with a
storm of tears cried out from her heart: 'Oh, Miss Knightly,
talk to me about my Lesley! Seems so many have forgot her,
but I know you haven't.'

'No, Mrs Ferguesson, I never forget her. Yesterday morning I took a box of roses that I brought with me from my own
garden down to where she sleeps. I was glad to find a little
seat there, so that I could stay for a long while and think
about her.'

'Oh, I wish I could have gone with you, Miss Knightly! (I
can't call you anything else.) I wish we could have gone
together. I can't help feeling she knows. *Anyhow*, we know!
And there's nothing in all my life so precious to me to
remember and think about as my Lesley. I'm no soft woman,
either. The boys will tell you that. They'll tell you they got on
because I always had a firm hand over them. They're all true
to Lesley, my boys. Every time they come home they go
down there. They feel it like I do, as if it had happened
yesterday. Their father feels it, too, when he's not taken up
with his abstractions. Anyhow, I don't think men feel things
like women and boys. My boys have stayed boys. I do believe
they feel as bad as I do about moving up here. We have four
nice bedrooms upstairs to make them comfortable, should
they all come home at once, and they're polite about us and
tell us how well fixed we are. But Miss Knightly, I know at
the bottom of their hearts they wish they was back in the old
house down by the depot, sleeping in the attic.'

Mrs Thorndike stroked her hand. 'I looked for the old
house as I was coming up from the station. I made the driver
stop.'

'Ain't it dreadful, what's been done to it? If I'd foreseen, I'd
never have let Mr Ferguesson sell it. It was in my name. I'd
have kept it to go back to and remember sometimes. Folks in
middle age make a mistake when they think they can better
themselves. They can't, not if they have any heart. And the
other kind don't matter – they aren't real people – just poor
put-ons, that try to be like the advertisements. Father even

took me to California one winter. I was miserable all the time. And there were plenty more like me – miserable underneath. The women lined up in cafeterias, carrying their little trays – like convicts, seemed to me – and running to beauty shops to get their poor old hands manicured. And the old men, Miss Knightly, I pitied them most of all! Old bent-backed farmers, standing round in their shirt-sleeves, in plazas and alleyways, pitching horseshoes like they used to do at home. I tell you, people are happiest where they've had their children and struggled along and been real folks, and not tourists. What do you think about all this running around, Miss Knightly? You're an educated woman, I never had much schooling.'

'I don't think schooling gives people any wisdom, Mrs Ferguesson. I guess only life does that.'

'Well, this I know: our best years are when we're working hardest and going right ahead when we can hardly see our way out. Times I was a good deal perplexed. But I always had one comfort. I did own our own house. I never had to worry about the rent. Don't it seem strange to you, though, that all our boys are so practical, and their father such a dreamer?'

Mrs Thorndike murmured that some people think boys are most likely to take after their mother.

Mrs Ferguesson smiled absently and shook her head. Presently she came out with: 'It's a comfort to me up here, on a still night I can still hear the trains whistle in. Sometimes, when I can't sleep, I lie and listen for them. And I can almost think I am down there, with my children up in the loft. We were very happy.' She looked up at her guest and smiled bravely. 'I suppose you go away tonight?'

Mrs Thorndike explained her plan to spend a day in the country.

'You're going out to visit the little schools? Why, God bless you, dear! You're still our Miss Knightly! But you'd better take a car, so you can get up to the Wild Rose school and back in one day. Do go there! The teacher is Mandy Perkins – she was one of her little scholars. You'll like Mandy, an' she loved Lesley. You must get Bud Sullivan to drive you. Engage him right now – the telephone's there in the hall, and the garage is 306. He'll creep along for you, if you tell him. He does for me. I often go out to the Wild Rose school, and over to see dear Mrs Robertson, who ain't so young as she was then. I can't go with Mr Ferguesson. He drives so fast it's no satisfaction. And then he's not always mindful. He's had some accidents. When he gets to thinking, he's just as likely to run down a cow as not. He's had to pay for one. You know cows will cross the road right in front of a car. Maybe their grandchildren calves will be more modern-minded.'

Mrs Thorndike did not see her old friend again, but she wrote her a long letter from Wiscasset, Maine, which Mrs Ferguesson sent to her son Hector, marked, 'To be returned, but first pass on to your brothers.'

1945

A NOTE ON EDITIONS

The stories in this selection fall into several textual
categories.

1. Stories which Cather published in magazines but which
were not reprinted in book form in her lifetime. These are:
'Lou, the Prophet', 'On the Divide', 'Tommy, the Unsentimental', 'The Sentimentality of William Tavener', 'The
Enchanted Bluff', 'The Bohemian Girl', 'Consequences',
'Ardessa', 'Uncle Valentine'. All of these have since been
published (with typographical errors corrected) in post-
humous collections, *Willa Cather's Collected Short Fiction 1892–
1912*, ed. Virginia Faulkner (Lincoln and London: University
of Nebraska Press, 1965, 1970), and *Uncle Valentine and Other
Stories: Willa Cather's Uncollected Short Fiction 1915–1929*, ed.
Bernice Slote (Lincoln and London: University of Nebraska
Press, 1973). I give these versions.

2. Stories which underwent revisions. These were the stories
published first in magazine form, then (revised) in *The Troll
Garden* (McClure, Phillips & Co, 1905), then (revised again)
in *Youth and the Bright Medusa* (Knopf, 1920), which was
reissued in the Autograph Edition of 1937–8. These are: '"A
Death in the Desert"', 'A Wagner Matinée', 'The Sculptor's
Funeral', 'Paul's Case'. As my selection is chronological, and
as the revisions made for YBM tended to soften and mature
the early work, I have chosen to give the first revised version
from *The Troll Garden*, in the text of *The Troll Garden by Willa*

Cather: A Variorum Edition, edited (with typographical errors corrected, and a table of the successive revisions of the stories provided) by James Woodress (Lincoln and London: University of Nebraska Press, 1983).

3. 'Coming, Aphrodite!', first published as 'Coming, Eden Bower!' in *Smart Set*, 1920, and revised for YBM. I give the YBM version. In both versions, Cather is inconsistent about Eden's home town, giving it as 'Huntington' and then as 'Livingston'.

4. Later stories, either not revised between magazine and book publication, or published in *Obscure Destinies* and *The Old Beauty* without having been previously published as magazine stories. These are: 'Neighbour Rosicky', 'Two Friends', 'Old Mrs Harris', 'The Old Beauty', 'Before Breakfast', 'The Best Years'. These are reprinted from *Obscure Destinies* (Knopf, 1932; Hamish Hamilton, 1967) and *The Old Beauty* (Knopf, 1948; Random House Vintage Books, 1976).

Throughout, I have kept to chronological order, of the first publication or of the order of writing where known; this means that I have not kept to the arrangement of the stories made by Cather for book publication. Inconsistencies in spellings between the different editions have been retained. For details of the publication of Cather's stories, see *Willa Cather: A Bibliography* by Joan Crane (Lincoln and London: University of Nebraska Press, 1982). I give a critical account of the stories and their place in Cather's work in *Willa Cather – A Life Saved Up* (Virago, 1989).

WILLA CATHER

A Life Saved Up

Hermione Lee

Willa Cather (1873–1947) is one of the great American writers of this century. Born in Virginia, she was uprooted in childhood to the newly settled prairie farmlands of Nebraska. This startling transition gave a first awakening to Cather's imagination and profoundly coloured her later life and work. Before she turned to writing fiction, she spent hard years working as a journalist and teacher, and as an editor of the famous New York magazine *McClures*. She made intrepid journeys to the American South West, a region which drove her 'crazy with delight'. An independent and professional woman, Willa Cather's deepest feelings were directed towards women. Her friendships – from Sarah Orne Jewett and Dorothy Canfield, to Stephen Tennant and Yehudi Menuhin – were deeply important to her, yet as she became more famous, she also withdrew increasingly from a modern world she disliked.

Willa Cather's fiction charts new, female versions of epic pioneering heroism and the extraordinary cultural encounters of 'New World' history. Usually read as a nostalgic celebrator of American pastoral, Hermione Lee's major reinterpretation of Cather's work explores that American context and those traditions, but finds a stranger and more disconcerting Cather: a writer of split identities, sexual conflict, dramatic energies and stoic fatalism. Travelling beneath the apparently simple surface of Cather's work, Hermoine Lee presents an illuminating and exciting new reading of this marvellous writer.

OTHER WORKS BY WILLA CATHER

"Her work has its own firm reason for existence ... a monument more unshakable than she might have dreamed, to the independent spirit she most adored" – **Eudora Welty.**

Death Comes For The Archbishop

In her most famous novel, Cather explores the importance of spiritual values and the nature of love, evoking too, with delicate mastery, the sensuous beauty of a land on the raw edges of civilisation.

A Lost Lady

Marian Forrester bewitches everyone by her brilliance and grace, but, ultimately betrays all. For Marian longs for life on any terms, and in fulfilling herself, she loses all she loved, all who loved her.

Lucy Gayheart

Lucy, a talented pianist, meets and falls in love with a middle-aged opera singer. She rejects the commonplaces of a small town life and seeks the splendour of an "invisible, inviolable world" glimpsed through her music.

My Mortal Enemy

The life story of Myra Driscoll Henshawe could be that of many young women reared in an age of romantic fictions. Myra is to discover the fallacy of love, the rewards and terrible punishments of human passions.

My Ántonia

A magnificent portrait of a pioneer woman seen through the eyes of a man for whom she can be only a memory, never a possession. Her struggle and splendour represent the very source of life itself.

One of Ours
In this Pulitzer Prize – winning novel Cather looks back through the figure of a young man to the idealism seemingly discarded by twentieth century values, finally epitomised in the War. The message is ambivalent – war may demand altruism, but, its essence is destructive.

O Pioneers!
Alexandra is driven by two great forces: her fierce protective love for her young brother Emil and her deep love of the land. Through this incredible woman we learn the story of those imigrants who came to carve out new homes for themselves in a wilderness.

The Professor's House
In his attic study, throughout one long summer, Godfrey St Peter reflects upon his life and the people he has loved. This haunting novel examines human love and human isolation in all its manifestations.

Sapphira and the Slave Girl
A retrospective portrait of the Old South, with its stain of slavery, seen through the relationship of Sapphira Colbert to her Black maid, Nancy. When Sapphira overhears a conversation linking her husband's name and Nancy's, the horrific potential of Sapphira's power is unleashed.

Shadows on the Rock
At the end of the seventeenth century a French family, the Auclairs, begin a life in Quebec very different from the one they knew in Paris. On her mother's death Cécile is entrusted with the care of the household, for her father it becomes a life of painful exile, but for Cécile life holds innumerable joys.

The Song of the Lark
"As long as she lived the ecstasy was going to be hers. She would live for it, work for it, die for it ..." The Cinderella story of Thea Kronborg born into provincial obscurity, she becomes a great opera singer but learns on the way that to be a true artist she must make the most bitter sacrifices of all.

AMERICAN MODERN CLASSICS

DOROTHY BAKER
Cassandra at the Wedding

DJUNA BARNES
Smoke and Other Early Stories

JANE BOWLES
Two Serious Ladies
Everything Is Nice: Collected Stories

KAY BOYLE
My Next Bride
Plagued by the Nightingale
Year Before Last

MARTHA GELLHORN
Liana
A Stricken Field

ELLEN GLASGOW
Barren Ground
The Sheltered Life
Virginia

ELIZABETH HARDWICK
The Ghostly Lover
The Simple Truth
Sleepless Nights

H.D.
Bid Me To Live
Her

ZORA NEALE HURSTON
Their Eyes Were Watching God
Jonah's Gourd Vine

GRACE PALEY
Enormous Changes at The Last
Minute
The Little Disturbances of Man

ANN PETRY
The Street

KATHERINE ANNE PORTER
The Collected Short Stories

AGNES SMEDLEY
Daughter of Earth

GERTRUDE STEIN
Blood on the Dining-Room Floor

EUDORA WELTY
Delta Wedding
Losing Battles
The Optimist's Daughter
The Ponder Heart
The Robber Bridegroom

DOROTHY WEST
The Living is Easy

EDITH WHARTON
The Age of Innocence
The Children
The Fruit of the Tree
The Gods Arrive
The House of Mirth
Hudson River Bracketed
Madame de Treymes
The Mother's Recompense
Old New York
The Reef
Roman Fever

ANZIA YEZIERSKA
Hungry Hearts